THE FIERY RING

BOOKS BY GILBERT MORRIS

THE HOUSE OF WINSLOW SERIES

The Honorable Imposter
The Captive Bride
The Indentured Heart
The Gentle Rebel
The Saintly Buccaneer
The Holy Warrior
The Reluctant Bridegroom
The Last Confederate
The Dixie Widow
The Wounded Yankee
The Union Belle
The Final Adversary
The Crossed Sabres
The Valiant Gunman
The Gallant Outlaw
The Jeweled Spur
The Yukon Queen
The Rough Rider
The Iron Lady

The Silver Star
The Shadow Portrait
The White Hunter
The Flying Cavalier
The Glorious Prodigal
The Amazon Quest
The Golden Angel
The Heavenly Fugitive
The Fiery Ring
The Pilgrim Song
The Beloved Enemy
The Shining Badge
The Royal Handmaid
The Silent Harp
The Virtuous Woman
The Gypsy Moon
The Unlikely Allies
The High Calling
The Hesitant Hero

CHENEY DUVALL, M.D.[1]

1. *The Stars for a Light*
2. *Shadow of the Mountains*
3. *A City Not Forsaken*
4. *Toward the Sunrising*
5. *Secret Place of Thunder*
6. *In the Twilight, in the Evening*
7. *Island of the Innocent*
8. *Driven With the Wind*

CHENEY AND SHILOH: THE INHERITANCE[1]

1. *Where Two Seas Met*
2. *The Moon by Night*
3. *There Is a Season*

THE SPIRIT OF APPALACHIA[2]

1. *Over the Misty Mountains*
2. *Beyond the Quiet Hills*
3. *Among the King's Soldiers*
4. *Beneath the Mockingbird's Wings*
5. *Around the River's Bend*

LIONS OF JUDAH

1. *Heart of a Lion*
2. *No Woman So Fair*
3. *The Gate of Heaven*
4. *Till Shiloh Comes*
5. *By Way of the Wilderness*
6. *Daughter of Deliverance*

[1]with Lynn Morris   [2]with Aaron McCarver

GILBERT MORRIS

the FIERY RING

BETHANYHOUSE

Minneapolis, Minnesota

Published by Bethany House Publishers
11400 Hampshire Avenue South
Bloomington, Minnesota 55438

Bethany House Publishers is a division of
Baker Publishing Group, Grand Rapids, Michigan.

Printed in the United States of America

ISBN-13: 978-0-7642-2972-5
ISBN-10: 0-7642-2972-9

The Library of Congress has cataloged the original edition as follows:

Morris, Gilbert.
    The fiery ring / by Gilbert Morris.
        p. cm. — (The house of Winslow ; Bk. 28)
    ISBN 0-7642-2622-3 (pbk.)
    1. Winslow family (Fictitious characters)—Fiction. 2. Women circus performers—Fiction. 3. Brothers and sisters—Fiction. 4. Missing persons—Fiction. 5. Revenge—Fiction. I. Title.
    PS3563.O8742   F545   2002
    813'.54—dc21
                                                            2002001341

TO RICKY LEACH

Nothing gives me more pleasure than to see a young man or woman begin a pilgrimage with Jesus—and especially those in my own family. I pray that you will be used in a mighty way for our wonderful Saviour for many years. He who has begun a good thing in you will surely complete His work. Love the Lord with all your heart and strength and might, Ricky, and run with patience the race that is set before you.

GILBERT MORRIS spent ten years as a pastor before becoming Professor of English at Ouachita Baptist University in Arkansas and earning a Ph.D. at the University of Arkansas. A prolific writer, he has had over 25 scholarly articles and 200 poems published in various periodicals, and over the past years has had more than 180 novels published. His family includes three grown children. He and his wife live in Gulf Shores, Alabama.

CONTENTS

PART FOUR
November 1928–November 1929

THE HOUSE OF WINSLOW

★ ★ ★ ★

THE HOUSE OF WINSLOW

★ ★ ★ ★

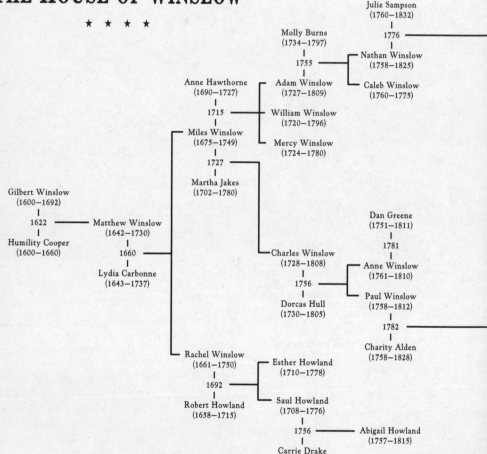

Julie Sampson
(1760–1832)

1776 ——————

Molly Burns
(1734–1797)

1755 ——

Nathan Winslow
(1758–1825)

Anne Hawthorne
(1690–1727)

Adam Winslow
(1727–1809)

Caleb Winslow
(1760–1775)

1715 ——

William Winslow
(1720–1796)

Miles Winslow
(1675–1749)

Mercy Winslow
(1724–1780)

1727 ——

Martha Jakes
(1702–1780)

Gilbert Winslow
(1600–1692)

1622 —— Matthew Winslow
(1642–1730)

Humility Cooper
(1600–1660)

Dan Greene
(1751–1811)

1781

Anne Winslow
(1761–1810)

1660 ——

Charles Winslow
(1728–1808)

Paul Winslow
(1758–1812)

Lydia Carbonne
(1643–1737)

1756 ——

1782 ——————

Dorcas Hull
(1730–1805)

Charity Alden
(1758–1828)

Rachel Winslow
(1661–1750)

Esther Howland
(1710–1778)

1692 ——

Robert Howland
(1658–1715)

Saul Howland
(1708–1776)

1756 —— Abigail Howland
(1757–1815)

Carrie Drake
(1720–1785)

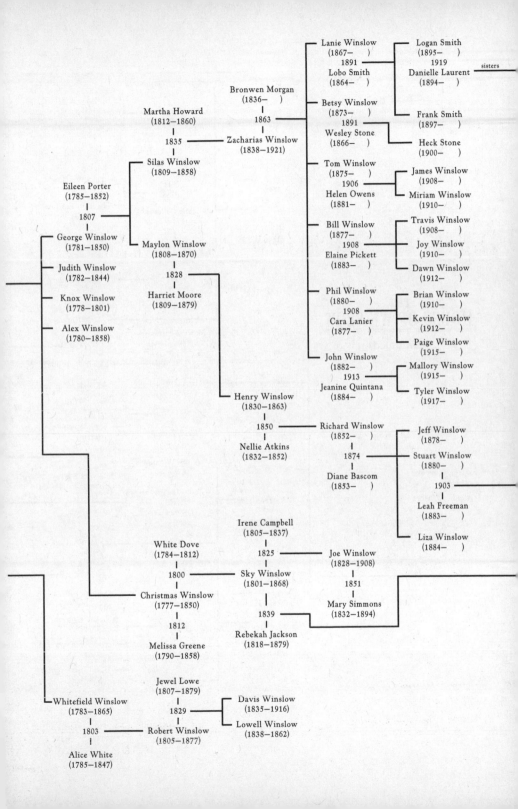

Eileen Porter (1785–1852)
1807
George Winslow (1781–1850)
Judith Winslow (1782–1844)
Knox Winslow (1778–1801)
Alex Winslow (1780–1858)

Martha Howard (1812–1860)
1835
Silas Winslow (1809–1858)
Maylon Winslow (1808–1870)
1828
Harriet Moore (1809–1879)

Bronwen Morgan (1836–   )
1863
Zacharias Winslow (1838–1921)

Henry Winslow (1830–1863)
1850
Nellie Atkins (1832–1852)

Lanie Winslow (1867–   )
1891
Lobo Smith (1864–   )

Betsy Winslow (1873–   )
1891
Wesley Stone (1866–   )

Tom Winslow (1875–   )
1906
Helen Owens (1881–   )

Bill Winslow (1877–   )
1908
Elaine Pickett (1883–   )

Phil Winslow (1880–   )
1908
Cara Lanier (1877–   )

John Winslow (1882–   )
1913
Jeanine Quintana (1884–   )

Richard Winslow (1852–   )
1874
Diane Bascom (1853–   )

Logan Smith (1895–   )
1919
Danielle Laurent (1894–   )   sisters
Frank Smith (1897–   )
Heck Stone (1900–   )

James Winslow (1908–   )
Miriam Winslow (1910–   )

Travis Winslow (1908–   )
Joy Winslow (1910–   )
Dawn Winslow (1912–   )

Brian Winslow (1910–   )
Kevin Winslow (1912–   )
Paige Winslow (1915–   )

Mallory Winslow (1915–   )
Tyler Winslow (1917–   )

Jeff Winslow (1878–   )
Stuart Winslow (1880–   )
1903
Leah Freeman (1883–   )
Liza Winslow (1884–   )

Irene Campbell (1805–1837)
1825
Joe Winslow (1828–1908)

White Dove (1784–1812)
1800
Sky Winslow (1801–1868)
Christmas Winslow (1777–1850)
1812
Melissa Greene (1790–1858)

1851
Mary Simmons (1832–1894)
1839
Rebekah Jackson (1818–1879)

Jewel Lowe (1807–1879)
1829
Davis Winslow (1835–1916)
Lowell Winslow (1838–1862)
Robert Winslow (1805–1877)
Whitefield Winslow (1783–1865)
1803
Alice White (1785–1847)

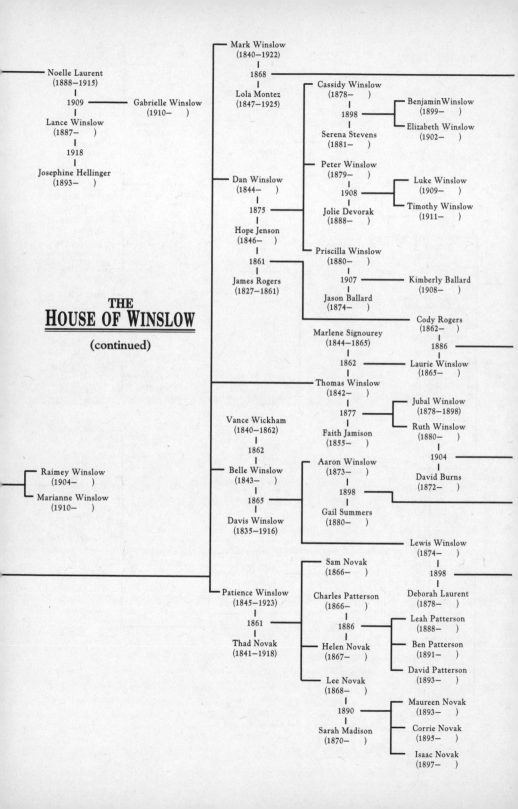

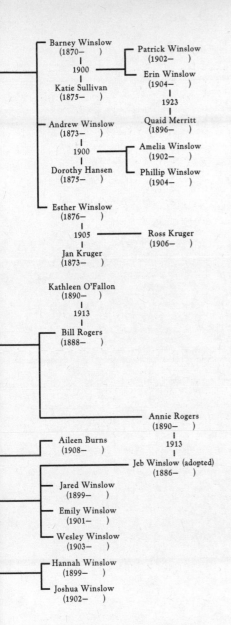

Barney Winslow
(1870–   )

1900

Katie Sullivan
(1875–   )

Patrick Winslow
(1902–   )

Erin Winslow
(1904–   )

1923

Quaid Merritt
(1896–   )

Andrew Winslow
(1873–   )

1900

Dorothy Hansen
(1875–   )

Amelia Winslow
(1902–   )

Phillip Winslow
(1904–   )

Esther Winslow
(1876–   )

1905

Jan Kruger
(1873–   )

Ross Kruger
(1906–   )

Kathleen O'Fallon
(1890–   )

1913

Bill Rogers
(1888–   )

Annie Rogers
(1890–   )

1913

Aileen Burns
(1908–   )

Jeb Winslow (adopted)
(1886–   )

Jared Winslow
(1899–   )

Emily Winslow
(1901–   )

Wesley Winslow
(1903–   )

Hannah Winslow
(1899–   )

Joshua Winslow
(1902–   )

PART ONE

November 1925–March 1927

★ ★ ★

CHAPTER ONE

PROMISED LAND

★ ★ ★ ★

The land lay flat in every direction, the horizon unbroken by mountains or hills, the gray land meeting an even grayer sky in an invisible seam. Two figures made their way across this vast openness, looking out on their dull, colorless world. Behind the pair, a quarter of a mile away, the monotony of the land was interrupted by the outline of a house, a barn, and a windmill, and even more faintly by a fence enclosing livestock.

Only the crunch of their boots in the snowy field of stubble disturbed the silence. The air was bitter cold, reddening their cheeks. The man wore overalls, a heavy dark brown coat, and a cap with flaps over his ears. The young girl beside him wore a long skirt over her boots and a plaid mackinaw. Her bright red scarf made a vivid crimson splash on the colorless world.

"I guess this ought to do it, Joy."

Bill Winslow fished in his pockets and produced two tin cans. He placed them on an upended ancient wooden apple crate, weathered to a pale silver. Turning to the girl, he smiled and winked at her. "Think you can hit anything today?"

"Sure I can, Dad." Joy Winslow took off her right glove and pulled a nickel-plated thirty-eight out of her pocket. "All loaded," she grinned. "I bet I hit better than you do today."

Winslow, a tall, lean man of forty-eight, had a pair of searching brown eyes and a face tanned by the sun and hardened by the wind. Small creases edged the corners of his eyes, and his wide, generous mouth turned upward in a smile as he studied the girl. *Hard to believe she'll be sixteen in a few months. Seems only yesterday she was just a baby.* "Bet you don't," he said. "I feel sharp today. Come on, we'll go back an extra ten paces."

The two moved away from the target, and when they halted, Joy held the thirty-eight firmly in her right hand and placed her left underneath. She held the pistol steady for two or three seconds, then squeezed the trigger. The explosion reverberated across the empty field, flushing out a flock of crows from the stubble. Rising with raucous cries, the birds formed a black cloud against the neutral gray of the sky. One of the tin cans lay on the ground.

"I got it, Dad!" Joy cried. Her eyes were laughing as she turned to him and said, "Bet'cha can't beat that."

"I'm not sure I can. You're a regular Annie Oakley." Bill aimed carefully at the second can with the forty-four but missed. He laughed and put his arm around her, pulling her close. "You're a fine shot, daughter. All right, your turn again."

The two fired at the tin cans for twenty minutes, laughing at their misses and shouting when they hit their target. Finally Bill said regretfully, "Reckon we better be getting back to the house."

"All right, Dad." Joy removed the spent hulls from her pistol, and as she did, Bill said, "I want you to have that thirty-eight for your own, Joy."

"You're giving it to *me*, Dad!" Joy exclaimed, astonishment sweeping across her face.

"Sure am—and the forty-four goes to Travis. I know you'll keep them always because they're more than just two pistols. They're part of our family history."

"I know," Joy murmured. She looked at the thirty-eight and then glanced up. "This belonged to my uncle, didn't it?"

"Yes, Lobo Smith. He carried it when he was a federal marshal under Judge Isaac Parker in Oklahoma Territory."

"Do you think he ever actually killed anybody with it, Dad?"

"Wouldn't be surprised. He's peaceable enough now, but he was pretty wild when he was younger."

"I'd like to meet him. Do you think we ever will?"

"Maybe someday." Bill quickly changed the subject. "This forty-four belonged to your grandfather, Zack Winslow. Zacharias, his name was. He fought in the Civil War. When he came home he did a lot of things. He went prospecting for gold out west and later became a successful rancher."

"Why don't we ever go see any of our relatives, Daddy?"

"Well, they live a long ways away, and besides I haven't always gotten along with all of them. Not something I'm proud of. I've always wanted to go back and make it up to them. Family is very important, and I've cheated you kids out of knowing your aunts and uncles."

The two pocketed their revolvers, put on their gloves, and trudged back over the icy wheat stubble. As they made their way home, they heard the lonely wail of a train whistle. Joy glanced west, where the rails ran, and spotted the plume of smoke. A fervent longing to travel swept over her, as it frequently did. The freight train was headed south, and her heart was in the South. "Daddy, do you think we'll ever go back to Virginia?"

Winslow did not answer, merely shaking his head. When Joy saw that he could not speak, she felt his sadness. She was twelve when they left the hills of Virginia to come to North Dakota, and she still longed and dreamed for those hills and the warm summers of the southland.

When they arrived at the house, Joy said, "I've got to go milk the cows, Daddy."

"All right, but we'll be leaving pretty soon, so don't dawdle."

"I won't."

Joy ran into the barn, where she took off her gloves and heavy coat, leaving on the two flannel shirts she wore for extra warmth. She noted that the cow's breath rose like steam in the cold air.

"All right, Sookey, I'm coming." Grabbing a three-legged stool and a bucket, Joy sat down, leaned her cheek against Sookey's silken flank, and grasped two of the cow's teats. The milk made a steady tattoo in the bottom of the tin pail, a rhythmic sound that Joy found soothing. Milking was one of her favorite chores. When she finished, she slapped the cow's side, saying, "Now, that's a good Sookey."

She was turning to pick up her coat when her brother, Travis, stepped inside. He was two years older than Joy, a tall, lathe-shaped young man with the same cobalt blue eyes as his sister. His tawny hair fell down over his brow as he pulled his cap off and said with a quick grin, "Better get your best dress on today, sis. Charlie Thompson will be waiting for you. You know how sweet he is on you."

"He is not either!"

"Sure he is. I saw him trying to give you a kiss after church last Sunday."

Joy's face flushed crimson, and she threw herself at her brother. Caught off balance, he went down, but he was laughing as she attempted to beat at him with her fists. He pinioned them, rolled over, and held her down tightly. "Don't be mad, sis. You can do better than old Charlie. Come on now." He rose quickly and helped her up. Dusting off the seat of his overalls, he said, "We're going to eat at the Royal Café tonight."

"Yes, and Dad said we could go to a movie. I hope it's Charlie Chaplin."

"I don't. I hope it's Buster Keaton. It probably won't be either one, though, but anything's better than nothing."

★ ★ ★ ★

"You about ready, Elaine?" Bill finished combing his hair and glanced over to where his wife was buttoning her dress. "Here, let me help you with that." He fumbled with the buttons in the back and then reached around and hugged her. "I remember the first time I ever helped you button up your dress. It was on our honeymoon. No, wait—I think I remember *unbuttoning* you."

"Well, I should think it was on our honeymoon and not before!" Elaine turned around and patted his cheek. She was a small blond woman with the same cobalt blue eyes she had passed on to two of their three children. She looked tired, for the work on a wheat farm was not easy. She never complained, how-ever, and now she said, "I'm glad you're taking us all out, Bill. Everyone needs to be cheered up."

Bill chewed his lip, then shook his head. "The drought this

year was bad. We haven't made any money at all. As a matter of fact, we've lost money."

Shooting a quick glance at her husband, Elaine abruptly said, "We should never have left Virginia. It was my fault."

"No more than mine. We made the decision together."

"No, I thought it would be better. We weren't getting anywhere there on the farm, and Opal made this sound like such a good way to get ahead."

Both of them thought of how they had left Virginia at the encouragement of Elaine's sister, Opal. She and Elaine had always been close, and when Opal married Albert Tatum and moved to North Dakota, the pair had missed each other. Opal had persuaded Elaine and Bill to buy a farm next to theirs. She and Albert had painted a rosy picture, but the move had proved to be more difficult than they could have imagined. The bitter cold winters had been followed with blistering summer heat. During their first two years there, drought had baked the land, and farmers all over the area had suffered dreadfully. All were praying that 1926 would bring them abundant crops and freedom from drought.

"We agreed to come, both of us," Bill said heavily. "Maybe it was a mistake, but we had no way of knowing that."

"I worry about our children."

"So do I. They don't like this place. Joy asked me today if there was any chance of our going back to Virginia."

Elaine longed to urge her husband to take them back home, too, but she held her tongue. They were locked into this land now. Nobody was buying property, and they would lose what little they had if they walked away and left it. Seeing the troubled light in Elaine's eyes, Bill pulled her close and held her. "I don't like this place either, and I know you hate it. But I've been thinking, all we need is one good year. If we have it this year, we'll sell out. Land prices will be higher then, and we'll go back home."

Elaine leaned back, excitement in her eyes. "You mean it?"

"Sure I do! You have to grow up here to get along with these winters, and I miss the hills. We'll do it the first good year we have."

"Then I pray 1926 is the year!"

*   *   *   *

Bismarck was already held in the dead grip of winter. The snows had fallen and melted before falling again and freezing, leaving the streets a mass of crusty mud and ice. Bill held on to the wheel of the truck tightly as it bounced roughly, then pulled up in front of Langley's General Store. "When this street thaws out it's going to be one big mess," he muttered. "Maybe they'll pave it."

Getting out of the truck, he helped Elaine out first, then his daughters, Joy and Dawn. Travis followed. The streets were filled with the usual Saturday crowd, mostly farmers coming to town for supplies. Bismarck was not Minneapolis by any means, just a small town of about nine thousand in the middle of the North Dakota prairie land, but the railroad did provide a connection with the rest of the country, pulsing two or three times a day with trains coming and going. As cold as it was, some had gathered at the station to watch the train arrive, even though they had no one coming in on it.

"Let's get in the store and thaw out," Travis said. "I feel like an icicle."

"Me too," Joy said. "Daddy, can I have some candy?"

Dawn piped up, "Me too, Daddy!" At the age of thirteen, she was the image of her father—a fact that delighted Bill Winslow.

"I think we can afford that. It'll give us something to chew on at the movies."

"What are we going to see?"

"Whatever's on."

"I know what's on," Elaine said. "It's the *Hunchback of Notre Dame*."

"Oh, phooey, who wants to see that old thing again!" Dawn exclaimed. "Why couldn't it be Charlie Chaplin? He's funny."

"Well, since there's only one movie theater here, we'll have to take what they've got. Come on, let's go inside. I'm cold too."

For the next half hour the family roamed around the store, going their different ways. Travis stayed close to the glass case full of knives, pistols, and rifles, while Joy inspected the yard goods and ready-made dresses. She spent a great deal of time at the shoe display but did not try any on. As for Dawn, she had not outgrown her love of dolls and examined the sparse stock with intense envy.

Bill and Elaine stayed together to select the staples they would need for the next week. They turned when a voice said, "Hey, Bill. Hello, Elaine."

Elaine went forward to greet her sister, Opal Tatum. Opal was a small, thin woman who had never been hearty. Her eyes were a faded blue, and as usual she had a worried look on her face. "So good to see you, Elaine. I've been meaning to come over, but it's been too cold."

"Yes, it has, but it's good to see you, Opal. Hello, Albert."

Albert Tatum was a tall, heavy man with a full stomach and a fleshy red complexion. A straggly mustache covered his mouth, and his eyes were a pale blue.

"Good to see you," he grunted.

Bill had never felt particularly close to Albert. He had always felt that Tatum had misrepresented the farm to them, although Bill had never complained. "Just came in to buy a few things and give the family a night out."

"We're going to the movies," Joy said. She spoke to the Tatums' daughter, Olean, who was a little older than Joy. Olean was wearing a new coat and new shoes. She was not a pretty girl but dressed better than any of her friends. Now she sniffed, "There's nothing on but that old hunchback thing. Last week we saw Harold Lloyd. Now *that* was good."

Witt Tatum, at eighteen, was a copy of his father, tall and already showing a heaviness that would catch up with him later. Witt reached out and pulled Joy's hair as she joined the group. Grinning, he said, "That picture will scare you to death. You'd better not go."

"I will too go!" Joy said, jerking away from him. He had always teased her, and now she resented being treated like a child.

Albert looked with displeasure at his brother-in-law. "These are hard times, Bill. Don't need to be spending your money foolishly on movies."

Bill Winslow put his level gaze on Tatum. "I don't expect

eating a meal out and going to a movie is going to change things much, Albert."

Tatum was a bluff, arrogant man. He bulldozed his wife so that she had practically no will of her own and had tried the same tactic on Bill Winslow. It had not worked, and the result was a coolness between the two men. "Have it your own way, then."

Travis waited until the Tatums had moved out of earshot, then said bitterly to Joy, "It's all his fault that we're here anyhow. He told all kinds of lies about the place. He talked Dad into buying it. You know what I heard?"

"What?"

"I heard he got a commission from the man that owned it for selling it to Dad."

Joy stared at her brother. "You don't mean that. He's mean, but he wouldn't do that."

"Wouldn't he? Look at the way he treats his wife. He spoils those kids rotten, but Aunt Opal has a terrible life. I don't know why she doesn't leave him."

Travis Winslow had always disliked the Tatum youngsters. He had had a knock-down, drag-out fight with Witt a year earlier, and though Travis was younger, he had won. Since then Witt had ignored him whenever possible.

"I miss our friends back in Virginia," Travis said. When he saw something stir on Joy's face, he regretted having mentioned it, but there was nothing he could do about it. "Of course," he said quickly, "they're changed now. They're all three years older."

"Still I'd like to see them," Joy said. "Robin told me she'd write, and she did twice, but then she quit."

Travis suddenly realized he had made his sister sad. "Come on, sis, we're going to eat at the Royal Café. I'm going to stuff myself like a Thanksgiving turkey!"

★   ★   ★   ★

The Royal Café was not a fancy or expensive place. It served meals to the farmers who came in only once or twice a week. But the food was good, and Joy loved eating there. She ordered meatloaf and mashed potatoes, and Travis ordered a steak and a baked potato. Dawn ordered a hamburger and fries, to the disgust of Joy and Travis. "You can get hamburgers anytime," Travis snorted.

"Hamburgers are my favorite food," Dawn insisted. "I wish we had them every day."

While they waited for the food, the three siblings entertained each other with stories about their neighbors, and then when the meal came, they threw themselves into it with gusto. The dessert choices were apple and cherry pie, and even though it was chilly in the restaurant, Joy wanted ice cream on hers.

As they were finishing their dessert Bill Winslow turned to the children and said, "Your mother and I have been talking, and I think it's something you three should know about."

With some apprehension all three youngsters looked up. "What is it, Dad?" Travis asked. "Something bad?"

"No. I think you'll like this." Bill's wide mouth turned upward at the corners. He loved his children dearly and wanted them to have good lives, but he did not see any possibility of that where they were. "The first good year we have—and I hope it's this next year—the price of land will go back up again. As soon as it does, we're going to sell out and go back home."

"You mean back to Virginia to our old house?"

"No, we can't go back to the old place, but we'll find someplace as close as we can get. I'm hungry to see something sticking up out of the ground, like a hill or a mountain."

Joy's eyes blazed with excitement, and she forgot the ice cream that was soaking into her apple pie. "Oh, Daddy, maybe it will be this coming year!"

"Maybe so, punkin'. I know it's been hard on all of us. One good year, and we can go back down south where we belong."

★ ★ ★ ★

Joy had drawn her chair closer to the coal oil lamp. Before her were four tablets, each of them with a date drawn in heavy black crayon across the front. Picking up the first one, she opened it and thought about how different she was from the time she had written these entries. She had started keeping the journal when she was only nine, and it gave her a great deal of pleasure to turn back the clock and read what had been on her mind then.

The first entry was dated May 20, 1919:

> I am going to keep a dairy. It won't be to hard because I like to rite. I will put down everthing in this dairy that is on my hart and someday when I'm a gron up I will look back and no what I was thinking wen I was only nine years old.

Joy smiled at the misspellings and the large childish scrawls. Her penmanship had improved and so had her spelling. She flipped through the journal, letting her eyes roam over the pages, and then picked up another journal. She had read them all so often she could practically recite them from memory. Her face flushed when she came to an entry in which she had tried to describe her thoughts about getting her first period. The writing was somewhat better but was still immature:

> It scared me very much. Mom had tried to warn me but I din't pay much atention. Now I wish I had. I was so scared but Mom talked to me for a long time and its all right. She said its very natural and it means that I'm becuming a full-grown woman. I hope I can talk to Dawn about this before it happens to her. She'll be scared to death!

Joy had been very honest in her journal, and she was always nervous that someone would find her writings. She kept them hidden as well as possible behind a drawer of a large bureau.

Picking up the current journal, she folded the pages back, placing at the top November 15, 1925, and then began to write:

> We went out tonight and had dinner at the Royal Café. I had meatloaf and mashed potatoes and for dessert I had apple pie with ice cream. Afterward we went to see The Hunchback of Notre Dame with Lon Cheney. It was not a good movie but very interesting. He is such an ugly man, the hunchback, but the real Lon Cheney isn't ugly at all. I tried to pretend I wasn't scared, but I really was. But the best thing of all was, Daddy said tonight while we were eating that if we have a good year next year and a good

crop, the price of land will go up. And if it does, we're going to sell this old farm and go back to Virginia.

Joy studied what she wrote and then continued:

I've been praying to God that He would get us all home again, and now I'm going to pray even harder than before.

She wrote for ten more minutes and then folded the tablet up and put it in the hiding place. Quickly she got into her narrow bed and, shivering, pulled the covers about her. The last thing she did before going to sleep was to pray, "Oh, God, get me and Mom and Dad and Travis and Dawn back home again!"

CHAPTER TWO

"You Can Have Anything You Want!"

★　★　★　★

Joy lay under the weight of the blankets, savoring the warmth and dreading getting up. Dawn lay beside her, sleeping like a hibernating bear. Joy had always envied Dawn's ability to sleep through anything, even the frigid cold. The worst of winter was over now, but March still retained some of its bitter traces. The dawn was just beginning to break, and she could hear her mother downstairs in the kitchen, the faint sounds of pots and pans clanging gently.

Finally, with resolution, she swept the blanket back and climbed out of bed, pulling off her long woolen nightgown. Shivering, she tugged on her underwear as quickly as she could, then her outer clothing. After blowing on her hands, she fumbled with a match to light the coal oil lamp that sat on a small table. The yellow light broke the semidarkness of the bedroom. Hastily, she removed the drawer of the bureau, pulled out the tablet with the red cover, sat down at the table, and began writing. She put the date, March 15, 1926, at the top, then wrote:

> It's my birthday today. I'm sixteen years old and have great hope for this year to come.

She glanced back momentarily at an earlier entry, read it, then went back to the present date.

I was looking back four months ago. We went to the Royal Café for supper in Bismarck and saw The Hunchback of Notre Dame, and that was when Daddy told us that if we had a good year, we would sell out and go back home to Virginia. I haven't said anything to him about it, but I think the drought has broken. We had a ton of snow this winter, so it looks like this could be the year we go back.

She wrote rapidly until she heard her mother's voice floating up to her. "Girls, come down and help with breakfast."

She replaced the notebook in its niche, put the drawer back, and went over to shake her sister. "Dawn, wake up. Time to get ready for breakfast." As she left the room she heard the train whistle and knew it was the six-thirty southbound freight. She wished she and all of her family were on it. True enough it was only a freight train, but she would be willing to ride on *top* of a train if it would take her back to Virginia.

Downstairs she found her mother busily putting breakfast together. Her mother gave her a hug and smiled. "Happy birthday, Joy."

"Thanks, Mom."

At that moment Travis came in, grabbed Joy, and swung her about. She protested but actually liked it very much. "Happy birthday, Joy," he said, kissing her on the cheek. He held her for a moment longer, then assumed a studious frown. "Now, the only question is—"

"What is the question?" Joy demanded, trying to get loose.

"The question is, do I put you under the bed now—or do I do it after breakfast?"

Joy struggled harder. "Let me down, you bully!"

Travis always felt it was his duty to put her under her bed on her birthday to show that she was still just a little girl. She struggled hard and kicked at him, but he merely laughed and avoided her blows and kicks. "I guess it'll have to be after breakfast. You're too rambunctious right now."

Her father entered to catch the last of this and laughed aloud.

"It'll be your birthday in a couple of months, Travis, and I'll have to put *you* under the bed."

"Oh, come on, Dad! That's just for little children like Joy."

"Everybody sit down. The food's going to get cold," Elaine said quickly. Dawn came sleepy-eyed to the table as Joy helped her mother set out the meal, which consisted of eggs over easy, the way they all liked them, fresh biscuits, fried ham slices, three different kinds of homemade jellies, coffee for the adults, and milk for the youngsters.

"When can I start drinking coffee?" Dawn protested as her father poured her a glass of milk.

"You can start right now." Bill grinned. He got up, grabbed a cup from the cupboard, and poured it full of black coffee from the battered pot. Picking up the cream pitcher, he added cream, then three spoonfuls of sugar, and stirred it. "There, you're just as grown up as anybody."

Dawn smiled. "Thank you, Daddy."

"She's too little to be drinking coffee," Travis protested. "Here, I'll take it."

Dawn slapped his hand as he reached over. "You keep your grimy hands off of my coffee!"

Bill Winslow laughed, sat down, and bowed his head. The others followed his lead, and he said, "Lord, we thank you for this food. We thank you for our home. We thank you for every blessing. And, Lord, we ask your guidance in all that we do this day and for the rest of our lives. In the name of Jesus. Amen."

"Amen," Dawn said, then discovered that during the blessing Travis had taken her cup and was sipping from it. "You give me that back!" she demanded.

"Give her the cup back, Travis," Bill said good-naturedly. "She's almost a grown woman now."

Travis handed the cup back with reluctance. "Grown woman! Why, she's a baby, and so is Joy." He grinned at Joy and winked at his father.

"And you're a long way from being a full-grown man," Joy said, sticking out her tongue out at him.

Elaine laughed. "Now, that's showing real maturity—sticking your tongue out."

"Well, he's so mean to me," Joy said.

They continued the lighthearted banter as they ate breakfast. When they were finished, Travis started to get up, but his father said, "Just a minute, Travis. I have an announcement to make."

Travis sat back down, and the three youngsters looked up expectantly at their parents' smiling faces. "What is it, Mom— Dad?" Joy asked curiously.

"Well, we didn't want to say anything until we were pretty sure it was all going to work out, but we've made a decision," Bill began. "I've been talking to the Tatums, and they've agreed to buy this place."

Joy stared at her father in disbelief. She could not say a word for a moment, then let out a screech. "Daddy, we're going back home!"

"That's the plan. We're not going to get much out of this place, since buyers aren't all that thick right now. Albert drove a hard bargain, but he's willing to take over the property and pay cash, so at least we'll have enough to go back home."

"Hey, that's the best news I've ever heard, Dad!" Travis said. "When can we leave?"

"Your mother and I need to talk about that and make a decision."

"Where will we go?" Joy asked. "I mean, where in Virginia?"

"Not sure about that, but we'll be starting all over. I'll have to get a job. My brother John is looking around for a place for us. Maybe we can get a good deal on a property the bank has taken over. At least that's what I'm hoping for."

"But what about all our furniture?" Joy asked. "We can't leave it here!"

"No, we'll take it with us," Bill said. "Almost all of it has belonged to our family for a long time. I thought our move here would be for good, so I wanted to keep it. I wanted you kids to have something that's been in the Winslow family for a long time. As a matter of fact, it's pretty valuable. Antiques cost more than new furniture."

"So we'll take it all back with us." Elaine smiled. "And one day you children will have it—and then your children."

For twenty minutes the family talked excitedly about the move. Finally Bill rose and said, "Your mother and I are going to town to sign the papers this morning. We won't get the cash today, but we need to sign the papers to make the deal legal. You kids get the chores done." He turned to Joy and smiled. "And tonight we'll go into town and celebrate. It's your birthday, Joy, so you get to eat anywhere you want to, go anywhere you want to go. You can have anything you want!"

Joy leaped out of her chair, ran around the table, and threw herself into her father's arms. "I'm so happy, Daddy! Moving back to Virginia will be the best birthday present any girl ever got. I don't care if I get anything else."

"Well then, we'll just have to take back all those presents we bought." Travis grinned.

"Oh no, you won't!"

Elaine took off her apron and said, "We're not sure how long it will take, but we should be back by noon or maybe before."

Dawn spoke up eagerly. "Daddy, let me go with you."

"You'd just be bored, honey."

"No I wouldn't! Please let me go."

Bill Winslow tried to fend her off but in the end threw up his hands. "All right! All right! But no complaining if you get bored."

"I won't complain, honest I won't."

Elaine smiled and shook her head. "You spoil her to death, Bill."

"We'll take care of things around here," Travis said. "I'd like to go with you, but I guess you won't need any help."

"No, I think we'll do just fine by ourselves."

Ten minutes later Travis and Joy were out front standing beside the truck. They took turns hugging both their parents. "Hurry back," Joy said. "We want to hear all about it."

At that moment Dawn came running out of the house, still pulling on her coat over her best dress. She stopped long enough to hug Travis. He lifted her off the ground and said, "You're not going to China, you know. We'll see you in no time."

Dawn turned to Joy and hugged her, then kissed her cheek. "Bye-bye, Joy. I love you!"

Joy laughed, "I love you too, little sister!" It touched her that Dawn said that to her so often. "We'll have such fun when we get back to Virginia."

Dawn smiled and said, "I'll be so glad to get home."

Bill opened the passenger door for Elaine, then went around

to the driver's side. "We'll see you soon, and then we'll be on our way to Virginia. Bye, kids." He got in, slammed the door, and started the engine. The ancient truck rumbled off down over the icy ruts of the road.

Joy and Travis watched them go. Then Joy turned to him. "Well, did you expect anything like this?"

"Not really. I knew we would go back to Virginia someday, but I didn't expect it this soon."

"I'm going to have trouble working on the same old chores today."

"Tell you what, you milk the cow, and I'll slop the hogs. Then we'll run down and see if we can't catch a fish or two. The ice has melted off part of the pond in the last few days, and I could sure use a bite of fried fish."

"I'll bet I catch more than you do!" Joy smiled brilliantly, then turned, and the two of them raced toward the barn.

★　★　★　★

The sun was high in the sky, and Joy looked out the window impatiently. "I don't know why they're taking so long."

"I don't either, but those legal things are pretty slow, I hear. I guess we might as well do the rest of the chores."

Joy sighed but agreed. As she went about cleaning the house while Travis took care of the outside work, she thought about the fun she'd had fishing with her brother. They hadn't caught anything big enough to keep, but they had enjoyed themselves. The two of them were very close, and even though Travis was two years older, he always included her in any activity. He took her hunting and fishing, and whenever he went to town in the truck, he brought her along.

Joy worked steadily, thinking with pleasure of returning to Virginia. She remembered so clearly the warm days of summer and the haze that sometimes topped the Blue Ridge Mountains, wreathing them in vapor.

Finally she heard Travis in the kitchen and went in to find him fixing a sandwich. "Don't you eat too much," Joy said. "We're going to eat out tonight."

Travis was putting a layer of peanut butter on a piece of bread. "I've got to have something to eat," he complained, "or I'll starve." He started to take a bite, then turned his head to one side. "Listen, I think I hear them."

Joy had heard it too. She rushed to the door, and the two of them arrived at the same time. They struggled for a moment, and then Travis stepped back and said, "All right, it's your birthday."

Joy rushed outside, but as soon as she was out on the porch she stopped. "It's not them!" she exclaimed with disappointment. "It's Uncle Albert and Aunt Opal."

"What are they doing here?" Travis wondered.

The two descended from the porch and walked out to the drive to meet their aunt and uncle as the car pulled up to the house. Joy lifted her hand to wave, but to her surprise her aunt Opal did not wave back. She had not expected anything like a cheerful wave from her uncle, for he never had a good word for anyone, as far as she could tell. Catching a glimpse of her aunt's face, a strange feeling swept over Joy. She could not explain it, but somehow she knew it was bad news.

"Travis," she whispered, "something's wrong."

"I think you're right," Travis murmured. "Look at their faces. I'll bet the sale didn't go through, and they've come to tell us."

The Oldsmobile came to a halt, and the engine shut off. The door on the driver's side opened, and Albert struggled to get out. He was such a big man it was difficult, and while he was still at it, Opal was already outside and had moved around the front of the car. Her eyes were opened wide, and Travis and Joy saw tears running down her face. "What's wrong, Aunt Opal?" Joy cried, but she did not want to know the answer.

Opal Tatum reached Joy and threw her arms around her. She began crying so violently she could not speak. Travis turned to his uncle and said, "What is it, Uncle Albert?"

Albert's face was pale, and there was a puckered look around his mouth.

"What is it? Is it Mom and Dad?"

"I'm afraid so, boy." Tatum cleared his throat and looked at the ground. He shook his head as if trying to clear it, then looked up and bit his lip. Finally he said, "It's your folks—they were—they were in a bad wreck."

At that moment Joy knew everything. She did not have to hear the rest of the story. She stiffened and her mind grew numb. It was as if the world had shut off and she was standing outside of it. She felt Travis put his arm around her, and she heard Albert say, "They got hit head-on by a big truck. They didn't have a chance, kids. They were both killed instantly."

Travis's face was pale as paper. "What . . . what about Dawn?"

"She's gone too," Opal sobbed, turning to Albert and pressing her face against his chest.

Joy couldn't take it all in. She could still see her father smiling and waving, saying, *"You can have anything you want!"* and her mother's smile, the last glimpse she'd had of her as the family truck had pulled out. And she knew she would never forget Dawn saying "I love you" before she left.

And now they were all gone.

Joy felt light-headed. She turned to Travis, and he caught her as she fell against him weeping.

★ ★ ★ ★

"I've got to tell you kids something, but I wish I didn't."

It was several weeks after the accident, and Albert Tatum had called Travis and Joy into the drawing room after supper. He had waited until his own children had gone out with some of their friends. Travis and Joy had been washing the dishes when he spoke to them. Now they all stood in the drawing room, Albert facing his niece and nephew and Opal standing partly behind him.

"What is it, Uncle Albert?" Travis asked.

"It's bad news for you."

"I guess we're used to that," Travis said bitterly.

Joy cast a quick glance at her brother. He was the man of the family now. The memory of the past weeks since the funeral ran through her mind. It had been a living death for both of them. They had not been permitted to stay on the farm but had come to live with the Tatums. This was bitter medicine in itself. Their aunt was kind enough, but living with Albert's gruff demands was truly a hardship. And Witt and Olean were thoughtless, spoiled, and at times even cruel. Albert spoke little with Joy and Travis, though he had insisted on their working from the very day they came in. "Work is good for you," he said. "It'll help you forget your grief."

And now as Joy stared at her uncle, bitterness gnawed at her heart. She had wept herself to sleep for weeks, glad that she had a place of her own where Olean and Witt could not hear her. She slept in a tiny room in the attic, no more than eight by ten, with only a bed, a table, and a small chest. It had become a haven for her; it was the only place she could go to be alone in this hostile environment. She had brought her journals with her and managed to conceal them between the joists of the ceiling under her.

"I've been meetin' with the lawyers," Albert said. "I guess you both knew that the farm hadn't done well."

Travis and Joy looked at each other but said nothing.

"There were a lot of debts on the place, and now the notes are all due. I had to settle for the best I could."

"What do you mean, Uncle Albert?" Joy asked. "Mom and Dad were going to sell out to you."

"Well, that was the plan, but when we got to looking into it, there were so many debts that there wasn't any money left over. I managed to pay the place off, but there won't be any inheritance. No money for you kids."

Opal came forward and put her hand on Albert's arm. "We'll take care of you. I promised Elaine long ago that I'd always do that if anything happened to them. We promised each other."

"Of course, that's right." Albert nodded. He chewed his lip as he always did when he was disturbed and said, "I'm right sorry that it didn't turn out better, but you kids will always have a roof over your head. You'll have to work, of course, and as soon as you get to be of age, I'll try to help you get started."

Joy stared at her uncle. She sensed that something was wrong with all of this. Naturally she had known little of her parents' financial situation, but she knew they had been confident of getting enough money out of the farm to get them all back to Virginia. Now she could not help saying, "I don't understand. There was money enough to get us back home. Daddy said so."

"That was before we found out how many debts were owed."

"I'd like to see those records," Travis said quickly. His face was flushed with anger.

"Are you saying you don't trust me, your own family?"

"You're not my family," Travis said hotly. "We're not blood kin."

"But we are, you and me," Opal said. "Your uncle wouldn't do anything wrong."

At that moment both Joy and Travis knew the hopelessness of it all. The look in their uncle's eyes revealed his character, and both of them were certain he had robbed them of their inheritance—as certain as they were of life itself.

But there was nothing they could do. They listened while Albert outlined his plans for them, and then when he nodded, they turned and left. As soon as they were outside the house, Travis said bitterly, "He's lying."

"I think he is too, but we'll never prove it."

"You won't have to stay here long, Joy. I'm old enough to go out on my own. I'll find a job, and then I'll come and get you."

"Will you, Travis?"

"Sure, sis, you can bank on it!"

CHAPTER THREE

"I'LL COME BACK FOR YOU!"

★ ★ ★ ★

The gray dawn had barely broken over the land when Joy awoke in her narrow bed. She lay there feeling the hopelessness of her existence. For six months, ever since the deaths of her parents and her sister, she had spent her days working hard for the Tatums. She welcomed her time alone at night in her tiny attic room, even though there was no heat in the winter and no way of cooling the room in the summer. After winter had passed and she no longer had to pile her blankets on so high she could barely breathe, the heat of summer had been even more oppressive. The tiny window did not allow in enough air to cool the room, and oftentimes the stuffy heat became suffocating. On many a summer night she had sneaked downstairs and slept outside on the porch. She rarely got a full night's sleep, and that made the days of cheerless labor even harder to bear.

This September morning was pleasant enough, with a touch of fall in the air, and she lay on her bed for a few extra minutes, listening to the muted song of a bird outside. She kept her eyes shut, dreading to open them. She did not know what sort of bird it was, but it made a cheerful sound, and for one moment she wished she could change places with the feathered songster. The song rose, then faded away as the bird flew off. Knowing she could no longer postpone the inevitable, she crawled out of bed and dressed in the faint light that filtered through the small window of her cell-like room. She thought about Travis out in the bunkhouse, where she knew he too was rising, along with the hired hands. There had been no room for him in the house, and he had been glad to make a spot for himself in the bunkhouse.

Travis had not yet been able to leave the farm to find a job, for Uncle Albert had gone back on his word and decided he would not give Travis permission to leave until his sister reached the age of eighteen. For that Joy was secretly glad. She feared being left alone with the Tatums, but at the same time, she hoped Travis could devise a plan for them to sneak away—far, far away from this hated place. Both of them lived for the day when they could shake the dust of North Dakota off their feet and find their way back to Virginia.

When she was dressed Joy went downstairs, pausing to look at the furniture in the living room. Her throat tightened each morning at the sight of her family's antiques sitting in the Tatum home. It not only brought back memories of her parents and of Dawn, but it also reminded her painfully of her uncle's betrayal. Albert Tatum had appropriated all of the Winslow furnishings and moved them into his own house without apology. "This stuff might as well be used, and you two don't have any place to put it," he had told Travis and Joy. Both of them had resented it but could do nothing to stop him. Fortunately, they had managed to rescue many personal items, such as pictures and treasured keepsakes, packing them up and storing them in the Tatums' attic without Uncle Albert's knowledge. "One day, Travis," Joy had said fiercely, "we'll have our own place—then we can come and get all of the furniture and our other things!"

Joy pushed the memories aside, as she had learned to do, and started the fire in the wood stove in the kitchen. Wood was scarce and Albert Tatum was stingy with it, so they used it sparingly. Albert didn't complain much about the wood they used for cooking, but they could only use it for heat when he was there to enjoy it. That had been the one advantage of working in the kitchen last winter—it had always been warm, even during the coldest days.

Joy had always been a strong girl, but as she gathered the

ingredients for breakfast, she felt a weariness that was more than physical. True enough she worked long hours, but that did not fully explain the fatigue that seemed to soak down to her very bones. It felt almost like a sickness, for she was without the vigor she had been so accustomed to all of her life. The deaths of her parents and Dawn—so sudden, so unexpected, so dreadful—had drained her vitality. It was a matter of heart and spirit rather than of flesh and blood. She moved about the kitchen mechanically, as she did every morning, forcing herself to go through the familiar motions.

From outside she could hear the farmhands rising, getting ready for another day in the fields. She knew that Travis hated this place too. He had never been afraid of work, but to work all day for nothing—not even a kind word—had worn down his resistance as well. It simply never occurred to Albert Tatum to pay Travis a wage, or even to commend him for work well done. The past few months had drawn all the smiles out of Travis Winslow, and he now went through his days as mechanically as Joy endured hers.

She heard the family gathering around the table in the dining room, and then Albert stuck his head through the door. "Hurry up, Joy, we're ready for breakfast!"

"I'm coming as quick as I can."

Picking up a platter of eggs and fried ham, Joy moved out of the kitchen. The family was seated, and as soon as she put down the plate, Olean took her fork and picked at a piece of meat. "These are too done! Can't you ever do anything right?"

Anger flared through Joy and she snapped, "If you don't like the way I cook, why don't you cook breakfast yourself!"

"That'll be enough out of you!" Albert said sternly.

"It wouldn't hurt her to come help me in the kitchen once in a while," Joy protested.

"Pa, tell her to shut her mouth!" Olean cried.

Opal tried to bring a little peace into the room by saying, "I'm sure she's doing the best she can, Albert."

Joy glared at her uncle, then turned and walked stiffly out of the dining room with her head high. She brought the rest of the food and filled the coffee cups. When everyone had been served, she sat down and said, "Please pass the eggs."

Witt picked up the plate and handed it to her but wouldn't let go of it. "Say please." He smirked.

Joy did not say a word, and with an annoying grin he put the plate back where she could not reach it.

Furiously, Joy got up from the table and stormed out.

"You come back to this table, Joy," Albert shouted at her.

Joy did not even pause. She went out the back door and ran to the bunkhouse. There were four hands there for the harvest besides Travis, and they would all have to have breakfast too, which they always ate out in the bunkhouse. They all looked up surprised when Joy walked in without so much as knocking. She was so angry her face was pale. Travis came toward her and said, "What's the matter?"

"Oh, nothing. I'll be a little bit late with breakfast for all of you."

Slim Whittaker grinned at her. "That's all right, Joy. We don't mind waiting for your fine cooking."

Joy studied the tall, slender young man, thinking, *These hired hands are so nice to me. Why can't the Tatums be like that?* "Thank you, Slim," she said. She turned back to Travis and said, "I'd better get back inside. I just got upset is all."

"I'll go back with you. Maybe I can help carry some of the food out."

Slim yelled, "Give me a call when you're ready. I'll help too."

Travis walked back inside with her, and as soon as they stepped in the door, he saw Albert standing there, his face florid with anger. "Don't you walk out on me, Joy, when I'm talking to you!" He grabbed her arm, and instantly Travis reached out and struck his arm away. "You keep your hands off of her, Uncle Albert!"

"Boy, don't you ever lay hands on me again!"

"Don't you lay hands on my sister again."

Albert shouted, "Get out of here!"

"I'll be glad to. Call me when you're ready, Joy. I'll help you take the food out." He gave Albert a defiant look, then turned and walked out the door, slamming it shut.

"You listen to me, Joy, you're gettin' too uppity. You're not an honored guest around here. You've got to work for your living."

"I work every day, and you know it."

Olean came into the drawing room to add her own com-
ments. "Don't let her talk to you like that, Daddy," she said. "She
needs a whipping."

Opal had followed her in. "Please, Albert, let's not have an
argument. You go on. I'll help Joy cook breakfast for the hands."

Albert stood there for a moment undecided, then scowled
and, turning on his heel, walked away. Olean glared at Joy and
spat, "You two are lucky to have a roof over your head. You're
nothing but paupers." Then she turned and followed her father.

Opal sighed and wrung her hands helplessly. "Don't pay any
attention to Olean. She doesn't mean it."

"Yes she does, Aunt Opal," Joy said quietly. She was really
fond of her aunt, for Opal tried her best to make life as pleasant
as possible. Several times she had given both Travis and Joy
money that she had managed to conceal from Albert.

Joy said wearily, "I'd better get breakfast for the hands."

"You haven't eaten anything yourself. Here, you sit down,
and I'll fry you a fresh egg."

At her aunt's kindness, tears came into Joy's eyes. She ate
breakfast but had little appetite for it. Then she called to Travis,
and the two of them carried the food out on covered trays. She
moved around the bunkhouse mess room, serving the coffee and
being teased by the hands. She never minded their good-natured
teasing, and she smiled back at them, thinking how much more
pleasant it was in the bunkhouse than in the farmhouse.

Finally the hands were finished and went outside, all of them
saying a word about how good the breakfast was. Travis stood
up but stopped long enough to say, "Try not to let it get to you,
Joy."

"I do try, Travis, but I just can't help it sometimes. The Tatums
are so mean."

"Aunt Opal's nice enough."

"Yes, she is, but she can't stop the others. Olean is downright
hateful."

"And Witt's no good either, but we'll have to tough it out for
a little while longer. Say, I forgot to tell you, I got a letter from
Uncle John last time I went to town."

Instantly Joy looked up. "Daddy's brother?"

"Yes. I wrote him and asked him if he could find a place for us, and he says he thinks he can."

"But Uncle Albert will never let us leave here, not until I'm eighteen. If you could get away, though, you're old enough to make your own way."

"I'd rather we sneak away together and get to Virginia. He'd have a hard time getting us back from there." He put his arm around her and hugged her. "We'll do it, sis. See if we don't."

Joy reached up and put her hand on his cheek, and he leaned over and kissed her on the cheek. He was a handsome young man, clean-cut and lean. Whenever Joy looked at him it made her sad, for she saw some of her father and her mother in his features. "We'll do it, won't we?"

"Yes, we will, Joy. One day soon we'll do it."

★ ★ ★ ★

It was exactly one week after the flare-up with Albert Tatum that Joy was out with her chickens. One of her chores was to take care of the chickens from their old home. Travis had made a fence for them to keep out the hawks and foxes, and he had also helped her build a chicken house, which now housed over twenty laying hens. There were plenty of eggs left over to sell to the neighbors, and without letting Albert know about it, Opal allowed Joy to keep that money. Opal hated going behind her husband's back, but she also knew the youngsters would need some cash to start out with when it came time for them to leave, and it grieved her that her husband was so stingy with them. Joy had accumulated a small sum, no more than thirty dollars, but it represented a start on an escape from the Tatum household.

"Chick-chick-chick-chick!" she called. As the hens came running out, she threw the feed to them and took pleasure in watching their heads bob up and down. They were beautiful to her, and she loved each one of them. She had named many of them and had tried to convince Travis that they knew their names.

"No, they don't know their names, silly," he always said with a smile. "They just come to you because they know you've got lunch."

Now as she watched the chickens, she was thinking of how

her uncle was mean enough to make her butcher some of her hens for the table. It infuriated her, and she knew she could never have any smidgen of affection for the man.

Joy was about to turn to go back into the house when suddenly a pair of arms went around her. She had not heard the gate creak, but suddenly she was held tightly, and she immediately knew who it was.

"Turn me loose, Witt!"

"Oh, come on, let's have some fun. You're gettin' to be quite a good-lookin' girl."

"Stop touching me!" Joy cried. "You'd better stop or I'll scream!"

She was powerless in Witt's grasp, for he was a big man. He put his heavy hand over her mouth and held her even tighter, laughing in her ear. She struggled and tried to kick him, but he merely laughed louder.

"You've got to learn how to make a man happy, Joy. You're growing up. You were just a skinny kid the first time I saw you, but now you've got a good shape on you."

Tears of rage filled Joy's eyes, and with all of her strength she reached up and broke his grip long enough to grab a handful of his thick hair and yank it with all of her might.

"Ow, cut that out!"

Joy squirmed around until she was facing him and struck him in the face. He instantly stopped laughing. "You're not so nice," he snarled and advanced toward her. But at that moment he was suddenly whirled around. "What—?"

Joy saw that Travis had entered the chicken yard, and before she could speak, he had drawn his arm back and struck Witt Tatum directly in the mouth. Witt stumbled backward as he tried to recover. Witt was probably thirty pounds heavier than Travis, but he was overweight and soft. He had done almost no hard work in his life, whereas Travis was nothing but lean muscle and much faster. His fist beat steadily on Witt's face while the big man swung ponderously. When Witt lifted his arms to protect his face, Travis drove a hard blow right in the stomach, then smashed him again over the eye, drawing blood.

"That's enough, Travis," Joy cried, trying to pull the men apart.

"Not enough for me," Travis panted, pushing her away. "I'm going to whip you so you'll never touch my sister again, Witt."

Witt cursed and moved forward, but then ran directly into a blow that smashed his nose flat, sending a spurt of blood over his white shirt.

Joy kept trying to pull Travis away, and finally several others arrived. She heard her uncle Albert yelling, and then Opal and Olean crying for them to stop.

Albert grabbed Travis, and the young man did finally stop. His eyes were narrowed, glaring fiercely at Witt as Uncle Albert held him back.

Witt said, "Pa, he came up and hit me. I wasn't doing anything."

"Yes, he was!" Joy cried. "He was putting his hands all over me like he always does."

"Don't you lie," Witt yelled. "I've never touched you!"

Albert reacted typically. He did not ask about the circumstances but simply shouted, "That's enough! You're nothing but a troublemaker, Winslow! Get your things and get off this place!"

"I'll go, but I'm taking Joy with me."

"No, you're not. She's a minor. She can't leave this place until she's eighteen. You try to do it, and I'll have the law bring her back and have you thrown in jail!"

"It's all right, Travis," Joy said. Her heart was breaking, but she didn't want to cause Travis any more trouble. "You do as Uncle Albert says."

Travis Winslow faced Albert with a look that was frightening. "You're a no-good, low-down skunk, Albert. If anything happens to my sister while I'm gone, I'll come back and I'll kill you."

Silence fell on the small group. Opal gasped and reached out to hold Albert's arm. "Don't do this, Albert."

"Keep quiet, woman! I'm not afraid of you, Travis!"

"Yes you are," Travis said quietly with steel in his voice. "You mind what I say, Albert. I'm not going to say it again. You hurt my sister, and one night you'll wake up, and I'll be there—and it'll be too late for you."

Turning on his heel, Travis walked out of the chicken yard with Joy hurrying after him. They went to the bunkhouse, where he pulled out his few belongings and started stuffing them into a pillowcase. "I hate to leave you here, Joy."

"Wait, don't leave yet. There's something I want you to take."

She ran from the bunkhouse and up to her room. She removed a floorboard by her bed to reach the hiding place where she kept her journals and the little store of money. She grabbed the money pouch and returned to the bunkhouse. "Here," she said, "take it. You'll need it."

"I'm not taking your money."

"I'll make more," she said.

Travis resisted, but finally he relented. "I'm not taking much. Still got the forty-four that belonged to our grandfather Zack."

"Oh, Travis, what'll I do without you?" Fear overcame Joy, and she held tightly to him. He put his arms around her and held her, and the two clung to each other. "I know it'll be tough, sis, but I promise I'll come back for you! As soon as I get a job and can save a little money, I'll come. I don't care what that monster says. He can't keep us apart."

"All right, Travis, if you say so."

The parting was quick. Travis kissed her on the cheek, then turned and left. The Tatums were all outside on the porch. Joy did not even look at them. She stood watching the figure of her brother as he walked down the road. He grew smaller and smaller and finally disappeared around the bend in the road. For Joy, it seemed as if the sun had gone out of the heavens. First her parents and younger sister, and now her brother. Her stomach lurched with the bitterness that welled up inside her, and she fiercely wiped the tears from her eyes. She was not going to let the Tatums see her cry, no matter what.

She walked back to the house, and the four of them stood watching her. Opal's eyes held kindness and pity, but the others stared at her with hard eyes. Joy turned to her uncle and said, "Albert,"—for the first time leaving off the word *Uncle*—"your son put his hands on me, and then he lied. He's a liar and a sneak." She turned to Witt and said, "Witt, if you ever touch me again . . ." She did not complete her threat but held Witt's eyes until he dropped his head. She went into the house and heard Olean screeching. "Why, the very idea! You ought to throw her out with him. Neither one of them is any good."

Joy went up to her room, found her journal, and wrote in it:

September 18, 1926
    Travis left today. One day he'll come back and get me. Until then I don't have anyone. No father or mother or sister, and now no brother, and I don't believe in God. If there were a good God, He wouldn't have let this happen.

She suddenly scratched out the words, fearful at what she had written. But she could not scratch out the hardness that had formed in her . . . and the regret over her loss of childhood and the end of gentleness.

CHAPTER FOUR

A Desperate Venture

★ ★ ★ ★

Through the cracks in the wall, the bitter cold fingers of winter entered, pulling the temperature of the attic room down steadily. Snow covered the ground in a six-inch-thick carpet, and the tree outside Joy's window had turned into a beautiful piece of fine glass. The rain the previous night had frozen, and now as the breeze stirred, Joy could hear the branches click as they turned upon themselves. The beauty of the scene outside held no attraction for her. It only meant that she would have to struggle harder to keep warm as she did her outside chores, and later that evening she would once again have to try to find warmth in her small cell of a room.

No mirror adorned the walls of her room, and the only three dresses she had were hung on a single nail. She shook her head in disgust, chose one of the dresses, and pulled it over her head. Just getting it on was a struggle, for in the months that had passed since her brother left, she had filled out even more. The dress was two years old, so now it was almost impossible to get into it. Her figure had swelled with womanly curves, which would have pleased her if she had been thinking about such things. Now her only thought was how to cover herself, and in despair she shook her head and picked up the wool coat. It had once belonged to Olean, but Joy had inherited it when she could no longer get into any of her coats. Her shoes were too tight for her, too, and the soles were as thin as paper.

She turned to leave, but first paused for a moment to look around the room. The lamp shed a meager light, twisting her own shadow into a tortured shape on the peeling wallpaper behind her. Its amber gleam on the walls and floor made the room gloomier instead of more cheerful. Hating the thought of going downstairs, she walked over to stare out of the window. She rubbed off the frost with her coat sleeve.

Outside, the early March sun bored a white hole in the sky, and the trees shed their shadows on the wintry ground like discarded rags. The barrenness of the scene saddened her beyond endurance. Life was unbearable to Joy. She woke each day as a galley slave must have awakened, with no hope of anything fine or good or wonderful happening—just another day of endless, meaningless labor. The night before, she had been reading a poetry book that had belonged to her mother, and part of a poem had stuck in her mind. She had gone to sleep thinking of it, and now it came floating back:

> . . . and beloved people push off from my life
>   like boats from the shore.
> They never come back, they never return,
> And I stand looking out on an empty sea.

A slight tremor passed through Joy as she stood there thinking of the lines. Then she quickly and firmly pushed them out of her mind and turned to go downstairs.

During the long winter months, she had only the family to cook for. Now that the hired hands were gone, her aunt never even helped her. Going into the kitchen, she started the fire. She raked the gray ashes away from the hot coals she had banked the night before. From the wood box she got a few scraps of rich pine and noted that she would need to bring more in. It would do little good to ask Witt to help with this, for he would only laugh at her. Besides, she avoided contact with him whenever possible. For a time after Travis had left, he had been decent enough, but it wasn't long before he was back to his old ways with her. His constant harassment left her exhausted, but if she tried to defend herself, it only caused her more trouble with Albert.

The rich pine caught, and she added larger pieces of wood until she had a good fire going in the cook stove. She held her hands over it, soaking up the warmth, not thinking of the day ahead, for what was there to think about? Another day of thankless work. The only pleasure she got out of life was caring for her chickens and reading in bed after her long day. She had formed the habit of bundling up, even wearing gloves in the freezing attic, which made it hard to turn the pages. Staying downstairs in the warm kitchen to read was impossible, for Albert always found more work for her to do, and Witt was a continual nuisance. There was nothing for it but to escape to her cold loft, the only place where the Tatum family left her alone.

She had breakfast ready and on the table when the family came in. As usual Opal spoke to her in a kindly fashion, and the others ignored her. The way Albert and his two children ate disgusted Joy. They were all big and bulky, even Olean, and they ate like hogs, gulping the food down rapidly, as if someone were going to take it away from them.

Joy had learned to fix her own breakfast either early or late, just so she wouldn't have to watch them while she ate. Today she was surprised, however, when her aunt Opal said, "We're going into town today. I'd like you to come with us. You can help me with the shopping."

Joy was pleased, for anything to get away from this house was a pleasure. "All right. When are you leaving?"

Albert said, "We're going right after dinner, but you can't go unless you get all your work done."

Olean looked sullenly at Joy. "I don't know why you have to take her. It'll be too crowded in the car."

"That car's big enough for all of us," Opal said rather sharply. "And you clean your room up or you're not going."

Olean waited until her mother's head was turned and then made a face at Joy. Witt saw it and laughed, then winked at Joy. "Maybe I'll take you to a picture show if you're good."

Joy simply gave him a hard stare, then turned and left the kitchen.

"That girl's too stuck up," Witt said angrily. "She forgets who puts a roof over her head and feeds her."

"I think she earns everything she gets," Opal protested.

"She *is* getting stuck up," Albert grunted. "Can't get a pleasant word out of her." He swallowed the rest of his coffee and called out, "Joy, bring some more coffee in here and hurry it up!"

★   ★   ★   ★

Wedged between Olean and Witt in the backseat of the new Packard, Joy tried to ignore Witt. It was a large car with plenty of room, but he pressed his thigh against hers and grinned at her when she gave him an indignant look.

The expensive car had been purchased only a short time after the death of her parents, and Joy suspected it had been bought with money that came from her own parents. She would go to her grave with the knowledge that Albert Tatum had robbed her and Travis of their inheritance.

The roads were rutty and tossed the riders around uncomfortably. Wishing she were not next to Witt, Joy turned sideways and stared out the window, ignoring him as well as she could. She watched a flock of red-winged blackbirds divide the air into a kaleidoscopic pattern against the featureless gray sky. From time to time flocks of crows would arise, shaking their heavy wings as they circled the shorn wheat fields. As they grew closer to Bismarck, the trees began to show themselves against the sky. They stood in disorganized ranks, and those nearest the road seemed to shoulder the sun out of the way, but the sun put long fingers of light through the trees, touching the frozen earth with pale white light.

The car bumped again, and Witt slumped against her, this time allowing his hand to drop onto her thigh. Joy knocked his hand away and said furiously, "You keep your hands off of me, or I'll scratch your eyes out!"

"Hey, what's the matter with you?" Witt said as his mother turned around. Innocence was in his voice, but his eyes were jeering. "You always think somebody's trying to touch you."

"He wasn't doing a thing, Mother," Olean said. "She's always blaming him. I told you we should have left her at home."

"Keep quiet back there, Joy," Albert grumbled. "I'm tired of always hearing your complaints."

Joy clamped her teeth together. She had resolved so many times simply to accept whatever happened without complaining, for she had learned the hard lesson that she could not ever win an argument with Albert or his children. Now she wished she had stayed home alone rather than endure the ride into town.

She breathed a sigh of relief when they reached the main street of Bismarck and Albert pulled up in front of the bank. "I've got to go in here and do some business. I'll meet you all at the general store."

As they got out Joy took a deep breath. She had planned her speech on the way to town and now said quietly, "Uncle Albert, I can't get into any of my dresses. Could I please have a new one?"

"She can have one of my old dresses. I need a new dress, Daddy," Olean piped up.

"There you are. Olean, you give Joy a dress and pick yourself out a new one."

Joy stared at her uncle. She kept hoping to find some bit of kindness in him, but it never happened. Now she said, "I'm five feet four and weigh a hundred and fifteen pounds. Olean is five feet eight and probably weighs a hundred and eighty pounds. How am I going to make a dress like that fit?"

Witt grinned at her. "Get your needle and thread out and sew it up. Maybe I'll help you."

Olean's face flushed, as she was sensitive about her weight. "Come on, Mother, let's go," she said.

Opal turned to whisper to Joy, "I'll try to do what I can."

"Never mind, Aunt Opal. I'm not asking anything of Albert ever again." She turned and left Opal standing calling after her. Her aunt was totally ineffectual, and the scene left a bitter taste in Joy's mouth. Angry thoughts raced through her mind, and she couldn't control her trembling as she walked along the frozen streets. *I'll never ask him for anything again. I'll steal. I'll do whatever I have to do!*

By the time she reached the post office, Joy had gained control of herself. Entering the small building, she waited in a short line until she came up to Mr. Higgins, the postmaster. "Do you have anything for me?"

"Not today, Joy."

"But my brother was supposed to write me in care of general delivery, and he's been gone for months."

"Well, he did write the one letter."

Joy stared at Higgins. He was a small man with delicate features and wore thick-lensed glasses. "What do you mean 'one letter'? I haven't gotten any letters."

"Why, there was one that came for you about a month ago. It came all the way from Texas, I remember."

"I never got it."

"Oh, your uncle was in, so I gave it to him and asked him to give it to you."

Shock raced along Joy's nerves. Speechless for a moment, she stared at the small man, then said, "I think it's illegal for you to give a person's mail to someone else."

"But he's your uncle."

"I'm going to report you," Joy said in a voice as cold as polar ice. She took some pleasure in seeing fear leap into the eyes of the man but turned and walked away.

He cried out to her retreating form, "But . . . Miss Joy, he's your uncle. I just thought it would save you some time."

Joy left the post office, blind with rage. All these weeks of waiting, and her uncle had kept Travis's only letter from her! She was trembling with anger and didn't even notice the freezing air. She did not remember walking to the general store. When she arrived there and threw the door open, she saw her uncle standing at the counter talking to Orville Wessicks, the owner. She walked straight up to Albert and demanded, "What did you do with my letter?"

Albert blinked in surprise. "What letter?" he said loudly. "I don't know anything about any letter."

"You're a liar! The postmaster gave it to you a month ago."

"Oh, one might have come. I don't remember."

At that moment all of the pain, anguish, and loneliness that had been building up in Joy Winslow erupted. She had no control over her words. She was aware that Mr. Wessicks was staring at her, as was every customer in the store, but she didn't care as she let her anger spill out.

"You're a liar and a cheat and a thief! There's not one kind or decent thing in you, Albert Tatum. You robbed me and my brother, and you're a filthy, rotten crook!"

Bismarck was usually a quiet town, so the people in the store were transfixed by this unexpected drama unfolding before them. They moved in closer so as not to miss a word. As for Albert Tatum, his face at first flushed with anger, then grew pale. He held his hand up. "Now, now, don't talk like that, Joy." He tried to quiet her, but her voice rose louder, and finally his own anger overflowed. "Shut your mouth, girl! You don't know what you're talking about!"

"Yes, I do too know what I'm talking about!" Joy saw that the gathering crowd was hanging on to her words. She pointed at her uncle and turned to the crowd. "He stole my dead parents' farm, and he's worked my brother and me like slaves! Now he's stolen mail from the United States Post Office, and I'm going to tell the sheriff!"

Joy whirled, but Albert caught her. "You're not going to do anything but go home. I've heard enough of your insolence." He would have said more, but Joy suddenly swung her arm and slapped him across the face. The print of her hand leaped into his cheek, and he slapped her back with his heavy hand. Joy fell backward and Mr. Wessicks caught her, saying, "Hold on there, Tatum. You can't strike a youngster like that."

"You don't know what she's done," Albert shouted. "She does nothing but make trouble." He looked around wildly and said, "Witt, take her home!"

"Sure, Dad." Witt came forward and took Joy by the arm. "Come on," he urged, tugging her out of the store. Before the door closed, she heard his father instructing, "Don't take her all the way home. Let her walk the last three or four miles. It'll cool her off."

Witt yelled back, "Okay, Dad."

Tatum turned back and saw the people staring at him. "Well, I hated for you to see her like that, but she's always screaming. We can't do a thing with her."

Mr. Wessicks said nothing, but he stared at Albert Tatum with his cold gray eyes. "Did you fail to give her the letter that came for her?"

"I gave it to her. She just wanted something to throw a fit about."

Opal stared at her husband. Later when they left the store, she said, "You didn't tell me about a letter."

"It was from that no-good bum of a brother of hers."

"You should have given it to her, Albert. Do you still have it?"

"No. Now enough about it."

★   ★   ★   ★

Joy wedged herself against the car door as far away from Witt as she could get. He had spoken to her several times on the drive back to the farm, but she had kept her face averted, returning not a word. The pain of losing a letter from Travis was overwhelming. Where was he? What did he say? He would think she didn't care because she hadn't answered his letter.

Her thoughts tormented her as the car moved along, and finally she was aware that it had stopped. She looked out and was surprised to see that Witt had taken her all the way to the farm. As the two got out of the car, Witt said, "I couldn't be mean enough to let you walk. Come on now. You're all upset, but it'll be all right. I'll talk to Dad."

"Stay away from me! Don't ever speak to me again, and if you touch me, I'll claw your eyes out!"

Joy turned and went into the house. She was so shaken she could not think properly, and she went to her room, trying to calm down. She collapsed on the bed weeping. After several minutes, she finally got control of herself. She began thinking, then suddenly sat bolt upright. "The letter—it's probably in his desk." She knew her uncle never threw anything away and suspected that the letter was still there.

With renewed hope in her heart, Joy ran downstairs and headed straight for the big rolltop desk. Sighing with relief that it was not locked, she pushed up the cover and began searching through the compartments in the top section. She found nothing and had just pulled open the bottom drawer when she spotted a package of letters with a string around them. She untied the bow and shuffled through them. Her breath caught in her throat when she saw Travis's handwriting. She threw the rest of the letters down and opened it. It was very short, but just the sight of his writing brought a pang to her heart.

> *Dear Sis,*
>
> *I've had a hard time finding work, but at last I've had some luck. I'm signing on with a ship, a steamer, that'll be leaving here to go to South America. It's not on a regular run so I don't know exactly where we'll be going. I do know we make one stop in Brazil.*
>
> *I hate to leave the country, but it was all I could find, and the pay is good. I'll save it all, and as soon as I get back, I'll come for you. Write me in care of general delivery in Galveston, Texas. I won't be here to get the letter, but I'll call at the post office as soon as I get home.*
>
> *Things have been bad, sis, but God's going to take care of us. I've been thinking a lot about how Mom and Dad served the Lord. I haven't done that, and I guess you haven't either, but I'm feeling more and more that I need to.*
>
> *Take care of yourself. I know it's hard for you. I'll be counting the days until we return, and I'll come as soon as we do.*
>
> *Love, Travis*

Tears came into Joy's eyes, and she stood there, shaken by the only contact she'd had in months with someone who loved her. She was so overcome she did not hear footsteps before two arms suddenly went around her. She cried out, knowing that it was Witt. She thought he had gone back to town to get his family, but instead, here she was alone with him! She squirmed, but he held her tightly. Raising her foot, she brought her boot down on his toe, and he cried out.

"Stop that! I'm not going to hurt you!"

"Let me go!"

Joy struggled fiercely, frightened by the thought of what he might do to her now that they were alone. "You've been running away from me," he sneered, "but I've got you now. Nobody's here. Go ahead and scream. I'm going to get what I want, Joy. Don't make me hurt you."

Paralyzing fear gripped her, for she saw the wildness in his eyes. She fought with all her might, but he wrestled her to the floor. She struck at him with her fists, but he was much bigger than she, and Joy could no more stop him than she could stop the wind.

Using the only weapon she had, she scratched her fingernails down across his face. One of them struck his eye, and he yelled with pain and released her. Joy scrambled to her feet and dashed across the room, but he was already coming after her, cursing loudly. She grabbed the front-door handle as he reached her, catching the back of her dress. She wrenched herself free, feeling the dress tear.

And then she saw the poker that rested beside the stone fireplace. She made a lunge for it, and as she turned back with the poker in hand, she saw that Witt was headed straight for her. She swung the weapon with both hands like a baseball bat. Witt never saw it coming, and it struck him in the temple. He staggered to one side, his eyes rolling upward, but he quickly recovered his balance and lunged at her again. Joy struck him again, and this time the poker caught him above the eye and blood spurted down his face. He fell to the floor, his legs and arms twitching. Then he became very still.

Panting and petrified at what she had done, Joy dropped the poker. She stood there trembling, waiting for him to move, but he did not.

"I've killed him!" she whispered. "I didn't mean to kill him!" Panicked, she knew she could expect no mercy from her uncle. *I've got to get away from here!*

She ran upstairs and began throwing her clothes together. She had no idea which way to go, but she knew she couldn't stay here. She took a deep breath and forced herself to think calmly. *I've got to get away, but where can I go?*

And then as if from outside of herself, a thought formed clearly in her mind: *The two-thirty freight—it'll be coming along in half an hour.*

The thought galvanized her. She knew that hobos sometimes rode in the empty cars. She had seem them sitting there dangling their legs, sometimes waving at her as they went by. They seemed happy enough, she thought.

But I'm a girl. I'll be easy to find among all those men.

Joy was terrified over what she had done, but some part of her mind still worked rapidly. "I'll put on boys' clothes, some of Travis's old ones," she said aloud. She ran to pull out a trunk in the attic next to her room where they had hidden some of their possessions. She found a pair of overalls Travis had worn when he was younger, a pair of his old shoes, several shirts, and a floppy hat he had once loved—an old fedora. It was shapeless now but big enough to tuck her hair into and pull down over part of her face. She also found an old green-and-white mackinaw, worn but usable. Quickly she stripped off her own clothes, shoved them in the trunk, and donned her disguise.

She ran back into her room and grabbed her journals, the thirty-eight pistol, and her egg money. It wasn't much, but it would have to last her. She stuffed the money into one pocket and the pistol into the other. Then she crammed the journals, some underwear, and a few other items into a gunnysack, knowing she could not carry much.

Moving cautiously downstairs, she started to leave. Expecting to see Witt's lifeless body on the floor, she was startled to see that he had turned over onto his back and was breathing regularly. Blood flowed from the cut over his eyes, but he was not dead!

Relief washed over her, and she tiptoed quickly past him toward the front door. She stopped only to glance at the clock and saw that it was fifteen minutes past two. The two-thirty freight was nearly always on time. She had to hurry. The train stopped to add water at a tank a mile from the farm. Realizing she was going to need some food, she went to the kitchen. She got a few cans of food from the cupboard, a can opener from the drawer, a tin cup and plate, some utensils, and some matches that were by the stove. Then she stopped dead still. Her lips set in a straight line as a thought occurred to her. Going over to the counter, she reached into a jar marked TEA. She pulled out some bills and some change and stuffed them in her pockets. "He's robbed me of everything, so I'm going to have this at least!" She did not count the money but knew she would need every penny.

She hurried outside and headed toward the train tracks, then suddenly thought, *I need to buy some time.* The ax was stuck in the chopping block beside the house. Putting down her sack, she ran and got the ax and carried it to the car. She drew the weapon back and struck one of the balloon tires with it. The tire made a mild explosion, then flattened. She flattened all four tires, then threw the ax down. Retrieving her sack, she hurried west toward the railroad tracks, with one thought replaying in her mind: *I've got to get to Galveston.*

She reached the water tank by the tracks, and within a few minutes she heard the lonely sound of a whistle. She hid herself behind a clump of dead grass, and when the train pulled up, expelling steam as it came to a stop, she watched to see if the brakeman would emerge. He did, and she saw him making his way to the water tank to release the water into the engine. She had watched him do it many times.

She picked up her sack and moved nervously along the line of dull red freight cars. She came to one with the door open and saw that it was empty. She threw her sack on, then sprang up and pulled herself into the car.

She pulled the door shut so that only a little light filtered through the bars. Then she sat down, her back against the side of the car. She closed her eyes and put her head back, pulling the soft cap over her face.

As she sat there aware of every sound, fear quickened her breathing. She had nothing, not even friends, and she knew that her uncle would soon have the law looking for her. The fear grew until it occupied her completely, and she cried out, "Oh, God, help me!"

As soon as she cried out, she remembered what Travis had said in his letter about wanting to serve God.

She tried to pray, but nothing came. She wanted to ask God for help, but she knew she had hardened her heart, that she was not the same girl she had been a year earlier. Now she sat in the gloomy interior of the empty boxcar with nothing to hold on to, and whispered bitterly to herself, "If God couldn't keep my mom and dad alive, He can't help me."

CHAPTER FIVE

TERROR IN A BOXCAR

★ ★ ★ ★

For a moment, as he struggled back to consciousness, Chase Hardin could not remember a single thing. All he knew was that his head was pounding and his mouth was dry. He lay still, trying to think, but the pain in his head was terrible—like a spike being driven through from temple to temple. His first conscious thought was, *My head is killing me. Why do I drink and bring on these awful hangovers?*

Using all his determination, he lifted his head and gazed around. He did not recognize the room but was mildly surprised when he realized it was not a jail cell. He usually awoke behind bars from his drunken binges, but this room, though small and plain, was obviously a dwelling. Coats were hung on nails on the wall, and a scarred and battered pine chest sat in the corner, looking forlorn. The window to his left let in pale beams of light filled with dancing dust motes, illuminating an ancient carpet with the pattern worn off down to the backing.

He was lying on a feather mattress in an iron bed, and a colorful patchwork quilt lay on top of him. Each quilt square had a chicken on it—some were red and some were blue. "I don't know this place," he muttered. "Where am I?"

From the next room he could hear someone moving around,

and he wondered who it was. He closed his eyes and tried to go back to sleep. Sleep was a refuge for him, a haven where he did not have to face the world. Drinking served the same function, but he always wound up like this—with a splitting headache, clothes covered in vomit, and quite often in a cell waiting to appear before a judge who would pronounce a fine he could not pay.

He lay there quietly hoping for sleep, but it would not come. Instead, memories ran through his mind like a motion picture. He remembered meeting a man called Mack, who had told him there were jobs to be had in Pierre, South Dakota. Mack had been a convincing fellow, and Chase had ridden the rails with him until they reached Pierre.

Sadly, there had been no jobs, and Mack had vanished. Chase had been disappointed too many times to feel anything more than a dull pain at the memory of yet another unfulfilled dream. He remembered spending his last two dollars on a bottle of bootleg whiskey. It had had an oily, vile taste, but he had gagged it down anyway, seeking oblivion—and he had found it.

Suddenly the door opened, and light from the other room fell across Chase's face. He blinked and turned away as a voice said, "Well, you're awake, I see."

Shading his eyes, Chase sat up and then swayed, for the pain jarred his head ferociously.

"That's some hangover you've got."

Chase gritted his teeth and waited until the waves of pain faded, then opened his eyes. A man stood before him—an older man with white hair and a pair of steady gray eyes. He was wearing overalls, a blue wool shirt, and a red sweater with one button fastened. "Do you think you can get up? I've got somethin' on the stove."

"I guess I can." Chase turned the quilt back and saw that he was fully dressed except for his shoes. He wore two pairs of socks, both of them full of holes, and he groped around for his brogans. He wouldn't put them on right away, though. He knew that leaning over to fasten them would destroy him. He had learned that much about hangovers. He got to his feet, swayed, and almost fell back.

"Hey, let me give you a hand." Chase felt a strong hand on

his arm steadying him and then urging him toward the door. "Come on, you can sit out here. I've got a good fire going."

Chase managed to move into the next room, which was obviously an all-purpose room for cooking, dining, and living. Soothing heat emanated from a wood stove to his left, on top of which were several pans. A table with two mismatched chairs sat over against the far wall, and his host led him to one of these. "Sit down there, and we'll get some coffee down you."

"That sounds good."

Chase leaned back, and when a cup was set before him, he picked it up with trembling hands. He tasted the boiling-hot black coffee and murmured, "This is good."

"How do you like your eggs?"

"Any way I can get 'em."

"That's the way I fix 'em. Scrambled is the easiest."

Chase watched as the man broke four eggs and mixed them in a large blue bowl. He poured them into a frying pan with some melted butter and then opened the door of the oven next to the firebox. "Got some biscuits from yesterday. They ain't fresh, but they ought to be good."

Chase felt he should say something, but he was still befuddled. "How did I get here?"

"I found you passed out down the street a ways. What's your name?" the man asked while stirring the eggs in the pan.

"Chase. Chase Hardin."

"My name's Thad Gilbert."

"How'd you get me here?"

"Oh, a friend and I, we carted you in and put you to bed." After the eggs were cooked, Thad occupied himself with finding some plates, knives, and forks. He set them out on the table, then dumped half of the eggs out of the pan onto Chase's plate and took the rest for himself. He moved back to the stove and picked up a plate covered with a white cloth. "Got some pretty good bacon here." He put butter, sugar, and cream on the table, then sat down. "You want to bless this, or do you want me to?"

Chase stared at the older man. "I guess it'll have to be you. I'm not on speaking terms with God."

"Well, that can be fixed." Thad bowed his head and said in a conversational tone, "Thank you for this good grub, Lord, and thank you for my friend here. Give him a good day. In Jesus' name." Without a change of breath, he said, "I got some black-strap molasses here. Put some butter on one of those biscuits and pour this on top. It'll go down pretty good."

Chase Hardin did not know how long it had been since he'd eaten a regular meal, but he was wise enough to know that on an empty stomach after a binge he needed to be careful. He ate half of the eggs and avoided the greasy bacon altogether.

"These are good biscuits," he said as he buttered one and put just a taste of molasses on. "And the molasses is good too."

"You'd better eat all you can. Looks like you're off your beat a little bit."

"You're right about that, but after a binge like I was on, I don't need to eat too much."

"Reckon that's right too. I've been on a few myself. Where you from?"

Chase had to think for a moment and then shook his head. "I guess from nowhere."

Thad Gilbert smiled. "A man from nowhere. Sounds like a book or a movie or somethin'. What's your line of work?"

"I'm a bum."

Thad had been chewing thoroughly, but he paused and stared at his guest. "You're too young a man to be in that profession for the rest of your life."

"Seems it's what I do best."

"What about your family?"

"Not much left, and they wouldn't want me around anyway."

Chase waited rather anxiously to see if the food would stay down, and it did. He felt compelled to make some conversation and said, "I guess no matter how run-down the rest of me is, I still got a good stomach. That was mighty good. I thank you, mister."

"Just Thad's good enough. Where you headed?"

"South."

"How'd you wind up in Pierre?" Thad listened as Chase gave him a brief history of his aborted journey and then shook his head. "Too bad. Not much work around here in March. Come April or May there'll be some. If you want to stay around, you can bunk with me. Might find you somethin' to do. I know quite a few folks here in town."

The offer warmed Chase's spirit. "I'm not used to falling in with kindness," he murmured, "but I think I'd rather go back down south."

Thad did not attempt to change Chase's mind, and finally he said, "I don't guess you remember tellin' me about your dad last night."

Chase stared at him. "I don't remember much of anything."

"You woke up when I was getting you in bed. You told me your dad was a preacher."

Chase was shocked, for he had not spoken of his family to anyone in a long time. "He was." He stared at Thad's lean face and asked curiously, "What'd I say?"

"About your dad? Just that he was a good man."

"He was," Chase said slowly. He dropped his eyes and swirled the black coffee around inside the white mug. "I guess it's a good thing he's passed on. It would have broken his heart to see what's become of me."

"What about your mother? Is she alive?"

"Yes, still alive, but I'd be ashamed to see her."

Thad Gilbert studied his guest, then shrugged. "Never too late to change, Chase."

"I used to think that, but I'm not sure of it anymore."

Thad began to speak of his own life then. He'd had a hard one, and as the two men sipped their coffee, Chase listened carefully. Finally Thad said, "If I hadn't found the Lord, I woulda been dead, I guess, or in the pen. I don't know if I'm succeedin', but I'm tryin' to be a good Christian now. I try to do what the Lord says."

"Is that why you took me in, Thad?"

"Sure. I wouldn'ta done it a few years ago, you can bet."

"Lucky for me."

The two men sat there, and finally Thad said, "You told me you were goin' to hop on the next freight out. Do you still plan on doin' that?"

"Yes."

Thad got up and went over to a small table beside the wall piled high with books and papers. He sorted through them for a moment and then came back. "Here, I'd like you to have this."

Chase took it and saw it was a New Testament. He also saw that it was well thumbed, and some of the passages were underlined. "I used to know this book," Chase said. "I knew it but didn't do it. Thanks a lot. I'll keep it always."

Thad reached into his pocket, pulled out a few bills, and separated two of them. "Here, buy a meal on me down the line."

"Aren't you afraid I'll drink it up like I did the last two dollars I had?"

"No, I'm hopin' not." He studied the young man before him and asked suddenly, "How old are you, Chase?"

"Twenty-six."

"You got a lotta livin' to do yet. Wherever you go, you remember there's an old man in a shack in Pierre, South Dakota, askin' God to look in on you and take care of you." He put his hand on Chase's shoulder and squeezed it. "And I believe He's going to do it, son."

Chase Hardin thought all emotion had been squeezed out of him, but a wave came over him at the touch of the man's hand. He could not remember the last time any man had helped him, much less put a hand on him and given him a word of encouragement. He kept his eyes down, for they suddenly stung, and he did not speak for a time.

Thad smiled, patted Chase's shoulder, and said, "You'd better get on down to the train yard. The three-oh-six will be leaving pretty soon."

"Sure." Chase rose and found that the food had strengthened him. He turned and found his coat hanging from a nail on the wall. It was old and too large for him, but he put it on, then pulled the floppy fedora down over his head. "Thanks for what you've done for me, Thad. I'll remember you."

"Jesus is on your trail, boy. He'll find you." As Chase moved to the door, Thad said, "Watch out for a bull named Kaufman. He's rough on hobos. Nearly killed one last month."

"I'll be careful." He turned and took one last look at Thad Gilbert, as if storing up a memory. "You've been a help and an encouragement."

"Remember your dad and go see your mom—and remember Jesus."

* ★ ★ ★

Chase had arrived in Pierre on the northbound freight. Now the southbound was waiting on the opposite track. Having learned the routines of railroad brakemen, he knew it was best to wait until just before the train pulled out. He spotted one car with the door slightly ajar, and when he heard the engine give two shrill blasts, he knew it was time. He carried only a small canvas valise with a few items in it, so he was not burdened down. As the train jerked forward, he ran over, shoved the door open, and threw his valise in. His head still hurt as he heaved himself on board, and he pulled the door shut as the train began to pick up speed. Nausea swept over him, and for a while he was afraid he would lose the meal he'd just eaten. He sat very still, and finally the feeling passed. His headache remained with him, however, and he lay down and put his head on his valise.

The car was cold and the wind was whistling between the slats, but he was on his way south. There was nothing there for him except for warmer weather, but that in itself would be a blessing. As he lay there, he thought about his encounter with Thad Gilbert. He thought of his dad and for some reason remembered a fishing trip he had gone on with him. They'd had such fun that day! He remembered his dad ruffling his hair and saying, *When you grow up, you may be a preacher like me.*

A wave of sadness washed over Chase Hardin at that thought, for he had gone far away from his father's God. And then the image of his mother floated in front of him, and he tried to shake it away. It always hurt him to think of her. She had been so proud of him, yet he had gone so far down. More than once he had started to go see her, but he always changed his mind at the last minute. What would she think when she saw the wreck that was left of all of her dreams?

The *clickety-clack* of the wheels passing over the joints of the rails echoed a rhythmic pattern, and he lay still, rolling with the swaying of the car as it traveled south. He tried to put everything out of his mind, but as always, this was impossible. Before he dozed off, his last thought was of Thad Gilbert and how he had given him a Bible and two dollars and a meal. He felt the warmth of the man's hand on his shoulder, and the sensation comforted him as the freight train rattled over the prairie.

★   ★   ★   ★

For two days Joy had mostly stayed inside the car, and her initial panic had worn away. She was hungry, having eaten only one can of beans each day. She did not want to use up her food supply too quickly. By now she was also very thirsty. She had gotten off the train twice to get water at the station when the train had stopped at night, but now as another day was ending, she desperately needed another drink.

As the train slowed she stood and looked down the length of the car. The man who had gotten on earlier in the day had slept most of the time. She had watched him cautiously, but he had made no move except to sit up for a while and stare into nothingness. She could not make out his features, for he never moved from the shadows and wore a large shapeless overcoat. Now he appeared to be sleeping again, his face against his small valise.

When the train stopped she moved toward the door but paused when she heard voices. She took a quick breath and glanced outside and saw two men running toward the very car she was in. She retreated quickly into a corner, and there was a rumble as the door opened. She heard curses, and then two men piled inside. They stood up, and the small guy said, "Hey, there's a guy over here, Earl."

The big man named Earl answered, "Who is it? What kind of a guy?"

"Just a guy."

Joy scooted backward silently, hoping the darkness would conceal her. She watched the two men as they approached the one who was sleeping. The bigger man rolled him over. She heard a voice protesting, "What do you want?"

"Everything you got. You got any whiskey?"

"No."

"You got some money, though."

"No, I don't."

"Don't lie to me." There was a meaty sound of a slap and a

muffled grunt, and then the big man straightened up. He held something up to the light that filtered in through the slats of the car and said, "Well, looky here, Roy. We got a preacher with us. See, he's got a Bible."

"I don't need no preaching," Roy said.

"He's got some dough too. We can use that."

"Give that back to me."

The big man laughed and said, "Shut up or I'll kick your head off."

Joy's heart froze, for these two men clearly had evil intentions. She made herself as small as possible, and the train started up again. The sunlight suddenly illuminated the end of the car as the train rounded a curve, and the man called Roy said, "Look, there's another guy back there."

"So there is. Maybe *he's* got somethin' to drink."

The two approached, and Joy pulled herself back as far as she could get into the corner.

"Hey, you got any whiskey?"

Making her voice as rough as she could, Joy said, "No, I don't."

"You got anything to eat?"

"A couple cans of beans."

"Let's have 'em."

Joy knew it was useless to argue. She reached into her sack and brought out the two cans of beans. The smaller man snatched them up. "Gimme a can opener." He waited until Joy handed it to him and then proceeded to open one. He handed it to the big man, who tilted the can up and began eating noisily. Roy opened the other can, and the two men ate like starved wolves.

"You ain't got nothin' to drink?" the big man said.

"No, and nothing else to eat."

"You got money though, I bet. A few bucks."

Joy panicked. What if she lost her egg money? "No, I don't have any. I'm broke."

Something about the voice suddenly caught Roy's attention. His hands shot out, and he snatched the cap from her head. Joy tried to prevent it but was too late. She felt her hair, which had been tucked inside the cap, fall around her shoulders and knew she was in bad trouble.

"Hey, Earl, this here's a girl!"

Earl had seen the shiny blond hair spill out and laughed. "How about that!" He reached out and grabbed Joy's arm. "You're in luck today, sweetie. What's your name?"

"Joy."

"Well, Joy, you got a couple of good-lookin' boyfriends here." He pulled her close and grabbed her hair, pulling her head back. "You're a pretty little thing, aren't you? Well, I ain't had me no lady friends for some time now." Earl laughed. He brought his face close to hers. Joy yanked her head away but felt his lips slide over her cheek. "Come on, don't be shy."

Joy knew there was little hope of being rescued from this situation. Earl was as strong as a gorilla, and his hand held her like a vise. She begged, "Please don't hurt me. Leave me alone."

"A little lovin' never hurt a girl," Earl said, his voice thickening. "Just relax."

"Let that girl alone!"

The grip on Joy's arm did not loosen, but she felt Earl turn around and saw Roy do the same. They were staring at the man who had advanced toward them. He was not an impressive figure. He was no more than average height and seemed quite young. He had black hair, dark eyes, and an olive complexion.

Earl stared at the man and said, "I suppose you want her, huh?"

"I said leave the girl alone."

"Why, preacher, you can have your turn with her—soon as we get through."

Joy felt a tiny ray of hope. At least one man had some decency, but suddenly Earl let go of her arm and stepped toward the other man. He shoved him backward and said, "You stay out of this or I'll break your face."

"You let her alone, and I'll stay out."

Earl laughed harshly. "Listen to this, Roy. He thinks he's gonna stop us. You couldn't stop anybody, mister."

And then Joy saw the smaller man strike a futile blow to Earl's chest. He ignored it except to laugh. "Why, you couldn't hurt a fly." Then his own arm swung, and his huge fist caught

Joy's defender high on the head. She saw him careening backward to fall full length, and then Earl advanced toward him. Before her terrified eyes, Joy saw him viciously kick the prone figure twice, then a third time. She heard his muffled cries of pain and heard Roy yelling, "Don't kill him, Earl."

"I ain't gonna kill him, but I'm gonna bust every rib he's got, and then I'll bust his face."

Joy suddenly remembered the gun. Moving slowly, she reached into her coat pocket and brought out the thirty-eight. Aiming over Earl's head, she pulled the trigger. The sound of the shot brought a startled response from Earl. "Hey!" he yelled and whirled around. He found himself facing the muzzle of the revolver and a pair of steady eyes behind it, feminine eyes but full of determination.

"Put that gun down, girl!"

"You two get out now!" Joy demanded, waving the gun at Earl.

Roy was startled. "We can't jump from this train. We'd break our necks."

"It's not moving that fast. Jump, both of you, or I'll shoot you."

"She's bluffin', Roy," Earl said. He took a step forward, and then another shot rang out. A blow struck Earl's left forearm and turned him around. He grabbed his arm and looked down wild-eyed to see the blood seeping between his fingers. "Hey, you shot me!"

"The next one's right between your eyes. I'll count to three, and on three you're a dead man. One—two—"

Earl stared at her wildly and then gave a startled cry. Holding his arm, he ran to the door, threw it open, and jumped from the car.

"Now you!" Joy said.

Roy whimpered but said nothing. He moved to the door, took a deep breath, and then casting a malevolent look at Joy, jumped with a wild yell.

"I hope you both break your necks!" Joy shouted after them. She put the gun down and found she was trembling all over. She moved across the car and knelt beside the still form of the man who had come to her defense. Blood was running down his face, and he was moaning. "Are you all right?" she said.

"My side . . ."

There in the boxcar Joy Winslow did not know what to do. This man had risked his life for her, taking away the attention of the two attackers. She had a horrifying image of what would have happened if he had not tried to help. Sitting down beside him, she pulled out a handkerchief and held it over his bleeding face to staunch the flow of blood. "We'll get some help at the next stop," she promised.

★　★　★　★

As soon as the train pulled to a halt somewhere in central Nebraska, Joy jumped to the ground. She saw a brakeman hanging on to the side of the car, and she cried out, "Help! I need help!" She ran forward, and the brakeman turned warily to face her. "You been on this train?" he demanded.

"There's a man in that car. He's hurt real bad."

The brakeman was a tall man with a deep chest and a pair of wide-spaced gray eyes. "What happened to him?"

"Two men beat him up. He's hurt bad."

"I'll take a look."

Joy felt a wave of gratitude. "He's down here," she said. She led the brakeman to the car, and the two entered. Leaning over, the man studied Chase's bloody face. "Can you hear me?"

"Yes." The voice was barely audible.

"Where are you hurt?"

"In my . . . side."

"They kicked him. I think his ribs are broken."

"Well, he can't stay on the train. I'll go get some help."

Joy knelt down, saying, "It's all right, mister. You're going to be fine."

"What's your name?" Chase whispered.

"Joy."

The man didn't respond; he simply lay there. His breathing was shallow, and Joy saw that his face was still bleeding. Then she heard footsteps approaching, and two men heaved themselves up into the car.

"There he is, Kaufman. I think he's busted up pretty bad."

"All right. Let's get him out of here."

Joy went at once and got her gunnysack. She also picked up the small valise the man had brought on with him. She hopped out and saw that the two men had simply laid the injured man down on the ground.

"You can't just leave him here," she cried.

"It ain't our problem," Kaufman said brutally. "Come on, Cam."

"She's right. We can't leave him here."

The older man stared at the one called Cam. "What do you propose to do? It's time to pull out."

Cam's eyes darted around, and he said, "Look, there's that old caboose. It's been there for months." He turned to the girl and said, "We could put him in there. There's a stove in it. It's been condemned, but at least you can get a fire going. Maybe you can find a doctor. The station agent's name is Powell. He'll help you."

"Come along, Cam. Leave him there."

"No, give me a hand, Kaufman."

Kaufman cursed under his breath but obeyed the younger man. Joy followed them and saw as they struggled to get the injured man inside that he had passed out. She followed them in, and the younger man said, "We've got to go. Go see Powell. He'll help you."

"Thanks."

"You're welcome."

"Come on, Cam. We're behind schedule."

Joy looked around. She had never been in a caboose before. There was an ancient potbellied stove in the corner, and she hoped she could find something to burn, either wood or coal. She leaned over the man and saw that his face was as white as chalk and he was still unconscious. They had placed him on the bunk, which was fastened to the wall. She glanced around and spied some old wooden boxes. Between her pocketknife and some good hard stomps with her foot, she managed to splinter one into pieces. She dug to the bottom of her pack to find the matches, then lit a fire in the stove. She added a few chunks of coal she found, and soon a fire was blazing.

She turned her attention to her patient. "Can you hear me?" she asked, leaning over the still figure. She got no answer and thought, *I've got to get help.*

Leaving the caboose, she went to the station, which was as small as a station could be, she thought. When she stepped inside she saw an older man with silver hair and bright blue eyes watching her. "Who was that the guys put in the car? Your man?"

"No, just somebody I met, but he's hurt bad. Are you Mr. Powell?"

"That's me. Well now, that caboose has been there for three months. It ain't goin' nowhere."

"Would it get you in trouble if we stayed there?"

Powell grinned, studying the girl. "I'm sixty-six years old, and nobody wants my job. Stay there as long as you please."

"I've got to take care of him. Could I get some water?"

"Sure. I got a bucket here. Plenty of water. What's your name?"

"Joy . . . Smith."

Powell did not miss the hesitation but did not press the issue. "What's his name?"

"I don't know yet. Two men jumped on the train and beat him and kicked him. He's hurt real bad, Mr. Powell. He needs a doctor."

Powell shook his head. "No doctor here. I'll stop in and take a look at him after I get off."

He looked at the girl, wondering about her history, then said quietly, "You've been in a bit of trouble, I take it."

Joy stared at the man. "Yes," she said. "Quite a bit."

CHAPTER SIX

SISTER HANNAH

★ ★ ★ ★

The smell of meat cooking awoke Chase. He blinked his eyes and started to sit up, but an unbelievable stab of pain in his side caused him to lie back and catch his breath. Something on his forehead was shutting out the vision of his right eye, and reaching up, he discovered a damp cloth.

For a moment he was confused, and then the scene in the boxcar started coming back to him. The last thing he remembered clearly was a tremendous blow to his side as he lay on the floor trying to get to his feet. And then other vague memories flitted through his mind—he recalled someone lifting him—but then he must have blacked out.

He lifted his head slightly and saw someone standing with her back to him, cooking at a stove. He cleared his throat and found his lips almost too dry to speak. The long blond hair that fell down the back identified the person as female, and he assumed she was the girl he had tried to rescue.

"Hello," he said feebly. The girl turned around, and he saw that she was very young. She came and bent over him, and by the sunlight that filtered through the window he saw that her enormous eyes were an intense shade of blue. She was wearing a pair of overalls and a blue wool shirt. "Where is this place?" he croaked.

"It's a caboose in Nebraska. Are you thirsty?"

"Yes."

"I'll get you some water." She dipped a cup down into a bucket, and then said, "I know you're awfully sore, but can you lift your head enough to drink?"

"I'll try." Very cautiously Chase lifted his head. Despite his care, the pain in his side made him blink, but he was so thirsty it didn't matter. He gulped the water down as she tilted the cup. He almost choked on it and then pulled his head away. "That's good," he murmured.

"You remember anything after the fight?"

"Not much. What happened to those two?"

"I'll tell you later. What's your name?"

"Chase Hardin."

"My name's Joy." She hesitated for a moment and then said, "Joy Smith. I introduced myself yesterday, but I don't expect you remember much from yesterday."

"How did I get to this place?"

"You were unconscious, and the men that work on the train helped me get you off at this stop. We're in an old abandoned caboose. The stationmaster says we can stay here until you get well."

"Must have some broken ribs. I can hardly move."

"I was waiting for you to wake up because I'm going to try to find a doctor. Do you want something to eat?"

"No, not hungry."

"Well, I'll put the water bucket right here. You can reach down and get water with the cup. I don't know how long I'll be gone."

Chase took the cup and considered the girl. She had a smooth complexion and regular features. "Well, Joy Smith," he said, "it looks like you're the boss. I can't do much to help you."

"You just lie there. I'll be back soon, and I'll bring you something to eat. Maybe some soup."

"That sounds good."

She stood looking down at him for a moment, then said,

"Your forehead won't stop bleeding, and it's a bad cut. I think it'll have to be sewn up."

"I didn't help you much, did I? Not much on saving damsels in distress."

The girl's face changed, and he saw a look in her eyes that hadn't been there before. She hesitated, then said, "You did your best, and that's all anybody can do." Finally she turned to leave, saying, "You lie still. I'll be back as soon as I can."

The sun was bright as Joy moved quickly down the tracks. She found Mr. Powell inside the station, and he asked how the patient was doing.

"He's not good at all. He needs to see a doctor."

Powell shook his head and took off his glasses. "That won't be easy," he said slowly. "The closest one I know is Dr. Thomas, but he's all the way over at Broken Bow. That's nearly fifty miles."

"I'll just have to go get him."

"Doubt if he'd come. He's not much on charity cases."

"I've got a little money."

"Not much I'd guess, Missy."

"But he needs help! His head needs to be sewn up, and I think his ribs are broken."

William Powell had seen a great many hobos in his day. They came and went, and in most cases, he was glad to see them go. But this girl was different. He thought for a minute and then said, "I'll tell you what I would do if I was you, Missy. There's a lady who lives not two miles from here—in a farmhouse all by herself. Gettin' on in years now, like I am. I think she must be pushin' seventy, but she's strong and able. Most folks go to her when they have hurts. She's a midwife, but she's done plenty of doctorin', including gunshot wounds. If I was you, I'd go see Sister Hannah Smith. Maybe she can help your man."

Joy's face flushed. "He's not my man. He's just someone who needs help."

"All right, then. In any case, Sister Hannah's on the main road. I can't leave here, but it's only a couple of miles if you don't mind a walk."

"I can do that."

"All right. Go out to that road and go east. Just stay on the road, and 'bout two miles from here you'll cross a little bridge over a creek. It's the only bridge around. Sister Hannah's house is the first one on the left. I 'spect she'll be home, unless she's out doin' some of her preachin'.'"

"Preaching? She's a preacher?"

William Powell scratched his head and grinned. "Yep, she's religious all right. Makes a fellow plumb nervous the way she lights in. She's a good healin' lady. She'll pray over your man—I mean that fella—but she'll do whatever she can for him in a medical way too."

"Thank you, Mr. Powell. I'll go right now."

Powell talked to himself as he watched Joy turn and walk rapidly down the road. "That girl's got a lot of grit. It's a pity she's gotta be out on the road like this. Gotta be a story behind her, but she didn't offer to tell none of it." He put his glasses on, took one final look, then shook his head. "Sister Hannah don't set well with ever'body, but that girl ain't got much choice—nor the fella over in that caboose, for that matter."

★   ★   ★   ★

After crossing the bridge over a gurgling creek, Joy saw a two-story white house to her left, with a driveway leading up to it. Quickening her pace, she strode down the drive. She saw a barn out back and a corral with two horses. A huge German shepherd snarled at her, but Joy saw that he was chained. She climbed the steps to the porch and knocked on the door. No one came for a few moments, and she thought, *If no one's home, I don't know what I'll do.*

Then she heard the sound of footsteps, and the door opened slowly. The woman who stood there was very tall for a woman and strongly built. Her silver hair was coiled behind her head, and she had a pair of penetrating blue eyes behind wire-rimmed glasses. She studied Joy carefully before asking, "What are you doing out here, young lady?"

"Are you Mrs. Smith?"

"Most folks just call me Sister Hannah. Come in outa the cold."

Joy stepped inside, and when she pulled off her hat, her hair fell down over her shoulders. "Mr. Powell, the railroad agent, told me about you, Sister Hannah. He said you're good with sick folks."

"The Lord Jesus is the healer. I'm just His instrument. Are you sick, child?"

"Oh no, it's not me. A man got hurt in a freight car last night. He was badly beaten. We got him off, and he's in an old caboose down by the station."

"I know that caboose. What's this man to you?"

Joy hesitated, then said, "I'd been riding the freight train when two men got in the car. They started to . . ." She hesitated, and color flooded her cheeks. "They started to bother me, and this man—he had been sleeping in the corner—tried to take up for me. But they beat him and kicked him. I thought they'd kill him."

"Did they bother you after they whipped him?"

"No, they didn't."

"I wonder why not. Wasn't nothin' to stop 'em."

Joy lifted her head and met the silver-haired woman's eyes. "I had a thirty-eight, and I pulled it out of my bag and told them I'd shoot them if they didn't get off the train."

"And they did it?"

"They did after I shot one of them. Oh, just in the arm a little bit. I'm a very good shot, Sister Hannah."

"Well, my stars alive, I can't believe it! You shot a man and then made 'em jump off a moving train?"

"I had to. I was afraid. I don't think they got hurt, but they would have killed the man that tried to help me."

Hannah Smith studied the girl in front of her and noticed that her lower lip was trembling. *No wonder,* she thought, *I'd be afraid, too, if I'd gone through that.* "What's your name, young lady?"

"Joy Smith."

"You got a home?"

"No. My folks died a year ago. I'm trying to get to Galveston so I can meet up with my brother, and then I want to get back to Virginia, where I used to live."

Sister Hannah knew there was more to the story than this, but first things first. "All right," she said. "I'll get my medicine bag. We'll hitch up the horse and go see what we can do."

"Thank you, Sister Hannah," Joy said with a gush of relief. "I . . . I didn't know what else to do, and Mr. Powell says that the doctor is fifty miles away."

"Well, we've got Dr. Jesus with us. Come along. We'll go hitch up that ornery mare."

Twenty minutes later the mare was hitched, and Sister Hannah was coming out of the house with a black suitcase. She put it in the back of the buggy and then asked, "What you usin' for sheets and covering?"

"Nothing. There's a bunk there, an old mattress, but no covers at all."

"Well, that won't do. I'll go get somethin'. Probably need some pans and pots to boil water in too." She disappeared into the house and soon returned with blankets, sheets, and a burlap bag. She put those in the back along with the medical bag, then slowly climbed in and picked up the lines. "Get up, Ginger!" she said forcefully, and the mare started up at a brisk walk. They had not gone a hundred yards before Sister Hannah turned and said, "Joy, are you a Christian girl?"

Joy ducked her head and swallowed hard. "No, ma'am, I'm not."

"Well, you can't get away unless you jump outa this buggy, so you sit there, and I'm going to tell you how Jesus saved me and filled me with the Holy Ghost."

Joy turned and smiled. "That'll be fine, Sister Hannah. I'd like to hear it."

"Not everybody does, but I like to tell it." She began speaking, and Joy was amazed to find out that Sister Hannah had been a wild young woman in her earlier days. She did not go into great detail but told enough to let Joy know that she had led a wild, sinful life.

"I got married and had six children, all married up now except for Susie. She lived with me until she died two years ago. My husband, Lester, he up and died on me five years ago. I didn't get saved until after Lester died, but when I did get religion, I got it good. The Lord convicted me of my sins, and I got saved in a holiness meeting. It took five nights at the altar, but when I got it, I got it good. I've been tellin' everybody ever since about Jesus and His precious blood and doin' all the good I can."

"Are your children far away?"

"Oh, land no! They're all here in the county except for Jeannie, and she married a fella from California. They're doin' good, though. The Lord gave me a promise. 'All thy children shall be taught of the Lord,' and that's what happened."

Sister Hannah turned to face Joy and said, "I know you're runnin' away, child. I don't know what you're runnin' from, but whatever it is, it ain't nothin' that Jesus can't fix. So I'm gonna tell you how to find the Lord, but first we'll take care of this sick man of yours. How old a fella is he?"

"I don't know—he looks about twenty-five, I guess. His hair is black, the blackest I've ever seen."

"Well, we'll see to him, and then we'll have plenty of time to talk to you about findin' your way to glory."

As the buggy pulled by the station, Mr. Powell came out and said, "Hello, Sister Hannah."

"Hello, Brother Powell. You wasn't at church Sunday. You be there next Sunday, you hear me?"

"I'll sure be there," he called back, smiling. "If you need any help with that feller, call on me."

Sister Hannah sniffed. "What good does he think he'd do? I'd just as soon have a gorilla around a sick man as him."

Sister Hannah pulled the buggy up next to the caboose and got out. She picked up her black bag and followed Joy to the steps at the rear of the caboose. Joy went on up and said, "Let me take your bag, Sister Hannah."

"Maybe you'd best do that. That's a pretty high step."

Joy took the bag and waited until Sister Hannah was on the rear platform. She opened the door, and Sister Hannah followed her in. She put the bag down and went to stand beside the bed. "Are you all right, Chase?"

"Sure."

"This is Sister Hannah Smith. She's going to help you. She's real good at doctorin' people." Then turning to Sister Hannah, she said, "This is Chase Hardin."

Chase looked up at the large woman with the bright blue eyes and said, "I'm in pretty pitiful shape, I guess, Sister Hannah."

"Well, the first thing we gotta get straight is that nobody can help you except the Lord Jesus. Dr. Jesus is the one you need. I can do some stitchin' and some bandagin' and a few things like that, but He's the one that's gotta help you."

Chase found himself smiling despite the pain. "My dad would have agreed with you."

"He was a Christian?"

"Yes. He was a preacher and a good one too. I'm sorry to say that I've gotten away from what my dad wanted for me."

"Well, first we're gonna pray, and then we'll go to work." Sister Hannah bowed her head and laid both hands on Chase's shoulders. She prayed with such vigor that her voice filled the space.

"Lord Jesus, this here man is hurt. He needs your help, and you know I can't do nothin' except as you help me. So I'm askin' you who gave sight to the blind and hearin' to the deaf and legs to them that couldn't walk and life to them that was dead to come down to this man and help us to do whatever you want done to him. And make him strong and hale, and do more than that, Lord—I'm askin' you to touch his spirit. In Jesus' name. Amen."

"Amen," Chase said. He was overwhelmed by Sister Hannah, and he watched as she took off her coat and picked up the black suitcase. She opened it and removed a large brown bottle. "Here, take three good swallows of this."

"He can't sit up, Sister Hannah. I'll hold his head."

Chase felt Joy's hand behind his head and ignored the pain. He tilted the bottle and took three quick swallows. He made a face and gasped. "What is that? It tastes terrible."

"Nothin' but paregoric. I give it to babies with colic and men that have had their heads kicked in or anybody else. You'll start gettin' sleepy in a few minutes. If you don't, you can take three more swallows."

"Isn't that dangerous?" Joy asked.

"We gotta make sure he don't feel much when we sew up that head of his. Then we gotta move him around quite a bit. Get him outa that bed and put some covers on this here bed, and then we best see about them ribs—if'n they's busted. It ain't gonna be no pleasure a'tall. What'd you say your name was?"

"Chase Hardin."

"Well, Brother Chase, we'll just wait a bit until that paregoric takes ahold of you." She turned to Joy. "He needs a bath. He's plumb filthy. Get them pans outa the buggy, and we'll heat up some water."

Joy left quickly and soon returned. She had to fetch another pail of water from the station, but the stove was an effective heater, and soon the water was warm enough for bathing.

"You ain't sleepy enough yet for me to do that stitchin' on your eyebrow," Sister Hannah said. "So I'm gonna tell you 'bout gettin' saved first. . . ."

★ ★ ★ ★

"He's just about unconscious, Sister Hannah," Joy whispered.

"Let's get started on sewing up that head. It may hurt him a little, so you gotta hold his head still while I do the stitchin'."

Joy swallowed hard, but she followed Sister Hannah's instructions, holding Chase's head firmly. It was necessary, she found, for he did flinch when the needle hit his flesh. When the stitches were done, Sister Hannah said, "You done good, Joy. Now, let me check them ribs. This is gonna hurt him."

It was a painful business, and the medicine was only partially effective, but finally Sister Hannah said, "As far as I can tell, there ain't none of 'em fractured. What I suspect is that they're just cracked, not broke, which is good."

"I'm relieved to hear that."

"Yep, me too. Let's get him down off that bed long enough to put some sheets on it, and then we'll give him a bath. He can't lay there on that filthy bed."

"How're we going to move him?"

"I'll take his head, and you take his feet. We'll just set him right down on the floor, and then we can fix the bed. I don't think he'll feel too much."

Following Sister Hannah's instructions, Joy took Chase's feet while the large woman slid her hands under his shoulders. "When I say three, we lift him. Just set him down easy. One—two—three."

Chase groaned as they lowered him to the floor, but Sister Hannah ignored him. "There, get them sheets." The two women put the sheets on quickly, then added two blankets. When they were done, she said, "We gotta give him a bath." She knelt on the floor and started unbuttoning Chase's shirt and said, "Pull his britches off, girl."

"Me?"

Sister Hannah paused and looked up. She saw that Joy's face was red with embarrassment. "Get them britches off. It looks like he ain't changed his clothes lately. Go on. It won't shock you too bad."

Joy's face was flaming, but she managed to get the wool trousers off. To Joy's relief he was wearing long underwear. "Okay, let's put him on the bed now, and then I'll clean him up. You ready?"

"All right."

At the count of three again, they picked Chase up and laid him down on the fresh sheet. Joy watched as Hannah washed him as if he were an inanimate object. She was appalled at seeing the deep purple-and-yellow bruises on his side. "His side looks awful, Sister Hannah."

"Ain't no doubt but them ribs are cracked, but Dr. Jesus can mend them. Now," she said, "that's clean enough. Hand me that there towel." Taking the towel, she dried Chase off. "Now we gotta get him bandaged—as tight as he can stand it."

The bandaging was difficult. Joy had to hold Chase up in a sitting position, and more than once he groaned as Sister Hannah wrapped him tightly. Finally she was finished, and she said, "All right, lay him back there." Joy carefully lowered Chase to the bed. "Let's cover him up now and keep him warm."

Sister Hannah covered him, then studied the man's drawn face. "He got hurt real bad, and he's gonna need lots of care, little sister. I'll come back tomorrow and check on 'im. You'll be all right tonight?"

"Oh yes, and, Sister Hannah, I want to pay you for coming."

Sister Hannah shook her head firmly. "I don't take money for helpin' folks."

Joy had started to pull money from her pocket, but she hesitated. "Then I can only thank you."

"I'm going to leave some of this paregoric here. He ought to stay out most of the rest of the night. If he does wake up, give him a big tablespoon full of it. I'll come tomorrow about noon maybe."

"Thank you, Sister Hannah."

After Sister Hannah had closed her bag and left, Joy closed the door. The fire was dying down, and she put two more chunks of coal on it. Mr. Powell had contributed some of his own for this purpose. She pulled up a box and sat down beside Chase. Sister Hannah had bandaged his forehead, and now Joy brushed back his black hair, noticing it had a curl in it.

For a long time she sat there, and then for the first time since the struggle in the boxcar, her thoughts turned to her own troubles. *Albert will have the police looking for me. He may even figure out I left on the freight train. If they start checking, those brakemen will tell him where I got off.* The thought troubled her, but she was too exhausted to worry about it. There was another bunk down at the other end, and Sister Hannah had brought enough sheets and blankets to fix it. She made the bed quickly and then slipped off her shoes and climbed under the covers. Her last thought was of how Chase Hardin had tried to help her, and she murmured aloud, "I'll stay until he's able to take care of himself."

PART TWO

March—May 1927

★ ★ ★

CHAPTER SEVEN

"It Ain't Fittin' . . ."

★ ★ ★ ★

As the freight slowed beside the small station, the engine released a burst of steam, and the brakes ground the train to a halt. The cars made a metallic clanging as the slack was taken out. Even before the train had fully stopped, Cam Freeman swung to the ground and headed purposefully toward the abandoned caboose that rested on the siding fifty yards from the station. He had often thought of the injured man and the girl, and now as he approached the caboose, he muttered, "Been three days—they might have moved on—but that fellow was in pretty bad shape." Stepping up onto the rear platform, he knocked on the door, calling out, "Anybody home?"

The door opened almost at once, and the girl stared at him apprehensively. Her eyes lit up as she recognized him, and he grinned at her. "Well, you're still here, I see."

"Oh yes. I'm glad to see you again. Come on in."

Cam stepped inside the caboose and saw that it had been made fairly livable. The small coal stove threw off a cheery glow, and on top of it a blackened coffeepot was giving off a delicious aroma.

Joy introduced Cam to Chase. "This is one of the men who

helped get you off the train and into this caboose. You were out cold when they moved you."

"I don't remember much about that day. Thank you for help-ing me."

"Would you like some coffee?" Joy asked.

"No, I can't stay," Cam said. "I've got to be on my way. I just wanted to check and see how you're doing." He nodded at Chase, who was sitting up on the small cot, his back braced with blankets. "Well, I see you didn't die."

Chase managed a grin. "No, but from what I hear I might have if you hadn't helped us. I sure appreciate your help."

Cam moved closer and studied the face of the injured man. The black hair was brushed back, and he was fresh shaven, but his lean face was tense.

"He had some cracked ribs," Joy said, "and we had to have his head sewn up, but he's doing fine now."

"Glad to hear it. You were in pretty bad shape for a while."

Chase's eyes went to Joy for a moment and he nodded. "Looks like I'm nothing but excess baggage."

Cam grinned broadly, shaking his head. "Don't be sayin' that. You'll be okay now. How long before you can get around?"

"Can't say, but it won't be too soon for me."

Cam heard the warning blast of the whistle and said, "Gotta be going. Just wanted to check on you. Is there anything I can do for you?"

"No," Joy said, "you've done a lot. We both appreciate it."

Cam turned and, with a wave of his hand, stepped outside the door. Joy turned to Chase, saying, "He's a nice man."

"Sure is. Not too many like him around."

"I've got to go to the store and get something to eat. You just lie there until I get back. Here, I'll give you a cup of coffee. Don't you get out of bed, now."

"I'm nothing but an overgrown baby," Chase grumbled. He watched as she filled the mug and handed it to him. "I feel like a charity patient, Joy."

"All of us have to have help now and then. I'll be back soon."

Leaving the caboose, Joy headed east, where the small town was located. There were no more than twenty houses in the town, and the only business on the main street was a general store with a gas pump outside. She had been to the store once and now felt the eyes of the few people who were on the street. She kept her head high, despite their suspicious glances. One man even made a crude remark to his friend, which she ignored.

Turning into the store, she saw a clerk behind the counter measuring beans into bags. The small man had oily hair plastered against his head and an unkempt mustache. He was wearing a white shirt with a black string tie and had old-fashioned garters around his arms. "Hello there," he said, putting down the scoop. "What can I do for you?"

"I need a pound of coffee, a pound of bacon, some bread, and a can of peaches." As Joy gave her order, the clerk moved around rapidly, piling the items on the counter. His eyes watched her furtively, and when she said, "That's all," he picked up a tablet and added up the total.

"That'll be sixty-three cents."

Joy reached into her pocket, pulled out a small roll of bills, and peeled off the top one. The clerk took the bill, and when he handed her the change, he managed to tickle her palm and then laughed at her as she pulled her hand back.

"Don't you want this change?"

"Just the change," Joy said, anger flaring in her eyes. "Just put it on the counter."

"Well, aren't we hoity-toity! Who do you think you are—the queen of England?"

"Put those things in a sack please."

The clerk tossed the items into a used paper bag. He shoved it toward her and sneered, "You're the one living with that guy out in the caboose, aren't you?" He saw the dismay sweep across the girl's face and laughed. "Everybody knows about you, so don't be acting like you're all holy."

Joy's face flushed as she snatched up the bag, whirled, and slammed the door behind her. A scrawny yellow dog that had been napping outside was startled by the explosion of sound. It jumped to its feet, looked around, and bared its teeth, but Joy paid it no heed. She stomped along the street furiously, ignoring the looks she got from two women, one of whom leaned over and whispered to the other as she passed.

When she got back to the caboose, Joy said nothing, not even a greeting. Chase knew something was wrong. She put the few items she had bought onto a shelf that she had added to the caboose by simply nailing an apple crate to the wall. She turned and saw Chase watching her.

"Is anything wrong?" he asked gently.

"No, nothing," Joy said shortly. "I wish I could make biscuits, but we don't have an oven." While she thought for a moment, Chase kept his eyes on her, aware both of her strangeness and of her pleasing appearance. Even dressed in the rough boys' clothing, she still appeared quite feminine, and he appreciated the graceful lines of her throat where her shirt collar fell open. She was always guarded, but he understood that a girl out on her own would have to be. *I'll bet she's had a hard time of it—maybe runnin' from somethin'. She wouldn't be out riding the rails alone for no good reason.* He lay still watching her, noting the hint of willfulness and pride in the corners of her eyes and lips. Even in the brief time he had known her, he had learned that beneath her cool exterior, she was a girl of deep feelings. Now her lips softened into a slight smile. She made a little gesture with her shoulders and looked at him. "I think I'll make stew today. It'll be a change."

Chase nodded, and as she turned and began her work, he wondered what went on underneath that façade she had assumed. He said nothing—just kept staring—and once she glanced over and said, "I wish you had something to read."

"Well, I've got a New Testament. Would you hand it to me? It's in that sack."

Joy studied him for a moment and then nodded. Turning, she walked across the narrow aisle, picked up the New Testament, and handed it to him. It was thick, and the black cover was worn. "Have you had it a long time?"

"No, a fella gave it to me just a few days back." He remembered Thad Gilbert's kindness. It was one good memory in a long list of harsh ones, and he had stowed it in a section of his mind where he kept other good memories. When things got bad he would go there, take them out, and examine them one by one. It had been a habit of his for a long time, and for the last few years the good memories had been rare indeed. Opening the New Testament, he began to read. Soon the aroma of frying bacon filled the small room, and he glanced up to watch Joy. Her back was to him, and her head was turned to one side, allowing him to study her profile without being noticed. The clean sweep of her jaw gave her a youthful look, but he found it hard to guess her age. For one brief moment he wondered what would become of her and was troubled by the possibilities. Suddenly she turned and met his eyes, and he smiled. "Been trying to read Revelation."

Joy laughed. "My dad had a dog once named Revelation."

It was the first time she had mentioned her family, and Chase picked up on it. "Why in the world did he call him that?"

"He said he called him that because he didn't understand a thing about that book—and he could never understand anything about that dog either."

Chase smiled. "I've known a few animals like that myself. Do you like animals?"

"Yes, we always had pets." Joy's face softened as she said, "Once I got to raise a wolf."

"Is that right! Where did you get it?"

"A friend of my dad's killed the mother, and then he found these little pups. He killed all of them but one, and my dad got it and brought it to me. It was so small. I had to feed it by hand."

"What did you feed it?"

"Oh, at first I would just dip a cloth in some milk and let it suck the cloth." The distant memory came back to her, and she said, "I called it Buck, like the dog in *Call of the Wild*."

"I would guess you didn't get to keep it, though."

Surprise washed across Joy's face. "How'd you know that?"

"Because wild animals don't make good pets after they're grown. They're cute enough when they're kittens and pups, but they eventually grow up. Even coons are wild animals, as cute as they are when they're babies."

"Why, that's right!" Joy exclaimed. "I raised one of those too. He stayed around a long time, but finally he went back to the forest. I cried all day, I think." She turned back to the stove, saying, "Oh no, I'm going to burn your dinner!"

Chase went back to reading the New Testament but contented himself with reading the Gospel of John instead of the mysterious book of Revelation. When Joy told him dinner was ready, he looked up with surprise. "I got caught up in the stories in the book of John," he said. "Are you a Christian, Joy?"

Joy had been spooning out stew with one of the two spoons the station agent had given her. "I used to think I was," she said tersely. "Now I don't know." She set the stew on an upended crate she had put beside his bunk. She returned with a piece of bread and said, "I wish we had some butter."

"This is fine. Why don't you sit down and join me?"

Joy got herself a bowl of the steaming stew and sat down on the box she used for a chair. She took a spoonful and tasted it cautiously. "It's hot."

"But good. You're a good cook, Joy."

"Anybody can make stew."

"Not me. I could never cook anything."

The two ate slowly, saying little, and just as they were finishing, Joy lifted her head. "Listen."

Chase had caught it too. "Buggy pulling up."

"I expect it's Sister Hannah. She said she'd come by about noon." She took Chase's empty bowl and put it on the small shelf, then went to open the door. "Hello, Sister Hannah," she said, smiling.

Hannah was getting out of the buggy. She tied the mare up to a small sapling and then nodded as she stepped up onto the rear platform. "How's the patient?"

"Much better. Come on in and take a look at him."

Chase greeted her with a big smile. "Hello, Sister."

"Lemme see them stitches." Hannah tilted Chase's head with one hand on the top of his head and the other under his chin. Her eyes narrowed as she studied her handiwork. "Not a bad job of stitchin' if I do say so myself. Have to take them stitches out maybe in a few days." She started unbuttoning his shirt without asking permission.

"You don't allow a fellow much modesty, do you?"

"When you've raised kids like I have and handled as many sick men, they ain't much time for modesty." She palpated his chest and sides, giving him instructions all the while. "Take a deep breath. Does that hurt? Can you turn thisaway?"

Finally she straightened up and said, "Good thing them ribs

wasn't broke. You'd be in bed for months. The Lord is doin' a good work of healin'."

"I just made some stew, Sister Hannah. Sit down and eat a bite."

"There ain't no time for that," Hannah said flatly. "Get your things together."

Joy exchanged a startled glance with Chase, then stammered, "But-but where are we going?"

"You're going to my house, that's what."

Chase shook his head. "Wouldn't want to be a bother."

"Ain't no bother about it, but it ain't fittin' for a man and a woman what ain't married to stay together. So don't argue with me none. You're goin', and that's the way it is."

Joy swallowed hard and felt her cheeks grow warm. "We haven't done anything wrong."

"The Bible says 'Abstain from all appearance of evil.' " Hannah's voice was sharp, but then a kindly light appeared in her eyes. She reached out and ran her hand over Joy's light hair. "I know you ain't done nothin' wrong, honey, but people talk, so you're comin' with me. Don't worry about crowdin' me. That big old barn of a house has got more bedrooms than you could shake a stick at. Back a few years ago I had it full of young'uns, but then my husband went to be with the Lord, and the kids all growed up, and I'm all by myself there. So get yourself ready, because we're a-goin'!"

★ ★ ★ ★

"You've gotta take it easy, Chase. Got plenty of time. Don't move them ribs around no more than you can help."

Chase held himself carefully upright in the seat of the buggy. Joy sat between him and Sister Hannah, and when they arrived at the house, both women got out and helped him get down. Pain shot through him as his heels hit the ground, and he took a deep breath. "Not too bad," he said. "I think I can make it."

"You just keep ahold of him, Joy," Sister Hannah admonished. "Men ain't got no sense about takin' keer of themselves."

As the trio moved through the gate of the picket fence, a

sudden barking startled Joy. She looked over to see the German shepherd that had barked at her on her first visit hit the end of its chain, fangs bared. She asked, "Is that your watchdog, Sister Hannah?"

"He's just a no-count dog, that's what he is. His name's Jake, but it might as well be Satan!"

"He looks like he could eat somebody up."

"I reckon you got that right. My grandson Caleb, he had the crazy idea that I needed protection and brought that dog here a couple weeks ago. Keerful now goin' up these steps—just take it slow and easy." As she helped Chase up several steps to the front porch, she laughed, "That Caleb! Sometimes I think that young'un ain't got a lick of sense! He gave me that dog to protect me, and I can't even get close enough to feed him. If he ever gets loose, I expect he'll half kill me."

They reached the porch, and Hannah opened the door. "Bring 'im on in here. I got a room on the first floor. You can stay upstairs, Joy."

Chase's room was large, and the two high windows admitted plenty of sunlight. A walnut bedstead with a red-and-white counterpane all turned back was waiting.

"You might as well get out of them clothes. You gotta have a bath."

"I guess I can do that myself."

"We'll see about that. Who's gonna wash your back? You answer me that."

Chase laughed. "All right, Sister Hannah, you're the doctor."

"You just keep thinkin' that, son! Come on, I'll show you your room, Joy," Hannah said.

Joy followed the large woman back into the hall, then up a flight of stairs. At the top she saw that there were two doors, one on each side. Hannah opened the one on the right, saying, "There ain't no heat up here, but you can come downstairs when you get cold. We got plenty of blankets for the nighttime."

"Oh, it's a beautiful room!"

"It is pretty, ain't it, now."

The room, not as large as the one downstairs, had a sloping ceiling to follow the roof and a large window at one end. A worn blue carpet covered the floor. The bed was made up with several blankets, and the pillow was fluffy and thick.

"One of my granddaughters, Lucy, she lived here with me a spell afore she went off to college in St. Louis. She left some of her clothes here. I reckon they'll jist about fit you. They're in that closet over there." She gestured toward the closet, then added, "Reckon you'd like to have a nice hot bath, wouldn't you?"

"Oh yes!" Joy said fervently. She felt gritty and grimy, and just the thought of a good bath warmed her heart.

"Let's let Chase get cleaned up first, then you can take your turn in the tub. Go ahead and pick out some of them clothes. There's some underwear over in the drawer of that bureau. Good thing Lucy's about yore size."

"But . . . I can't take her clothes!"

"Them clothes is goin' to waste. Pick somethin' out, and I'll start heatin' the water for Chase."

★　★　★　★

Joy sank down in the tub and luxuriated in the hot water—as hot as she could stand it. Her knees stuck out, and she closed her eyes and laid her head back.

"Might as well wash your hair while you're in there. The well water here is pretty soft. 'Course I use rain water sometimes, but I ain't catched any lately."

"Oh, that would be good! My hair is so dirty and grimy."

"I got some store-bought hair soap from the Sears 'n Roebuck catalog. Ain't even out of the box." Sister Hannah rummaged in a cabinet, located the soap, and handed it to Joy. "You just enjoy a nice bath. I'll lock the door so cain't nobody get in. Not that I'm expectin' anybody."

Joy soaked until she felt like a prune, then scrubbed herself with a washcloth and washed her hair. Finally she got out of the tub and dried off with the fluffy white towel Sister Hannah had left her. She slipped into the underwear she had found in the drawer. The clean garments delighted her, and the dress was a perfect fit, better than any of her old dresses had fit her. It was light green with small white flowers. She slipped on a pair of stockings and a pair of black shoes that were a little large, but not by much. She unlocked the door and sat down beside the kitchen stove, drying her hair with a towel. She was trying to comb it with her fingers when Hannah returned.

"Land sakes, you can't comb your hair like that! Let me get you a comb."

Hannah disappeared and was back almost at once. "You set still whilst I comb it out."

Joy sat upright, and an unfamiliar feeling of luxury swept over her. No one had helped her with her hair since her mother had died, and a lump rose in her throat as Hannah gently pulled the comb through her hair. It always made her drowsy when someone combed or brushed her hair, but it was a comforting drowsiness. Finally she said, "Thank you, Sister Hannah. I'll just tie it back."

"You got right pretty hair. Always was partial to blond hair. Ain't none of my children exactly blond. My youngest—her name was Fairy—she had kinda reddish hair with a light streak, but yours now is a real pure blond color."

"What can I do to help with chores, Hannah?"

"Well, be time pretty soon to be thinkin' about supper. You know how to kill a chicken and cut it up?"

"Oh yes."

"Well, go pick out a nice one, and while you get it ready I'll do the rest."

Joy started out the door, but Sister Hannah said, "Put on a coat, young lady! It's cold out there—always is in March. And put that sweater on first." She pointed to a sweater draped over the back of a chair.

Joy put on the blue sweater, then the coat Hannah handed her, and went outside. She heard the clucking of the chickens and followed the sound around to the back of the house, where she found a large area fenced in with chicken wire. She chose a fine young chicken that came trustingly up to her. She reached down, stroked the hen for a moment, then said regretfully, "I'm sorry, but we've got to have something to eat." Expertly she reached down, grasped the chicken around the neck firmly, and with one practiced motion, swung it upward in a wide circle. The head separated, and the headless body hit the ground. As she knew it would, the hen got to her feet and began running around wildly. It fell twice, kicking and bloodying the ground with bright red blood. Finally it lay still, and Joy went over and picked up the body. It always troubled her to have to kill chickens—but she'd learned that such things were a part of life. She sat on a stump in the yard and plucked the chicken, and then finally she went back into the warmth of the kitchen.

Sister Hannah nodded. "I watched you take care of that hen. Ain't it a caution the way they run around after they have their necks wrung?"

"I never could understand it," Joy said, laying the chicken on the cutting board. "If you've got a sharp knife, I'll gut it and cut it up."

"Right there in that drawer." Hannah studied the hen and then laughed aloud. "Reminds me of some church members. Some of the most active ones ain't worth nothin'. I always say the most active chicken in the barnyard is the one that just had its neck wrung—and some church members that make the most commotion ain't got nothin' in 'em."

Joy had a good laugh, and it was the first time Sister Hannah had seen the girl release the tension that had bound her. As Joy expertly prepared the chicken, Hannah said, "You remind me of my middle girl, Susie. She's the one who went to be with Jesus two years ago."

Joy looked up. "That must have been very difficult."

"She was never healthy. Had a lot of sickness, but I loved her. She was always my favorite, but I tried not to show it." She came over and stood beside Joy and stared out the window. The big dog, Jake, had come to the end of his chain, and was filling the air with savage snarls directed at a man who was walking down the road. "That's a bad dog. I'm gonna have to get rid of him." She turned then and said quietly, "You know, Joy, I got mad at God when He took my daughter Susie. I wouldn't even speak to Him for nearly a year."

Startled by this revelation, Joy stared at the older woman. There was strength and character in every line of the old face, and she thought, *That's what I'm doing. I'm mad at God because He took my parents and my sister. . . .*

"But then, you know, that all changed one day. I was poutin' and wouldn't read the Bible and wouldn't do what God told me to do. I was just downright mad. And then I remembered somethin'. I remembered when I was just a little girl, no more than five or six years old, I pulled up some of my mama's prize flowers. Well, she cut a switch from the apple tree and took me by the arm and started switchin' my legs." A smile touched the older woman's lips as she said softly, "I tried to get away, and the further I got, the more room she had to swing that switch—and the more it hurt. And you know what happened then, Joy?"

"What?"

"I was tryin' to get away, and somehow I ran right into her. I grabbed her around the legs and held on to her, and I started cryin' out, 'I love you, Mama!' and I found out somethin' right then about God."

"About God? I don't understand."

"Well, when I was tryin' to get away, my mama had plenty of room to swing that switch, but there I was holdin' on to her, and she couldn't swing it with her whole arm. She could just pat me, sort of. It didn't hurt near so bad, and then I kept tellin' her I loved her, so she quit switchin' me. She put her arms around me, and I remember she cried that day—and my mama wasn't a cryin' woman." The distant memory caused Sister Hannah's face to grow soft. "Not long after that, I run across a verse in the Bible. It said, 'Kiss the Son, lest he be angry.' So I learned somethin'. When God's whippin' us, we don't need to be tryin' to run away. We need to turn to Him and throw our arms around Him and tell Him we love Him."

The kitchen was silent then, and Joy Winslow felt tears rise in her eyes. The story had touched her, and she could say nothing. Her throat grew thick, and she turned away and began fumbling with the pieces of chicken. "Do you want me to fry these?"

"We'll wait a spell, so they'll be hot for supper." Hannah's hand fell on Joy's shoulder. She said nothing, but there was a warmth to her touch that made Joy feel even more vulnerable. After a moment Hannah changed the mood, saying, "Can you make biscuits?"

★   ★   ★   ★

"What are you doing up?" Joy asked with surprise a few days later. She stepped into the kitchen to find Chase fully dressed and sitting at the kitchen table. Sister Hannah had gone to visit a sick member of her congregation, and Joy had just come inside after feeding the livestock.

"I couldn't stand that bed anymore," Chase said. "I had to get up and stretch my legs."

Chase had been getting out of bed more each day, but he usually just sat in a rocker in his bedroom. Now he had more color in his cheeks, and Joy said, "You look better."

"I feel better." Chase carefully took a deep breath and shook his head. "That feels good. I feel like I can get some air down in my lungs."

"Well, what do you want for breakfast?"

"Anything!"

"I doubt that. I think I'll fix pancakes."

She began pulling the ingredients out of the cabinets. During the five days they had stayed at Sister Hannah's, Joy had learned everything about the house. She rose early, washed, cleaned, ironed, took care of the animals, and worked in the kitchen. Sister Hannah had shaken her head. "You are a working machine. Slow down, girl!"

It pleased Joy to work hard. She had tried once to express her thanks to Sister Hannah, but the silver-haired woman had said, "Just pass it on, child. You'll find somebody that needs help. As a matter of fact, you already did—with Chase in there. That's what we live for. To love God and to love each other."

Now as she poured the batter into the large black frying pan, Joy thought back to the day she had met Chase. She asked him, "Do you miss drinking, Chase?"

"I haven't even thought about it. That surprises me too. I haven't gone this long without drinking in ages."

"I'm glad."

"Pretty hard way to stop drinking."

Joy was hesitant. "Have you been drinking a long time?"

"Couple years."

It was on the tip of Joy's tongue to ask him why he had started drinking, but she knew that would not be right. She gave

Chase the first two pancakes, then said, "You start on these while I fix some more."

Chase looked at the golden brown pancakes and shook his head. "You are a fine cook, Joy."

"My mother taught me."

The two ate breakfast slowly, coating the pancakes with rich, fresh butter and dousing them with cane ribbon syrup. The fried ham not only tasted good but also left a delicious aroma in the air.

"I haven't eaten this good in a long time," Chase murmured.

"Neither have I. I'll be fat as a hog if I don't slow down."

"I doubt that."

Joy was wearing another of Lucy's dresses that had been hanging in the closet. It was pale blue with a white collar and nipped in at her waist. Chase noticed that the dress fit her perfectly, and he admired the easy way she moved about the kitchen. When she refilled his coffee cup, he said, "We can't stay here forever."

"No, but it's sure been nice compared to the caboose."

★　★　★　★

The next day as Sister Hannah was returning from another one of her visits to a sick church member, she pulled the buggy into the driveway, then stopped abruptly and stared at Chase. He was sitting on an empty apple crate in front of Jake. The dog was staring at him, his lips drawn back from his teeth. Hannah wanted to tell the man to get away from the dog, but she was afraid she would startle the animal. Quietly she went inside the house and found Joy mopping the kitchen floor. "You know what that fool Chase is doing?"

Joy looked up, wiped her hands on a towel, and said, "What?"

"He's out there tryin' to make friends with Jake. Might as well make friends with the devil himself!"

Joy went to the front room and looked out the window. "He shouldn't be doing that," she whispered. "That dog could tear him to pieces."

"I guess he knows that. Kinda funny, ain't it? He's the first one I ever seen come anywhere close to that dog."

"I thought he'd gone back to his room. He must've been out there the whole time you were gone."

The two women were puzzled by this, and when Chase came in thirty minutes later, Sister Hannah said, "Chase, you stay away from that dog."

"Why? He's a fine dog."

"Fine? He'll bite your head off!"

"No, he won't do that."

"What were you doing out there with him, Chase?" Joy demanded.

"Just getting to know him—and letting him get to know me. There's a good dog down in that animal somewhere. He just has to find out about it himself." He smiled, and there was a winsome look about him. His olive skin and black hair went well together, and even in the few days he had been at Sister Hannah's, he had put on enough weight that his cheeks were no longer sunken. His eyebrows were dark and arched in an unusual fashion.

"You're gonna get dog bit," Sister Hannah warned.

"Why, Sister, don't you think God can take care of me?"

"If Jesus told you to do it, it's fine. But if it's jest somethin' you thunk up, you'll get bit. The Bible says, 'Thou shalt not tempt the Lord thy God.'"

"Yes, that's in Matthew 4:7."

Hannah was surprised at Chase, and a look of grudging admiration flickered in her eyes. "Well, you ain't got completely away from your raisin', have you, boy?"

"I've gone pretty far."

"Well then, you're goin' to church tomorrow, so make up your mind to that. If you're strong enough to sit out by that worthless dog, you're strong enough to sit through a sermon!"

CHAPTER EIGHT

THE WOMAN AT THE WELL

★ ★ ★ ★

As Sister Hannah halted the buggy beside a grove of pin oak trees that bordered a plain white church, Joy felt strange. She glanced at Chase, who was clean-shaven and wore the same clothes she had always seen him in, only freshly washed and pressed. She was wearing the blue dress that had belonged to Sister Hannah's daughter. She felt strange about coming to church and wondered if Chase felt the same. He said nothing, however, as he braced himself against the jolts of the buggy and the dirt road.

"Well, good morning, Sister Hannah." The speaker was a tall, broad man with bushy brown hair and cheerful brown eyes. He smiled and reached out to help Hannah to the ground.

"Good morning, Brother Felix. We've got some visitors this mornin'. This is Chase Hardin and Joy Smith. This here is Elder Felix Bone."

"Kinfolk of yours?" Elder Bone asked.

"No, not a bit of it," Sister Hannah replied. She scanned the churchyard, which was covered with wagons, cars, and trucks. She looked at the church building and said, "The church house looks plum good. That coat of white paint shore makes it stand out. I like to see the Lord's house lookin' sprite."

"It does look good, don't it? Well, I hope you got a good sermon for us this mornin', Sister. I think the congregation needs a little brimstone."

Hannah smiled and shook her head. "A little fire and brimstone goes a long way, Brother Felix. What folks need to know is the love of Jesus."

"Amen! Hallelujah! Praise God, you're right." Elder Bone nodded his head with each word and then said, "I'll go in and prime the pump, get the singin' started."

Hannah turned back to Chase and Joy. "A good man, Felix Bone. Used to be a bootlegger. He got saved by the grace of God and now leads our singin'. C'mon, I'll see you get good seats right down in front."

Joy thought, *I'd rather have one in the back*, but she did not argue. She and Chase followed Sister Hannah as she made her way into the church. Joy took in the simple meeting place in a glance. The ceiling was high and formed of rough pine, and bare light bulbs hung from naked wires. The walls were whitewashed, and the smell of pine filled the building. Hannah directed them into the second pew, and when Joy sat down she found it impossible to assume any position except one—bolt upright. The seat was so narrow she could not possibly slump, and the back went up at an uncomfortable right angle.

Chase was more interested in the people than he was in the architecture. The women all wore long-sleeved dresses, buttoned down to the wrists, and their skirts brushed their shoe tops. None of them, he noted, wore jewelry, and most of them had their hair plaited and bound up in a roll. One woman's hair was done so tightly it pulled her eyes into a slanting position. None of them, of course, wore makeup.

The men, for the most part, wore overalls or jeans, but all of them wore white shirts and ties. It appeared to be a poor congregation, Chase noted. He leaned over and whispered to Joy, "This reminds me of some of the churches my dad pastored—everybody wearing their Sunday best, even if their Sunday best wasn't much different from their everyday clothes."

Joy had no chance to answer because Brother Felix had loosed a booming greeting on the congregation. "Well now, we're mighty glad you're here in the house of God this morning. I want you to let God know how much you love Him and appreciate Him. We'll start by singin' 'When I See the Blood.'"

The congregation all stood without being urged and sang vigorously to the accompaniment of an out-of-tune piano. As Joy glanced around she saw that most of the worshipers were enthusiastic. Some of them clapped their hands, and more than once someone would lift his hands and shout, "Glory to God!" or "Praise be to God forever!"

Joy was not accustomed to such enthusiasm in church. Her experience had been with more sedate churches and sour-faced participants. These worshipers actually looked like they were happy to be here. She glanced over at Chase and saw that he looked as uncomfortable as she felt. He was not singing, for like her, he probably did not know the words to any of the songs. His whole body looked tense, and he clasped the seat in front of him with splayed fingers and white knuckles.

I wonder what's wrong with Chase. He grew up in church. This is not like anything I've ever seen myself—but I don't know why it's affecting him so. . . .

The singing went on for some time, much longer than Joy was accustomed to. There was a pause while the ushers took an offering, and then Sister Hannah said, "Now the Scripture tells us that if any of you are sick, you should call for the elders of the church. The elders shall anoint the sick with oil, and the prayer of faith shall save the sick. Any of you who have a sickness in your body, I want you to come down to the altar, and we're going to see miracles."

This was certainly outside of Joy's experience, and she watched with astonishment as an older woman walked down the aisle and knelt at the front rail. Several other people came forward—the elders, Joy assumed—and laid their hands on the woman's shoulders. Sister Hannah put one hand behind the woman's head and with the other hand rubbed oil on the woman's forehead. She then clasped the woman's head firmly with both hands and began to pray in a loud, piercing voice, "O God, this here is your daughter, and she is sick in her body. I pray, Lord Jesus, that you would heal her as you healed blind Bartimaeus, as you healed Naaman the leper. . . ." The prayer continued on, and with each phrase Sister Hannah would firmly shake the old woman until she almost reeled back and forth. Finally Sister Hannah opened her eyes and said, "Do you feel the power, Sister Irene?"

"I feel it! Praise God, He done healed my body."

A chorus of amens and shouts went up, and then Sister Hannah turned to a bulky man who said, "I got me an ailin' in my stomach, Sister, but I believe in the power of God."

The healing prayers went on for half an hour, and all the time the congregation remained standing. Finally, however, everyone who went forward was prayed for, and Sister Hannah cried out, "Let's everybody lift our hands and shout glory to God!"

As the congregation lustily shouted and raised their hands, Joy felt completely out of place. She did not know whether to imitate the worshipers—which would have been hypocritical in her mind—or simply keep her hands down and feel like a total alien. She saw that Chase simply stood there, neither lifting his hands nor saying a word, but his face was still full of tension.

Finally Sister Hannah said, "All right, you can sit now." She waited until the congregation sat down and then picked up a black leather-covered Bible and said, "I intend to preach the Gospel to you this mornin', and we're goin' to take our text from the fourth chapter of the Gospel of John. Find your Bibles now, and you follow along as I read."

Chase pulled the New Testament from his pocket, opened it, and leaned forward, holding it so Joy could see it. They both followed along as Sister Hannah read a large portion of the chapter. It was a familiar enough story to Joy, and she assumed that Chase knew it well too. She had heard more than one sermon preached from this chapter, and when Sister Hannah finished reading, she prayed loudly, "O God, let your spirit rest on me. Anoint me with the power of the spirit of God, and may every sinner in this house see himself as condemned and lost, held over the pits of hell! And then may he see the Lord Jesus as the only hope he's got in this world. In the name of Jesus. Amen."

Sister Hannah paused only to let her eyes sweep over the congregation and then plunged into her message. "Every one of you has read this story about a poor, sinful woman who had no hope until she met a man called Jesus at Jacob's well." She continued to speak about the setting of the story. She finally said,

"Women had a hard time in those days, even harder than they have today in this country. They was almost like cattle. If a man wanted to divorce his wife, all he had to do was to say, 'You're divorced. Now get out.' They had no rights, and the poor women of that day didn't expect anything good to come to them. I expect this here woman was plumb surprised when Jesus spoke to her. That's why she said, 'How is it that thou, being a Jew, asketh drink of me, which am a woman of Samaria?' The first point of my sermon this morning is that Jesus found this woman *on purpose*. In verse four it says, 'And he must needs go through Samaria.' That means, beloved friends, He had to go that way. He could've gone half a dozen other ways, I reckon, but He knowed at that time of day, at that place, there would be a woman there who had to hear the Gospel. When He got there, verse six says Jesus was weary from his journey. Can you imagine that now? The Son of God weary! Does God ever get weary? No indeed, and in Isaiah 40:28 it says, 'Hast thou not known? hast thou not heard, that the everlasting God, the Lord, the Creator of the ends of the earth, fainteth not, neither is weary?' But the Lord Jesus, He became a man, and He had come lookin' for this woman on purpose."

Sister Hannah's eyes again swept the congregation, and Joy felt the power of them as they locked onto hers. Hannah's voice dropped, and almost in a whisper, she said, "Jesus is looking for *you*."

Joy knew that this was meant for everyone, but it felt as if Sister Hannah had taken her by the shoulders and spoken only to her. She dropped her eyes, unable to endure the gaze of the older woman.

Sister Hannah continued, speaking about how God saw everybody. She quoted Scripture after Scripture, including Titus 3:5. " 'The grace of God that bringeth salvation hath appeared to *all* men.' " Sister Hannah waved her Bible around and said, "There ain't no rich or poor, jest sinners."

Finally Sister Hannah moved on to the second point of her sermon, saying, "And the second thing is this poor woman back in John four didn't understand very much about what the Savior was sayin'. He told her she needed living water, but in verse eleven, the woman said, 'Thou hast nothing to draw with, and the well is deep.' You see what's happenin'?"

Hannah thumped the Bible with her free hand. "*He* was talking about spiritual things, and all *she* could think of was physical things. Ain't that just like us today? When God tries to come to our hearts, He wants to tell us about the glories of what He is and who He is and the glories of heaven—and all we can think about is how am I going to pay my bills? Who's going to take care of my sick chil'uns? What am I goin' to do with that boy of mine? Where am I goin' to get money?"

Hannah leaned forward and said, "Jesus said in verse thirteen, 'Whosoever drinketh of this water shall thirst again.' And what does that mean? It means that there ain't nothin' in this world that'll satisfy a person except Jesus. But then in verse fifteen the woman said, 'Give me this water, that I thirst not, neither come hither to draw.' Don't you see what she's doin'? She's still talkin' about the water, the physical water in that well, and Jesus was tryin' to save her soul."

The sermon went on for a considerable time, and when Joy glanced at Chase, she saw he was listening intently. His eyes were half closed in a fixed expression, but it didn't look like he was missing a word.

"And then Jesus put His hand right smack dab on this woman's problem! He told her to go call her husband. But in verse seventeen she says, 'I have no husband.' Well, that was true enough. Jesus said, 'That's right. You've had five husbands, and the man you're livin' with now, you ain't married to him neither.' You see what happened? Jesus knew the very thing in her life that was keepin' her from bein' saved. And I suspect every sinner in this house this mornin' has got somethin' that's become so big you cain't see over it. You cain't hear God because of it. There's something in your life that's not worth havin', and I want every one of you to ask yourself—what is it that's keepin' me from God?"

Joy immediately thought of her bitterness against God. She thought of how much she had loved her parents and her sister and how her heart had been broken when she lost them all on that terrible day. She recognized, as she always had, that her bitterness was wrong, but she couldn't release it. She bowed her head and tried to shut out Sister Hannah's words.

Sister Hannah preached for over an hour. The last part of her message was brief. "This woman, she got saved, and she couldn't keep quiet about it. And her revival come to that whole part of her world because of what Jesus had done for her. And that's what every Christian ought to be, a voice. John the Baptist, he said, 'I'm just a voice crying in the wilderness, and I'm pointin' at Jesus, and I'm sayin' behold the Lamb of God that taketh away the sin of the world.' "

Sister Hannah paused and lifted both her hands, clutching her worn black Bible in one hand. She said, "I'm goin' to ask everyone in this house today who don't know Jesus to come and ask Him to save you."

Joy knew what was coming. Brother Felix stood to lead the congregation in another song, and Joy heard the words she had heard in her own church: "Jesus is tenderly calling today...." Sister Hannah begged and pleaded, but no one went forward.

Finally a young girl, no more than eight or nine, went down to the front, and Sister Hannah talked with her, then put her hands on her and prayed loudly. She asked, "Are you saved, honey?" and when the girl spoke in a muffled voice, Sister Hannah threw her hands up and shouted, "Glory to God and the Lamb forever! Another sinner come into the kingdom!"

The service ended shortly after that, and Chase and Joy found it difficult to get out because so many people wanted to shake hands with them. The hands were hard with work, and the voices were earnest as they invited the two young people to come back. Joy murmured polite words in response, and finally, when the congregation had dispersed, she and Chase stepped out the door and walked over to the buggy. They waited for Sister Hannah as she stood outside shaking hands with the last few people, her voice carrying over the distance.

"Some sermon," Chase murmured.

"Never heard anything like it. Have you?"

"Yes, I have."

"You believe it, Chase?"

Chase Hardin turned, and his eyes were sad. "I believe it, but it's got away from me, Joy. I've lost it somewhere along the line."

Joy looked up. "So have I, Chase. So have I."

★ ★ ★ ★

That afternoon the sun was starting to angle to the west when Joy went outside to find Chase sitting beside Jake. His hand was on the big dog's head, and she approached cautiously. When he looked up he said, "You can put your hand on him now. Just move slow and easy."

Joy moved cautiously. The big dog eyed her as she approached, and she felt a moment's fear. This huge dog with the sharp teeth and powerful jaws could do some serious damage. Carefully and slowly, she put her hand out and ran it over the coat of the shepherd. "Good dog, Jake," she said.

"He *is* a good dog," Chase said.

"But he was so vicious. What did you do to him?"

"He just needed somebody to trust him. I don't think he's ever had that."

"How did you do it? All I ever saw you do was just sit with him."

"I talked to him. Animals don't know many words, but they know the tone of a voice, and they sense it when people have confidence and trust in them."

"He's a beautiful animal."

"Yes, he is." Chase hesitated, and the two sat there quietly for a moment. Finally he remarked, "I used to work with animals in a circus, Joy."

"Really! That must have been fun." She expected him to say more, but he did not. Finally the silence grew uncomfortable, and Joy said, "I've got to get to Galveston, Chase."

"To Galveston? What for?"

Joy hesitated and then began to tell him about Travis. She told him little of her problems, saying merely, "He's gone in a steamer down to South America. He doesn't know where I am, so I've got to be there when he comes back."

"You two are pretty close, I take it."

"He's all I've got left, Chase, after..." It was hard for her to go on then, but she swallowed and said, "Well, I just need to be there is all."

Chase wondered about Joy—why she had been riding the

rails and where the rest of her family was, but he didn't press her to say any more. "Well, I guess Galveston's not all that far away."

His words encouraged Joy. She studied him for a moment, then turned and said, "I've got to go start supper." She leaned over and put her hand on the big dog's head. "Good dog, Jake."

Jake licked her hand, and she smiled and then looked at Chase. "You've done a good job."

At that moment Sister Hannah came out and saw what had happened. "Well, I never!" she exclaimed. "What kinda spell you put on that there dog?"

"Come over here, Sister Hannah. You've got a new friend here."

Joy smiled at Hannah's surprise that she was able to pet the dog. The big woman could not get over it, and finally she laughed. "I got some sinners in this community I should put you onto, Chase. They're as vicious as that dog was."

"I think I can only work with animals. You'll have to handle the people, Sister Hannah." Chase smiled at her.

Joy went inside, and as she worked on the supper, she was surprised by a sensation of fear. She had been so occupied with helping Chase recover from his wounds that she had almost forgotten the circumstances under which she had left the Tatums. Now as Chase was recovering his health, it occurred to her that the law might be hot on her trail. As she cut potatoes into small chunks, she wondered if she was safe living here. She clasped her trembling hands together, and she almost burst out and asked God to help her, but the memory returned of the church service and how even there she had refused to let God come into her life. She continued with her work, resolving not to tell anyone about her feelings, nor the reason why she needed to leave as soon as possible.

★ ★ ★ ★

That night at supper Chase ate heartily, and Sister Hannah said, "You're a fine cook, Joy."

"Thank you very much, Sister Hannah."

"You look a little bit peaked. Don't you feel well?" Sister Hannah inquired.

"No, it's not that. It's just . . . well, I'm afraid I'm going to have to leave soon."

"Leave?" Hannah was taken aback. "Why would you do that?"

"Because of my brother. I need to go to Galveston." She explained that her brother would be coming back on a ship and would have no way of finding her.

"Well, just write this address down. He can come here."

"I don't know if he'd have the money to get here, Sister. No, I'll have to go."

"Well, how will you get there? That's a long way. All the way down to the big water."

"I'll have to hitchhike or ride the rails."

Sister Hannah stared at her, then shook her head firmly. "No, I don't want you to do that."

"I don't have a lot of choice, Sister Hannah."

Hannah leaned forward and said firmly, "Jesus owns all the railroads and all the trucks and all the cars and all the horses too. If he wants you to go to Galveston, I think He can find you a ride."

Joy smiled faintly. "That would be nice, but I'll have to leave soon."

Sister Hannah put her hands down flat on the table. "Well, I'm glad you told me about it. I'll pray about it. Say, I've been wondering—how old are you, child?"

"I'll be seventeen in two days."

"Is that right! I thought you were a mite older. Well, we'll have to give you a party."

"Don't bother. I don't make much of birthdays."

Hannah exchanged a glance with Chase, who shook his head slightly, and they wondered about what a strange girl this was. Hannah shook her head and said, "Well, I'd better get to prayin' if I have to git you to Galveston. . . ."

★ ★ ★ ★

When Joy awakened two days later the first thought that entered her mind was, *It's my birthday*, and the second was the memory of her parents and sister who had died one year ago. She got out of bed, forcing the dreadful thought out of her mind, washed her face in the basin at the washstand, then dressed and went downstairs to fix breakfast. She found Hannah already there and was greeted with a cheerful, "Happy birthday, child!"

"Thank you, Hannah."

"How does it feel to be seventeen?"

"Just like it felt to be sixteen."

"Well, I'm makin' you a cake, and we're gonna have a birthday celebration whether you like it or not."

"I wish you wouldn't."

"Don't be foolish. It'll give me an excuse for bakin' a beautiful cake."

★   ★   ★   ★

Sister Hannah did indeed make a beautiful cake. It had white icing with pink roses, and she put one big candle in the middle. She brought it to the table after supper that night and said, "Well, I couldn't find seventeen candles, but you can blow this one out."

"It's a beautiful cake," Joy smiled. She leaned forward, and Chase said quickly, "Make a wish."

Joy nodded, then blew the candle out.

"What'd you wish for?" Chase demanded.

"Oh, that I could get to Galveston."

"Well, I don't have no doubts about that, but right now it's birthday time." Hannah opened the door to the cabinet and brought out a package wrapped in red paper. "Happy birthday, Joy."

Taking the package, Joy could not speak for a moment. "I wish you hadn't done this. I wasn't expecting anything."

"Well, you got a surprise, then. Open it up."

Joy took the paper off, opened the box, and stared at the gift, unable to speak.

"What is it, Joy?" Chase said, leaning forward.

"It's . . . it's a comb and brush." She put the box down on the table, took the comb and brush out, and examined them. "They're beautiful," she whispered.

"They belonged to my sister. She gave 'em to me. They ain't hardly been used. That's mother-of-pearl. A girl with hair like yours needs good brushes and a good comb."

Joy ran her hands over the smooth surface of the mother-of-pearl and could not speak. When she looked up there were tears in her eyes. "Thank you so much," she whispered.

Chase saw that Joy was moved but embarrassed at showing it. Quickly he said, "Well, I got you a present too. It won't do to brush your hair with it, though." Reaching into his pocket, he pulled out a slender package wrapped in brown paper. "No pretty paper either, I'm afraid."

Joy took the package and blinked the tears away. Unwrapping it, she exclaimed, "It's a fountain pen! Look, Sister Hannah."

"Looks good. Is that real gold around the edges?"

"I guess so," Chase said. He smiled and pulled a bottle of ink from his pocket. "I've seen you tryin' to keep pencils sharpened while you write in that diary of yours. I thought you might do a better job with this."

Joy felt elated. "Let me fill it up and try it."

"Go ahead. I'll get a piece of paper," Hannah said. By the time she had brought the paper back, Joy had filled the pen. She glided it over the surface of the paper. "Look at how smooth it is," she marveled. She wrote several lines and then turned the paper around. *Thank you—thank you for everything!* she had written.

"It's the nicest birthday I could've had," she whispered. "Thank you so much."

"It ain't over yet. I got one more present for you."

Joy turned to stare at the woman. "What is it?" she said.

"Well, this present's from the Lord Jesus, at least that's the way I see it."

"What in the world is it?"

"It's a ride all the way to Texas." Hannah laughed at the expression on Joy's face. "It ain't all the way to Galveston, but it's almost there."

"Who will I ride with?"

"I've got this grandson named Caleb who drives a truck. He's makin' a trip from Helena, Montana, to Fort Worth, Texas. He called me last night on the phone. Said he didn't know why he wanted to call, but he just felt an itch to do it." Sister Hannah smiled and said, "I told him that was the Lord doin' that to him. Anyway, he'll be here around the eighteenth. That's Friday."

"Well, Fort Worth isn't that far from Galveston," Chase said.

"Have you been there?" Joy asked.

"Sure, a couple times. It shouldn't be too much trouble to get from Fort Worth to Galveston."

Joy suddenly looked down at the comb and brush and ran her hand over them. The other two watched as she caressed the surfaces, and a glance passed between them. Sister Hannah said gently, "I think we'd better give thanks to the Lord Jesus for His birthday present."

Joy bowed her head, and as Hannah prayed, she felt herself agreeing, and when the woman had finished, she said, "Amen."

CHAPTER NINE

END OF THE ROPE

★ ★ ★ ★

Sister Hannah came upon Chase as he was sitting outside stroking Jake's head. Hannah considered his taming of the vicious animal a miracle. Chase had helped her actually become friends with the big dog, and now as she watched the two sitting in the sunlight that fell in long golden bars across the yard, she smiled slightly. *I wish it was as easy to get people to change as it was for Chase to change that dog's meanness.*

"Almost time for dinner, Brother Chase."

Looking up, Chase smiled. It amused him and yet troubled him that Sister Hannah had started attaching the title *brother* to his name. He had once told her he wasn't worthy of such, but she had simply shrugged, saying, *"You're a brother to me, and God's goin' to do somethin' with you. I'm just looking ahead a little bit, is all."*

Getting to his feet, Chase looked up and said, "Going to be good weather for it."

"Good weather for what?"

"For Joy to make that trip to Texas."

"I want to talk to you about *that* girl."

Chase turned his eyes on Sister Hannah. "Sure. You want to sit down?"

"No, this is all right. It won't take me long to say what I got to say. Truth is, I been troubled about Joy. She's been on my heart right smart the past few days."

"Mine too. She's so defenseless, even though"—he smiled broadly—"she carries a thirty-eight. Still there's an air about her that makes her seem sort of vulnerable."

"That's what I've been tellin' the Lord, and now, Brother Chase, the answer came. It was right sharp."

Chase studied the tall, strongly built woman. She had character built into her features—strong features they were—and he had learned that she'd had a difficult life, yet had not let it embitter her. Now he thought about how she'd come to their rescue and saved their lives, so it seemed to them.

"What has God told you?" he asked.

Hannah grinned at him. "So you *do* think God tells people things."

"He tells *some* people things. I've always known that," Chase replied.

"Well, brother, I believe God will speak to *anyone*, if'n they're willin' to listen. My daddy heard from God, and my mama too. And you will too, Brother Chase. It's jist a matter of time." Sister Hannah tucked a silver lock back under her bonnet and said, "Seein' as you're not listenin' to Him yet, though, God told me that you're supposed to go to Texas with Joy and see to her."

Chase stared at Hannah in disbelief. "Why, I can't even take care of *myself*, Sister."

"I know that. None of us can, but this time you've got the Lord Jesus on your side. He'll help you through it." She smiled heartily, and warmth flooded her eyes. "God don't sponsor no failures, Chase."

Chase laughed shortly. "Well, that proves I'm not one of His, because if there ever was a failure—"

"Now, you stop talkin' like that. God's got somethin' for you to do, and it's got somethin' to do with takin' care of that girl. If I'm hearin' God right, you gotta be her protector for a while."

Chase bowed his head and studied the ground. A big yellow tomcat strolled by, and he saw Jake consider the animal. "No, Jake, that's not for you. Live and let live," he murmured. He put his hand on the big dog's head, and Jake sat down and looked up at him as if he understood the words perfectly. "I don't know what to say," Chase went on.

"We don't always know what to say, and we don't always know what to do. That's the way it is on this earth. Most of us would like it if God would just write down every morning what we're supposed to do for that day, but God don't do it that way. We're supposed to walk by faith. One of the psalms says, 'The steps of a good man are ordered by the Lord, and he delighteth in his way. Though he fall, he shall not be utterly cast down, for the Lord upholdeth him with his hand.' What that means is every man—and every woman too—has got God's hand on 'em. You been runnin' away from the Lord, Chase, but someday He's goin' to catch up with you, and this may be one of His ways."

Chase looked up and shook his head. "The last time I tried to help Joy, she wound up having to help *me*."

"That may be true, but from what she tells me, if you hadn't been there, she would have come to real grief."

A silence fell between the two, and from the distance came the lonesome sound of a train whistle. Chase waited until it faded away, then shrugged his shoulders. "What do you want me to do?"

"Stay with her until she finds her brother."

"All right, Sister Hannah, I'll do the best I can."

"And, Brother Chase, don't you harm that girl." She saw Chase's eyes open wide and then said, "You know what I mean. You're a man, she's a woman, and you'll be alone together. God will be watchin' you."

Chase Hardin grew serious. His lips drew together tightly, and then he nodded. "Sister Hannah, you can believe this—I'd rather cut my arm off than hurt Joy!"

★ ★ ★ ★

"I reckon Caleb will be in pretty soon," Hannah told Joy while the two women were in the kitchen finishing up the break-fast dishes. "He didn't give me no exact time. He jest said some-time today. Come upstairs with me."

At Hannah's blunt command, Joy took off her apron and

followed her out into the hall, then up the stairs. When she entered the bedroom Joy had been using, Sister Hannah leaned over and pulled a suitcase out from under the bed. "This here belonged to my granddaughter Lucy," she said, "but I want you to take it. You can't be carryin' that sack around with you."

"But I wouldn't want to take your granddaughter's suitcase."

Ignoring Joy's protest, Hannah walked over to the closet and said, "I want you to pick out the best of these clothes—shoes, too, and underwear. They ain't doin' a livin' soul no good jest sittin' here, and you don't need to be runnin' around all over creation in boy's garb. You're a woman, and you need to dress like one."

Joy had become accustomed to Sister Hannah's ways. Her gruff manner covered a heart as warm and generous as any Joy had ever known. The days she had spent in this house had been the most pleasant she could remember since the deaths of her parents and sister. She had arrived with a troubled heart and an angry, bitter spirit, still grieving and blaming God for taking her family away. But the faith of the older woman had touched her and changed her—almost, at first, against her will. She had resisted for a short time, but then the genuine goodness of Hannah Smith's very being had won her over.

Joy went over now and put her arm around the older woman and said gently, "You've been so good to me, Sister Hannah."

Hannah warmed to the young woman. "I got a special love for you, daughter," she said quietly, "and after you leave, my prayers are goin' to be with you every day. There's goin' to be temptations and hardship—no doubt 'bout that, my sister—but the Lord Jesus will build a ring of fire about you. The devil said of Job when he accused him before God that God had built a hedge about him so thick that he couldn't even get at 'im! And that's what I aim to do for you, Joy."

"I know I need it."

"Yes, you surely do, and there's somethin' else I gotta tell you. I been prayin' 'bout how in the world you're goin' to make it, and God spoke to me and gave me some instructions."

"Instructions? What kind of instructions?"

"He told me that Chase was supposed to go with you and take care of you until you find your brother."

"I couldn't ask him to do that."

"You don't have to. I done already told him."

"What did he say?"

Hannah chuckled. "Well, young'un, he said the last time he tried to help you, he just about got beat to death!"

"He was trying to help. He did all he could," Joy said defensively.

The girl's quick response pleased Sister Hannah. "I know he did, and I'll always think it was God who made him do his best. But, anyhow, he's goin' with you now, and I want you to be careful."

"Be careful of what?"

"You're just comin' on to bein' a woman, Joy. You ain't a little girl no longer, and women are weak where men are concerned."

Joy dropped her eyes for a moment and then looked up. "I . . . I don't know what you mean."

"I mean you and Chase are going to be throwed together a lot. I've already seen you have a special kind of likin' for him."

"That's just because he tried to help me."

"It's that, and it's that you nursed him back to health. He's been like a baby, but he's not a baby at all, so you gotta be careful. A woman has a treasure, and she needs to keep it for the man she'll marry one day."

Color rose in Joy's cheeks, and she did not speak for a time. The older woman studied her face, admiring the beautiful large blue eyes, her best feature. Hannah had often seen the dance of laughter in those eyes, and once or twice a joy that bubbled up from within. But now there was an inexpressible gravity in them as she said, "I'll remember what you've said, Sister Hannah. . . ."

★ ★ ★ ★

The roar of an engine followed by the squeal of brakes caught Hannah's attention, and she rushed to the kitchen window and looked out. "Well now, Caleb's here. He drives that there truck like Jehu his own self!" She smiled at Joy. "He's a feisty one, he is, but he's a good man."

The door opened, and a large young man wearing worn jeans

and a checkered shirt rolled up to the elbows hustled in. He had tow-colored hair, bright blue eyes, and a breezy manner. He strode across the room, threw his arms around his grandmother, and lifted her clear off the floor. He swung her around, laughing. "You're puttin' on weight, Grandma."

"Put me down, you fool!"

Hannah's words were sharp, but Joy saw the affection in her eyes. She watched as the old woman collected a kiss on each cheek, then reached up and patted the young man's face. "Your manners are as bad as they always were."

"Aw, c'mon, Grandma, you're glad to see me. You don't get a good-lookin' man to hug you every day of the week."

Hannah Smith laughed and turned, saying, "This here is Miss Joy Smith. Joy, this is my grandson Caleb."

The large young man put his eyes on Joy and stuck out his hand. She took it, and her own was swallowed up. "Well, are we cousins or somethin', Miss Joy?"

"I don't think so, but we might as well be because your grandmother's almost taken me into the family."

He nodded. "Ain't she a caution, now? I'd hate to tell you about the time she took a hickory switch to me when I was growin' up." He turned to his grandmother and winked. "Remember the time Rob Peterson and me stole your eggs and sold 'em so we could go to the dance over at Callaway?"

"I remember it all right, and then I guess you remember what happened when I caught up with you."

"I sure do." He winked knowingly at Joy, saying, "I was sixteen then and already bigger than Grandma, but she made me stand up while she walloped me. I couldn't sit down for a week."

"Well, Joy don't hanker to hear any more of your stories. Dinner's ready."

"I want to see that dog I gave you first."

"Dog! That weren't no dog! That monster tried to take a leg off of me."

"He's just spirited," Caleb protested.

"Well, you meant well, but he was a lot more than 'spirited.' Joy, go out and round up Chase for dinner. I think he's out back with the animals."

Caleb gave the young woman a curious glance as she went

out the back door. "Pretty girl," he said. "Who's this fella Chase?" He listened as his grandmother told him briefly what she knew of the pair. She ended by saying, "Her brother's gone off on a ship, and he don't know where she is. She's gotta get to Galveston before he returns there."

"I'm only goin' as far as Fort Worth."

"I know that, Caleb, but if you can get 'em that far, Chase says they can get the rest of the way on their own."

They were still talking when Chase and Joy entered. Hannah stood up to introduce the men. "Caleb, this here is Chase Hardin. And, Chase, this is my grandson Caleb Smith."

The men shook hands. Caleb was taller and bulkier than Hardin, and the two made quite a contrast.

"It was Chase what tamed that dog," Hannah said. "I never seen anythin' like it. Nobody could get near that devil, but he's just like a pet now."

"Well, I appreciate that, Chase," Caleb said. "How'd you do it?"

Hannah didn't give Chase a chance to answer. "He says he just shows the animal respect." She went on, "Whatever he's done, I've gotten pretty fond of that big dog. Well," she said, changing the subject, "I know you must be hungry, Caleb."

"I gotta be on my way pretty soon, Grandma."

"Well, you gotta eat."

"All right. Are you two all packed and ready to roll?" he asked.

"Sure are," Joy said. "As soon as we eat, we can be on our way."

The two men sat down at the table while the women put the food on. Caleb, without appearing to do so, studied Chase carefully. He was trying to put together the facts that his grandmother had given him, but he was still puzzled about the relationship between the man and this girl. He did not ask anything specific but tried to get Chase to talk about his past. Caleb soon saw that Chase Hardin was not proud of his past, and he couldn't get much out of him.

"My grandma tells me you been laid up lately, Chase."

"Sure have. I got me a few cracked ribs, and your grandma patched up this eye. The stitches are out now, but I'll probably always have a scar." He touched the eyebrow and looked over at Joy. "Guess you might say your grandma and Joy have made a patient out of me."

The table was soon loaded with chicken fried steak, boiled potatoes, golden corn, and freshly made biscuits. The milk was rich and creamy, and Caleb ate as though he had not seen food in a week. His grandmother kept urging him on, and finally when she set a wedge of cherry pie in front of him, he grinned at her. "Still the best cook in the world, Grandma."

"You don't eat right bein' out on the road like you are."

"Well, cookin's not as good as yours, but I make out."

Joy had said little during the meal. Although she was excited about meeting up with her brother again, she was also quite sad at leaving the haven that had provided such a time of peace for her.

After the meal was over, Caleb got up and announced, "Well, if you two are ready, we'll be on our way."

"I'll get my suitcase," Joy said and went upstairs.

Chase left to get his few belongings as well. When they returned, Caleb said, "Well, Grandma, thanks for the meal. I'll stop and see you next time I come by."

Hannah took his kiss and patted his cheek. "You take care of yourself, boy. I pray every day for you while you're in that truck."

"You keep it up, Grandma. I need all the prayers I can get."

Caleb took the suitcase from Joy, saying, "Here, let me tote that," and led the way out to the large truck. Caleb opened the back gate of the truck, wedged the suitcase in, and took Chase's canvas bag as well. Shutting the door, he nodded. "We're on our way."

Joy walked to the front of the truck, climbed in the cab, and slid to the middle of the seat. Chase got in beside her, still moving cautiously, and then Caleb plopped himself down and slammed the door. "Bye, Grandma," he shouted as the engine broke into a roar. Joy waved at Sister Hannah, keeping her eyes on her until the truck had pulled out into the road and, making a wide, sweeping turn, headed out. A sense of loneliness settled over Joy, and she said, "I'll miss your grandmother, Caleb."

"So will I," Chase said. "You're a lucky guy to have someone like that in your family."

"I know it," Caleb said. "There ain't nobody like her. Never has been, I don't reckon. One of these days I hope I'll believe in God just about a hundredth as much as she does." He pulled off the dirt road onto the main highway and stepped on the gas. The engine responded, and the big truck lumbered down the road. Joy was tossed back and forth against Caleb and Chase. "Sorry," she murmured.

"It's all right. These roads are pretty bad. It'll get better, though, a few miles up the way."

"How long will it take to get to Fort Worth, Caleb?" Chase asked.

"Well, let's see. I reckon we'll stay at Russell, Kansas, tonight and then maybe we can make Ardmore, Oklahoma, tomorrow night. We'll be pullin' into Fort Worth the day after that, I reckon."

★ ★ ★ ★

"Well, here's where I deliver my load," Caleb announced as they crossed the Fort Worth city line. "Been a pretty good trip."

"It sure has, Caleb." Joy smiled up at the big young man. "I can't tell you how much we appreciate your giving us a ride."

"Why, shore, no trouble at all, Joy. You and Chase have been good company. It gets lonesome bein' by myself all the time. Maybe someday they'll figure out a way to put a radio in a truck. Be mighty nice."

The trip had been pleasant enough. They had left on March eighteenth and now after three days on the road were finally in Fort Worth. Texas was a different kind of country—flat with low hills in places, and the mesquite trees were ugly, at least to Joy. They made twisted forms as if they were in pain, she thought. Now as Caleb pulled the truck up in front of a large warehouse, she turned to Chase. "Well, we're here."

"Yes, and not too far to go."

"It's too late to head to Galveston tonight," Caleb said. He backed the truck up carefully, watching the mirrors on each side, pulled the emergency break on, and cut the engine. "Tell you what. Let me ask around, and I'll see if I can find you a place to stay tonight."

"That would be nice of you," Joy said. She waited until Chase had climbed out, then got out herself. She looked around curiously at her surroundings and said, "Somehow I thought there'd be cowboys here."

Chase laughed. "I think you're about fifty years too late for that, but at one time you would have seen plenty of them."

The two waited for no more than five minutes before Caleb came back, smiling. "I had some good luck," he said, "or maybe you did. I talked to the guy that manages this place. He says he has a room with some cots in there you two can stay in tonight." He grinned at Joy. "When I told him you were a young lady he kind of balked, but I sweet-talked him into finding you a place where you could have a little privacy."

"Thank you, Caleb. That'll help a lot." Joy smiled up at him.

"C'mon. I'll introduce you to the manager, and you can get your stuff stashed. Tell you what. I'll buy you some dinner and show you a little bit of the town."

★　★　★　★

Caleb was as good as his word. He took them out to a café close to the terminal called Ma's, and Ma herself served them the specialty, barbecued ribs. Ma was a small, sprightly woman with gray hair and a face lined with many years. Apparently Caleb knew her well, and she stopped by their table more than once to inquire if the food was good.

"It's great, Ma, as always. How's that no-good son of yours?"

"Which one? They're all pretty worthless."

"Why, you don't believe that, Ma. I mean Denny."

"Got him a good job over at Abilene. Gettin' married too. About time. About time for you too, Caleb."

"You hustle me up a fine-lookin' young blonde that comes from a rich family, then I can retire."

Ma laughed. "You'd do it too, wouldn't you?"

As she moved away, Caleb continued his stories of his adventures on the road. He had an easy way about him, and his stories were amusing. Finally, he said, "Guess I'd better get you back. I expect you'll want to leave early in the mornin'."

"I'd like to," Joy said. She sipped her coffee and nodded. "I'm anxious to find out if there's any news of my brother."

"Well, let me make a call before we go." He got up, and as soon as he disappeared, Joy said, "He's such a nice guy."

"Yes, he is. Of course, he's got good blood in him from Sister Hannah."

"To tell the truth, I miss Sister Hannah already."

"I know; so do I."

They talked idly until Caleb returned, and they saw he had a satisfied smile on his face. "Had good luck," he said. "A friend of mine makes a run down to the coast three times a week. He's leavin' tomorrow. He owes me a favor. He said he'd haul you all the way down to Galveston."

"How wonderful!" Joy said. "I don't know what we would have done without you, Caleb."

"That's right." Chase nodded. "You've been a good friend."

"No trouble at all," Caleb said cheerfully. "Well, if you're ready, we'll go catch some shut-eye."

★ ★ ★ ★

Hack Wilson, their ride for the next day, was a rough fellow. A big, burly man of some thirty years, he had obviously been in a few fights in his life. His nose was crooked from having been broken, and there was scar tissue around his eyes. Despite his rough appearance and coarse language, Joy and Chase enjoyed his company. As he told it, he had done just about every kind of job there was to do, and as he steered the big truck down the highway, he told them about every one of those jobs.

He kept up his storytelling almost without a break from the time they left Fort Worth early Monday morning until they arrived in Galveston late in the afternoon. As they approached the city Hack asked where they wanted to be dropped off and agreed to take them to the main post office. When he stopped in front of the building, he said, "This is it. Hope you find your brother, miss." He jumped out and got their luggage, and Chase shook hands with him. They both thanked him, and he waved his big hand, saying, "Good luck to you both."

"Well, we're here," Chase said, looking around. "Let's see if there's anything from Travis."

"Yes, I can hardly wait! Say, would you mind staying out here with our bags while I go check for a letter?" Joy had suddenly realized she would have to inquire about a letter for Joy Winslow, and she was still reluctant for Chase to learn her real name.

"Sure. I guess that's easier than hauling them into the building."

Joy's expectation turned to disappointment when she found there was no mail for her. She turned away sadly and rejoined Chase outside.

"Well, we'll just have to find a place to stay until his ship comes in."

"All right," she agreed with a sigh, "and we'll have to find jobs."

They started down the street. "I don't know what to do, Chase. We don't have enough money to go to a hotel."

"I know. We'll have to be hobos, I guess. Maybe we can find an empty building to sleep in tonight, and tomorrow we can look for jobs."

They headed for the outskirts of town, thinking there might be an abandoned warehouse to spend the night in. They passed by a small grocery store, and Chase stopped and looked in the window. Joy saw that he was staring at a poster advertising the circus. "The Carter Brothers Circus," Chase read. "It says they'll be here on the twenty-fifth and twenty-sixth. That's just four days from now."

"You still like to go to circuses?" Joy asked, curious. "Didn't you tell me you worked in one once?"

Chase did not answer the question. Instead, he said, "We'd better go in here and get somethin' we can cook up tonight. Maybe some beans and sausages and a pot to cook them in."

After buying their groceries, they continued out of town and reached the far outskirts as the sun was nearing the horizon. A few factories were scattered along the highway, but they couldn't see any abandoned warehouses. Joy had about given up when Chase shouted, "Hey, look over there!"

Joy turned to follow his gesture and saw a burned-out house. "What is it, Chase?"

"Look, the barn didn't burn down with the house. I bet we could hole up there tonight. Come on, let's take a look."

They found that the barn, although in poor condition, was good enough to sleep in. There was even some hay in the loft, and although they had no blankets, Chase said, "This should be okay, I think. Might be a little chilly during the night, but it's a lot warmer down here than it was up north."

"This'll be fine. Maybe we can do better tomorrow."

Chase started gathering firewood, and out behind the barn he coaxed up a small fire. By the time darkness settled in, the two had hot beans and sausages ready to eat.

"Not as good as Sister Hannah's cooking, or yours either," Chase said. "But it's filling."

Joy took a spoonful of the beans and sausage pieces from the small saucepan they had bought and asked, "Do you think we can find work here?"

"Well, it might be a bit tough. I don't think you'll have any trouble, though. You can always be a waitress or a cook. Might be harder for me."

"You won't be able to do any heavy work yet, Chase. Your ribs are still too tender."

Chase did not answer. He took a sip from the bottle of soda pop they had bought at the store and looked up at the stars. "There's Orion."

"You know the stars, Chase?"

"Not many of them. I know that one, though. You see, it's supposed to be a big hunter." He pointed out the four stars that made the shoulders and then the lower part of the shape of a man. "Those stars across the middle are called Orion's Belt."

"They're so far away."

"When I was a kid I used to wonder who lived there."

"Do you think anybody does?"

"I don't know. We're not likely to find out."

Chase shivered and said, "It's gettin' kind of cold. We should have gotten a couple of blankets."

"We can do that tomorrow, or maybe if we get jobs, we can find rooms."

"That'd be a lot better. You don't need to be out like this."

The two fell silent, enjoying the warmth of the fire. Finally Chase said, "Why don't you go up in the loft and see if you can get comfortable on the hay? I think I'll just sleep here by the fire."

"All right, Chase." Joy rose and said quietly, "I guess Sister Hannah will be praying for us. We need it." As she studied Chase's features in the firelight, she saw that she wasn't the only one who was troubled.

Chase turned to Joy. "It'll be all right," he said. "Don't worry."

"And you either. Good night, Chase."

Chase watched her leave and then turned back and put his gaze on the fire. He poked it with a stick, releasing a puff of sparks into the darkness, then stretched out on his side and lay still until finally sleep overtook him.

★   ★   ★   ★

"We've got to do *something*, Chase! We can't go on like this."

"You're right about that." Chase shook his head. "There's just no work here."

The two had returned to the barn, for they had no money to stay in a hotel. For three days they had searched diligently, but neither of them could find a job. The town seemed to be filled with people looking for work, many of them Mexicans. Their clothes were dirty now, and both of them were low in spirits. They had made another poor supper of beans and bread, this time with two doughnuts to add a little sweetness.

"I don't know what we're going to do, Chase."

Chase was silent for a time, and then he looked up from the can of beans he held and stirred the remainder with his spoon. "I've been thinking about something. But maybe it's not a good idea."

"What is it? Anything's better than what we've got."

"You know how I used to work with a circus."

"I remember."

"Well, it was the Carter Brothers Circus. That sign said they're coming to town tomorrow. I could get us jobs there, I think. It wouldn't pay much, and we'd have to travel."

"But what could I do in a circus?"

"Always things to do in a circus. Never enough hands. I had friends there once, but I don't know if they're still there or not."

"Do you really think they'd take us?"

"I think so." Chase ate the last of the beans and set the can aside. He wiped the spoon on his handkerchief and stuck it in his coat pocket. "It won't be much of a life, though, Joy."

"I always thought being with a circus would be exciting."

"The performances are, but you wouldn't believe how much work there is just getting from one place to another and getting set up." He shook his head and said, "I don't know if it's a good idea or not."

Joy waited for him to say more, but he sat there cross-legged and silent in the darkness. The fire crackled, and a heavy truck lumbered down the road. When the sound died away, she said, "I think we're at the end of our rope, Chase. We'll have to try it."

The flickering flames highlighted the sharp planes of Chase's face, and he sighed heavily. "Well, I suppose you're right. It's the only thing I can think of. Other than going back to Sister Hannah. She'd take us in."

"No, I don't want to do that. My brother would have to come all the way north, then. I'd rather wait for him here. Let's try the circus first."

"All right."

The two sat in silence, watching the stars in the night sky. Feeling despondent, neither of them spoke until Joy rose and murmured, "Good night, Chase."

"Good night, Joy."

For a long time Chase Hardin sat in front of the small fire. From time to time he looked up at the stars, but finally he lay back and closed his eyes. *The circus is probably not a good idea— but I don't see any other way. At least we'll eat and have a place to sleep. . . .*

CHAPTER TEN

A NEW WORLD

★ ★ ★ ★

Chase and Joy awoke early and washed up as well as they could. Joy shook out one of the dresses she had not yet worn, a tan dress with white lace around the neck and sleeves and a dropped waistline. The weather was still cool, so she slipped on a lightweight wool jacket and donned a pair of black patent leather shoes. As she stepped out of the barn, she found Chase waiting for her. He was wearing the only outfit he had, which was much the worse for wear. His black hair needed cutting and curled over his coat collar.

"Pretty dress," he commented. "Are you ready?"

"Yes, I am."

The two left and paused at a diner to inquire the way to the fairgrounds. It sounded like finding their way would not be difficult, but it was a long walk, and they decided a good breakfast first was in order. They ordered the special—two eggs, bacon, and toast. The portions were not particularly generous, so they wolfed them down quickly and left.

They walked steadily and reached the fairgrounds just before ten o'clock. Chase scanned the grounds, then nodded. "They must have gotten here early. The big top's almost up."

Joy was confused by the activity, and her eyes darted everywhere as she followed Chase across the field. The tent was up, but there were still people running every which way stretching ropes and driving stakes into the ground. She gasped when an elephant strolled by, led by a handsome man with olive skin and flashing black eyes. Joy saw a look of astonishment cross his face as he spotted Chase.

"Well, if it isn't Chase Hardin!" he called out and stood waiting as the two approached. The man's bright green shirt contrasted with his crisp black curls spilling out from under a wide-brimmed gray fedora. He put his hand out, and his white teeth flashed against his dark skin. His eyebrows were black, as was the neatly trimmed mustache. "Good to see you, Chase. Where you been?"

"Oh, around, Dan."

Chase turned and said, "This is Joy Smith, Dan. Joy, this is Dan Darvo."

Darvo swept off his cap, and dark curls fell over his forehead. "Gypsy Dan is good enough." His obsidian eyes studied Joy as she murmured a greeting. Then he turned back to Chase and asked, "How have you been?"

"Not too good. Is the colonel still in charge?"

"Sure. You need a job?"

"That's why we're here."

The two were interrupted by another voice yelling, "Hey, Chase!"

Joy turned to see a midget hurtling across the lot. He skidded to a stop in front of Chase, slapped his hands together, and then stuck one of them up. Chase smiled and said, "How are you, Oz?"

"Better than you could guess. You old son of a gun, it's good to see you! Who's this? You done went and got married up on me?"

"Oh no, this is just a friend of mine. Her name's Joy Smith." Turning to Joy, he said, "Oz is one of the clowns in the circus."

"I'm right proud to know you, Miss Smith. I'm Phineas Oz. Everybody just calls me Oz, though."

"I'm glad to know you, Mr. Oz."

"No 'mister.' Just Oz. You comin' back to the show, Chase?"

"I thought I'd hit the colonel up for a job." Then Chase

added, "Just as a roustabout. And we need something for Joy here too."

Oz chewed his lip thoughtfully and turned his head to one side. "Things have changed a little bit since you left, Chase. Mrs. House passed away about a year ago."

Gypsy Dan added, "Had a heart attack. Dropped dead right in the middle of Ella's dog act."

"I'm sorry to hear it. She was a good woman," Chase said regretfully. "The colonel's missed her, I bet."

"Well, you know how close they were," Oz said, stroking his blunt chin. "He took to drinkin' pretty hard. Next thing we knew he married up with Stella."

Joy sensed Chase stiffen next to her, and she turned to see shock spread across his features. He recovered quickly and murmured, "Well, that's a surprise."

"Yeah, it was for all of us. I guess he was lonesome."

A silence fell on the small group, and then Oz said, "Stella pretty much runs things now, but you can probably get a job."

"Karl Ritter is doing the big cage now. You know him?" Gypsy Dan asked.

"No, never saw his act."

"Well, he's flashy, but I've seen better. You can probably find the colonel in his tent. He doesn't get out until pretty late."

"The tent's around on the other side of clown alley. Just where we always put it." Gypsy Dan turned to Joy and studied her carefully. "Do you like animals?"

"Oh yes, I do."

"Maybe you'd like to come into my act. We could always use a pretty girl on top of an elephant."

"Oh, I wouldn't know how to do that."

"Nothing to it." Gypsy Dan turned and said, "Trunk, Ruth." The elephant swung her trunk around, and Gypsy Dan put it toward Joy. The trunk came up in front of Joy's face, and she reached out tentatively and stroked it. The tip of the trunk touched her shoulder with its fingerlike appendage on the end of it. Dan reached into his pocket, saying, "Give her a bit of this. She'll love you forever."

Joy took the quarters of apple and handed them to the elephant, which immediately stuck them in its mouth and came back asking for more. Joy stroked the trunk again. It was very rough and hairy, but the elephant's eyes seemed to gleam with pleasure. Joy said, "She's really sweet."

"Sure, sweet just like me." Gypsy Dan winked at her. "We'll talk later."

Chase turned abruptly, and Joy had to hurry to catch up with him. He wound his way through the maze of equipment and canvas, and Joy noted that many of the circus workers looked at him in surprise. When some called out to him, he nodded but did not stop. He finally paused before a tall, broad-shouldered man with red hair and blue eyes wearing stained and wrinkled khakis.

"Hello, Pete."

"Hello, Chase." The broad-shouldered man studied him carefully, his eyes flickering over to Joy. "What's goin' down?"

"Bad pennies come back. I'm lookin' for a job and one for this young lady here. Her name's Joy Smith."

"Well, I hope the colonel can find something for you. It'll be good to have you working with us again."

"We're heading over to the colonel's trailer right now."

"Have you heard about Stella?"

"Yes, Oz told me."

"Might be a problem for you."

"No, it won't." Chase's voice was clipped and short. "Guess I'll go find out. Come along, Joy."

Joy hurried along after Chase, saying nothing. This world was not hers, and she was confused by it. The strong smell of animals overrode most other smells, and she almost fell over a tent rope because she was so busy looking around.

Chase led her around to the back of the lot, where he saw a man in a white suit and a white straw hat. "That's the man we're looking for—Colonel House," he said.

Colonel House did not turn until Chase spoke his name, and when he did, shock flickered across his florid features. He had been a big man, but now the flesh had sagged. He pulled off the straw hat, revealing his white hair. "Hello, Chase," he said. "Surprised to see you."

"Good to see you, Colonel. I'm sorry to hear about your wife. She was very good to me. I'll miss her."

Colonel House bowed his head for a moment, and sadness colored his eyes when he looked back up. "It was like the sun went out of the sky for me, my boy." He shook his head and asked, "What can I do for you?"

"Need a job, Colonel. Not my old one, though," he added. "Just pulling down, setting up, washing dishes. Anything. This is Miss Joy Smith. She could be handy too, I think."

"How do you do, Miss Smith?" House had a courtly manner, and although he appeared tired, there was still an air of gallantry about him. He addressed Chase again. "Don't know if you've heard about me and Stella."

"Yes, Oz told me. Congratulations."

A look passed between the two men, and Joy saw that both of them were uncomfortable. "We'll have to ask Stella, but I think we can find something."

At that moment the trailer door opened, and a woman stepped out. She was wearing a short yellow dress, and her hair was bobbed in the current flapper fashion. Her green eyes flickered over Joy, sized her up, and then moved on to Chase. She came down off the steps and walked forward with a swagger. "Hello, Chase," she purred, keeping her eyes fixed on his.

"Hello, Stella. You're looking well."

"You don't look so good yourself."

"Little down on my luck. I was asking the colonel here for any kind of a job for me—and for Miss Joy Smith here."

"We could certainly use some help," House said. His eyes narrowed, and he shook his head slightly. "Karl Ritter lost his helper. But he's pretty hard to please."

"I can do it, Colonel."

"Won't be very pleasant for you," the colonel suggested. "Cleaning out cages."

"It doesn't matter."

The colonel glanced at Joy and stroked his goatee. He looked a great deal like the pictures Joy had seen of Buffalo Bill, with the white mustache and white goatee to match. She wondered if he had adopted the mannerisms as well. "What about Miss Smith, Stella?"

"Annie needs some help over in the cook tent. Can you cook?"

"Yes, I can."

"All right. Chase, you wait here. I'll take you to Ritter after I talk to Annie about the new help." She turned to the young woman, saying, "All right. Come along—what's your first name?"

"Joy."

"Come along, then, Joy. I'll take you over and see if you can handle the job."

Joy obediently followed the woman, who rapidly threaded her way through the circus maze. She stopped abruptly and turned to her. "How did you get hooked up with Chase?"

"Well, it was mostly because of an accident." Joy struggled to choose the right words, not wanting to say too much. "He got hurt, and I stayed around to take care of him."

"Is he your boyfriend?"

"No!"

Stella stared at the girl while Joy tried to guess how old Stella was. She appeared to be in her late twenties or early thirties. There was a hardness about her, attractive though she was, both in face and form. It was more in the glint of her eyes than in any outward mark of age, and she exuded a callous boldness.

"Well, I find that hard to believe, a guy and a girl traveling around together."

"It's the truth, though." Joy changed the subject. "What did Chase do when he was with the circus, Mrs. House?"

"He didn't tell you that?"

"No, we haven't known each other very long, and he's just getting over his injuries, so we haven't talked all that much." This was not entirely true, but true enough, Joy felt. Chase hadn't talked about his time with the circus except to mention it once or twice.

"He was in charge of the big cats. He was the best man in the business," Stella said.

"You mean he trained them?"

"You mean tell you never heard of the great Chase Hardin?"

"I guess I don't keep up with circuses. I haven't seen one since I was six years old."

"Well, he was the star of this circus," Stella said flatly. "But he's not a star now, as you can see. C'mon, I don't have time for this." As she strode rapidly along, Stella said nothing more until they stopped in front of a tent off to one side. "Listen, you cause trouble with our men here and out you go."

"I won't do that, Mrs. House."

"Be sure you don't. That's Annie Delaney over there." She stepped inside the tent and called out, "Annie, I want you to meet someone. This is Joy Smith. She says she can cook and she's looking for work. See if she can handle the job and let me know." She turned and left the tent without even so much as a good-bye.

Joy was somewhat nonplussed by Stella House. She knew the woman didn't like her—that was easy enough to discern—but then perhaps she didn't like anybody. Joy looked more hopefully at the woman who was standing by a wood-burning cook stove stirring a steaming pot, and went over to her. The cook was a woman of average height with reddish hair and intense blue eyes. When she stepped toward Annie to speak to her, Joy noticed she had a limp, but otherwise she appeared strong and able.

"Well, Joy Smith?" she said, with her hands on her hips. "You say you can cook?"

"Oh yes, ma'am!"

"Well, we'll see about that. I don't want any prima donnas in here. I just need somebody who can cook, wash dishes, and peel potatoes. Are you a prima donna?"

"A what?"

"Do you want to be a star in the circus?"

Joy smiled. "Why, no, I never even thought of such a thing."

"You come all by yourself? Where are you from?" Annie demanded.

"I came with Chase Hardin. He's going to work with some-body named Ritter."

The woman's eyes widened with surprise. Then she asked suspiciously, "What are you doing running around with Chase? You're not married to him, are you? You're not old enough for that, although I guess you're big enough, and that's old enough these days."

Joy knew then that she was going to get very tired of explain-ing her relationship with Chase, but it had to be done. "There was an accident, and Chase got hurt. He needed somebody to take care of him, so we stayed with a woman in Nebraska, Mrs. Hannah Smith. I had to get to Galveston, and Chase came along to look out after me."

Annie Delaney listened to this with a suspicious air. "All right. You're not telling me everything, but I'm not telling you everything either." She turned abruptly. All of her motions were swift, and she pointed at a basket full of potatoes over against the tent wall. "Wash those potatoes and peel 'em. I'll give you a try, but we don't need anybody around here who can't carry their own weight."

★ ★ ★ ★

"I'm all through with those potatoes, Miss Delaney."

Annie turned and exclaimed, "Well, that didn't take long!" She picked up one of the potatoes and looked at the peelings. "You can peel potatoes anyhow. Some of the help I get leave peelin's a half-inch thick. It'll be time for lunch soon. I want you to start cooking steaks. You ever cook steaks before?"

"Not that many," Joy said, staring at the small mountain of steaks on a table beside the stove. "How do you want 'em cooked? Well . . . medium well . . . rare?"

Annie laughed, and it made her look much younger. She was probably in her midthirties, Joy guessed. "They don't care," Annie said. "They'll be so hungry they could eat 'em any way. Just make 'em medium well. If you get a few of 'em too well done, somebody will like 'em that way. If some of 'em are rare, some will like 'em that way too."

Joy threw herself into the work of cooking the steaks while Annie went outside to where the tables were lined up. Her husband, Pete, came over and said, "How you doin', sweetheart?" He leaned over and kissed her, pulling her close for a hug and a love pat.

"Keep your paws to yourself, old man! Can't you see I'm busy?"

"Aw, come on now. Be sweet." He kissed her again, and she

held on to him a moment, then said, "Did you hear about
Chase?"

"Yeah, I met him and the girl that's with him. Who told you?"

"Stella brought the girl by and wanted me to see if she could
handle the work here."

"What do you think about her?"

"She's a funny little kid. I don't know how old she is. Probably no more than sixteen or seventeen, I would guess, but she's
a good worker so far."

"Well, hope it works out for you. You've needed some help.
I've been gripin' at Stella about that for a long time."

"She might work out, but I don't know about Chase. Has he
been drinkin'?"

"Couldn't tell it if he had, but he's lost a lot of weight."

"The girl says he was in an accident of some kind. Just gettin'
over it."

"Well, we don't need any cripples around here. But he's a
pretty good guy, Chase is."

"I don't think he'll make it. Remember what he said when he
walked out? 'I'll never go in the big cage again!' "

"Nothin' I can do about that." He kissed her again and picked
up an apple and left, munching it. Annie went back to join Joy at
the stove. She started opening huge cans of beans and dumping
them into a cast-iron pot. "We need to get another stove," she
complained. "It's hard to cook everything at once. Just see that
these get heated up."

"Yes, ma'am."

"You don't have to be so formal. First names are all right,
except for the colonel." She had a sudden thought and said, "Say,
you and Chase aren't married, are you?"

"No, we're not."

"You don't look like a bad girl."

Joy's face flushed, and she said indignantly, "I'm not! We're
just friends. I helped him out, and he's doing me a good turn, is
all. There's nothing between us."

Annie was not completely convinced, but she shrugged her
shoulders. "Well, it's his business and yours."

Joy flipped the steaks over and said, "Why did Chase leave
the circus?"

"You don't know?"

"No, he never talks about it much."

"I guess I can understand why not. It was a pretty hard time for him."

"Mrs. House says he was the best wild-animal trainer in the world."

"Well, in America at least," Annie agreed. "I don't know about Europe, but he was world-class in my book."

"What happened to him?"

Annie hesitated for a moment, but the girl had an open air about her, and although it was hard to believe a guy and a girl could travel around together and be innocent, somehow she suspected this girl was telling the truth. "Well, it's not a happy story. Chase rose up pretty quick in the business. He was the youngest there was, really, and the best. I was performing then too."

"What did you do?" Joy interrupted.

"I was a bareback rider, but I got thrown and hurt. Had to quit. Good thing I was married to Pete. I couldn't perform anymore, so I started working in the cook tent." She looked down for a moment, regret in her blue eyes. Then she shook it off and said, "It was a real tough break for Chase."

Joy sensed a tragic story coming, and when Annie hesitated, she asked, "What happened, Annie?"

"One of the tigers went wild one night. The lights went out for just a minute, and the tiger lunged at Chase. When the lights came back on, the other cats were beginning to jump off their perches. He was lucky he didn't get killed!"

"How awful for him."

"It ruined him. He was clawed up pretty bad. Was laid up for three months. He tried to come back, but he couldn't do it. He'd lost his nerve, and in his business, that's all a man has. He walked away from the circus without a word. Just left everything. That was two years ago, and this is the first anybody has heard of him. Where did you run into him?"

"In South Dakota."

"Does he drink all the time?"

"No. I haven't seen him have a drink in all the time I've known him."

"I remember the night he left. I wasn't performing then, but I was watching. Everybody was. Chase tried to go into the cage, but he couldn't do it. Pete was standing there beside me. Chase came over, and his face was white as paper. He said, 'Pete, get somebody else. I've lost my nerve. I'll never go in a cage again!' He disappeared that night, and this is the first we've heard of him."

Joy was so caught up with the story she had forgotten the steaks. Annie called out, "You're burnin' those steaks! Get to work, girl."

★　★　★　★

Karl Ritter was speaking with a beautiful young woman when Stella House interrupted them. She said, "Karl, this is Chase Hardin. Chase, this is Karl Ritter."

Ritter was surprised. "Why, sure! I saw your act several times. Always thought you were the best."

"Thank you, Mr. Ritter."

Stella said, "You need a helper, Karl. Chase needs a job."

Ritter stared at Chase. "But you can't be serious! I mean, I just need someone to clean cages and move the cats in and out of the big cage."

"I can handle that." Chase knew Ritter was familiar with his background and said, "I got out of the animal training business, but I'm pretty good with sick animals—and I don't mind cleaning the cages."

Ritter was a fine-looking man pushing thirty. He had Nordic good looks—blond hair, piercing blue eyes, strong features, tall and well built. He was usually self-assured, but this troubled him. "I need a helper, Chase, but people will talk. I mean, you were the best!"

"Ancient history," Chase said. "I can handle it."

Ritter looked at Stella, then shrugged. "Fine with me, Stella."

"All right, Chase," Stella said in a businesslike tone. "Get settled in and then we'll talk terms."

Ritter watched Stella as she turned and walked away, and Chase could almost read his mind. *He knows that Stella and I were lovers—and he's wondering how to deal with me.* "I'm ready to go to work, Mr. Ritter."

"Just Karl is fine. Come along. I'll introduce you to the cats— but you'll remember some of them. . . ."

★　★　★　★

Joy had worked furiously getting the tables set and the food out. She was aware that everyone was staring at her, and more than one of the men had grinned and made a pass at her, but she ignored them.

Through the tent flap, Annie watched the young woman as she moved around the tables efficiently, pouring coffee and refilling plates. Joy was moving about so quickly she was out of breath when she came back in.

"Slow down, girl!" Annie admonished her. "No sense in killing yourself."

"I don't mind. Work never hurt anybody."

Annie lifted one eyebrow. "No, it didn't, but most people these days don't know that." As the women worked side by side, Annie asked, "Do you have a place to stay yet, Joy? You can share our trailer. Even help me do some of the cleaning. You'll have to sleep on the couch, though."

"That's fine," Joy said. "I appreciate it." She looked outside and said, "Look, there's Chase."

Joy put a steak on a plate and carried it out to him. Chase had taken a place at a table next to Oz and across from Gypsy Dan. "Here, Chase. Did you and Mr. Ritter work something out?"

"We're all set. I'll start right after we eat."

"Will you be careful not to work too hard?" she asked. "Your ribs won't take it."

"What's wrong with your ribs?" Gypsy Dan asked, leaning forward.

"He had an accident and got some ribs cracked," Joy explained.

Oz whistled. "That's a bad one. I had that happen once. The

test's center pole slipped and nearly killed me. Nothing worse than cracked ribs."

Joy left, but from time to time she glanced out at Chase. He was eating slowly. She saw a big man with blond hair and steely blue eyes approach Chase's table. "Is that Karl Ritter?" she asked Annie.

"That's him."

Joy went out to the tables and approached the trainer. "Mr. Ritter, I'm Joy Smith."

Ritter stopped and smiled at her. "Good to meet you, Joy. You're helping Annie, I understand."

"Yes. I . . . I know Chase wouldn't tell you, but he's been hurt. He's got some cracked ribs."

Ritter was surprised. "He didn't mention that. Hey, Chase, you should have told me."

"They're healing up just fine."

Ritter smiled at Joy. "Thanks for telling me. I'll look out he doesn't do too much."

Joy smiled, relieved. "That's nice of you, Mr. Ritter."

"Just first names in the circus. Karl is fine. Welcome to the big show. Hope you can cook as good as Annie." He turned, made his way to a table, and took a seat.

Pete Delaney had been listening to this. "Didn't know about the ribs, Chase."

"I'll be okay. Thanks, Pete."

"You got a place to bunk yet?"

"Not yet."

"He could stay with me," Oz piped up. "I've got room."

"That sounds good. Thanks."

Pete Delaney left, and Joy wanted to speak to Chase, but everyone seemed to be watching them. Instead, she turned and went back into the cook tent, and as she left, Oz said, "You ain't gonna have it easy, Chase. It's been a while since you worked with the big cats, and then there's that history with you and Stella. Think you can handle that?"

"That's been over for a long time, Oz."

"If you say so. But it's going to be rough cleaning out cages when you been a star."

"I can handle that too."

Phineas Oz was a small man but had a large amount of wisdom. He knew something was going on in Chase Hardin, but he didn't know what. He stared at his friend for a moment, then said, "Okay, just holler if it gets too bad."

CHAPTER ELEVEN

FALL FROM GRACE

★ ★ ★ ★

As soon as Joy awoke she plucked her journal from the suit-case, then picked up the fountain pen Chase had given her for her birthday. She leafed through until she found the last entry and then wrote:

March 26, 1927
Well, I'm a part of the circus now. I don't know how it will work out. Chase doesn't seem happy, but at least we found a place to work until Travis gets back. Somehow I think it is Sister Hannah's prayers that are helping us, and although I feel about a million miles from God myself, it gives me a good feeling to know that she's still on our side.

Joy read what she had written, then added:

I try to forget what Albert Tatum did to Travis and me—but I just can't! I'll always believe he stole my daddy's farm, though I can't prove it. And I know he stole all of Mama's furniture! I don't know how, but someday I'll make him pay for all he's done to us!

Hearing sounds in the bedroom of the trailer, Joy capped the pen and closed the book, then put both back into her suitcase. By the time Annie stepped outside fully dressed, Joy was ready to greet her. "Good morning, Annie."

"You sleep all right?"

"Oh, just fine."

"We don't fix any breakfast here at the trailer. We go over and cook for everybody else, and then have a late breakfast ourselves."

"That suits me fine."

As the two women left the trailer, dawn was just beginning to break, lightening up the eastern sky. When they reached the cook tent, Annie said, "Why don't you start the fire, and I'll make the batter. It's pancake morning."

Joy nodded and built up a fire in the stove, then asked, "What else can I do?"

"Why don't you cook the pancakes, and I'll fry the ham."

No sooner had Joy flipped the first batch of pancakes than she heard the murmur of voices outside as the circus people gathered around the tables. The griddle was sizzling hot by now, and soon the pancakes were being sent to the tables in a steady stream. She got into the rhythm of it, pouring out a dozen pancakes at a time on the large griddle, serving those that were ready, then coming back in time to flip the others. It was not hard work for her, and she threw herself into it with gusto.

While setting down a platter of pancakes on one table, she stopped to speak to Chase, and he asked her, "How are you making out with Annie?"

"Oh, just fine. What about you?"

"Yes, I'm okay. It was good talking with Oz again."

There was no time for more conversation. The circus people ate fast and worked fast. Soon everyone had eaten, and Annie said to Joy, "Now, let's sit down and have a bite. I think we deserve it."

They dug into tall stacks of their own pancakes with cane syrup and thick slices of ham. Both women ate as though they hadn't had a decent meal in a month. Annie did most of the talking while they ate. She finished her last bite, took a sip of coffee, and nodded. "You're a hard worker, Joy. I'm glad you're here."

"It's good for me and Chase too."

"I guess everybody's curious about you and Chase."

Joy shook her head. "I know they are. Everyone has managed

to ask me if we're sleeping together."

"Well, it's a natural enough assumption."

"That may be, but honestly, we're not."

Annie smiled at the intensity of the young woman's reply. "How old are you, Joy?"

"Just turned seventeen."

Joy liked Annie very much and felt grateful for her hospitality. At Annie's questions about her past, she opened up a little, but her answers were still guarded and evasive. She said nothing about losing her family, only that she had been unhappy at home and had been forced to go out on her own. She spoke of the incident on the train when Chase had come to her assistance and been badly beaten.

Annie listened with interest, then asked, "If Chase was down, what kept those guys from turning on you?"

Joy smiled and said demurely, "I discouraged them."

"How'd you do that?"

Joy laughed out loud. "I shot one of them."

Annie's eyes flew open. "You didn't!"

"Yes, I did. My father gave me a thirty-eight. It's an old family treasure. I had no doubt that creep on the train was going to hurt me, so I just pinked him a little. I'm a very good shot. And then I made them jump off the train."

"Good for you!" Annie exclaimed. She liked the girl's spunk. "And so you stayed with the woman you told me about until Chase was able to move again?"

"Yes. Sister Hannah Smith. She's no relation of mine," Joy added hurriedly.

Annie sipped her coffee again and said, "I've always liked Chase."

"Have you known him for a long time?"

"Oh yes. We were both performers before I had my accident."

"What was he like then?"

"Not like he is now. He's been beat down so bad now that the hurt shows in his face. Back then he was on top of the world. He was a star of the circus world, Joy, and he could make those tigers do anything—and I mean anything!" She went on describing a younger Chase and concluded, "He's changed so much, I hardly know him."

"I'd like to have known him then. Do you think he'll ever get over it?"

"I don't know. It doesn't seem likely. Once someone in the circus loses his nerve, it's usually for good." Annie rose to her feet and said, "Help me clean up, and then you can have the rest of the morning off."

"All right. I'd like to look around."

★ ★ ★ ★

The circus world fascinated Joy. She discovered an area called Clown Alley, where the clowns practiced. She stood watching them for a long time with great amusement. With Oz shouting directions, they were working on an act that simulated a burning building and involved throwing a baby off the top of it. Joy could not help laughing as the clowns ran around wildly.

She moved on into the big top itself and was enthralled by the sight of an aerialist troop practicing their act at a dizzying height above the floor. She had never seen anything like it! There were four of them: a man and woman perhaps in their late thirties and a boy and girl probably in their teens. The man caught the boy and the girl as they sailed through the air after turning somersaults, and the woman stood beside the man, seeing that the trapeze got back in place to catch them as the flyers returned. Joy was so immersed in watching that she was startled when a voice said, "Hi. Watching the Martinos, are you?"

Joy turned to see a girl perhaps no older than she was. The girl had blond hair and large green eyes, and was dressed in tights and a body suit.

"I've never seen anything like this."

"They're good, aren't they? You must be Chase's friend." Without waiting for an answer, she said, "I'm Angel Fontaine."

"My name's Joy Smith. What do you do in the circus, Angel? Are you a flyer like them?"

"No, a wire walker. My mother and dad and my brother Bert and I."

Joy suddenly said, "Well, go ahead and ask."

Angel blinked with surprise. "Ask what?"

"Ask about me and Chase. Everybody else has."

Angel noted the rather sharp tone and laughed. "Well, it's only natural. Chase stays gone for two years without a word and then shows up with a girl. Naturally we're curious."

"We're just good friends." Joy pronounced the words slowly and carefully so there would be no mistake.

"I'll take your word for it. I saw you over in the cook tent this morning at breakfast. You're not a performer?"

"Me? No, nothing like that." She looked up at the aerialists and shook her head. "I think you'd have to start when you were just a baby to do a thing like that."

"That's right," Angel said. "The circus works that way. Most of us have circus backgrounds. My grandparents were wire walkers, and Dad and Mom just took over. I've never known anything else."

"Did you know Chase when he was here before?"

"I sure did." Angel smiled broadly and then laughed aloud. She seemed like a happy girl and very outgoing. "As a matter of fact, I had the world's biggest crush on him. I was only fourteen when he was with the show. I made a real pest of myself, but he was always nice."

The two girls stood talking for a few minutes. When Angel turned to leave, she said, "Too bad about Chase. He was the best."

Joy said good-bye to Angel, and then wandered around until she found the animal cages, which Annie had already informed her was called the menagerie. Chase was cleaning one of the cages with a garden hose. She immediately went up to him and greeted him.

Chase shut off the hose and said, "Hi. Taking a tour of the circus world?"

"Yes. I met Angel."

"She's a nice girl. Her whole family's very fine. Been in show business forever, I think."

"She said she had a crush on you when she was younger."

Chase smiled slightly and shrugged. "That happens a lot. Who did you have a crush on when you were just a kid?"

"The quarterback of the football team, I guess."

"Did you ever go out with him?"

"No, he never even saw me." She looked over at the tiger that had come to press its head against the cage. "Why is it doing that?"

"She wants to have her head scratched." Chase went over and scratched the big cat's furry head.

"Can I do that?" Joy asked.

"Sure. Why not. This is Mabel, a good friend of mine."

"She was here when you left?"

"Oh yes. She was always my favorite. Mabel, I want you to meet Miss Joy Smith."

Joy reached in and ran her hand over the tiger's head. The animal made a rumbling noise deep down in her throat, and Chase said, "That means she's happy." Joy continued to rub the tiger's head. "She's so beautiful!" she whispered. "And she's just like a big kitten."

"No, she's not," Chase said firmly. "She's a wild animal."

"But she's so tame."

"Don't ever make that mistake. Animals like Mabel here can be very well behaved and seem to be affectionate, but in a flash that wildness can leap out, and suddenly they're not pussycats anymore. They're killing machines. Look at those teeth." He pulled the tiger's head up, and Mabel opened her mouth. "See those teeth? You wouldn't want her to bite you with those pearly whites! And get a load of these claws. Sit up, Mabel."

Mabel sat up and waved her paws in the air, making Joy laugh with delight. Chase grabbed her paws and said, "Once these get into you, she doesn't have any way to get them out easily. She just pulls back, and whatever they're in rips wide open. If that's your face, then good-bye face."

Joy was struck with Chase's affection for the animal as he continued to talk about Mabel. At one point she interrupted him. "You really love her, don't you, Chase?"

"I guess so." The admission embarrassed him for some reason, and he changed the subject. "Well, stand back. I gotta wash out these cages." He turned the hose on and aimed the spray at Butch, who plunged his head into the water and turned around with obvious pleasure. "Some tigers are scared to death of water, but some love it—like Butch here. And elephants, now, they love water of any kind. They'd love to have a bath every day, but then they love to get out and roll in the dirt, and then they have to be washed off again."

Joy listened attentively, soaking up everything he said as they went from cage to cage. When she stepped close to one particular cage, Chase grabbed her arm and pulled her back. "Don't get too close. That's Sultan."

"Is he bad?"

"Yes, very bad. They should have gotten rid of him after he—"

"After he what?"

"This is the one that—" He broke off and shook his head. "He's just a bad tiger."

Joy swept his face with a quick glance and saw pain in his eyes. *This must be the one that mauled him so badly.* She did not ask Chase then but determined to find out later exactly what had happened.

They were almost to the last cage when a voice rang out. "Hello! How are they this morning, Chase?"

"All right, Karl. They all look healthy."

"How are you this morning, Joy?"

"Just fine, thanks." She smiled broadly at Ritter, for he had a winning way about him.

"Looking over the cats?" he asked.

"Yes. Chase was just telling me some things about them. I don't really know anything about tigers."

Ritter slapped Chase on the back. "Well, he's the man who can tell you. He wrote the book on them."

Chase shook off the praise and said, "Princess has got a touch of asthma, I think."

"Do tigers get asthma?" Joy asked with surprise. "I thought that was just humans."

"No," Karl said. "They're strong, but they're delicate. That's why the cages have to be washed out every day. If they're not, the urine fumes aggravate asthma in cats. Are you just looking around?"

"Yes. I've never seen anything like this."

"Well, if you're through here, why don't you come with me and I'll introduce you to some more folks."

Joy liked the trainer and said, "All right. I'll see you later, Chase."

"All right, Joy."

Ritter said to Chase, "I'll be back pretty soon. I'll have them set up the cage, and we'll have a practice session and get you back into the old routine."

"All right, Karl, I'll be ready."

Joy walked alongside Ritter, and when they were out of earshot, the trainer shook his head sadly. "Too bad about Chase. He was the best there was, and he hadn't even reached his peak when the trouble came."

"Were you with the circus then?"

"Not with this one, but everyone in the circus world knew about it. It really tore him up. I guess that would hurt any man."

"It must be hard on him, Karl."

"I expect it is. I'm surprised he came back."

"Why is that?"

"Well, he was a star. Now he's cleaning out cages. That's bound to hurt."

Joy did not answer. She spent a pleasant hour with Karl Ritter. He was witty and outgoing, and when he left her, he said, "Those were good pancakes this morning. You made them, I guess."

"Oh, I just helped Annie."

"I'm glad you're here. Annie needed some help. I told the colonel she was being worked to death in that cook tent, and so was I with the animals. So you and Chase are like a gift from heaven." He smiled and said, "Welcome to the circus."

"Thank you. This is going to be much more exciting than working back on the old farm."

"Come around later on, and you can watch how tigers and lions get trained."

"I will. Thanks for showing me around."

★ ★ ★ ★

Karl's words about Chase stuck in her mind. She knew there was truth in the tall trainer's remarks. It certainly must be hard to come down from being a star to cleaning out animal cages. She was thinking of this as she was taking a meal tray to Colonel House. They had been told he was under the weather. "Most likely a hangover," Annie had grunted.

Reaching the trailer, Joy knocked on the door, and Stella opened it almost immediately. "Here's the colonel's food, and yours too, Mrs. House."

"Good. Oh, by the way," she said, taking the tray, "you'll be in the spec today."

Joy stared at her. "The spec? What's a spec?"

Stella laughed. "I forget you're really a private person."

Joy looked puzzled. "Well, I guess I am. I'm not very out-going."

"No, a 'private person' is what we call somebody who's not a member of the circus, but you're not really that anymore. A spec—well, that's the parade before the performance. We have one opening every performance and another closing it."

"Why, that's just for performers, isn't it?"

Stella laughed. She appeared to be in better humor today. "It's for everybody, Joy. Go find Mamie—she's our costume lady—and tell her I said to put you in a costume. One of the harem costumes. And then tell Pete that you can ride Ruth."

"You mean the elephant Ruth?"

"Yes."

"Why, I can't ride an elephant!"

"Yes you can. Gypsy Dan will help you. There's nothing to it. Just don't fall off." She shut the door, then without further instructions, Joy turned away, filled with consternation. "Me ride an elephant?" she murmured. At first the thought was alarming, but then she was intrigued by it. She remembered Ruth's gentle manner. She straightened up and smiled broadly. "All right, I'll ride an elephant."

She saw Oz coming toward her and asked, "Oz, where do I find a lady called Mamie?"

"Oh, that's Mamie Madden. Come on, I'll take you to her."

As Oz scurried across the lot, talking as fast as his legs moved, Joy grew more and more excited. He stopped and motioned toward a tent. "She's probably in there. You gonna be in the show?"

"Mrs. House said I should ride Ruth in the spec."

"Great! You're a real kinker."

"A kinker?"

"Sure, that means a circus person. Now, go on and tell Mamie I said to do you up right."

"All right, Oz, I will."

Raising the tent flap, she stepped inside and saw an obese woman with black hair sitting at a sewing machine. The big woman looked up and said, "Who are you?"

"My name's Joy Smith. I'm—"

"Oh, you're Chase's woman."

Joy was sick of explaining her situation, so she ignored the remark. "Mrs. House wants you to give me a costume. I'm supposed to ride an elephant in the spec."

Mamie Madden had several chins, and they all quivered with indignation. "How does she expect me to do all this, I ask you? She don't have no respect for my art."

"I'm sorry," Joy said contritely. "Maybe I could come back when you're not—"

"When I'm not so busy? That ain't never gonna be. Well, let me see what we got."

"She said something about a harem costume."

"Oh, well, that's easy enough." A smile creased the woman's face, and she got up and shuffled through a collection of costumes hanging from a steel rod. "Let's see." She ran her practiced eye over Joy and said, "This one oughta do."

Joy look with astonishment at the garment Mamie was holding up. "Why, I can't wear *that!*" she gasped.

"Why not? It'll fit you perfect."

"It's not that. It's . . . it's so revealing."

Mamie's eyes closed, and she shook as laughter passed through her. "Of course it's revealing. Why do you think men come to the circus? To see elephants? Not much! They want to see girls in scanty costumes."

Joy took the garment and stared at it doubtfully. It was composed of an abbreviated top and bottom of a bathing suit under a pair of filmy pants and a top that puffed out and tightened at the wrist and ankles.

"Go on. Put it on, and let's see what you look like."

Joy swallowed hard. "Don't you have anything else?"

"Sure, I've got an overcoat you could put on. You think that would thrill anybody? If Stella said a harem costume, you'd better put it on. I found out it pays to keep that woman happy."

Joy felt trapped, but then she decided, *I can do it. Nobody knows me here except Chase, and he's used to circus things.* "Where can I change?"

"Why, change right there."

"But—somebody might come in!"

Mamie chuckled, sending the fat rippling across her array of chins. "Well, they wouldn't see nothin' they ain't seen before. Look, honey, there ain't no privacy in the circus. What we have to do is just have good manners, and when we walk in on somebody half dressed or even worse, we just pretend we don't see nothin'." Seeing the young woman's alarm, however, she softened. "Well, go back on the other side of them racks. I'll station myself here. I'm so big nobody can get around me to see you."

Joy followed Mamie's advice, undressing and pulling on the costume as fast as she could. She came out barefooted, since her black shoes did not go with the rest of the outfit.

"Well, ain't you pretty now!" Mamie exclaimed. "Believe it or not, I looked just about like you when I was your age. Now there's enough of me to make three of you."

"Do I go barefooted?"

"No, we got some slippers here. Let me see." Mamie rummaged through a trunk and pulled out a pair of soft gold slippers. "How's that?" She straightened. "You better hurry up if you're gonna be in that spec. The crowd's a-comin' in. Sounds like a straw crowd too."

"What's that? A 'straw crowd.'"

"What we call a full attendance. You better git now."

Feeling indecent, Joy stepped shyly outside. The costume tent was attached to the smaller tent where the parade was made up. She saw Gypsy Dan Darvo and ran to him. "Dan," she said hastily, "Mrs. House wants me to ride Ruth."

"Well, don't you look pretty! Sure, I think that's a great idea."

"I've never been on anything but a horse and not too many of those."

"Don't you worry," Dan grinned. His white teeth flashed

against his dark complexion. He was wearing a splendid costume with the loudest possible colors and a turban on his head.
"Come on, you've already met Ruth. She'll remember you."

"No, she won't."

"That's what you think! You heard about having a memory
like an elephant? Well, it's no lie. I don't think they ever forget
anything. She'll know you all right."

Indeed, Ruth did seem to remember her. When Darvo
stopped in front of her and said, "Ruth, you remember Joy?" the
elephant reached her trunk out and tentatively brushed it across
Joy's shoulder.

"See, I told you so."

"But how will I get on, and what keeps me from falling off?"

"Gettin' on is easy enough. Ruth, *leg.*"

Ruth obediently lifted one leg, and Darvo said, "Here, step
on this leg. I'll give you a hand. Just swing your leg over her
neck."

Joy had little choice. Dan practically picked her up, and in
one swift motion, she threw her leg over the big animal's neck.
There was a wooden collar there, and she grasped it with both
hands.

"You're all right. Just hang on. Ruth knows this drill better
than anybody."

Darvo wheeled and left her alone on top of Ruth. Joy found
herself trembling—but partly with excitement. She had never
done anything like this, and she looked around curiously at the
rest of the parade.

Everyone she had met was there in costume, and then she
saw Chase. He was in a chariot pulled by two beautiful white
horses. He grinned at her and waved, and she waved back and
called out, "Hi, Chase! Look at me!"

"You look beautiful, Joy!"

Joy flushed at his compliment and then suddenly the flap of
the tent opened, and she felt Ruth move under her. It took her
only a few paces to get the rhythm of the elephant, and she was
delighted at the sensation. She patted Ruth on the head and said,
"Good, Ruth. Good girl."

The parade was a blur to her, but she soon forgot the brevity
of her costume and her nervousness about the spectators. They

were applauding, and she found herself waving at them and smiling.

The spec did not take long, and as soon as they were back out of the main tent, Darvo appeared again. "*Leg*, Ruth," he said, and without being instructed, Joy slipped down, stepped onto the animal's leg, and jumped to the ground.

"You did fine—fine! I'll make an elephant girl out of you if you're not careful. You could do it too. You're not afraid of animals, are you?"

"No, I never have been. Not unless they're mean."

Joy turned and started toward the costume tent to change back into her regular clothes. She was almost to the flap when a hand seized her and turned her around. The young man with nearly white hair held on to her arm painfully. "My name's Benny," he said. "Benny Yates. How about you and me steppin' out sometime?"

"No thanks." She tried to pull away, but the man was stronger than he looked. "Aw, come on, I heard about you. I know you're Chase's girl, but you need a little variety."

"Let me go!" Joy tried to pull away but did not succeed.

To her even greater surprise, the man rose almost magically up in the air, and his grip on her arm loosened. Joy did not understand at first what had happened, and then she saw that Yates was being held by a massive black man, who held him by his neck with one hand and his belt with the other. The big man was well over six-four and must have weighed at least two hundred fifty pounds.

His voice was deep, like a threatening rumble on a stormy night. "Now, Benny, this here young lady is a particular friend of mine."

Yates reached up and grabbed the giant's hand to support himself. "Hey, I didn't know that, Doak. You shoulda told me."

"Of course you didn't know, but you do now." The giant set the young man on the ground and dusted him off. "Now, you run along—and you pass the word to the other young men of our fine establishment. Miss Joy here is a good friend of mine, and I'd purely *hate* to have trouble with anybody."

"Oh, you won't have no trouble, Doak. I'll tell 'em," Yates

said nervously. He disappeared, and the big black man turned to say, "Sorry about that, Miss Joy."

Joy looked up into the man's face and realized he was as black a man as Joy had ever seen. "We haven't met."

"No, but my name is Doak. Doak Williams."

"Thanks so much, Doak."

"Why, I always aim to stay on the good side of the cook."

Joy found herself liking this man with a gentle smile and a handsome, pleasant face. "You deserve a reward. I'm going to make you a pie of your very own. What kind do you like?"

"How 'bout apple?"

"That's my specialty. I'll have it for you at supper tonight, Doak."

★　★　★　★

When Joy entered the costume tent and began changing her clothes, Mamie interrupted her. "No point in that. You'll just have to change back for the closing spec. Here, put on this robe instead."

Joy took the tan satin robe, slipped it on, and went back to watch the performance.

She loved all of it but was especially interested in Karl Ritter's act. She had never seen a wild-animal act before, and she froze in anticipation when he stepped into the cage with six lions and six tigers. Any one of them looked capable of destroying him, and she gasped as he put them through their paces. She was also aware that Chase and two other men were stationed outside the cages with long sticks, and one of them carried a gun.

Ritter was very energetic. He held a chair in one hand and a whip in the other, and had a pistol at his side. More than once he'd pull the pistol and fire it at a lion or a tiger that seemed to be ready to charge. He fended them off with his chair, cracked his whip, and shouted a great deal.

When the act ended, Joy felt weak with excitement.

She had no time to speak to Chase, for she had to get right back to Ruth and be ready for the closing spec.

* ★ ★ ★

By the next day, Joy was already getting more proficient at fixing meals for a large crowd. She had learned the names of many of the performers, and most of them were friendly. She finished the supper dishes in time to go back for the evening performance and enjoyed her ride in the spec again.

At the end of that performance, everything exploded into action.

"We're pulling down!"

She remembered then that they were taking the tent down and moving on. She flew back to the cook tent, and for two hours helped Annie get the kitchen gear packed and ready to be loaded onto a big truck. She was vaguely aware of the shouts and activities as the big top was being pulled down. Everyone worked feverishly, and as the trucks were being loaded, it seemed like utter confusion to Joy. She learned, however, that the circus workers and performers knew their jobs so well that it all fell together without a hitch.

The big diesels were beginning to roar when she saw Pete stop to speak with Annie. Joy was close enough to hear him say, "We'll just have to leave him here."

"You can't do that, Pete," Annie protested. She noticed Joy standing nearby and looked her way. Joy approached the couple to ask what the trouble was.

"It's Chase. He's dead drunk. He was drinking tonight before the performance."

Joy saw the anger in the big man's face. "Do you know where he is?"

"Somebody said he was over where the menagerie tent was."

Joy took off in that direction, and Pete called after her. "We'll leave him here. He's no good, Joy!"

But Joy ran quickly, dodging and threading her way through the activities. She found Chase curled up on the ground, unconscious, reeking of alcohol. She shouted at him to wake up and shook him hard, but he simply curled up tighter.

Giving up, she ran back toward where the activity was the thickest. She had to have help, and her eyes lit on the enormous form of Doak Williams. She raced up to him, shouting, "Doak! Doak!"

"Yes, Miss Joy, what's wrong?"

"It's Chase."

"What's wrong with him?"

"He's drunk, and Pete says he's going to leave him here. Please, he can't do that. I'll have to stay if he does."

"What do you want to do?" Doak asked.

"Help me get him into one of the trucks."

"Why, shore, we can do that. Show me where he is."

Joy led the big black man to where Chase lay, a shapeless lump on the ground. Without a word Doak stooped over and picked him up as easily as if he were a child. "I'll put him in the truck I rides in."

"Can I ride with him?"

"That'll be fine, Miss Joy. Plenty of room."

★ ★ ★ ★

The space in Doak's truck was cramped, but Joy had wedged herself in beside Chase. He was lying flat on his back, and she had her own back braced against the side of the truck. The diesel fumes were sickening as the truck rumbled through the night. She felt Chase stir and heard him groan.

"Are you all right, Chase?"

"Where am I?"

"You're in a truck, and we're going to Lake Charles, Louisiana."

Chase struggled to sit up. By the flashlight, she saw that his face was twisted and contorted. "How'd I get in here?"

"I had Doak put you in. Pete was going to leave you behind."

"He should have, and you should have left me too."

"No, remember what Sister Hannah said. God told her you're supposed to take care of me until Travis gets here."

Chase stared at her for a moment, then closed his eyes and lay down flat again. "I can't even take care of myself," he muttered, falling once more into a stupor.

CHAPTER TWELVE

FIRST OF MAY

★ ★ ★ ★

Joy took out the pen, removed the cap, and then bent over the table. She had returned to the Delaneys' trailer after doing the breakfast dishes and had gotten out her journal, as well as the writing paper and envelopes she had purchased at the ten-cent store in Lake Charles. She carefully wrote the date at the top of the paper, *April 2, 1927*, and then began writing with smooth, easy strokes. She was an expert penman, and her handwriting was as legible as print. Travis's had always been bad, and he had envied her ability to write so beautifully. Now as she wrote, she found pleasure in watching the words flow out from the pen, and the scene flashed in her mind of the moment she had unwrapped it on her birthday. She also treasured the comb and brush Sister Hannah had given her, and now as she addressed a letter to her she felt a pang of nostalgia for those brief days she and Chase had spent at the older woman's house.

Dear Sister Hannah,

We are now in Baton Rouge, Louisiana. After we left Galveston we went to Lake Charles, Louisiana, for three days, to Lafayette for three more, and then to Baton Rouge. You would not believe how much work it is to move a circus from one place to another. I sup-

pose the old hands, the kinkers as they call themselves, are used to it, but for a day after such a move I am stiff and so sleepy I can barely do my work.

The work itself is demanding, but it's so interesting. I cook three meals a day and clean up afterward. I also ride an elephant named Ruth in the specs—those are the parades before and after the shows. Gypsy Dan, who is the elephant man, wants me to be in his act, and I think I probably will. I'm not afraid of Ruth at all. She's such a sweet thing! I always take her some goodies, and she always puts her trunk around my neck and gives me a very gentle squeeze.

I am enclosing a copy of the schedule—the towns and dates where the circus will be. I left one at the post office in Galveston for Travis, so when he comes back he can find me no matter where the circus happens to be. You can write me in care of general delivery at any of these towns.

I have made so many new friends here. One of my best friends is Doak Williams, a huge black man who saved me a lot of embarrassment. One of the hands was trying to get too familiar, and Doak simply picked him up by the scruff of the neck and in the gentlest voice you can imagine told him that I was his special friend, and that he would hate to have trouble with anybody over me. The word got around because nobody wants trouble with Doak! He's such a gentle giant and so kind, and the strongest man I've ever seen.

Joy leaned back and read what she had written. The memories ran through her mind like a motion picture, or perhaps more like a kaleidoscope—scenes of the performances, tearing down and setting up, cooking the meals, the voices and faces of the performers. She smiled then and leaned forward to begin writing again.

I like it so much in the circus. My life has always been so boring that I don't mind the hard work at all. You would think the people here a little strange. They are cut off from the rest of the world. Their world is the circus. They're very possessive of their parts in the show. Sometimes they get into terrible arguments when someone feels slighted, but Pete usually settles them. He's very firm. Colonel House is the owner, but he's not in good health, so his wife, Stella, does most of the actual operation of the show. Colonel House is the ringmaster, and that's about all he's capable of doing right now. He's a very nice man, and he stopped me today to say that both Chase and I are going to be paid for our work. Up to now we've just gotten our room and board. Well, not a room actually but board at least. We'll get twenty dollars a week, which isn't much, but we don't have any expenses. I'll save my money until Travis gets home, and then we'll have something to start with.

Once again she paused and tapped her teeth with the base of the fountain pen. She did not know exactly how much to tell Sister Hannah about Chase's problem, but she suspected the woman already knew.

I'm very worried about Chase. He started drinking almost as soon as we got here, and he's so unhappy. I can understand that, because he was a star here. Everybody applauding him and everybody in the circus admiring him. Now he's just got the rough job of cleaning up after animals and doing menial work. I know he stays here only because you asked him to take care of me. Everyone says he'll never get in the cage again with the big cats because of what happened to him, and they're probably right.

Well, I must leave now. Dan is going to show me how to do some things with Ruth so I can be in his act. I'm excited about this, Sister Hannah.

I know you're praying for Chase. Please keep on. Give Jake a hug for me and Caleb, too, when you see him.

> Yours truly,
> Joy Smith

She folded the letter and put it in an envelope. She addressed it, put a stamp on it, and left the trailer. She heard the cats roaring and went inside the big tent to watch Karl as he put the felines through their paces. The act was almost finished, and she watched as Chase stood at the gate of the tunnel that led back to the menagerie. The big cats, one by one, leaped from their perches and ran down through the tunnel to their cages.

When Karl stepped outside, he saw her watching and came right over with a smile on his face. "That was a great breakfast this morning! You're a better cook than Annie, even if you are a first of May."

"But—it's April!"

"First of May—that's what we call newcomers to the circus."

"Oh, I see. But I'm not a better cook—and don't you ever dare say that to her."

"No, just to you. Where are you heading now?"

"I'm going to find the post office."

"Mind if I go along?"

"Why, no, it'd be good to have the company."

"I'll borrow the colonel's car, and we'll go in style."

The two left and went straight to the colonel's trailer. He was sitting outside in a folding chair, his legs crossed and watching the people in the backyard. This was the area where the performers congregated and dried clothes on a line and rehearsed their children in some of their skills. She watched as an acrobat helped a child no more than two learn to do a back flip. Joy smiled and said, "They start very young, don't they?"

"They have to in this business," Karl said, then turned to the colonel. "Colonel, can I borrow the car? Miss Joy and I need to go to the post office."

"Yes, of course, Karl. Stella has the key. I think she has some things to be mailed."

Karl went to the door and knocked, and when Stella opened it, he repeated his request. She agreed and handed him a handful of letters and the keys. "Don't wreck it, now," she said, smiling and batting her eyelashes.

"Why, I've never had a wreck in my life. You can trust me, Miss Stella."

The two left and got into the Packard. It was practically a new car, one of the few luxuries the colonel allowed himself. Karl was an expert driver, and instead of going straight to the post office, he simply drove around pointing out the sights. He had been to Baton Rouge before, and although there was little to see, Joy enjoyed it.

Finally he pulled up in front of the post office, a red brick building on Main Street, and got out, then ran around the car to open the door for Joy. They went inside, and Joy mailed her letters. She wanted to ask if there was any mail for her, but Karl was standing right beside her, and she did not want him to know that her name was Winslow. She hesitated and then said, "Karl, would you please wait for me in the car?"

Karl looked at her with surprise. "Why, sure." He turned and left the building. As soon as he was gone, she hurried to the window, and a cheerful-looking woman with bright red hair said, "Can I help you?"

"Do you have a general delivery letter for Joy Winslow?"

"I'll see." The woman turned to a small desk and shuffled through several letters, then came back and said, "Sorry, miss, nothing today."

"Thank you."

Joy went outside and found Karl leaning against the fender. "All ready?"

"Yes. I need to get back fairly soon and help Annie with the dinner."

"Oh, we've got plenty of time. How about an ice cream?"

"All right."

The two went into the drugstore that was down the street from the post office and took seats at the counter. A round-faced young man came over and said, "What'll it be?" He was short, and his hair stuck up in several wild cowlicks.

"I'll have a chocolate soda. What about you, Joy?"

"The same for me."

While they waited, Karl spoke lightly of the affairs of the circus, and when the sodas arrived, Joy took a straw and plunged it in. "Why, it's too thick to drink."

"That's what the spoon's for," Karl said. "Eat up. It'll make you fat and pretty."

Joy laughed. "I don't think I'd like that." She blew her cheeks out and said, "If I keep on eating things like this, I'll be as big as Mamie."

"It's hard to think of her as a young girl, isn't it? Some of the older people say she was the prettiest thing around."

"She's still pretty. It's funny how so many overweight people, women especially, are really pretty."

Karl nodded. "I'll bet your mother is pretty. And I'll bet you look just like her."

Joy said nothing but dropped her eyes, and Karl asked, "Did I say something wrong?"

"My mother's not living, Karl."

"Oh, I'm sorry. I'm always putting my foot into it." He reached over and squeezed her arm. "I'm sorry, Joy. I'm just an ill-mannered, uncouth tamer of lions."

"No, it was natural enough. I do look like my mother."

"No more family? Your father?"

"He's gone too. They died in a car wreck together with my younger sister. There's just my brother, Travis, left. He's at sea now, but when he comes back, he'll be at Galveston. That's why I came to Galveston."

The two continued talking, and Joy found herself enjoying Karl's company. She wasn't sure why she had so easily shared with him what had happened to her family, since she had not been able to bring herself to tell others, not even Chase. But it felt good to finally tell someone. She decided it was Karl's easy manner when he wasn't in the ring. He seemed to be two people: one, the rather gentle person he was now, witty and very charming; the other, the fearsome man he became when he stepped inside the cage. She had been curious about this and asked him now, "Why do you treat those animals so harshly, Karl?"

Ritter shrugged. "You have to keep them afraid of you. The second they get the idea they're stronger than you are, they'll jump you. Didn't Chase ever tell you that?"

"He never talks about his days in the cage."

"Well, his style was a lot different than mine, and I think that's why he got jumped. He just didn't put enough fear into those beasts."

This explanation did not seem quite right to Joy, but she said no more about it. Karl began telling her amusing anecdotes, keeping her entertained until she quite forgot the time. Finally he paid for the sodas, and they went back to the car. "This has been very pleasant. I get lonesome, you know."

Joy laughed, and he turned to her with astonishment. "What are you laughing for? Don't you think I could get lonesome?"

"Lonesome? The way women throw themselves at you?" Joy had indeed noticed that when Karl was not in the cage, he was subject to quite a bit of attention from women in the audience. She knew that he was also popular with the female performers, especially Angel Fontaine, the wire walker. Joy's eyes sparkled as she said, "I don't think you get very lonesome, Karl."

"Oh, well, you know how it is." He shrugged and grinned.

"Yes, indeed, I do know how it is, so don't try your wiles on me anymore."

Karl laughed and took her arm. "All right, I'm guilty as charged. All the same, it's been fun."

"Yes, it has. Thank you for bringing me."

★ ★ ★ ★

The days turned into weeks and weeks into a month. Joy could not understand where the time had gone. By the time they arrived in Pensacola, she had become part of Gypsy Dan's act. When he had first invited her to join his act, she'd thought it was impossible. But he had insisted, saying, "Really, it takes less talent to do the elephant act than anything else in the circus. All you have to do is hold on. Ruth will do everything else."

Joy had found this to be true. Mostly it consisted of posing in different positions, throwing her hand out and taking the audience's applause, stretching backward when Ruth rose up on her hind legs. She had learned to hang on tight to the harness, and it was no trouble at all.

The most difficult part was the spin. This simply meant sitting in the curl of Ruth's trunk and hanging on to the front of her headdress while Ruth turned rapidly in a circle. All she had to do was hang on with one hand and throw her arm backward, looking as graceful as possible. It was a great deal of fun, and she found she enjoyed the applause, even though she knew there was no great talent involved.

She stopped one day beside Dan, whose other job besides the elephant was being the human cannonball. It was an act that had frightened Joy when she had first seen it performed. Dan had to slide into the bore of a cannon mounted on a truck. A net was stretched out more than a hundred feet away, and with a tremendous explosion, Dan was thrown through the air, managing to turn in the air and land in the net. As the ringmaster, Colonel House made it sound terribly dangerous and emphasized the number of men who had broken their necks trying this very difficult stunt.

Now as she stood beside Dan, she asked him, "How dangerous is it really, Dan, this human cannonball stunt?"

"Safest trick in the circus."

"That's not what the colonel says," Joy protested. "He says a lot of men have broken their necks trying it."

"Oh, a few have been hurt, but it's their own fault. There's really nothing to it."

"But to be shot out of a cannon and all that noise . . ."

"Aw, the noise is nothing." Dan grinned. "It's just added to make the act more spectacular. Down at the base of the cannon is a plunger. It's pulled back by hydraulic pressure, and when I slide down I put my feet against it and block up. When it's released, the charge goes off, but it has nothing to do with pushing me out of the cannon. The plunger shoots me out the end, then I turn one graceful turn and land in the net. That's all there is to it."

"I don't believe it's that easy."

"Well, I hope the customers feel the same way. If they ever found out how easy it was, they'd stop watching, and I'd be out of one of my jobs."

★   ★   ★   ★

Joy loved being in Pensacola, where she could savor the ocean breezes and lush tropical climate. One morning after breakfast Chase came by and said, "Let's go down to the beach. Have you ever been on the Gulf?"

"I was close to it in Galveston, but I didn't actually see it."

"It's beautiful here. Nothing like it. Bring your suit if you want to go swimming."

"I haven't got one, but I'd like to see the beach and maybe find some shells."

"Okay. Doak is going into town to run errands. He can drop us off."

The two of them made arrangements with Doak, and Joy said, "After we go to the beach, I need to go to the post office. Maybe I'll have a letter from Travis."

"Sure. Nothing easier than that."

Doak let them out at the Pensacola beach, and after he drove away, the two took off their shoes and started walking along the white sand. "It's so beautiful. And the water's so green."

"Look at that!" Chase said excitedly. He turned her around and pointed. "Look right there."

"Oh, I see! What are they?"

"Dolphins. A pretty sight, aren't they?"

Joy watched as the sleek creatures rose out of the sea, then arched themselves in the air and slipped back under the waves. There were four of them, one after the other, and Joy was thrilled at the sight. "They're so beautiful," she said.

"Nothing much prettier than that."

They watched until the dolphins disappeared in the distance, and then Joy and Chase continued their walk. The sun was high and the sand was already too hot on their bare feet, so they waded in the water, searching for shells. Once Chase caught her arm and warned, "Watch out. Don't step on that."

"What is it?"

"Jellyfish. They sting like crazy when you get involved with them. I was swimming one time out in the Gulf, and I got in a big bunch of them. I thought I was gonna die."

It was a clear day with the sun gleaming on the crystalline sand and farther out from shore the water glistening green and blue. Joy felt exhilarated, and when it was time to turn back, she sighed, "I hate to leave."

"Maybe we could become beach bums. Doesn't pay very well, though."

"I suppose not."

The two went back to the street and waited until Doak drove up; then they got in the truck. "Run by the post office, will you, Doak? Joy needs to check to see if there's a letter for her."

"Sure enough, Chase."

Doak found the post office with little trouble, and Joy said, "You two can just wait here. I'll go in."

Slipping out of the truck, she ran into the post office. When she got to the window, she asked the clerk, "Is there anything in general delivery for Joy Winslow?"

"Let me see. I'll check." The man disappeared for a moment, and Joy's heart leaped when he returned with an envelope in his hand. "One letter for Joy Winslow."

"Oh, thank you!" Joy took the letter and stepped away from the window to read it. She trembled with excitement and ripped it open. Her brother's writing was as bad as usual, and it seemed he had written on a piece of brown paper sack. Her eyes scanned the lines:

Dear Joy,

   I have bad news. I'm sending this from a prison close to Veracruz on the Gulf of Mexico. The crew went ashore and there was a fight. I wasn't part of it, but one of the Mexicans got badly hurt. He was a prominent man, and we had no chance at all. Three of us were sentenced to a year in prison. You can't do anything. I'll find you when my term is up. I love you, Joy. This is the worst thing that's ever happened to me. The prison's bad. Write to me, and let me know what's happening. I've been so worried about you.

Love, Travis

★　★　★　★

"It's takin' her a long time," Chase said, a puzzled look on his face. "I'll go check and see what's happenin'." Getting out of the truck, he ran up the steps to the post office and passed through the doors of the building. He glanced to his left and saw Joy standing at a tall desk. Her head was bent over, and he saw that her shoulders were shaking. He immediately went to her side. "What is it, Joy? What's happened?"

"It's . . . a letter from my brother."

Chase took the letter and read it. He put his arm around her and said, "It's a tough break."

Without meaning to, Joy leaned against his chest. Sobs racked her body, and she clung to him. He could only hold her and pat her shoulders, knowing there was nothing he could say to make her feel better. Finally her sobs subsided, and he fished a handkerchief from his pocket. "Take this," he said gently. He watched as she cleaned her face, and then he said, "This is bad news, but we'll make it. We'll make it, Joy. It'll be okay."

When Joy looked up to him from the circle of his arms, her eyes held a tragedy that went right to Chase's heart. "We'll make it," he said softly. "You and me, we'll wait. We'll do what we can."

"Will you do . . . will you do one thing for me, Chase?"

"Anything."

"Please . . . would you not drink anymore?"

The question stunned him. Chase said nothing for a minute, seeing himself at a crossroads in his mind. He was facing two diverging roads—one, the path of drinking in order to forget, the other, Joy's way. She did not understand what she was asking of him, he thought. The liquor had gotten ahold of him now and seemed like the easy way to avoid his pain. But looking down at her tearstained face, her lips trembling, he knew he had no choice. Finding the courage to take the more difficult road, he said to her, "Yes, I'll do that."

Joy laid her cheek against his chest and relaxed in the comfort of his arms. "Thank you, Chase," she whispered.

Chase held her for a long moment, then said, "Come on, we've got a ways to go, Joy—but we'll make it."

PART THREE

March–August 1928

★ ★ ★

CHAPTER THIRTEEN

STELLA

★ ★ ★ ★

Joy came out of a deep sleep abruptly, and when she opened her eyes, a beam of sunlight slanting down from the window blinded her for a moment. Shutting her eyes quickly, she rolled over and pushed her face into the pillow, burrowing down under the blankets. She lay there for a moment savoring the warmth, for the March mornings in Asheville, North Carolina, were still cool and the trailer she occupied with Ella Devoe was not an efficient unit to heat. She had been glad when Ella invited her to share her trailer last summer. Living with Pete and Annie Delaney had been inconvenient. Not that it bothered Joy, but she just felt like she was in the way. Ella had said, "Come on and bunk with me, Joy. You can come and go as you please, and we'll see how we get along."

The trailer had only one bedroom, which Ella occupied, but the kitchenette, which consisted of two bench seats and a table, folded down cleverly to convert into a bed. It was not overly soft, but it was better than most had in the circus. She had learned that Ella went to bed fairly early, so Joy did not have to disturb her except on rare occasions.

The busy hum of the circus waking up captured Joy's attention. Muted by the walls of the trailer, voices seemed thin and far away, but the muffled roar of a lion added an exotic flavor to the sounds.

She threw the cover back, sat straight up, and opened her eyes wide as the thought seized her, *I'm eighteen years old today!*

She had not given much thought to her birthday, for her life was so busy she'd had little time to think about it. No one except Chase knew it was her birthday, so she was not expecting anything in particular—maybe just a good wish from him.

Leaning over, she picked up the tablet and the pen that lay on the floor beside her, flipped the tablet open, and began to write. The pale yellow sunlight illuminated the page as she wrote the date, *March 15, 1928,* hesitated, then started:

> *I'm eighteen years old today, but I don't feel any different than I did yesterday. I suppose birthdays are like that for adults—but they were very special when I was young. I remember Travis always put me under the bed, and I would kick and scream and try to keep him from doing it, and then we would both wind up laughing. And then on my last birthday at home I remember that Daddy—*

She broke off, for the painful memories of her sixteenth birthday ran through her like a razor. For a long time she'd had nightmares about her family going off in the truck and never coming back. Thankfully, those nightmares had finally stopped, and she could finally enjoy some of the happier memories. One of the silly little memories that came back to her now was the particular way her father used to peel an apple with his sharp pocketknife. He always peeled it in one single spiral, which had delighted Joy. She could see him now with his lips turned upward in a grin and a merry light in his eyes, winking at her as he handed her the peel and saying, *"Here, you eat this, and I'll eat the rest."*

She was able to smile now at such memories, remembering the good times. She began a new sentence:

> *I remember I got this pen a year ago today from Chase at Sister Hannah's, and I've used the comb and hairbrush she gave me every single day. That was a good day. I don't suppose I'll get any presents today, but I'm not complaining.*
>
> *No matter how hard I try, I can't feel anything but hate for Albert Tatum and his rotten kids! I know it's wrong—but I just can't help it! In a way Albert is responsible for Travis being in jail.*

If he hadn't been such a rotten man, we'd still be living at his place. I don't believe much in prayer, but if I did, I'd pray for him to die!

She stared at the lines, then shook her head. *Why can't I forget all about him?* She glanced at the clock and decided to go help Annie, although she had been released from morning duties to do other things. She replaced the pen and tablet in the box that she kept in one of the trailer's small overhead compartments. She slipped out of her pajamas and jumped into the shower as quickly as she could, savoring the hot water. Coming out shivering, she dried off with a large, fluffy pink towel and dressed with an efficiency of motion. She transformed the bed back into a dining table and bench seats, and since she would be eating breakfast later with Annie, she didn't make any now.

By the time she reached the cook tent, Annie already had most of the work done, but she smiled at Joy. "I'm surprised you're here today. I thought I gave you the day off. I'm almost done now."

"I decided to come help after all. I can set the tables, and then I'll clean up."

As Joy moved back and forth between the kitchen and the tables, she had a smile for those who greeted her. It occurred to her then that, in less than a year with the circus, she had immersed herself in the lives of the people there. Her eyes swept over them, picking out the Flying Martinos—Juan and Maria with their children, Mateo and Lucia. They chattered together in Spanish as Joy refilled their coffee cups.

The Fontaines sat at the next table, and their son, Bert, who was twenty, reached out and grabbed Joy by the arm as she passed by. He was a small, well-built young man with a pair of jaunty blue eyes. "How about you and me go out and do the Charleston somewhere, doll?"

"No, you've got too many girlfriends, Bert. They'd probably beat me up."

"Aw, I'd dump them all in a second for you, Joy."

Joy laughed. She couldn't help liking Bert despite his constant teasing, and his sister Angel had been a good friend to her. She chatted with them for a minute, then moved down to where the clowns formed a group. Oz, the loudest, was sitting with Red

Squires, Mack Button, and Oleander Jones.

The roustabouts kept to their own table, not being of the stature of the performers themselves. She smiled at Benny Yates, remembering how Doak had picked him up by the neck on her first day at the circus. Despite that introduction to Benny, she had come to like him. He played the trumpet in the circus band, and she admired his musicianship. She pulled his hair, and when he turned to grin at her, she said, "I'm going to cut off that hair of yours, Benny, before it gets down to the floor!"

"I thought women liked long, beautiful hair," Benny said.

"Not on men, silly! You'd better keep it short if you ever want a girlfriend."

Slim Madden, Mamie's husband, grinned at her. He was tall and thin, in contrast to Mamie's round form, and his glasses rode on the bridge of his nose. "Just shave it all off. He couldn't look any worse."

Breakfast disappeared quickly, but most of the performers and workers stayed around for extra coffee. When the dining area finally cleared out, Joy began picking up the last of the dishes and carrying them back to the washtub. She washed while Annie dried, and the two talked about their next engagement in Chattanooga, Tennessee.

"I've always liked Chattanooga," Annie said. "Pretty scenery and lots to see around there. There's a Civil War battlefield I'll take you to see when we get there."

Joy said, "I love all this traveling around. It's so exciting."

"Well, when you've done it as long as I have—and that's since I was born—you can't imagine staying in one place."

The two were interrupted when Karl stuck his head through the flap and grinned. "Hey, is it too late to get breakfast?"

"Yes," Annie said.

"No, that's all right, Annie. I'll fix something," Joy offered. "Eggs and bacon be all right? And I think there's some biscuits left."

"That'll be fine, and you can sit down and listen to me eat it."

"Don't you wish!" Joy teased back, laughing, as Karl left her to the preparations.

While Joy threw the elements of the meal together, Annie put away the last of the dishes, then turned and crossed her arms.

"You're not getting sweet on Karl, are you?"

"No, of course not."

"That's good."

Surprised, Joy looked up. "Why? Don't you like him?"

"Oh, I like Karl. I think everybody does, but he's a ladies' man."

"Well, I'm a lady, aren't I?"

Annie saw that Joy was smiling at her and noted the clean lines of the girl's face and the youthful curves of her figure. "You're not a baby anymore, and you need to watch out for yourself."

"Oh, Annie, I went through that last year when I first joined the circus. Doak would have broken anybody's neck that offended me—even Karl's."

Joy took the plates outside and set them before Karl, who was reading a newspaper. She walked over to the coffeepot, filled a large white mug, and placed it beside him, then sat down across from him. Putting the paper down, he took a bite of the eggs and bit off a chunk of the biscuit. "I thought you weren't going to listen to me eat." Karl grinned at her.

"I'm not. I just thought I'd keep you company, since you're so lonesome all the time."

Karl winked at her and took another bite of eggs. "Hey, did you listen to Will Rogers on the radio last night?"

"No, I missed it."

"That guy kills me! He's the funniest man I ever heard." Karl chuckled. He chewed thoughtfully for a moment, took a swig of coffee, then said, "Last night he reported on the state of the nation, and you know what he said? He said, 'The nation is prosperous as a whole, but how much prosperity is there in a hole?'" Karl guffawed and shook his head. "How does he think of that stuff? I'd sure like to see him at the Ziegfeld Follies. I went one time. It was great."

"Was that in New York?"

"Sure was. I would love to play New York sometime, but I don't guess we will. The Ringling Brothers have about got that sewed up. I'm going to be with that circus one day. The biggest show on earth! That's what I aim to do."

"Wouldn't you hate to leave your friends here?"

"Oh sure, but I'd make friends there."

"I like it here. It's a bit like a family to me."

"Why, sure it is, but a man's gotta make a place for himself."

He reached over and tapped the newspaper and said, "Look at that."

Joy picked up that section and looked at the drawing on the front page. "What's this?" she said.

"Something new. That's a cartoon character they call Mickey Mouse."

"Mickey Mouse?"

"Yeah. It's something that a fellow called Walt Disney has come up with. He draws a series of pictures and somehow makes the pictures look like they're moving. They're called animated cartoons."

"I've never heard of it."

"It's pretty new, I guess. I'd like to see it sometime. This mouse is the star of a movie called *Steamboat Willie*. I hear it'll be on at one of the local theaters in Chattanooga. Maybe we can take in a matinee."

"That would be fun," she said.

"You know what my favorite radio program is?"

"Can't guess."

"Amos and Andy. Funniest stuff I've ever heard."

"Funnier than Will Rogers?"

"Oh yeah, even funnier."

Joy had to agree with him about Amos and Andy. "Yeah, they're good all right, and from what I hear they're getting rich."

Karl glanced up at her and took a swig of coffee. "What do you say after I eat, we have another lesson with Mabel?"

Joy's eyes lit up, and she smiled. "Oh, I'd like that!" She had grown very fond of the big tiger, and as soon as Karl finished his breakfast, the two left the cook tent. They made their way to the menagerie, where Karl guided Mabel through the tunnel into the big-top cage for the morning's practice.

"You ready?" he asked Joy.

"Sure am."

"As I've said before, always remember that you've got to make her know who's boss," Karl warned. He looked fresh and handsome as he stood beside the door wearing a navy blue shirt, open at the throat, and a pair of light blue wool trousers.

"Come on in and see if she'll sit up for you today."

"She always sits up for me," Joy said, entering the gate without a moment's hesitation.

For some weeks Joy had been entering the cage with Mabel, the most docile of all the circus cats. She went toward her now without a trace of fear, and Mabel made a rumbling sound. Reaching out with a stick, Joy rubbed the top of her head, and the rumble became more pronounced. "Sit up," Joy commanded.

Instantly the huge tiger rose up and pawed at the air. Joy laughed at her. "She looks just like a kitten—a really big one!"

Karl, who was standing with his chair close beside them, had strapped on his pistol with the blanks. He kept his eyes cautiously on the cat and nodded. "She's safe enough all right, but just remember she weighs nearly five hundred pounds. She could hurt you by accident, Joy."

Joy went through the tricks Mabel had learned. She could easily make her sit up, lie down, and roll over. Then she led her to one of the high perches and got her to leap at her command. "Up, Mabel!" The tiger gracefully leaped to the top of the perch and then, again at Joy's command, sat up.

"That's great. You're going to be taking my job one of these days, Joy."

"I love the animals."

"Well, Mabel's one thing, but it gets a little harder with some of the others."

Karl unlocked the door for her, and as Joy went out, she saw that Chase had been watching. He was wearing a pair of coveralls—his usual attire for cleaning out the cages. "Hello, Chase. Did you see me make Mabel do her tricks?"

"Yes, I did."

Something about the spare tone of Chase's voice caught at Joy. While Karl was busy getting the cat back into her cage, she asked Chase, "What's the matter?"

Chase just shook his head, but something dark glowered in his eyes—like a permanent shadow. "You shouldn't be getting in the cage with that tiger."

"Why, she wouldn't hurt anybody!"

"She can kill you, Joy."

"But Karl's always in there with me."

Chase did not answer but turned away. "I guess I'd better get to work," he said.

Joy had felt alienated from Chase in recent weeks. She knew he did not like her getting in the cage with Mabel, but she thought there was more to it than that. He had made it known that he did not like Karl Ritter's methods of training animals. He felt they were cruel and dangerous. Joy wasn't sure what to think, but now she said simply, "Don't worry about me. I'll be all right."

★　★　★　★

At the performance that afternoon, Joy played a new role for the first time. As usual, she had ridden Ruth in the spec, then had been a watcher at the animal cage along with Chase and Benny. No problems there—the act had gone well. Immediately after that she had rushed to change into a tight-fitting silver costume covered in gold spangles. She no longer felt uneasy in the immodest circus costumes, accepting that it was all part of the show. She wore a spangled top hat and a coat with a frock tail also covered in spangles. She loved putting on this particular costume, and now she met Gypsy Dan, who grinned and winked at her. "You ready to send me to my death?"

"Don't talk like that, Dan."

"You know I'm just kidding. You look great. Go on out and get the crowd to liking me."

As Joy moved toward the entrance of the arena she thought about how Gypsy Dan had asked her to become a part of his human cannonball act. She had been reluctant at first until he had explained that she wouldn't actually be doing anything with the cannon. Her part was very simple.

Joy started paying attention when she heard Colonel House saying with a dramatic flair, ". . . and this young lady holds the life of Dan Darvo in her hands. If she does not aim the cannon right or does anything at all wrong, we'll have a tragedy on our hands. So I give you Miss Joy Smith!" Joy smiled and ran to the back of the cannon, which was mounted on a large truck bed, turned a pirouette, and took a bow.

"And now, Mr. Dan Darvo, the human cannonball!"

Gypsy Dan came running lightly out into the spotlight wearing a sparkling white uniform with a cape. The young ladies in the audience always cheered and applauded louder than anybody else for this handsome, dark-skinned man with dark hair and flashing eyes. Joy helped him remove his cape and handed him his silver helmet. He fastened it on, then leaned forward and gave her a kiss on the cheek, surprising her. "Just a little extra special bonus for being my helper." He winked, then climbed swiftly to the top of the ladder and slid feet first into the barrel. He paused to wave to the crowd and then disappeared.

She had actually done nothing yet, nor would she do anything really, but she understood that her part was simply to help create the illusion. The cannon was already pointed in exactly the right place. The net where Dan would land was securely in place. The control knobs on the back of the cannon were absolutely meaningless, but she would fiddle with them for show before the cannon was fired.

The colonel shouted out, "And now the final adjustments will be made, and in a few seconds you will see a human body doing what no human body was ever made to do. It will become a projectile—not of death, we trust, but there's always that possibility."

Joy turned wheels and pulled switches, none of which did anything to the cannon. Finally she heard Colonel House say, "When you're ready, Miss Joy, you may send our brave friend into flight."

Joy put her hand on a large lever. She paused dramatically and then pulled. There was a loud explosion—and a gasp from the crowd—while Dan was flung into space by a hydraulic spring inside the cannon.

Joy held her breath as the human projectile flashed out of the cannon and arced into the air. He held his body perfectly straight, his hands before him in the manner of a diver. As he rose higher the crowd uttered a sustained "Ahhhh!" Joy had watched this many times, but her heart still seemed to stop. As always, Dan made a perfect slow turn and landed on his back in the net. Joy began applauding as he sprang to his feet, flipped over the edge of the net in the manner of an aerialist, and then took his bows. He came running back and pulled off his helmet. When Joy reached out to him, he kissed her hand and then turned to wave at the audience. The applause was long and enthusiastic, and when the two left the ring, Benny got into the cab and slowly backed the truck that was hauling the cannon out of the arena.

"You did great," Dan said to Joy, giving her a big hug.

"I didn't do anything, Dan. Just pretended to push buttons."

"Are you going out with Ritter?" Dan asked.

The sudden question took Joy aback. "Why . . . what do you mean?"

"I mean are you two going together?"

"You know we're not. I've been a few places with him but that's all. It's nothing like that."

Dan reached out and put his hand under her chin. His black eyes were dancing as he said, "You went out with him just two days ago."

"Yes, he took me to an ice show. It was the first one I'd ever seen."

"Watch out for him."

"I'll watch out for *you*, Dan Darvo. You're the one who gives girls trouble."

★ ★ ★ ★

Joy was exhausted after the evening performance. The day had been long and hard. She had taken another lesson from Karl after the afternoon performance, and then had worked with Dan, learning more about the elephants. She headed back toward Ella's trailer as the crowds filed out and the equipment was put away. She was mentally reviewing everything she had learned about elephants in the past year. *I used to think that big hook Dan uses would hurt the elephants, but you couldn't hurt an elephant with a thing like that.* The hook was used only to give the animals direction and not to hurt them. She smiled at her own innocence. *If people realized how strong those animals are and how impossible it would be to hurt them with the hook, they wouldn't think like that.*

She had almost reached the trailer when Oz caught up with her. She looked down, smiled, and said, "You sure were good today, Oz."

"You think so? I try. Hey, Joy, there's a meeting. Everybody's got to be there."

"What's it about?"

"Don't know. Come on. It's over at the cook tent."

Puzzled, Joy went with Oz and found a considerable number of people there. Colonel House saw her and announced, "All right, Miss Smith, we've called this meeting just for you. You have created a problem."

Joy blinked her eyes, and she felt everyone watching her. She racked her brains trying to think of something she had done, but could not. "What . . . what did I do, Colonel House?"

A silence fell, and the Colonel glared at her. Joy glanced around and saw that Chase was standing over to one side, also watching her with a sober expression. Everyone seemed to be angry with her, and she whispered, "I don't know what I've done. What kind of problem have I caused you, Colonel?"

Much to her surprise, Colonel House suddenly grinned. He had a fine grin, and he called out in his best ringmaster voice, "You've become a beautiful young woman—and that's always trouble. Happy birthday, Joy!"

Joy found herself surrounded by people—some touching her arm and several kissing her on the cheek, including Gypsy Dan and Karl Ritter. She glanced around to find Chase standing back, a smile on his face.

"You did this, Chase. You're the only one who knew it was my birthday."

"Guilty as charged." He came over to her and took her hand. "Happy birthday," he said.

Joy was disappointed that Chase did not kiss her on the cheek as some of the others had, but she had no time to talk to him. Annie came out bearing a huge cake with eighteen candles on it, and there were drinks for everyone. Annie had fixed stacks of sandwiches and a baked ham, and they had a delightful party. She finally got a chance to speak to Chase, who was sitting down beside Angel Fontaine. "I use the pen you gave me on my last birthday every day, Chase."

"Well, I got you another present this year." Reaching into his pocket, he pulled out a small package, this time wrapped in red paper. It had a small bow on it, and when she opened it she found a delicate silver ring with a small turquoise stone. "I got it from one of those Indians that was with the circus for a while. He made it himself."

"Oh, it's beautiful, and it fits perfectly too!"

She reached over and kissed Chase's cheek, and he blinked with astonishment. "You didn't have to do that," he said, grinning.

"Take what you can get," Angel said, laughing, then she turned to Chase and said, "My birthday's on August the twenty-second. Write it down."

"I'll remember."

Chase left the party early. He was happy he had engineered the surprise celebration for Joy. He was almost halfway back to the trailer he shared with Oz when a voice turned him around. He stopped and said, "Hello, Stella."

"You left the party early."

"Yes, I'm a little tired."

Stella fell in beside him. "You gonna check the cats?"

"Yes, always like to put them to bed. You know, those cats get upset if I don't visit them after every performance and last thing at night."

"You're good with them, Chase—much better than Ritter."

Chase did not answer, for there was no answer to it. "I'll never get in the ring again."

"That's a shame. I'll never forget the first time I saw you in that ring, Chase. There must have been a dozen tigers. You had everybody in the palm of your hand, including the animals."

"Ancient history, Stella."

The two made their way to the menagerie, and Chase spoke to every animal. Some of them were already asleep, but others pushed their heads against the bars. Stella followed him, occasionally reaching out and touching one of the gentler ones.

When he was finished with his rounds, he turned and saw her watching him in a peculiar way. She stepped close to him, and in the semidarkness he saw that her eyes had grown large and her lips were parted. "Chase," she said in a sultry voice, "do you ever think about the times we had together?"

"I try not to."

He turned to walk on, but Stella caught him, pulling him back to face her. She put both hands on his arms, caressing his muscles gently. "Why don't you want to think about it? Those were good days."

"Better not to think about things like that."

"You mean because I'm married?"

"That's reason enough." He removed her hands gently and turned once more to leave, but she planted herself firmly in front of him.

"It's not a marriage, Chase. Maurice just wants somebody to take care of him. He's sicker than people know, and it's all he can do to get out there and be the ringmaster. I have to take care of everything else. I need more than that."

"He's your husband, Stella, and he's a good man."

"I know he's a good man, Chase, but he's an old man."

She put her arms around his neck. Chase knew he should pull away and leave while he still could, but the memory of their times together came flooding back and he remained rooted to the ground, his hands at his sides. She pulled his head down and drew nearer. Chase caught the fragrance of her perfume and felt her lips on his, soft and demanding. He surrendered himself to them, putting his arms around her waist and pulling her close. He knew it was wrong, but he told himself he couldn't help it. He dropped whatever inner restraint he was struggling with and succumbed to the luxury of her embrace. They remained in each other's arms for a long time, until he heard a noise and lifted his head. Stella had heard it too, and she dropped her arms and stepped to one side. Together they saw Joy, standing dead still at the corner of the animal cages watching them.

Chase saw the pain and disappointment in Joy's eyes and wanted to call out to her. But without a word she whirled and ran away.

Stella brushed her hair back with her free hand, then looked at Chase and laughed. "She's easily shocked, isn't she?"

CHAPTER FOURTEEN

HOTEL PEABODY

★ ★ ★ ★

The last of March found the circus located in West Memphis, Arkansas. This small town was separated from Memphis by the Mississippi River. Joy had gone earlier in the day to watch the mighty river as it flowed by. Rivers had always fascinated her, and she had spent over an hour simply sitting on the bank and watching the magnificent flow of the Father of Waters.

She had returned in time to help with the noon meal, then had done her part in the matinee. She had fallen into the routine of the circus world. There were very few variations, and it seemed that her time was almost as regimented as that of a soldier. At first it had seemed to her she would grow weary of repeating the activities time and again, but it had not been so—she loved circus life.

After the matinee she had spent some time working with Mabel. She had grown very fond of the beautiful tiger and was now trying to teach her to walk backward on her hind legs. Mabel could stand on her hind legs, but whenever she tried to go backward she stepped on her tail.

"No, no, Mabel, hold your tail up."

Without thinking, Joy stepped forward and lifted the tiger's tail. Mabel suddenly fell on her front feet, turned, and reached out with her paw. It caught Joy's sleeve, and the claws ripped the sleeve all the way down to the wrist. "Oh, Mabel, look what you've done!"

"It could have been worse."

The voice caught Joy unaware, and she turned to see Chase, who was watching her attentively through the bars. She was embarrassed he had caught her at such a moment and said testily, "She didn't mean to do it."

Chase was wearing a pair of faded jeans and a light blue cotton shirt. He shook his head and said, "I know she didn't mean to do it, but I've been trying to tell you, Joy, an animal can hurt you without meaning to."

"She would never hurt me."

"Suppose she'd gotten her claws in the flesh of your arm. She wouldn't have meant to, but they would have ripped it wide open just the same."

Deep down Joy knew Chase was right. He had more knowledge of these animals than anyone she knew, but she was too stubborn to admit it at this moment. "It's just a shirt. I can patch it up again."

For a time she continued to work with Mabel but was very aware of Chase's eyes on her. Finally she gave the command, "All right, back into the cage, Mabel."

Obediently the tiger turned and walked into the tunnel that led back to the menagerie. Leaving the big cage, Joy started back to the menagerie to make sure Mabel got properly caged. Chase walked alongside her and said, "I haven't seen much of you lately."

"I've been busy." Joy's reply was curt, and she was aware that she was behaving badly. Chase said nothing but turned and walked away without another word.

Suddenly Oz was beside her. "What's the matter with you? You're right snippy with Chase lately."

"Nothing, Oz. I'm just in a hurry."

Oz had to take two steps to Joy's one, but he trotted along beside her, looking up to study her face. "You know, when you and Chase first came here everybody thought you were lovers."

"I know. I spent enough time trying to convince people otherwise."

"Well, I guess you convinced everybody. Anyway," he said, "I ain't sure Chase has gotten over Stella."

"She's married, Oz."

Oz reached up and caught Joy's hand. He had large hands for such a small man and was very strong. He pulled her around abruptly, and dryness rustled in his words. "I've heard a time or two when a woman being married didn't matter to a man."

"Let me go, Oz!" Joy protested.

But Oz held her still. "Being married doesn't mean much to Stella."

"Well, why don't you talk to Chase, then? Tell him he's asking for trouble."

"I try not to mix in other people's business, but since you mentioned it, let me give you a warning about Karl."

"I've heard all that too," Joy said. "We're just friends."

"Karl's a nice guy, but he's never happy to be 'just friends' with women."

Joy wrenched her hand loose with an effort and shook her head. "You'd better go practice your act and stop minding everybody's business, Oz."

As she walked away rapidly the memory of Chase and Stella kissing after her birthday party flitted through her mind. She knew she'd been upset ever since then and was being unusually snippy with everyone. The incident had been more than a week ago, but she still thought of it every time she saw either one of them. She had not realized how strongly she felt about Chase until that night. The sight of them holding each other had greatly angered her, and she could not get it out of her mind, nor could she help the coolness she showed now to both Chase and Stella. With Stella it did not particularly matter, for she had little contact with the woman. But up until that night Joy and Chase had spent time together every day. They had always had things to talk about, and now that their communication had been interrupted, Joy felt empty, and it bothered her.

"Were you practicing with Mabel?"

Joy turned and found Karl coming toward her. "Yes, I was trying to teach her to walk backward."

"Hard to teach a tiger that. They always step on their tails."

Joy laughed loudly. "That's exactly what she does."

"Hey, what happened to your sleeve? Did Mabel do that?"

"She didn't mean to," Joy said defensively. "She was just going to pat me, and her claw got caught."

"Ruined a good shirt," Karl observed. He was wearing a pale green shirt and a pair of dark brown trousers and looked very handsome indeed. "I've been looking for you," he said. "I've always liked Memphis. Why don't we go out for a late supper after the performance tonight?"

Joy hesitated, thinking of what Oz had said, but decided Karl looked harmless enough. "I'd like that a lot, Karl."

"We'll go to the Peabody Hotel. It's where everybody goes to dance."

"I don't have a very fancy dress to wear."

"Go get one, then. You deserve it."

The idea appealed to Joy. "I think I will," she said. "I haven't bought a new dress in I don't know how long."

"You'll be the belle of the ball!" he said, then added, "It'll be a little past your bedtime, but we'll have a great time. Just you wait!"

★ ★ ★ ★

The ballroom of the Peabody Hotel was still crowded at eleven o'clock when Joy and Karl arrived. He said, "What'll you have to drink, Joy?"

"Oh, nothing for me." She had expected to get a meal but saw no signs of that possibility.

"Let's have some champagne, then. That's not really drinking. Waiter, bring us a bottle of your best bubbly."

"Yes, sir."

"C'mon, Joy. You know how to Charleston?"

Joy laughed. "I've seen it often enough, and I practiced a little by myself. It's such a funny-looking thing."

Actually, the Charleston had passed the high mark of its popularity. It was fabulously popular during the early part of the decade. Joy watched the dancers swiveling, kicking, and knocking their knees together. Then she moved out onto the dance floor with Karl to try it. Having always had good rhythm, she found she could do it very well but felt silly. "This is ridiculous!" she shouted over the noise of the blaring saxophone that led the band.

"Of course it is. That's why we come out, to be ridiculous. We're just gonna have fun tonight."

The evening was fun. It seemed like her first real date, and she found herself laughing nonstop. She did not attribute it to the champagne, which she drank sparingly, at least at first. Karl was a wonderful dancer, and he taught her a dance called the Black Bottom, which she thought was even sillier than the Charleston. The band was playing songs she had heard on the radio. They played the lively tunes "Ma, He's Making Eyes at Me" and "There'll Be Some Changes Made," and then some slower numbers, including "Look for the Silver Lining" and "It Had to Be You." She particularly liked "It Had to Be You," and as Karl led her around the dance floor, she found they were perfectly matched.

"You're as pretty a girl as I've ever seen, Joy. Where'd you get that dress?"

"Oh, I went shopping with Angel and Jenny this afternoon."

"Well, you look great."

The dress was more expensive than she had hoped, but she loved it. It had a bright floral print with a black ribbon sash and trimmings. She was wearing high-heeled court shoes with decorative bows, and she had bought a bottle of designer perfume by the famous Elsa Schiaparelli. Angel had urged her into it, for the perfume was called "Shocking." Angel had winked at her, saying, "Don't use too much of it. They say it drives men wild, and they become beasts!"

Taking this dare, Joy had bought a bottle and then had felt guilty over paying such an exorbitant price.

Karl held her closer and put his cheek against hers. "What is that perfume? It's great."

"It's called 'Shocking.' Do you really like it?"

"Love it." He kissed her cheek, then twirled her around. "We ought to go on the stage as dancers. We could call ourselves the 'New Castles'!"

The Castles had been a famous dancing duo of earlier years but were still well known. Karl's remark was not particularly witty, yet she found herself laughing at it. Karl laughed with her and said, "Now you're getting with the party."

The evening sped by, and Karl encouraged Joy to help finish the champagne. Joy had never been drunk before and, as a matter of fact, had never tasted champagne. Karl had insisted it was not really liquor, and anyone could drink all they wanted without becoming intoxicated. She had started by sipping at it, but then, without realizing it, had been taking longer swallows. At first it had just made her feel rather silly, but as they finally left the ballroom, she found that things were fuzzy. She held on to Karl's arm, for her steps were unsteady.

When they got outside she stumbled on the way to the car, and Karl put his arm around her. "Hey—let me give you a hand here."

Joy found the world whirling about, and she slumped into the car and put her head back. When Karl started the engine, she murmured, "I shouldn't have . . . drunk all that . . . champagne."

"You'll be all right, sweetheart. Come on, we'll go home now."

Joy remembered nothing of the trip back to the circus. When she closed her eyes the whole car seemed to be revolving in huge circles.

Finally she heard the engine shut off and knew they were back. She could hardly raise her head. Then the door opened, and Karl was half lifting her out. She leaned against him and staggered through the darkness. Her mind was not clear, but suddenly she opened her eyes and realized that he was leading her not to her own trailer but to his. His arms were tight around her, and he opened the door with his free hand. "Come on, sweetheart," he said.

"I can't go in your trailer."

"Sure you can," Karl said. "It'll be the perfect ending to a great evening!" He put his arms around her and kissed her. His caresses were demanding, his hands moving on her body.

In a flash Oz's warning came back to Joy, and she put both hands on Karl's chest and shoved backward. She almost fell to the ground, but when he moved to catch her, she cried out, "Leave me alone, Karl! You shouldn't have done this!"

Ignoring his protests and urgings, she turned and stumbled

through the darkness toward the trailer she shared with Ella. When she reached it, she was so dizzy she could hardly stand.

The door opened, and Ella appeared wearing a robe. "Come on in, babe. It looks like you had too much to drink."

Joy managed to get inside the trailer and then collapsed on the bed, which Ella had already made up for her. She opened her eyes and had to struggle to focus. Ella was looking at her in a strange way, and Joy began to cry. She put her head forward and felt the cushion move as Ella settled beside her. "He finally got to you, did he?"

"Who?"

"You've been out with Karl, haven't you?"

"Yes, but I just wanted to—"

"I know what you wanted," Ella said, and then her voice turned harsh. "And I know what *he* wanted too. Did he have his way with you?"

"He tried to get me to go to his trailer. He got me drunk, Ella."

"That's Karl, all right." Bitterness tinged her voice, born of a lifetime of unhappy experiences with men. "I'm glad you got off so light. Come on now. Get undressed and go to bed. We'll talk about it tomorrow."

Joy managed, with Ella's help, to get into bed. She lay down and let the tears flow. The light went out and silence filled the trailer. She wanted to cry out but did not know how or to whom she could cry. "I'm such a fool!" she whispered. "How could I be so stupid?"

★ ★ ★ ★

The next day was hard for Joy. She learned very quickly what a small world the circus family was. The first three people she encountered asked her, "Did you have a good time with Karl?" She gave them noncommittal answers but was miserable and embarrassed. Karl himself seemed unchanged. When their paths crossed that morning, he said, "Well, I guess we both found out you can't handle liquor."

Joy demanded, "Why did you do that, Karl?"

"Do what?" Karl said, his face showing surprise. "We just went out and danced and had some drinks. How was I to know you'd act like that? Some people just can't handle liquor, and I guess you're one of them."

"You tried to get me into your trailer."

Karl shook his head. "I guess I did, but didn't you know I'd try that?"

"I didn't think you would."

"I guess that's just the way I am with women. I can see you're different. Sorry, Joy, it won't happen again."

Joy accepted his apology, but was still embarrassed. Later on she found an opportunity to speak to Chase. "I'm sorry I was so rough with you, Chase. I've been . . . I've been having a hard time lately."

"Sure, it's okay." Chase smiled gently and put his hand on her arm. Joy was certain he knew all about what had happened the night before. She wanted to explain, to tell him she hadn't meant for it to be like that, but she could not put it into words. She looked up at him and touched the lapels of his coat.

Indeed Chase did know more than she thought. He had stayed up waiting for her to come home and had been standing in the darkness when Karl had tried to get her into his trailer. Chase had been about to interrupt when she had turned and stumbled home.

Now he saw that she was flushing, and her lips were taut in an uncertain, crooked smile. He had become very fond of her, and whatever mistake she had made with Karl, there was still an innocent sweetness about her. She loved life as much as any young woman he had ever seen, and he knew she was finding her way in a world that could be cruel. He could see a depth of maturity in her beyond her years, but also a childlike simplicity, and he remembered his promise to Sister Hannah to watch out for her. "Why don't we go to the zoo today after the matinee?"

Relief rushed through her, and she said, "That would be wonderful. I've never been to a big zoo."

"Good. I'll see if I can borrow Dan's car. We'll get a bite to eat if Annie will let you off from cooking tonight."

★　★　★　★

Stella sat at the small desk inside her trailer, her eyes intent on the books in front of her. From time to time she wrote down some figures and added up columns. The silence was broken by a knock at her door. "Who is it?" she snapped, annoyed at the interruption.

"I need to see whoever's in charge."

Stella shook her head in disgust. "Never a moment's peace around here. I'll never get these books straight." She threw the pen down, strode to the door, and flung it open. A tall young man stood before her. "What do you want?" she demanded.

"My name is Travis Winslow. I'm looking for my sister."

"Winslow? There's nobody here by that name."

She studied the cobalt blue eyes on this fine-looking, but skinny, young man. She wondered about the pallor in his face and his shoddy clothes for an instant, then decided she didn't have time for him and was about to close the door when he interrupted her.

"Is there a man called Chase Hardin here?"

Stella opened the door fully then and said, "Yes. Do you know Chase?"

"Never met him, but I understand that my sister is with him."

"What does your sister look like?"

"She's a blonde with dark blue eyes, about this tall." He motioned with his hand.

Stella's eyes narrowed. "I think she may be here, but she doesn't call herself Winslow. Come along."

She stepped outside, locked the trailer door, and said, "Follow me." She threw a glance at the young man, who she reckoned was no more than twenty, and said, "Where are you from?"

A hesitancy punctuated Winslow's reply. "I've . . . uh . . . been in Mexico for the past year."

★　★　★　★

Joy was in the backyard, that part of the circus where the performers sat outdoors when the weather was nice. April was kind, the sun shining down brightly. They had come to the small town of Forest City, Arkansas, two days earlier, and the crowds had been good. Joy was sitting beside her big friend Doak Williams. Hearing her name called, she glanced up, and then her eyes flew open. She leaped to her feet and ran over to grab Travis, hugging him as hard as she could. "Where'd you come from? I didn't expect you!"

Travis held Joy tightly. "It's good to see you, sis. I got out a month early for good behavior."

Stella's ears caught this. "You been in prison?" she said.

Travis turned and nodded. "Yes. I was working down in Mexico and got caught in the middle of a fight."

Stella demanded of Joy, "So your name is really Winslow, not Smith?"

"That's right."

"Are you running from the law too?"

"No, Mrs. House," Joy said. She clung to Travis, fearful of Stella's suspicions. She didn't want to try to explain that she was indeed hiding from the law, but not for any wrongdoing of her own. "We had some family problems, and we ran away. But I'm eighteen years old now, and they can't make me go back."

"I don't need any trouble from families or from the law," Stella snapped.

"It's all right, Mrs. House," Travis assured her. "There won't be any trouble."

As Stella turned and left abruptly, Joy laughed up into Travis's face. "It's so good to see you. It's been such a long time."

"A long time for me too. You're looking great, sis."

"Come on. You're nothing but skin and bones. I'll fix you a good meal."

On their way to the cook tent, Joy saw Chase. He had been sitting with Dan and Oz watching all this, and now she said to her brother, "Come on, I want you to meet Chase."

As they approached the table where the men sat, Chase rose to his feet. "I'll bet your name is Travis." He smiled and put out his hand.

"Yes, it is. I've got to thank you for all the help you've been to my sister."

"No trouble at all. It's good to meet you."

Joy introduced Travis to Oz and Dan, then said, "Come on, I've got to feed you."

They entered the cook tent, and Joy beamed as she introduced him to Annie.

Annie studied his lean face and said, "You look like you need
a decent meal. You two go sit down. I'll fix you somethin'.
What'll it be?"

"Anything you've got," Travis said. "If it'll stand still, I'll eat
it."

Joy led him out to a table. She filled two cups with coffee and
watched as he savored the strong-smelling brew. "Did you have
a hard time finding me?"

"Well, I had to hitchhike all the way up from Mexico but no
trouble." He shook his head. "I can't get over how you've grown
up since I left. You seemed like such a little girl then, and now
you're a woman."

"A lot can change in a year, Travis. Do you remember back
when we lived in North Dakota, and we just couldn't wait to get
back to Virginia?"

Travis nodded.

"Well, I'm having so much fun with the circus," Joy went on,
"that I don't even think about going back to Virginia anymore."

"I know what you mean, Joy. My focus has changed since
then too."

They sat quietly for just a moment, and then Joy said, "You
look so thin, Travis."

"Well, the pickin's have been pretty slim."

"Was it awful? I know it must have been." Joy reached over
and took one of his hands in both of hers. "I've been so sad, and
I've missed you so much."

"I want to tell you something," he said as a joy lit up his eyes.
"When they sent me to prison I just about went crazy. I couldn't
take it. I even thought of killing myself once, but something happened. A missionary named Jerry Golden came to preach. He
tried to talk to me about being saved, and I cussed him out. But
he never gave up." He smiled then and shook his head. "That
man was sure persistent. He kept coming back, and he never
showed anything but love for me. And finally, sis, well . . . I got
saved!"

Annie appeared at that moment with a plateful of food, and
when she left, Travis went on, "I thought I'd been a Christian all

my life, but I made a mistake somewhere. And in that jail when Brother Jerry was praying with me, I began to weep. I realized I'd never let Jesus into my life, so I just called out like Brother Jerry asked me to do, and something wonderful happened to me. From that moment on I've been filled with the joy of the Lord."

"Oh, Travis, I'm so glad for you!"

"Well, you may not be glad about the rest."

"The rest? What's the rest?"

"God's calling me into the ministry. I'm going be a preacher. Isn't that something? I don't know how in the world I'll do it, but I'm going to."

Joy was rocked by Travis's declaration, but as she looked into his face, she felt nothing but love and gratitude. "If that's what you think God wants you to do, then you'll have to do it."

"Well, I want to go to Bible school first, but I'll have to work until I can save enough money."

"I'm sure Colonel House would give you a job."

Travis laughed. "My jaw about fell to the ground when I read in your letters what you've been doing—getting into a cage with a tiger. I don't think I could do that, sis."

"No, but you can do everything else. You could always make an engine run when nobody else could, and these trucks are always breaking down. There's plenty of work to do." She ran around the table and flung her arms about him, hugging him tightly. "I'm so glad you're back, Travis. We're a family again!"

CHAPTER FIFTEEN

"I'M NOT A LITTLE GIRL!"

★ ★ ★ ★

Spring had spread over the land, bringing forth tender green shoots, carpeting the fields and softly rolling hills surrounding the circus in lush emerald. Travis Winslow, after pulling the carburetor off of a greasy engine, stopped long enough to rest his eyes on the scene. He'd had no trouble getting a job with the circus, for Colonel House was always happy to find cheap help. Despite the low wages, Travis was happy just to be out of prison. He knew deep in his heart that someday he would be in Bible school, and after that he'd be serving Jesus Christ somewhere in the world. It was enough for now that he was free. Being able to breathe the fresh air was intoxicating, and the work wasn't difficult. He had always liked tinkering with engines, and the trucks that hauled the circus from town to town were as temperamental as any he had ever seen.

"How's it going, Travis?"

Travis turned to find Chase Hardin approaching with a big smile.

"It's going better than snuff," he said, grinning.

"I don't see how you keep these engines running. Some of them are as old as Methuselah." He smiled at Winslow and added, "You sure made a place for yourself here."

"Just for now." Travis nodded. "It's so good to be out of that cell. I just thank God that I'm here."

"I guess you were surprised at Joy."

"You mean that she's grown up? Sure was. She's always been a pretty girl, but when I first saw her I couldn't believe it was her. She's just radiant. I don't know about getting in with that tiger, though. That seems dangerous to me."

"It is dangerous, Travis, and I wish you could talk her out of it."

"No use." A grimace twisted Travis's mouth slightly to one side. "She's got a stubborn streak in her—as you've probably discovered."

"Yes, I have, but she's had a rough time of it, so it's understandable. I'm sure glad you're here now."

A sudden shout caught the attention of both men, and Travis shook his head. "What's that? Sounds like trouble."

"It may be. Let's go take a look."

The two men hurried quickly into the main tent and saw a crowd gathering. Travis said, "I hope it's not Joy."

They ran across the sawdust, and Chase saw Gypsy Dan lying on his back, his face twisted in pain.

"What happened?" Chase asked.

"I was . . . helping with the rigging, and I fell. If I'd hit the sawdust, I'da been all right, but I hit this ring instead."

He referred to the ring that marked the limits for the acts. It was made into sections that could be easily disassembled. Joy had explained it to Travis. He had learned that every circus ring is the same size, forty-two feet across.

Colonel House suddenly appeared, his face worn and pale. "Dan, this doesn't look good." He bent down, and when he touched Dan's leg, the prone man cried out. "We'll have to get you to a doctor."

"Doak, you get some men and carry him to the truck. I'll join you in a minute."

Despite the severe pain, Dan kept from crying out as Doak and several of the other men picked him up carefully and carried him toward the opening.

"Well," House said gloomily, "there goes our elephant act."

Joy had heard the commotion too, and now, without thinking, she spoke up. "I can take Dan's place until he gets better."

Every eye turned toward Joy, and she flushed but lifted her head. "I can do it. Not as good as Dan, but at least we won't have to cancel it."

Colonel House brightened up. "Well, by George, I believe you can, Joy. Dan was telling me just yesterday how well you've done. So that's your new job."

House ran his hand over his thinning white hair and shook his head. "We'll have to take the human cannonball act out. Hate to do that. People want to see everything that's advertised."

"I can do that act, Colonel."

Colonel House blinked with surprise, for it was Travis who had spoken. All the colonel knew about this young man was that he was a magician at getting stubborn ancient engines to run. "You're not a performer," he said.

"No, but I talked to Dan a lot about that act," Travis said. "He always said it was the easiest act in the circus."

"I don't agree with that," House said. "It's dangerous."

"You can't do it, Travis. You've never done anything like that!" Joy exclaimed.

"I've never done that, but you know what a good diver I've always been."

"This is different from diving."

"I don't see why. If I can do a full gainer with a double twist, I can make one simple turn in the air. That's all it is, isn't it? You go up in the air, you keep your body straight, and before you hit, you do one turn. Why, I can do it."

Juan Martino, the trapeze artist, shook his head. "You can break your neck if you miss."

"How can I miss? If the cannon's aimed right and the net's in the right place, I'll have to fall into it, won't I?"

Chase shook his head. "I wouldn't want to tackle that myself. People have been hurt doing that act. Dan's been lucky."

Stella had appeared from somewhere, and now she interrupted their conversation. "I say we give him a chance, Maurice. Juan, why don't you let him take a few falls into your safety net? That's similar, isn't it?"

"Sure, Stella," Juan said eagerly. "Come along, Travis, we'll give you a try."

The net for the trapeze act was already set up, and Travis did not even change clothes. Joy stood beside Chase, watching her brother as he climbed up the ladder to the perch where the flyers did their act. They heard Juan speaking clearly, and everybody, it seemed, had gathered to watch, except for Colonel House, who had gone to the hospital to stay with Dan. Everyone was fascinated with the idea of a man just out of prison volunteering to be the human cannonball. Word of Travis's prison experience had gotten around, but it troubled no one.

"All you do is just fall forward and make a slow turn," Juan explained. "You want to land on your back in the middle of that net."

"Sounds easy enough," Travis said.

"Hitting the net's not hard. The hard part is what happens afterward."

"What do you mean?"

"I mean you're going to bounce up. Most people get hurt on the rebound. The net throws them up into the air, and they come down on the edge or miss it altogether. So always keep your mind on hitting squarely and not being thrown sideways. Here, let me show you."

The Martinos had been ready to practice their act when the accident had happened. Now all four of them—Juan, Maria, Mateo, and Lucia—gave a quick demonstration.

Joy watched all of this, then cried out to Chase when she saw her brother standing on the edge of the high platform ready to jump. "I'm afraid for him, Chase!"

"He'll be all right. He was a good diver, wasn't he?"

"He was great, but this is different."

Joy and the others watched as Travis launched himself out, made a slow turn in midair, and landed on his back in the net. He rebounded and then came to his feet and let himself down off the net. "No problem," he said.

Stella nodded. "You try that a dozen times, and then if you've got the grit for it, we'll try the real thing. Doak, set up the net for the cannonball act and bring the cannon out."

All too soon, it seemed, the practice was over, and Joy

watched with apprehension as Travis approached her. "Well, wish me luck." He grinned recklessly and said, "You're not worried, are you, sis?"

"Yes, I am. I don't care what you say, Travis, this is dangerous."

"I don't think so. It's something I can do without any circus background, and if I make it, I'll ask for a raise."

Reluctantly, Joy assumed her usual position at the back of the cannon. There was silence in the tent as Travis lowered himself into the mouth of the cannon. He stopped just before he went down and said, "Praise the Lord! Hallelujah, I'm going to fly with Jesus!"

He disappeared then, and his muffled voice came from the interior, saying, "All right, Joy, I'm ready. Let her go!"

Joy reluctantly put her hand on the lever that released the coiled spring. Even though she felt too far away from God to do such a thing, she prayed. "Oh, God," she murmured, "take care of Travis."

She pulled the lever, but there was no explosion this time, for without an audience, there was no need for the illusion. The truck shook slightly, and she saw Travis shoot from the mouth of the cannon. His experience as a diver led him to make all the right moves, and now his hands were held forward, his body perfectly straight. He sailed through the air like an arrow, and as he approached the net, he began a slow turn. He hit the net dead center and rebounded perfectly. The tent exploded with the cheers of the watching performers.

Joy ran toward Travis, whose hand was being shaken and his shoulders thumped with hearty congratulations, and threw her arms around him. "You did it!"

"It was fun," Travis said, smiling from ear to ear.

"All right," Stella said, "you're it."

"Well, Mrs. House, it seems I'm moving into a new position—from lowly mechanic to star of the circus. 'Captain Travis Winslow, the human cannonball.' Maybe we could talk terms."

Stella laughed. "I'm surprised you haven't got an agent. Come on, Winslow. I'll see what we can do."

★　★　★　★

Ever since Karl Ritter had gotten Joy drunk and tried to seduce her after their date at the Peabody Hotel, Joy had been standoffish with him. One day he came to her, however, and said with a troubled expression, "I've been thinking about what happened in Memphis, Joy, and I want to tell you that I was wrong."

Joy was taken off guard. She searched Karl's face, looking for any insincerity, but he seemed utterly truthful. More than that, he seemed embarrassed, and she relaxed enough to say, "It was a bad night, Karl. I never want anything like that to happen again."

"Oh, it won't, Joy," he promised. "You can bet on it." He stuck out his hand, tilted his head to one side, and smiled winningly. "Let's start all over again and put that behind us. All right?"

"All right, Karl." Joy managed a conciliatory smile.

"Good!" Karl shook her hand firmly and then changed the subject. "Stella and I have been talking about your act with Mabel, and we think it's time you did your act in the show."

Joy was surprised. "How would that work?"

"I think we'll let you come on first. It'll be a treat for the folks to see a beautiful woman alone with a vicious five-hundred-pound tiger."

Joy laughed. "She's about as vicious as a kitten."

"Well, the audience doesn't know that. Then after you've made Mabel do all her tricks, why don't you ride her around the ring once? It'll make a great ending."

"Sure, I've done that in our practices." Joy felt a rush of excitement. "It'll be fun, Karl."

"It'll help the act too. We'll bill you as 'Beauty and the Beast.' Stella said to go with it whenever we're ready, so I say let's start tonight."

★　★　★　★

When Mamie heard that Joy was going to be featured in the ring with the tiger, she insisted on updating Joy's hairdo. She cut several inches off Joy's long hair, then curled it up into a curly bob. "There," she said, "now you look like a real star!"

"Thank you, Mamie!" Joy exclaimed. "I don't know if you

should call me a star, but I do feel rather glamorous with this hairdo."

"You go on out there tonight and show them your stuff."

That night Mabel performed perfectly for Joy's premier performance under the big top. The tiger ran through her tricks without hesitation and acted believably vicious. She even walked backward without stepping on her tail. Joy was elated as she rode the big animal around the ring, then hopped off before Mabel ran into the tunnel back to her cage. The crowd roared with pleasure as Joy ran out of the big cage and took her bows. Colonel House announced, "Let's hear a great round of applause for the daring Miss Joy Winslow, the most beautiful and talented woman under the big top!"

Joy smiled, thinking, *The real performers won't agree with that, but they'll understand.*

She stepped outside and took her place as an animal watcher while Karl did his act. One of the things she had discovered about being a watcher was that the job was critical, yet could be very boring. After so many successful and safe performances, there was a tendency to become lackadaisical about the danger, which was still present all the time. She glanced over and saw that Chase was extremely attentive, watching every move of the cats, and more than once he would call out to Karl, "Watch out for Sultan—Mazie's getting upset—watch her."

Joy was amazed that Chase seemed to be able to read the mind of every cat. She glanced over and saw Doak in position with a rifle. It chilled her to think that one day he might have to shoot one of the animals, but that was always possible.

She watched as Karl moved around the ring, always challenging the cats. He had learned how to make them move toward him, slashing at the chair and growling, and he had a genius for making them look vicious. From time to time he would appear to be almost overwhelmed and would pull out his pistol and fire a blank. She remembered then that Chase did not like this treatment of the animals, and she had heard from Oz and others that his own act had been far different. His technique had been to gain the cats' confidence, never carrying anything but a small stick to tap their heads with or a whip—only to make noise, not to strike them with.

When the cats left the cage, Joy joined Karl when he came out to take his bows. He held her hand, and the two of them bowed together. Then he reached over and pulled her close, his arm around her. "Smile—they love us."

Joy felt the pressure of his arm, but since his apology, she had felt safe enough with him.

They left the arena and went to the menagerie, where Chase already had all the animals safely in their cages. "Look, Joy," Karl said, excited, "I've got an idea. Why don't you try your act with *four* tigers?"

Joy stared at him. "But I wouldn't know how. I've only worked with Mabel."

"It's no harder than with one. With only four cats, you'll never have to turn your back on them. And I've got three other cats that are as docile as Mabel. I wouldn't want you in the ring with Sultan or Rajah, but we could put you with Mazie, Sammy, and Lucy." Karl was excited. "It'll be great, and the audience will love it."

"Well, if you'll help me, Karl, I'll try it."

"Help you? Of course I'll help you! I'll always be right by the door. It'll look better if you're in there alone. Something about a beautiful young woman facing four fierce Bengal tigers. You'll be a star. You'll have me taking second billing."

Joy was excited about the act, but she knew Chase would be opposed when he heard about the plan. Later in the day she was not surprised to see him approaching her with a scowl on his face, demanding, "What's this I hear about you going in with four tigers?"

At his severe tone, she swallowed and tried to reply nonchalantly. "Karl thinks it'll make the act more dramatic."

"It'll make it more dangerous is what it'll do."

"But I'm not taking any of the bad cats, Chase," Joy pleaded. "It's something I want to do."

"It's something you *shouldn't* do." Chase stared at her and then shook his head. "I'm against it, Joy. I don't want anything to happen to you."

Joy could not answer. She knew he was just concerned for her safety, but she felt as though he was trying to control her. This was an exciting opportunity for her, and he had no right to deny her that. Rather than consider his warnings, her inner arguments held sway and her stubborn streak had its way. "Well, I'm going to do it, Chase. If you want to help, then teach me all you can. Otherwise, just stay out of it."

"All right, I will. I won't have anything to do with it. I've told you what I think you should do."

Chase turned and walked away, leaving Joy angry and frustrated.

★   ★   ★   ★

Joy was surprised at how challenging it was to be in the big cage with more than a single tiger. Karl had started her out with just two, Mabel and Mazie. Mazie was almost as gentle as Mabel was, and soon, after half a dozen practices, he added Sammy and Lucy. The four of them worked well together, and Joy threw her heart into learning the act. By the end of the week Karl felt she was ready.

★   ★   ★   ★

On Sunday morning after breakfast, she headed to the big top to attend an informal service at her brother's invitation. Travis had gone around inviting everyone to come. Joy looked around, surprised at the number of performers and workers who had gathered. There were at least thirty people there, including some she would never have guessed would respond to such an invitation. Most of them were wearing their usual work clothes, but surprisingly some had dressed up as if it were a regular church service.

After Travis got the group quieted down, he said, "I thank you all very much for coming, and I want to tell you how much I appreciate your taking me into the circus family. Joy and I haven't had a family for a while, and I know I speak for her too when I say we're really grateful for your kindness."

Travis opened the service with some familiar hymns, which he led with his clear tenor voice. Joy knew them well, as did several of the others—"Amazing Grace," "The Old Rugged Cross," and "What a Friend We Have in Jesus." Travis then said, "Rather than preach a sermon this morning, I'd like to tell you how Christ came into my life. It happened in prison in Mexico."

Joy listened as Travis related the story of his conversion. She found tears in her eyes as he told about the terrible circumstances in the prison and how he had been beaten more than once—something she had not known.

"The great preacher Reverend Dwight Moody used to say that every generation needs *re*generation. Well, at least I needed it," Travis said, smiling. He had a Bible in his hand, and from time to time he would read a Scripture passage. At the end of his testimony, he said, "Everything in me belongs to Jesus. If any of you want me to pray with you or need me to do anything, I'm always available." He closed the service with a prayer and was immediately surrounded by well-wishers.

Doak, who had been sitting beside Joy, said in his deep bass voice, "That brother of yours is truly a man of God."

"You're right, Doak. I wish I were as good as he is."

"What's stoppin' you?" Doak said and touched her gently with his elbow. "God don't shut nobody out."

Joy turned and looked into the black face, seeing great kindness there. Doak had become a dear friend and had saved her from some embarrassing moments by being her protector. "I know, Doak. I just haven't found my way yet."

"You're gonna find it, Miss Joy. The good Lord's gonna take care of you."

★ ★ ★ ★

Night had fallen, and the circus was bedded down. As was usual on Sundays, the crowd had been small for that day's performances, since many Southerners still believed that the Sabbath should be set apart for God, not taken up with frivolous entertainment. Despite the smaller audience, Joy had been excited to do her act with the four tigers for the first time, and she'd been thrilled at the crowd's reaction. Now as she enjoyed the warm night and walked slowly around the perimeter of the circus grounds, the stars were shining overhead. She had become so familiar with the smells of the circus that they now seemed entirely natural to her. She was thinking of Travis and how much he had changed. He had never been particularly religious before, but now she knew he was filled with a spirit that she herself did not have. *He really loves God with all his heart.* The thought was comforting, yet somehow disquieting as well.

"Hello, Joy." She turned quickly and could barely make out the dim form over to her left, but she knew Chase's voice.

"Hello, Chase."

"You out for an evening walk?"

"I just couldn't sleep. I was so excited." She wanted to ask his opinion of her act, but she knew he didn't approve of it and felt she was being foolish.

"Mind if I join you?" Chase asked.

"Oh no. I'd like some company."

The two moved away from the circus grounds, where the quieter sounds of the night became more distinct. They could hear a chorus of frogs from a nearby pond, the soft hooting of an owl, and the muted hum of cars and trucks on the distant highway.

Joy stopped and turned to face Chase. The moon was bright, and she looked up at it. "I used to think somebody lived on the moon."

"So did I, and on the stars too."

"Maybe they do."

"I doubt it. I think God made the earth for man, and all those stars and the moon and the sun are for our benefit, but who really knows what's up there?"

Chase looked down at her, noticing how the moonlight softly illuminated her features. "You look so different from the first time I saw you, Joy."

"I know," she said. "I was wearing that awful boys' garb. I've never forgotten that night in the boxcar when you saved my life."

"No, I think it was you who saved me. Do you still carry that thirty-eight?"

"I still have it. It's a family heirloom."

While the two talked, Chase watched the shadows of the

night move across her face. At one time she had seemed like just a girl to him, but now a complex and unfathomable woman stood before him. She surprised him by suddenly blurting out, "Chase, please don't be mad at me for doing the act."

"I'm not mad. I'm worried about you."

"I know you are, but really, there's no reason for you to be worried."

"You know my reasons, Joy."

As they stood together in the moonlight, Joy admitted to herself that she'd always been attracted to Chase. It began when she had nursed him back to health like a helpless baby. Then later her feelings for him had turned to infatuation, although she had never spoken of it to anyone else. Lately when she looked at him, she felt a deep stirring, and she often wondered what it would be like to be completely in love with this man.

"Chase . . ." She started to speak, but then for no reason she could think of, she had to struggle to keep her composure. She looked up at him and whispered, "Chase, I've always had a special feeling for you, and I'm worried about you."

"You mean about Stella? There was nothing to that. That's ancient history."

"Really?"

"Yes."

"I'm so glad, Chase."

She looked in his eyes as he gazed intently at her. She had little experience with men, but she knew desire when she saw it, and she saw it now in the face of Chase Hardin. When he put his arms around her, she did not resist. She let herself be enfolded in his embrace, responding in kind to his ardent kiss.

The moment surprised Chase as much as it did Joy. Her nearness drained him of his strength, and he held the kiss for a long time, not wanting to let her go. But then he stepped back and held her at arm's length. "Well, I've made a mess out of this just like I've handled everything else."

Joy was more than shocked . . . she was hurt. It was as if he had just slapped her in the face. She had been deeply stirred by the warmth of his arms around her and the touch of his lips as they clung to each other in the moonlight. The moment would have been perfect and complete if he had declared his love for her; instead, he had pushed her away and uttered this inane comment.

"Whatever do you mean, Chase?"

"I promised Sister Hannah I'd never do anything wrong with you."

These words hurt Joy even more. Her feelings rushed out in a torrent of anger and confusion. "How can you say that? We haven't done anything wrong!"

"I don't have any right to feel anything for a woman, Joy. I'm nothing but a roustabout and a drunk. I always will be."

At this Joy gave full vent to her anger. "You don't have to be a failure, Chase. You're just giving up on yourself and on life."

"You don't understand."

"Oh, I understand all right. You just refuse to be a man." She turned and started to walk away, the anger and hurt obvious in the stiffness of her body.

Chase started after her, now feeling even more confused and wondering why she was so angry with him. He ran to catch up with her, grabbing her arm and spinning her back around. "Wait, Joy! Why are you so mad at me?"

"Don't you know? You treat me like I'm a little girl! Well, I'm not a little girl, Chase!"

"Of course—I know that."

The whole situation was so frustrating Joy just wanted to scream. She knew she had a lot to learn about men, but her feelings for this man were now in a worse jumble than before. How could he kiss her like that, then just push her away? Fighting back tears, she turned and fled into the night.

In desperation, Chase called after her, "Joy, please don't do that act with the tigers."

She shouted back, "You're not my boss, Chase Hardin! Don't you dare tell me what to do!"

★　★　★　★

A week went by, and every night Joy could not avoid the memory of Chase's embrace and warm kiss. She could almost feel his arms around her, and she was disturbed and confused at what she felt. She was fairly certain he had deep feelings for her but was just afraid to admit it. She also knew that unless he got over his fear, it would never come to anything. Throughout that week the two avoided each other, speaking only briefly and only when necessary, both of them hiding their emotions.

Travis came to Chase one day, his face troubled, and said, "Chase, we've got to do something about Joy."

"Why? What's wrong with her?"

"You haven't heard what they're going to do?"

"What who's going to do? What are you talking about, Travis?"

"Karl's talked her into going into the ring with him—both of them in the ring together with all fifteen of those lions and tigers. She can't do it, Chase. You know that better than anybody."

Indeed, Chase did know. He said quickly, "You're right. You've got to stop her, Travis."

"She won't listen to me. Will you talk to her?"

"I think I'm the last one she'd listen to."

Travis considered Chase carefully. "I think she's got something in her heart for you, Chase. She's never said anything to me about it, but I've noticed that she watches you all the time."

"There can't be anything like that between us. I'm not good enough for her. I'm not going anywhere in life."

"Will you at least try to talk to her?"

Chase sighed. He didn't want Joy to do the act any more than Travis did, but he felt helpless to change her mind. He finally said, "I'll try, Travis. But I can't make any promises."

★ ★ ★ ★

The confrontation with Joy was short and more disturbing than Chase had imagined. He had gone to her trailer and found her there alone. When she answered the door, he said immediately, "Joy, listen to me. I know you're mad at me, but please don't do this thing with Ritter. I'm worried about you and so is your brother. It's a very bad idea."

Joy had expected this and had braced herself for it. "I know how you feel about it, Chase, but I've got to do it."

"Why do you have to do it?"

"Maybe I should have said I *want* to do it. I love the circus, and I think I can do this job. Why did you do it when you were performing? You loved it, didn't you?"

Chase dropped his head. He could not answer for a moment. "It's a different kind of thing."

The argument went on for some time, and finally Chase took a deep breath. "You won't listen to Travis or to me?"

"I have to do it—and you can't stop me."

Chase suddenly pulled himself up. "Well, I won't be here to see it."

Joy felt a surge of fear. "What do you mean you won't be here?"

"One of these days you're going to get badly hurt or killed, and I won't watch it. So I'll leave before it happens."

"Leave? But where will you go?"

"I kept my promise to Sister Hannah to stay with you until your brother got back. Well, he's back, so you don't need me anymore." Chase was angry, yet at the same time a gnawing fear lurked in his heart. He knew at that moment how much he had come to care for this young woman, and he felt bitter that he could not do more to dissuade her from getting in the cage with all the cats. Despite the guilt that swept through him, he told her, "I'm leaving."

"But, Chase—where will you go?"

Chase studied her briefly, then said, "I'm going back to ask my mother to forgive me for all the wrongs I've done her. I'm going to get a job selling shoes or carrying sacks out to a car for a grocery store. I'm going to find a good woman and have five kids." The words bubbled out of him, and he took a deep breath. "I'm going to be *normal* for a change. Good-bye, Joy!"

CHAPTER SIXTEEN

"GO FIND YOUR WAY"

★ ★ ★ ★

Jacksonville, Florida, was a flat place. No mountains rested on the horizon, nor even low rolling hills such as Chase had learned to love in other parts of the country. He walked down the street scanning the numbers on the Spanish-style houses. They were not ornate, just durable working-class homes, mostly one-story and covered with stucco. Many of the yards had palm trees and yuccalike plants called Spanish bayonet, but had no grass; they were as much white sand as soil.

Chase blinked at the bright late afternoon sun as he scrutinized the number on a house sitting farther back from the road than most: 2920. It was the right number, but he hesitated. The suitcase in his hand pulled at his arm, and he was weary from the long bus ride. He had relived his last painful encounter with Joy so many times that his nerves were frayed. His leaving her had been an impulsive decision, he knew, and more than once he'd wanted to go back and catch up with the circus. But some inner urge drove him here. Now as he stood in front of the gray stucco house with the red-tile roof, he was certain this was something he had to do.

Throwing his shoulders back, his lips grew thin with determination as he pressed them together. He walked down the paved driveway and onto the front sidewalk, stepping up onto a small porch with an overhang. Giving himself no time to think, he pushed the bell. He could hear it ringing inside the house, and a few seconds later the door opened. Chase suddenly felt a great sadness as he looked at his mother. "Hello, Mom."

"Chase—it's you!"

Lucille Matthews threw her hands up. Chase dropped the suitcase and embraced her. He felt her arms around his neck and his own tears on his cheek. For a time he simply held her, not wanting to let go. Then when she drew back and began wiping the tears from her face with her apron, his voice was unsteady. "The bad penny's come home again, Mom."

"You come right in the house." Taking his arm, Lucille pulled him inside. "Put that suitcase down there. Come into the kitchen. I'll bet you're hungry."

"I am a little bit, but I thought we might talk first."

Lucille Matthews was an attractive woman of fifty. She had the same black hair and dark eyes as her son, and a trim figure. One white streak ran through her hair, no more than half an inch wide, but it did not age her, Chase noticed. He stared at it, and she reached up and touched her hair with a faint smile. "I almost dyed it once but decided not to."

"It's very attractive, Mom."

"Here, come sit down."

They entered the kitchen, a cheerful room that was broad and long, with a dinette set at one end. Chase sat down, and when she brought him a glass of iced tea without asking, he gulped it down in a single breath. She got the pitcher and put it beside him. "Your letters have been an encouragement, Chase. Is the circus close by?"

"No, I left the circus."

"But you said you liked it so much."

"Things happen. Tell me about yourself."

Lucille reached out and took his hand, holding it and stroking it with her other hand. "I'm very happy with Jack. I'm anxious for you to meet him."

"I'm not sure he'll be so glad to meet me."

"Don't be foolish. You'll like him a lot."

Lucille had married Jack Matthews two years earlier. She had told Chase in her letters that Jack was an electrician with his own business, and was one of the kindest men she had ever known.

Now as she studied her son's face, she said, "I'm going to cook up a big supper for you. You still like steaks?"

"Sure, Mom, but don't go to all that trouble. I really thought I might get a room somewhere."

"If you want to hurt my feelings, that's the way to do it!"

Chase smiled. "All right, I'll stay—provided you have plenty of room."

"Yes, we've got a guest room. Jack built this house himself. It has three bedrooms. He's very proud of it and so am I."

"It's a fine house, Mom."

"Come along," she said. "I know you're tired."

She led him to a bedroom with an adjoining bath and said, "Why don't you shower and get comfortable? Lie down and take a nap. Jack will be home in about an hour, and we'll have supper."

"All right, Mom." Before she could turn to leave, he reached out and touched the silver streak in her hair. "I expect I put that there," he murmured.

Lucille took his hand and held it against her cheek for a moment. "I'm glad you're back, son."

★　★　★　★

"I can't eat another bite, honest, Mom."

Jack Matthews grinned and shook his head. "She doesn't believe a man's happy unless he's so full he can't even roll over." Matthews was a big, red-faced man with a cheerful smile and a pair of direct blue eyes. He was losing his hair in front but, even at the age of fifty-nine, was one of those men who get stronger as they get older. His hands were rough and callused, and the Florida sunshine had baked his skin to a brick-red hue.

"She always was that way," Chase said. He liked Jack Matthews, even on such short acquaintance. The man's bluff honesty made it difficult not to like him. Chase noticed that his stepfather did not ask him any questions, yet as they drank coffee after the meal, he felt obliged to give them a brief history of his recent whereabouts.

Both of them listened attentively as he spoke, and he didn't spare himself any embarrassing details. When he related how

Joy had shot the hobo and made the two men jump off the train, Jack laughed and slapped his meaty thigh.

"Good for her! She sounds like a girl after my own heart."

"You'd like her a lot, Jack. She's fit in well with the circus. And her brother's there now. He's a fine fellow too."

"How old is Joy?"

"She's eighteen, and her brother's twenty."

Matthews held his coffee cup, dwarfing it with his big hands, swirled his coffee, and said, "I'm glad you came, Chase. This may be a bit premature, but if you want to stay around, I could always use a good man."

"I'm no electrician, Jack."

"I could make you into one. You're smart enough, and all it takes is a little hard work."

Chase felt grateful to Jack Matthews. "I may take you up on that. I've gotta find a job."

"You don't think you'll be going back to the circus?"

"Nothing there for me now."

Both Lucille and her husband felt the terseness of that reply, and Lucille covered by saying, "Well, won't that be nice? You can stay right here with us."

"Oh, that wouldn't be convenient for you."

"Yes it would. You know I love to cook, and it would be good to be with you."

Chase could not speak for a moment. Finally he smiled faintly and said, "Well, what time do I go to work in the morning, Jack?"

★   ★   ★   ★

"There's a letter for you. I put it on your bed, son."

"Thanks, Mom."

Chase had come in from work and went right to his room. He had put in another hard day, but after a month of working alongside Jack Matthews, he felt a sense of satisfaction. *At least*, he thought, *I can make a living once I qualify as an electrician.* He stepped into his room, shut the door, and picked up the letter. He did not recognize the handwriting, but when he opened it, he let his eyes go to the bottom of the single sheet, where he saw Travis Winslow's signature.

He scanned the letter:

Dear Chase,

I was glad to hear that you have a good job working with your stepfather, and it sounds like your mother is in hog heaven to have you back. I am still traveling with the circus doing the human cannonball act and working on the trucks. Saving money to go to Bible school.

I wish I had better news for you about Joy. I'm worried sick about her, Chase. That fellow Ritter hasn't got a lick of sense. He's got her in the cage now with him and all those animals, and I've got a bad feeling about it. I've tried to talk to her, but she won't listen.

One thing I guess I might tell you. She really misses you, Chase. I don't know how you feel about her, but I suspect, from the little I saw, that you had some feeling for her. I think she loves you too. I wish you'd come back.

Write me, and let's keep in touch. You can write to general delivery at Denton, Texas. We'll be there next week, and I'll pick up the mail there. God bless you, dear brother, and may the Lord make His face to shine upon you.

For a long time Chase sat staring at the letter, and even as he did, depression settled on him. He had been contented enough to throw himself into his work with Jack, but deep down he knew he would not be content forever. Getting up, he went to stare out the window but saw only the house next door half hidden by spiky Spanish bayonet plants. The thought of Joy in the cage with over a dozen ferocious beasts scraped against his nerves. He stood at the window for a long time, and still he could not move. He heard his mother calling, "Supper's about ready, Chase," and he broke away from the window. He scrubbed his hands and face before going in to eat.

At supper, he ate mechanically and spoke little. When Jack left the house to attend his meeting at the Lions Club, of which he was a proud member, Chase went into the living room and sat down in an overstuffed chair by the radio. He tuned in to a news report and heard a politician by the name of Herbert Hoover delivering a campaign speech in his bid for the presidency. Not having paid much attention to politics, Chase did not know the man, but his ears perked up at Hoover's catchy slogan: "A chicken in every pot and a car in every garage."

The announcer then spoke of Miss Amelia Earhart of Atchison, Kansas, an aviator who had flown across the Atlantic in a plane, the first woman ever to do so, albeit as a passenger, not the pilot.

Chase half listened to the rest of the news, but then a program of music from a ballroom in New Orleans began, and he lost himself in his thoughts. He was startled when a hand fell on his shoulder, and he glanced up to see his mother looking down at him.

"What's the matter, son? Was the letter bad news?"

"I guess it was, in a way."

Lucille sat down on the couch across from him and said, "Is it anything you can tell me about?"

"I guess I can, Mom. Maybe that's why I came all the way back home. I've been wanting to tell you something."

"I bet I can guess what it is—part of it anyway."

As Chase's mother watched him calmly, waiting for him to explain, he remembered how she would do this when he was just a small boy. He had always thought she could read his mind. Testing her, he asked, "What do you think it is, Mom?"

"I think it has to do with Joy Winslow."

Chase dropped his eyes, unable to meet her gaze for a moment, then looked up and nodded. "You're right. I left because of her." He went on to explain how he had failed to convince her to stay out of the cage with all the big cats. "I've been worried sick, Mom, and I don't know what to do."

"Do you love this young woman?"

"I . . . I think I do."

"Then do something about it."

"What can I do, Mom?" Chase asked almost desperately. He got up and paced the floor, stopped, then wheeled to face her. "I have nothing to offer a woman."

"Then *get* something! I hated it when you were risking your life with those tigers, but at least you had a life."

"I can't go back. I don't think I could ever go back in the cage again."

"You can do anything you have to do if God helps you."

Chase stared at his mother, then got up and sat beside her, taking her hand. "What do you think I should do?"

"You know what I think. I think you need Christ in your life."

"I've gone a long way from God."

"Then come back."

"Why would He want me back?" Chase asked, a note of despair in his voice.

"Why would He want any of us? Don't ask me why God loves sinners. He just does. You know your Bible. Did He go looking for righteous people? Of course not. He always reached out to those who were in trouble."

Chase sat in the living room with his mother for over an hour before saying, "You know, I think I know what I need to do."

"What is it, son?"

"I need to go back to Nebraska and see Sister Hannah Smith."

"She had quite an impact on you, didn't she? You wrote about her so often in your letters."

"I don't know why, but I need to go see her."

"All right. Go find your way."

Chase nodded. "I'll check with Jack to make sure he can get along without me, and if it's okay with him, I'll leave in the morning."

"Jack and I will be praying for you. God isn't through with you yet, Chase."

★ ★ ★ ★

Sister Hannah's eyes flew open, and her hands went up. "Well, glory be to God and the Lamb forever!" She sailed out onto the porch, shoving the screen door back, and it slapped against the wall of the house with a loud bang. She grabbed Chase and hugged him so hard he protested.

"Sister Hannah, you're gonna break my ribs again."

"You come in this house, boy. I had a feelin' you were comin' back one of these days."

Chase followed Sister Hannah into the house, and as he did, old memories rushed through him. He allowed her to drag him into the kitchen and shove him onto a cane-bottom chair. "I just made some blackberry cobbler. Fresh out of the oven. You think you could arm wrestle a bite or two down?"

"I think I could." Chase grinned broadly and allowed her to fuss over him. He was tired, for it had been a long trip from Jacksonville, Florida, to Arnold, Nebraska, but as he sat in the kitchen enjoying the warm blackberry cobbler, he knew he had done the right thing.

"I've been hearin' pretty regular from Joy," Hannah said. "She told me about you leavin' the circus. What'd you do that for?"

Chase put the spoon in the bowl and shoved it away, saying, "That's what I've come to talk to you about. I don't know what to do with myself."

"Well, thank God you've finally realized you can't handle your own life." Sister Hannah pushed her glasses up over her head into her hair, and her eyes sparkled as she spoke. "I knowed all the time you'd come to your senses, and you're gonna stay here with me until you get right with God."

Chase couldn't help smiling at her forwardness. Her brusque ways were refreshing, and he put out his hand, which she took in both of hers. He felt the roughness of them, callused from a lifetime of hard labor. "That may take a while," he said, "but at least I can chop your wood and feed the chickens."

Time seemed to slow down for Chase as he settled into a peaceful life once again at Sister Hannah's home. He felt separated from the rest of the world there. Her house became his world, and each day he would rise, eat breakfast with her, and study the Bible with her. This consisted mostly of Sister Hannah opening the worn black Bible and reading to him. Some days she would read for almost an hour without commenting. Then finally one day, she said, "Sometimes I think we talk too much, Chase, and we don't let God talk enough. The Bible says, 'The entrance of thy words giveth light,' so we're going to put the Word into you until you're all light on the inside."

After their Bible study, Chase would spend a good part of his day sawing down trees, cutting them into lengths, and splitting them with a maul. He soon had enough wood for Hannah to go through two winters, all good white oak that split like cloven rock each time he hit it.

The nights were the same as the mornings. He would again listen to Sister Hannah read the Bible to him, then explain what she thought the good Lord meant. At no time did she ever accuse him or make him feel guilty. One evening after reading from the Gospel of John, they talked for over an hour about the encounters of Jesus.

"There ain't no better book than John," Sister Hannah said quietly. A single bulb dangling from a chain overhead illuminated the room dimly. They sat at the kitchen table with their cups of coffee, but they were forgotten now. He listened intently as Sister Hannah murmured, "Jesus kept hunting people down, or else they searched him out. Nicodemus in chapter three comes lookin' for Him. Didn't have the vaguest idea what the Lord Jesus was talkin' about or who He was. When Jesus told him, 'Ye must be born again,' old Nicodemus didn't have a notion in his head what the Lord was talkin' about. Then the woman at the well—how that woman must have felt to find someone who loved her no matter what she'd done!

"Then a little further on, there was that fellow born blind. I've always loved this story. You notice, son, that he didn't get saved all at once. After the blind man was healed, the Pharisees asked him who healed him, and he said, 'Jesus. He put clay on my eyes and I washed and now I can see.' He didn't know anything about Jesus. But later on, Jesus sought *him* out—all this is in chapter nine—and he asked that feller, 'Dost thou believe on the Son of God?' right here in verse thirty-five." Sister Hannah put her finger on the Bible, and Chase followed the lines. "You know, I've thought lots of times, Brother Chase, that this is the most important question. 'Dost thou believe on the Son of God?'"

The room was quiet then. A fly was buzzing around, making an unsteady hum, and Chase read the next line. "'Who is he, Lord, that I might believe on him?'"

"That's right." Sister Hannah nodded. "And Jesus said, 'Thou hast both seen him, and it is he that talketh with thee.'"

Chase read the next line aloud. "'And he said, Lord, I believe. And he worshipped him.'" Chase had felt little or nothing in his heart during the few days he'd been with Sister Hannah again, but for a reason he could not explain, his heart all of a sudden seemed to break. He looked across the table at Sister Hannah, and tears formed in his eyes. "I don't know what's wrong with me, but somehow that touches my heart."

Sister Hannah leaned over, and her eyes were also filled with tears. "That's the Spirit of God, son, and He's asking you, just like He asked that blind man, will you believe on the Son of God?"

"I've always believed that Jesus was God as long as I can remember."

"Then will you ask Him to be Lord of your life and let Him do anything He wants with you?"

Chase Hardin had never felt as he did at that moment. He was filled with a mixture of fear, joy, and excitement, and yet he could not speak. He watched Sister Hannah get up and walk around the table. "Son, let's kneel right here before Jesus. I'm gonna pray, and you're gonna pray, and when we get up, you'll be a new creature."

Without a word, Chase fell on his knees. He felt Sister Hannah's arm go around his shoulder, and he began to tremble and weep. He could hear her calling out to God in a loud voice, and then he heard his own voice crying out in agony, "Oh, God, I need you! Save me in the name of Jesus and by His blood!"

Chase never remembered how long he called out like this, but he did recall later that at one point weakness overcame him. Finally Sister Hannah pulled him to his feet, and spoke in a voice of exultation. "That's what you needed, son. God's done a work in you. Ain't that right?"

Chase Hardin knew she had spoken the truth. "Yes, Sister Hannah," he whispered, "He has."

★ ★ ★ ★

It had been three days since Chase had accepted Christ, but somehow he felt the need to stay on. He and Sister Hannah continued to study the Bible morning and night. He attended church with her that Sunday, and at the end of the service, when she gave an invitation, he came forward and saw the joy in the old woman's eyes. "I want to be baptized, Sister," he said.

And so baptized he was that very morning in a horse pond under the blue July sky. Sister Hannah did not baptize him herself; rather, a tall, strong elder put him under the water.

When Chase stepped out of the water, Sister Hannah grasped him, soaking wet as he was, and said, "I ain't never been happier. Now God's ready to go into business with you, son."

★ ★ ★ ★

Two days after his baptism, Sister Hannah received a phone call for Chase. It was Travis Winslow.

"Bad news, Chase."

"Is it Joy?"

"No, she's all right, but the cats turned on Karl. They didn't kill him, but he'll be out for a long time. Maybe for good."

Relief washed through Chase that it wasn't Joy. "I'm sorry about Karl, but I'm glad Joy's all right."

"Well, she's not all right. Stella's got Joy talked into takin' Karl's place. I know it's crazy, but that's the plan."

Chase did not hesitate. "Where are you?"

"In Yazoo City, Mississippi."

"I'll be there as quick as I can. Don't let her get in that cage, Travis. Tie her up if you have to!"

"All right. I'll do whatever I can—but please hurry, Chase!"

Chase turned to Hannah. "I gotta go, Sister Hannah." He explained the nature of the phone call and said, "I gotta get there quick. She shouldn't be getting in the cage all alone with those cats."

"Get your things, boy, but you're not hitchhikin'. I got the cash for a railroad ticket. I'll take you down to the station. You can catch the three-forty. Ought to have you there maybe tomorrow, or the day after for sure."

Things moved so rapidly then that within an hour Chase was saying good-bye to Sister Hannah on the railroad platform. He hugged her and kissed her cheek. "I'll call as soon as I get there, but please pray that whatever happens, we'll keep Joy out of that cage."

"I'll do that, and you do whatever God puts in your heart, boy. You're His child now, and He'll take care of you."

The conductor called out, "All aboard," and Chase tore himself from Sister Hannah's grasp. He ran to catch the train as it was moving out. Turning, he waved to her, then went inside and found a seat, knowing that God was sending him on his first mission.

CHAPTER SEVENTEEN

STELLA MAKES AN OFFER

★   ★   ★   ★

As Chase entered the circus grounds, he could hear the band playing and knew by the tune that it was the final spec. He shifted his suitcase from one hand to the other, then marched resolutely across the grounds, where he encountered Doak Williams. The big man turned to him with a flash of surprise in his eyes.

"Why, it's you, Chase! Hey, real good to see you." Doak put out his huge hand, and Chase shook it. "I 'spect you heard about Karl."

"Yes. Did you see it, Doak?"

"Was standin' right there. We was lucky to get him out alive, Chase."

"What happened?"

"You know how Sultan's always lookin' for a chance to fight somebody, do some damage. Well, he found a chance all right, and it seemed like the rest of them cats was just waitin'. We got in as quick as we could, but Karl was clawed up bad. One of them got him right across the face, laid it right open. You know how them tiger claws catch better'n I do. He ain't never again gonna be the good-lookin' fella he was, the doctors say."

"Where is he?"

"He's in the hospital. They took him to Jackson, but I don't think he's ever gonna be the man he was. A man can't go through a thing like that and be the same—but I reckon you know all about that, don't you, Chase?"

"I sure do," he said, nodding grimly.

"I guess you heard about the deal that Miss Joy made with Miss House."

"Yes, Travis called me and told me about it."

"I sure hope you can put a stop to that. You know that girl ain't got no business bein' alone in a whole cageful of them critters. You'd think seein' Karl clawed up like that woulda changed her mind, but that girl's stubborn as a blue-nosed mule!"

The blare of a trumpet sounded, and Chase turned to face the entrance. The spectators were filing out now, talking and babbling as usual, and Chase said, "I think I'd better try to talk to Travis first."

"You can talk to him," Doak said, nodding, "but he's already told me he's used every argument he can with Miss Joy. Says she just won't pay no attention. She's bound and determined to do it."

"I have to stop her, Doak."

"You comin' back to work, then?"

"I don't know what I'm gonna do—I've just gotta do *something!*"

Chase made his way inside the big top. He scanned the crowds and saw Travis standing beside the center pole. Chase hurried toward him, and at the same time Travis saw him and came forward to meet him. The two men shook hands. "Glad to see you, Chase." Relief washed across Travis's features, but then he shook his head. "I've said everything I can think of to get her to reconsider, but maybe you can talk some sense into her."

"I'll try. But first I've got some news for you."

Travis Winslow straightened up and stared at Chase. "What is it?"

"While I was gone I got converted. It took me long enough, but I finally found the Lord."

Travis reached out, his eyes bright and a smile on his lips. He gave Chase a hug and said, "Well, brother, I'm glad to hear that! I've been praying for you."

"So have a few others. My mother and Sister Hannah. You'll have to help me along. I need lots of counsel."

"You're going to do fine, Chase."

"Well, I better go find Joy."

"She's probably with the cats. She didn't do the act today, but like I said, she's determined to do it soon."

"I'll see you later, Travis."

Chase made his way back to the menagerie, and as Travis had predicted, Joy was there. She was stroking Mabel's head, which was pressed against the bars. Chase came up behind her and said, "Hello, Joy."

She turned quickly, her lips parted in surprise. Then she smiled and put her hands out. When he took them in both of his, she said, "I'm glad to see you, Chase, but I didn't expect it. You heard about Karl, of course."

"Yes, Travis called me. I hope Karl's going to be all right."

Joy realized he was still holding her hands, and when she looked down at them, he dropped them. "I don't think he'll ever be the same, Chase. His face was terribly clawed. They had to put in a lot of stitches, and the doctor says he'll always be scarred."

"I'm so relieved you weren't hurt. How did you get out of there in one piece?"

"The cats just went after Karl. I clung to the cage, and they stayed away from me." Joy fell silent then and looked at him in a strange way. "Why did you come back, Chase?"

"Because I was worried about you. I was at Sister Hannah's when I got the word."

"Yes, Travis told me. What were you doing there?"

"I needed some help, and I thought she was the one I needed. So I spent some time with her."

"I miss her a lot. I'd love to go back too."

"She'd love to see you." He hesitated, then said, "I gave my heart to the Lord while I was there this time."

Joy looked stunned, then said quietly, "I'm glad for you, Chase."

"It's a beginning, but as Sister Hannah says, it's easier to become a Christian than it is to *be* the Christian you've become."

A silence fell between them, each of them aware that something unpleasant lay ahead. Chase finally said simply, "I don't want you to do the act alone with all these cats. You're not ready for that, Joy."

"I can get ready for it. Karl used to do the act by himself all the time. I can learn to do it by myself too."

"Karl's had a lot more experience than you have. When you're alone in there you have to turn your back on half of them."

Joy shook her head. "I can do it. I'll just have to be careful."

"Why do you want to do it, Joy? Do you just love applause so much—is that it?"

Joy's face flushed. "That's part of it, I confess, but Travis wants to go to Bible school, and my raise will help pay for it."

"I doubt if he'll take your money. He doesn't want you to do it, and he's got sense."

Joy straightened up and said in a businesslike voice, "I'm glad you're back, Chase. It's good to see you again, and I'm happy for you that you've found God, but I'm going to do this act no matter what you or anybody else says."

★   ★   ★   ★

"I heard you were back, Chase." Stella stood at the door of her trailer and put her hands out. When Chase took them, she gave him a firm grasp and smiled. "Somehow I thought you'd come back."

"I guess you've got a pretty good idea of why I'm here."

"Sure—you're worried about Joy Winslow."

"That's right. Stella, you've been around circuses a long time. You know how dangerous that act is. I've been worried sick about her being in that cage with Karl, and here she's talking about getting in all alone with fifteen lions and tigers." He shook his head in despair, a pleading look in his eyes. "She can't do it. It's too dangerous."

"You're worrying too much about Joy, Chase. Come on in and sit down. Maurice is sleeping right now, and we have to talk."

Chase sat down on the couch, and Stella sat beside him—so close that her arm brushed his. She looked at him with a searching gaze, which put him on the defensive. He had felt guilty about their last kiss, knowing it was wrong, and yet realizing too that she still had power over him. Their romance years earlier had been earthshaking for him, especially since he had been young and inexperienced. She was the first woman he'd ever been intimate with. He had been deeply in love with her, or so he'd thought. When he had returned to the circus and found her married to Colonel House, he had felt great disappointment, realizing then that he'd always hoped they would get together again. Now he was on his guard and asked, "Has Maurice been to the doctor?"

"Oh yes. He says he needs to retire—that circus life is too demanding—but he never will. He'll die out there in his job as ringmaster."

Chase was aware of her perfume. The familiar fragrance stirred old memories in him, but he firmly shoved them aside and said forcefully, "You just can't let Joy do this thing, Stella. What if she gets hurt or even killed? You'd blame yourself. I know you would."

"You can help her, Chase."

"Me? I can't get in that cage."

"You could talk to her. You could teach her without getting in the cage."

"That's not the same thing, and you know it."

Chase spoke earnestly, ignoring the pressure of her thigh against his as they sat close together. He knew she was sending a signal, and he desperately tried to ignore it.

When Chase finished with his impassioned plea, Stella said, "There's something you don't know, Chase. Before the accident, Karl had already made a deal with Ringling Brothers. He told me last week. He was going to finish the season out here and then go with them next year."

"That's hard to believe. He's just not that good."

"They thought he was. Right now there's not a first-class cat-taming act in the country. Here's something else you don't know. If this circus doesn't find a really big act—and soon—it's going to fold."

"But I thought—"

"Oh, we've had some good attendance and a few good months, but overall we just don't have the drawing power." Stella's lips twisted bitterly, and she shook her head. "I've juggled the books and tried to come up with a way to save the circus, but it's not looking good."

"And you think Joy will do it for you?"

"I'm grasping at straws, Chase. Maurice is old and sick. He

can't live long, and I'm not getting any younger either. What am I going to do if this circus goes bankrupt? And another thing you don't know—Karl was so sure he was going with the Ringling Brothers that he sold his cats to them. Now I find out that they still want the animals, even without him."

Chase stared at Stella and shook his head. "That means no big cat act."

"We have these cats for the rest of the season, but we've got to come up with a plan for next year."

"Maybe you can find another act, but that settles it as far as Joy's concerned."

"Yes, for next year, but I've got to carry on this year." Stella reached over and put her hand on Chase's knee. It was an intimate gesture, one he could not mistake. He did not know what to do. To shove it off would be an affront she would never forget, but to allow it to lie there would be a surrender to an intimacy he could not agree to. He jumped up and ran his hand through his hair. "I'm stiff as a board from sitting all that time on the train. Could I have some water please?"

Stella hesitated, then rose and went to get the water. When she handed him the glass, he drank it dry, handed it back, and thanked her. Then he remained standing, walking back and forth within the limits of the trailer. "I wish you wouldn't let Joy do it, Stella. I know you have to do what you can to save the circus, but—"

"I've got an idea, Chase," Stella said. She stood before him, measuring him with her eyes. She suspected that the relationship they had once shared still had a hold on him. "Here's what I've thought of. I'm ready to gamble everything on you."

"On me!" Chase blinked with surprise. "What are you talking about?"

"Your name is still big, Chase. It'll be a powerful draw. I need a great new act, and I need your name. You come back and do your act, and I'll hock everything we've got to buy a complete stock of new cats. We'll put all our eggs in one basket. If we get one headlining act, it could work."

"Why, Stella, you know I can't go in there with those cats." Chase shook his head. "Even if I could, it would take two years to make them into a first-class act."

"That's why your name is important. People will come out

just to see you at first. If you have young animals, you could train them to be the best in the world. You think I've forgotten how we used to talk about this back when we were together?"

Chase suddenly remembered his youthful enthusiasm when he had been in love with Stella. He had talked endlessly with her about working with brand-new animals and training them to do things no cats had ever done before.

Stella put her hand on his chest, and he could not avoid it. "You and I had something once. You know why I was so crazy about you?" She did not wait for his answer. "Because you had more courage than any man I'd ever seen. That's why people came out to see you, Chase. They saw raw courage. A man not afraid of anything. I want to see that man again. If you really care about this girl, you'll do it."

"That's not fair, Stella!"

"It's the way it is, Chase. I'm hanging on by my fingernails. My whole life is tied up with this circus, and Maurice was good to you. His life is in it too. You say the girl's important. Well, we're all looking to you. You used to be a man without fear. I want to see that man again."

Chase could not answer. A denial rose in his throat, almost making it to his lips. But instead he heard himself say, "I'll have to think about it."

"You'd better think fast because Joy Winslow's going in the cage with those cats unless you do."

★   ★   ★   ★

For two days Chase wandered around the circus looking almost like he was in a trance. He said so little that people wondered what was the matter with him. Oz spoke to Travis about him. "That's not the same Chase I knew. He hardly says a word now. What's wrong with him, Preacher?"

"I don't know, but something is bothering him. He won't tell me about it. He won't even talk."

Oz shook his head sadly. "Everybody's wondering why he came back at all. He won't have anything to do with any of us."

"I can tell you one thing, Oz," Travis said, "he's seeking God.

I know that much. He's got some kind of decision pressing down on him, and I know what that's like."

"Well, I liked him better the old way."

"I don't know, Oz. I'm praying for him, and once he makes his decision, I think we'll see a new Chase Hardin."

★   ★   ★   ★

Joy was alone in her trailer. She had performed with the elephants and with Travis as the human cannonball. She had even done a stint selling tickets at the red wagon, but for two days she had wondered about Chase. He had said so little to her, she thought he must be angry with her, but it did not show in his countenance. He seemed preoccupied, and Joy wondered what was eating at him.

She had washed her hair and was combing it out, and as she looked down at the mother-of-pearl brush and comb, she thought of Sister Hannah and smiled. A knock at the door caught her attention, and she heard Chase's voice. "Joy?"

She got up and opened the door. "Come in, Chase." She stepped back and allowed him to enter. "Would you like some coffee? I can make some."

"No, thanks. I've gotta talk to you, Joy."

Joy stiffened her back and shook her head, a willful set to her lips. "You can talk all you want to, Chase, but it won't do any good."

Chase stared at her for a moment, thinking of all that had happened in the year and a half or so he had known her. He thought of the time he had first seen her in boys' clothes, fighting off her assailants in the boxcar. He thought of the days she had spent nursing him back to health and how he had thought of her then as no more than a child. Now he saw the stubbornness on her face and knew that what he was going to say might hurt her and certainly would shock her.

"I don't know how to say this any differently, Joy, but you're not going into the cage with those cats."

"Oh yes I am!"

"No, you're not," Chase said resolutely. "I'm going in."

Joy stared at Chase in disbelief. "You can't."

"You may be right, or at least I may go in only once, but I'm gonna try to do the act again."

"Chase, you know you can't do that. You've told me those cats can smell fear. If you go in there afraid of them, they'll jump you."

"Then I'll have to get rid of the fear. There's no other way."

Joy was shocked, even confused. "Chase, what makes you think you can do this?"

"We never know what we can do until we try. I've been running from myself for years now. It wasn't the cats I was afraid of. It was myself. I was afraid to show fear."

"That doesn't make much sense."

"I guess not. I don't know how to put it, Joy," Chase said slowly. "But here's the situation. Do you know that the circus is about to fold?"

Shock reflected in Joy's eyes. "What do you mean? I haven't heard that."

"You must have noticed that the crowds have been off."

"Well, I suppose I have, but—"

"I've been talking with Stella, and she says if something big doesn't happen, she's going to have to shut down the show. But she has an idea. She says with one big headlining act everything can be turned around. Did you know that before Karl got hurt, he was planning to leave the circus and go to Ringling Brothers?"

"No, he never told me that."

"Well, he told Stella, and he already sold the animals to them, so at the end of the season they'll belong to Ringling Brothers."

Joy stared at him in disbelief. "I never knew any of this," she whispered.

"Stella made me an offer. She says my name will still draw the crowds. She wants to gamble everything on a brand-new act that will bring in the people, and I'm it."

"But you've been out so long, and you don't have any animals if these are going."

"Stella says she'll hock everything and buy a complete new set of cats, and I'll train them the way they should be trained. I've never liked the ones that Karl has anyway. He wasn't smart about buying them. Many of them had been pets, and pets don't make good cats to train."

Joy found she was trembling. "I don't understand. You don't even know if you can go in the cage, and she's going to gamble on you?"

"For some reason she believes in me, Joy." Chase hesitated and then said, "I wish you would too."

Joy could not speak for a moment, but her dream seemed to be crumbling around her. She knew she was not good enough to go to Ringling Brothers with the cats, nor could she stop Stella from carrying through with this plan. If Chase went through with it, Joy would be left out. Despite her own disappointment, however, she felt a vague hope that Chase might regain his courage through this.

"Are you really going to do it, Chase?"

"Yes, and I want you to help me."

Joy blinked with surprise. "What do you mean help you?"

"You don't know how hard it is to train new animals, Joy. You've never seen it. You have to start from scratch, and you have to work with each animal every day. It's a tremendous job, a hard job, and there are so many failures. Some animals don't work out at all, but you don't know until you start working with them. I want you to help me train them, and then you can be in the act."

"I can?"

"Yes, we'll work it out. It'll be something we can do together."

Joy looked into his eyes. "Why are you doing this?"

"I don't really know. Maybe a lot of reasons. I don't want you to get hurt. I've always wanted to prove that I was a man even after I walked away. I don't know."

"Are you sure you can face the cats, Chase?"

"If God gives me grace, I can. But listen, in the meantime, I don't want you working with a whole cageful of cats. You can do the bit with Mabel like you used to, but no more. I'll finish out the season if God gives me the grace. And then when we get the new animals, we'll look to next year. Do we have an understanding, Joy?"

Joy Winslow felt she was at a fork in the road. She had made up her mind to do the act, but at the same time knew it wasn't a good idea. Now as she looked at Chase, a myriad of thoughts flooded her mind. After several moments of silence, a smile touched her lips. "All right, Chase. You take over the act for this year, then after that we'll do it together."

CHAPTER EIGHTEEN

THE BIG CAGE

★ ★ ★ ★

Very few environments are as conducive to gossip as a circus. The performers and workers that make the circus come alive twice a day are never very far from each other's lives. They live in glass houses, and the most intimate parts of life that would be kept secret in the outside world are practically blazoned among circus people. Perhaps sailors confined to a small space and isolated for months at a time experience a similar climate of whisper and innuendo; girls' schools situated far away from the hustle and bustle of civilization probably share a similar atmosphere. These people would understand how the circus is a cosmos of its own, with the constant traveling together, men and women with their families facing their co-workers morning and evening, day in and day out, their struggles and joys, victories and defeats intertwined.

In this small world the news that Chase Hardin was going to attempt a comeback in the cage was passed around so quickly that by the following morning, everyone knew exactly what was happening. Most of them were not optimistic about Chase's decision. Mamie Madden, who had been with the circus all of her life, had simply shaken her head and said darkly, "He's gonna get hisself killed. That's what he's gonna do!"

When Joy told Ella Devoe of Chase's plan, she remained quiet for a moment, then shook her head to say, "I wish him well, but he's been out of the cage a long time. I doubt if he can do it. Don't get your hopes up, Joy."

When Stella had told Maurice what the plan was, he had panicked. "We'll lose everything we've got! You know once a man runs away, he can't do anything else but run." Stella had merely answered, "The circus is going under. Chase is our only hope, Maurice."

Word had gotten around that Chase would have a rehearsal with the cats on Tuesday morning after breakfast. When Chase sat down at one of the tables outside the cook tent, the buzz of conversation fell off almost to nothing. Chase glanced around and raised his voice. "That's all right. Just go ahead and talk about it."

Frances Fairchild, one of the showgirls, sat down beside Chase as he was eating, her eyes big. "I hope it turns out good for you, Chase. I'd like to see your name all over the papers again just like it used to be."

"Thanks, Frances. It's in God's hands now."

Frances looked surprised but said no more.

Joy had been observing Chase's reception from the kitchen tent. She turned to Annie and said, "What do *you* think?"

"Well, anything's possible. When I fell, I couldn't come back. Of course, I'd lost too much use of this leg, so it was just a physical thing. But with Chase, it's a matter of losing his nerve. I wish he wouldn't try it. You remember what Karl looked like after the attack? I'd hate to see Chase slashed up like that."

★ ★ ★ ★

There was no shortage of hands to put up the big steel cage. Everyone had gathered to watch as Doak led the crew in erecting it. As they worked Oz said to Doak, "I wish he wouldn't do it, Doak. He's going to get himself butchered."

"Maybe not," Doak said. "A man don't always know what's in him until he's throwed in the crucible."

"What are you talking about?"

"Why, don't you remember the story of them three Hebrew chil'un in the Bible?"

"Don't know that much about the Bible."

"Well, these three Hebrew chil'un was commanded by the king to bow down and worship the image this king had made of himself, and they wouldn't do it. So he said he was gonna throw 'em in the furnace and burn 'em up."

"Did he do it?"

"Well, that'd be gettin' ahead of the story, Oz. Here, help me fasten this section." The two men fastened the section of cages, and then Doak smiled. "I always liked what one of them Hebrews said. 'God can deliver us if He wants to, but even if He don't want to, He's still the Lord God.' Somethin' like that."

"But did they get burned up?"

"Nope, they shore didn't. They got throwed in, and the soldiers what throwed 'em in got burned up, but the king, he looked inside and got quite a shock. He said, 'We throwed three fellas in there, but I see four, and one of 'em's like the Son of God.' Ain't that a caution, Oz? They come out of that furnace and didn't even have the smell of smoke on 'em."

"Why, I would just about as soon be thrown into a fire furnace as in with all those cats. You know how mean they are."

"Yeah, Mr. Karl he liked to make 'em mean. Reckon he shore paid for it, though." Doak straightened up and said, "Look, there's Chase. Wonder what he's thinkin' right about now."

Chase, in all truth, was not thinking clearly. He had been up practically all night praying, and his prayer had not been so much for his safety, although he asked for that too. Rather, he had prayed that he might not have fear, and as he stood there watching the workers put the cage together, he realized with a shock that at this moment he did not have any fear. *Thank you, Lord, that you're with me.* He turned then, for he caught a movement to his left, and he saw Joy, who had come to stand beside him. Her face was pale, and she said nervously, "Chase, please don't do it."

Chase smiled at her and reached out to touch a lock of her blond hair. "Well, that's quite a switch. I've been beggin' you not to get in that cage, and now you're beggin' me not to."

"I've been thinking about it. I didn't sleep a wink all night.

Karl had these cats trained one way, but it's not your way from what I've heard."

"No, I never believed in Karl's methods."

"But these cats—that's all they know. He fought them and delighted in making them charge him. Are you going to carry a chair and a whip?"

"I guess I'll have to with Karl's animals, but it's not the best way." He looked around and saw that every member of the circus was waiting. "Well, I've got the best audience in the world. These people know what's going on."

"Please don't do it, Chase!"

"I've got to."

He lifted his voice and said, "All right, bring them in."

The command was relayed, and soon the cats, as they were trained to do, ran out of the entrance that led into the cage. Chase stepped inside and locked the door behind him, his face intent. He glanced around at Doak, Joy, and Travis, who were his watchers, and saw that their faces were all fixed. He said to Travis, "Pray for me, brother."

"I am, Chase," Travis Winslow said. "God be with you."

The watching circus workers were quiet as the lions and tigers entered the cage. As they filed in they turned alternately to the right and the left. When the animals were new, Karl had watched them carefully, noting which way each cat naturally turned. Then he had arranged the cats in their natural order, making it appear that they knew how to make an orderly entrance into the cage.

The only sound under the big top was the cats' growling. The animals were rambunctious, which was the way Karl had liked them. Rajah, one of the biggest Bengal tigers, reached out and swiped at the biggest of the lions, a black-maned giant named King. King would have turned and answered the challenge, but Chase stepped forward and spoke sharply to him. "Back, King—Rajah!"

The lions and tigers circled the cage, knowing their routine as well as anyone who was watching. Chase saw, however, that they were confused because Karl was not there, and he had difficulty directing them to their perches. He had known this would be a problem, for any change in their routine disturbed the big cats; even a change of costume for the regular trainer could be disturbing. They were creatures of habit, and now they were staring at Chase in confusion, slow to obey his commands.

"He's not going to be able to do it, Stella," Colonel House said. He shook his head nervously. "Look, he's having trouble even getting them up on their perches."

"He's doing fine, Maurice," Stella snapped, her eyes narrowed to slits. "He got into the cage. That's the first big step. Now if he can just get out without getting hurt, it won't matter. It's this first time that's the hardest. You know that. Remember when that wire walker fell? It took all his courage for him to go back up that first time after he healed. After that he was fine." She whispered, "Come on, Chase. Come on, you can do it."

Indeed, all of the spectators were pulling for Chase. They had all seen the lions and tigers perform hundreds of times, but they knew this was the crucible for Chase Hardin. None of them knew exactly what he felt like, but they'd all been painfully reminded recently of the real danger in that cage.

Don Fontaine whispered to Gloria, his wife, who stood beside him. "He can do it! He can do it!"

"Yeah, maybe, but those animals sure are nervous. Look at 'em."

The animals were indeed restless and obeyed the commands reluctantly. Chase was everywhere, it seemed, giving commands, cracking the whip with his right hand, using the chair to fend off the big tiger named Rajah that slapped at him as he went by.

"That big tiger ought to be put down," Pete Delaney said. He slipped his arm around Annie and held her close. "Just one false move, and they'll explode just like they did with Karl."

"God won't let that happen," Annie said fiercely.

"He let it happen to Karl."

Annie had no response to this, and the two of them stood there, silently willing the animals to go through their paces without trouble.

As for Joy, she was watching their every move carefully. She knew these animals well now, and suddenly she yelled, "Watch out for Mazie!"

Hearing this warning, Chase whirled around to find Mazie charging him. He shoved the chair at her and popped the whip close to her head. At the loud crack, she sullenly backed up and resumed her place on the perch.

The silence of the tent was broken only by the growls and snarls of the animals and Chase's sharp commands as he put them through their paces. The act was ragged, and he had to struggle to get the animals to do even the simplest of tricks, but as Joy watched his face, she saw no sign of fear—just intense concentration. She unexpectedly felt a rush of pride for Chase. *Nobody knows what it's costing him to do this,* she thought, *but I do.* He had told her about some of the nightmares he'd had over the last two years of being back in the cage with the animals going wild.

Now the strain both inside and outside of the cage was tremendous, but the animals were slowly making their way through their act. He got them all to lie down before him in a line and then roll over, but only after an intense struggle.

As they stood up again, Prince, a large Siberian tiger, took a swipe at Rajah, and the two slashed at each other. When Chase ran to break it up, they both did what tigers often do. They forgot their own fight and charged the trainer. Chase looked into their fierce eyes and snarling faces and thought for a moment he was gone. But he fended them off, snapping the whip within an inch of Rajah's face, startling the big cat. He shoved the chair into Prince's face, and they finally gave way before him.

"It's almost over," Joy whispered. She grabbed the bars, still watching intently for any threatening behavior. Finally, with relief, she heard Chase call out, "Rajah, out!" The big tiger dropped off of his perch and padded toward the opening that led back to the cages. One by one the other animals followed, needing no command.

"He's done it!" Stella cried out. "He's done it!"

But even as she shouted in her excitement, Maurice stiffened. "Look out!" he cried, and other voices rose in a shout of alarm.

Chase heard all this, and then he heard Travis yelling, "Look out for Jackie!" followed immediately by Doak's mighty shout, "Chase—get back!"

Jackie was a heavy-maned lion really past the age for performance, but Ritter had kept him in the show. He was a temperamental animal, but a bit lazy and usually went through his routine in a halfhearted fashion. From time to time, however, a fit of rage would seize him, and he would charge the trainer without warning.

In this instance Chase's back was toward him as he watched the other cats disappear, and for no reason that anyone could see, he suddenly launched himself at Chase.

Chase turned and barely managed to get the chair up before the lion struck. Jackie had a ferocious look on his face, and Chase knew that the chair was all that stood between him and having those claws rip his flesh. As he raised the chair and tried to back up, he shouted, desperate to distract Jackie. It did no good, however, and he realized with despair that no human intervention could dissuade an animal that had gone mad like this. He had seen it before.

A shot rang out, sharp and clear, and then another.

The heavy beast collapsed onto the chair, knocking Chase over in the process. He smelled the animal's rank odor and rancid breath as they lay almost side by side. But Jackie was limp. As Chase stood, he saw that the bullet had caught him in the side of the head by the ear. Another bullet hole, he saw as he got to his feet, was in the animal's side—the brain and the heart. He looked over at the huge form of Doak Williams, who was lowering the rifle. He walked over and put his hand through the cage. "You saved my bacon that time, Doak."

"He was plumb crazy, Mr. Chase. I hated to do it." Then Doak said, "He got you on the arm there."

Chase looked down and saw that his sleeve was ripped to shreds and blood was soaking through the fabric. "It's not very bad," he said.

"Every one of them animals has got bad claws, old rotten meat under them. You gotta get cleaned up."

And then Joy was there. Chase felt her hand on his arm, and when he turned, he saw she was pale, and her eyes were enormous. "Chase, I thought he had you."

"So did I. If it hadn't been for Doak here, he would have."

"Come on, I'll have to clean that arm out."

This was easier said than done because now that it was over, everyone wanted to congratulate Chase. Hands appeared from everywhere, and he shook those he could get, and others pounded his back as he and Joy struggled to get through. Raising her voice, Joy said, "I've got to get that arm cleaned out. Let us through!"

The crowd parted then, and she led him out of the tent and to her trailer. "Sit down there," she ordered.

He slumped in the chair. "I don't want to get blood all over everything."

"Don't worry about it. Here, put your arm on the table."

Chase rested his arm on the dinette table and pulled his shredded sleeve back. "It's not very bad. It just looks bad."

"It's got to be cleaned out. Take your shirt off."

Chase obeyed and sat back down. Joy heated some water in a pan and found bandages and a bottle of antiseptic. She washed the wound carefully, then said, "This is going to sting." She applied the antiseptic liberally, which drew a sharp breath from Chase.

"That does sting," he said.

Joy did not answer. She bound up the arm with a bandage, saying, "It doesn't need any stitches, but you'll need a bandage on it for a day or two."

There was a knock at the trailer door, and before Joy could rise to open it, it opened and Stella waltzed in. She stared down at the two, who were sitting opposite each other at the dinette table. "Is it bad?" she asked swiftly.

"No, just a scratch."

"That's good." Stella stood beside Chase, her hip touching his shoulder, and brushed his coal black hair away from his forehead. "You had us all worried there, Chase."

"Jackie had me worried. He shouldn't have been in there at all. He's too old and temperamental."

"I'm glad you're all right, Chase. You gave me a bad fright."

Joy was watching these two and realized that the ties between them were still strong. Chase had never talked to her about his past relationship with Stella, but she couldn't forget the kiss she had seen that night by the menagerie. Chase had insisted that it was nothing, but now as she saw the two of them together, she knew the tie had not been completely broken. Stella might be married, but Joy believed it was more a marriage of convenience than love, and it wouldn't stop Stella from pursuing the man she truly wanted. And Joy also knew that because Chase was a man, he was weak where women were concerned.

Stella smiled then and said, "Do you feel like talking about our deal?"

"Sure." Chase got to his feet and picked up the bloody shirt.

"You can't wear that," Stella said. "I'll get one of Maurice's shirts. Come on."

Chase turned and said, "Thanks for the patchwork, Joy, and thanks for being a watcher."

Joy could think of nothing to say in return other than, "Take care of that arm, Chase."

"I will."

"Come on, Chase. We've got a lot to discuss." Stella's voice was insistent, and she turned swiftly and stared at Joy, who had stood up. "Chase is the man for this job, Joy. You won't be going into any cage unless he says so. You understand that, don't you?"

"Yes, Mrs. House."

"Good. Come along, Chase." She put a possessive hand on Chase's arm and led him out of the trailer. Joy stood unmoving and then sat down again. She whispered, "He's never gotten over her, and she's still in love with him. That's easy enough to see." This thought angered her, and she got to her feet and began to clean up, furiously telling herself, "I'll show him. My name will be up there just as big as his!"

PART FOUR

November 1928–November 1929

★ ★ ★

CHAPTER NINETEEN

BITTERNESS WILL KILL YOU

★ ★ ★ ★

The mighty body of the elephant beneath Joy swayed from side to side. So accustomed was she to riding Ruth that she no longer grasped the harness, but threw her hands straight up in the air and smiled at the crowd, which applauded as the last spec of the season drew to an end. A pang went through Joy as her eyes swept the audience. She looked both ahead of her, then back at the line of performers, and thought, *I'm going to miss all of this so much!*

The circus had reached as far north as Omaha, but that was the end of the line for the circus until early March. With all the big cats going to Ringling Brothers and no other big act to draw the crowds, Stella had decided to shut the show down entirely while Chase trained the new lions and tigers.

The crashing notes of the circus band reverberated as Joy tried to absorb all of it—the sounds, the colors of the brilliant costumes, the smells. Now that it was over—at least for the winter break—she wondered with panic, *What am I going to do with myself?* The uncertainty that swept through Joy had become too familiar. Since Chase had returned, her peace of mind had fled. She had worked hard doing her part of the act with Mabel and continued doing the human cannonball routine with Travis. She had also done the elephant act, but somehow everything seemed out of joint. Her relationship with Chase, she knew, lay at the heart of her discontent, and now as she looked around, he was not there. She knew he was back with the new cats, for he spent every spare moment of his time working with them.

Karl Ritter's mother had kept in touch with Stella by mail, giving her an update on his condition periodically. The wounds had been bad, and Karl had spent a full six weeks in the hospital in Jackson. In mid-September he had finally been stable enough to continue his recovery at his parents' home in Monroe, Louisiana. His face was severely scarred, and he would never again be the handsome man he had been before his accident. Even though he was finally healthy and active again, rejoining the circus wasn't something he would consider.

Chase had performed almost a miracle, everyone said, finishing out the season with cats he had not trained himself and which were not amiable to his own style. He had spent an enormous amount of time locating new animals, and two weeks ago he had taken the train across the country to view a group of young lions that had suddenly come on the market. He had returned with them and had been working with them every moment he could spare from other duties.

Ruth lifted her trunk back over her head, and as always, Joy plucked apple quarters out of the small bag she kept tied around her waist under the spangled cloak she wore. She fed Ruth the pieces one by one as the animals rolled back out of the tent. When she was clear of the main tent, without waiting for Ruth to lift her leg for a footstep, Joy slipped to the ground. She saw Slim Madden, who was an elephant man himself, and said, "Take care of the bulls, will you, Slim?"

"Sure will, Miss Joy."

It sounded strange to call female elephants "bulls," but that was the way of the circus. Slim said, "Well, it's home sweet home, ain't it?"

Joy turned and stared at the gangly individual. "What do you mean 'home sweet home'?"

Surprise swept across Slim's homely face. "Oh, I guess you wouldn't know, since we worked right through the winter last year. That's what we call the last show of the season—home sweet home."

"I guess I'm still learning the circus lingo after all this time." Joy made her way through the milling crowd, avoiding the animals being herded back to the menagerie. There was a great hubbub of voices and laughter, and she wished she could join in, but the best she could do was to put an artificial smile on her face as people greeted her.

Pete Delaney suddenly stepped in front of her, causing her to stop abruptly. He had a harried look on his face, even more so than usual. "As you know, Joy, we're gonna break up in the morning and go to Sarasota for winter quarters. We're short a driver for one of the trucks, so I want you and Travis to drive it back."

"All right, Pete."

As she left the hubbub of activity and made her way to the trailer, Joy tried to put her uncertainties out of her mind. All she wanted at the moment was to be alone.

When she entered the trailer, she took off her costume and took a shower. After drying off and changing into her pajamas and robe, she pulled out her journal and began to write.

> Well, it's all over until next spring. I've just found out that the last show of the season is called "home sweet home." We'll be tearing down in the morning and going to Sarasota, Florida. I've never been there, but they say it's a nice place to spend the winter.
>
> Travis and I will be driving a truck through, Pete has just told me, but it won't be long before Travis is going to Bible school. He's going to a place in Chicago called Moody Bible Institute. I'm glad for him. He's so happy and so anxious to get started on his training.

She paused for a moment and listened to the noise that filtered through the trailer. There was a celebration going on, and she expected there would be quite a bit of liquor flowing. By now she was used to the fact that quite a few of the circus people were hard drinkers. The thought of drinking made her think of Chase, and a frown creased her brow as she began to write again:

> Chase is spending too much time with Stella. Ever since he came back and took over the big cat act, they have had their heads

together. I know sometimes she just wants to talk to him about his plans for next year and about the business of buying new animals, but she never misses a chance to touch him. I'm afraid he's going to make a fool of himself over her.

Writing this down depressed Joy, and she took the pen and held it up before her eyes, remembering how thrilled she had been when Chase had given it to her for her seventeenth birthday. She noted also the silver ring with the turquoise setting that he had given her on her last birthday. She treasured both of them.

Her thoughts returned to Stella's behavior with Chase. It was obvious to everyone that she was trying to get him back. Why couldn't Chase see it?

A loud burst of laughter somewhere near her trailer caught her attention, and she listened, but then wondered why she had deliberately chosen not to go to the celebration. She had learned to love her circus family, even those who had some pretty glaring faults. As she thought about the shortcomings of some of her friends, her mind wandered to the Tatums. She stirred uneasily as she tried to shove them out of her mind. Finally she picked up the pen and wrote, pressing down with unnecessary hardness:

I can't forget what Albert Tatum did to Travis and me. I had hoped to put the furniture that belonged to Mom and Dad in my home someday, and now they've taken it. And they put all of Mom and Dad's other stuff in the attic, and the mice are going to get at it. Travis tells me I ought not to have hard feelings toward them, but I can't help it.

Joy lifted her head as an idea came to her. She impulsively threw off her robe, changed into a dress, and left the trailer. She went to find Pete and discovered that he had gone back to his own trailer. When she reached it and knocked on the door, he opened it and looked at her with surprise. "What are you doing here, Joy? I thought you'd be celebrating."

"I've got a favor to ask, Pete."

"Well, you don't ask many. What is it?"

"You know how we'll be driving that trailer down south to Sarasota?"

"Yeah, what about it?"

"We're not too far from my old home, Pete. Would it be all right if Travis and I took the truck and went there first before we go to Florida? I'd like to get some of our things. I'm afraid they'll get lost if we don't."

"Sure, if you'll pay for the extra gas."

"Thanks, Pete, we'll take care of that."

Joy whirled and half ran away from the Delaneys' trailer. She had no trouble finding Travis, who was with a group of the web-sitters, the men who held down the ropes as the performers did their acts.

"Travis, come here. I have to tell you something."

"Sure, sis." Travis followed Joy with a surprised look as she tugged on his arm. She took him away from the crowds, then turned and faced him squarely. "Did Pete say anything to you about driving one of the trucks back through to Sarasota?"

"He just told me about it. He said the two of us could go together. That'll be good. We'll have some time together that way."

"I just talked to Pete," Joy said quickly. "I asked him if we could use the truck to go back to our old home first and pick up some things, and he said we could."

"You mean go back to Uncle Albert's?"

"Yes. They've got things that belong to us, Travis."

"They're not going to give up that furniture, sis. You might as well make up your mind to that."

"It's our furniture, not theirs!"

"Well, you know how he is. I don't think it's a good idea." As a matter of fact, Travis had been disturbed about Joy. He had discovered the streak of bitterness that lay not deep beneath the surface concerning the Tatums, and he had tried to gently dislodge some of it. But she had been adamant, and now as he stood there hesitantly, he said, "Well, I think it's a bad idea, but they'd probably let us get the things out of the attic, I guess."

"Good," Joy said. "We'll leave first thing after tearing down in the morning."

★　★　★　★

The truck was old but ran passably well as Travis and Joy pulled out of Omaha. The weather was cold, for it was now the beginning of winter, and once, as they ambled across Nebraska, Travis grinned at her. "I'm sure glad we won't have to stay here long. I had enough of these cold winters up here. It'll be great to be in Florida again."

Joy was enjoying the trip. She put her problems with the circus out of her mind and turned to smile at her brother. "Me too," she said.

Traveling across Nebraska gave Joy an idea. "Let's stop and see Sister Hannah, Travis. It's not that far out of the way."

"Say, I'd like to meet that lady. From all you've told me about her, I think she and I would get along."

As they pulled into Arnold, Nebraska, Joy pointed excitedly. "Look, that old caboose is still there, the one where Chase and I stayed for a couple of nights. Turn here," she said, directing him to Sister Hannah's house. The truck stopped, and Joy scrambled out eagerly, with Travis following close behind. As they approached the house a large German shepherd started barking, and Travis said, "I hope he doesn't bite."

"Come here, Jake. Good boy."

The big shepherd, hearing his name, quieted down and came forward, wagging his tail, to get a pat on his head. "Chase tamed him. He was as wild as a tiger," Joy said. "I hope Sister Hannah's at home."

No sooner had she said it than the door swung open and a voice sang out, "Well, I never! Look what the wind blowed in. Come on in out of the weather."

"That's Sister Hannah," Joy said. "Come on, Travis."

She led Travis to the house, and Joy found herself enveloped in the big woman's arms. "Well, look at you, now! Done growed up and everything. And who's this with you? I thought it was Chase at first."

"No, this is my brother, Travis. Travis, this is Sister Hannah Smith."

Travis had pulled his hat off and smiled and put his hand out. "I'm proud to meet you, Sister Smith. I've wanted to thank you for everything you did for my sister and for Chase."

"Oh, don't mention it! Come on in. I'll bet you two could eat a little bit, couldn't you?"

"We sure could," Joy said. "I've thought about your cookin' ever since we left."

"Well, come on in. It won't take long to whip up a bite."

★ ★ ★ ★

Sister Hannah's "bite" turned out to be a meal fit for royalty—pork chops, mashed potatoes, green beans, pickled beets, fresh baked bread, and an apple pie. Hospitality was Hannah's middle name, and she was always ready to serve unexpected visitors. Travis leaned back and patted his stomach as he surveyed the remnants. "I can't eat another bite, Sister Hannah. I've never had a better meal."

Sister Smith peered at him with alert eyes. "So you're gonna be a preacher, Joy tells me."

"That's right. Don't guess I'll be as good a preacher as you, from what Joy says."

"I reckon you will be. I feel the Spirit of God in you, young man. Now"—she leaned back and took a sip of the sassafras tea she had chosen over the coffee that the other two drank—"you tell me everything you've done. Letters are nice, but there ain't nothin' like a real live conversation."

Sister Hannah listened eagerly as Joy spoke of what had happened since they'd left. She knew much of it, for Chase wrote to her regularly and kept her posted. She interrupted once in a while to exclaim, "Well, landsakes alive, I'd love to see you on top of that elephant—or in that cage with that tiger!"

"I love the circus," Joy said, "but that's enough about me. Tell me all about yourself, Sister Hannah."

"Oh, there ain't nothin' to tell. I keep preachin' the Word. What are you two doing way up here in the middle of winter almost?"

"We have to take this truck back to Florida for the winter. Chase is going to train a lot of new lions and tigers, and I've got to help him. But right now Travis and I are on our way to our old home."

"Oh, you're gonna see your people?"

"No, we're not!" A frown leaped across Joy's features. "We're going back to get what's ours."

"How's that?" Sister Smith asked carefully, glancing over at Travis. She saw something in his expression that warned her of family problems, and she listened as Joy explained angrily how her uncle had robbed the two of them of their inheritance and how determined she was to get some of their things.

This was the first time Joy had ever shared all of this with Sister Hannah, and the older woman said little, just quietly listened while Joy let it all spill out. When Joy was finished, Hannah said simply, "Well, it's a shame when families have trouble. Let's wash these here dishes, and young man, you go out there and chop some wood."

The two women began to clear the table while Travis went out back, and as soon as they heard the sound of the splitting maul hitting the white oak, Sister Hannah said, "I'm a mite worried about you."

"Why, I'm fine, Sister Hannah."

"No, you ain't. You got hard, hard feelin's agin that uncle of yours and his young'uns. I know they done you wrong, but bitterness will kill you dead."

Joy's face flushed, for she knew that with her usual discernment, Sister Hannah Smith had seen right into the heart of what she had been feeling. "I can't help it, Sister," she said, her lips drawn in a tight line. "They stole my father and mother's place, and they made slaves out of us. Travis wouldn't have been in jail if it hadn't been for them. I'm going to get back at them—you see if I don't!"

A sorrowful expression crossed Hannah's face, and she fell silent. She tried to think of something to say, but she had seen far too many people looking for revenge. She knew that bitterness would not kill someone as quick as a bullet, but it could be far more painful. She had seen so many lives wrecked by those who were unwilling to give up their hard feelings. Now she said simply, "I'll be prayin' for you, Joy. There ain't no happiness for you until you let the Lord Jesus get this thing out of your heart."

* * * *

"It looks about the same," Travis said mildly as he pulled the truck up in front of the two-story farmhouse. "They'll be pretty shocked to see us, I guess."

Joy's face was set. Usually she had a pleasant smile, but now anger flickered in her eyes. "They should be! If I had my way, we'd have the sheriff here to arrest them!"

"Ah, come on, Joy, let's just be nice and get the things out of the attic."

"I'm going to take some of the furniture too. We've got room for that!"

Joy got out and slammed the door of the truck with unnecessary force, and Travis followed. He was worried about this visit and had prayed much, but his prayers had not seemed to affect Joy. As the two mounted the porch, he said again, "Remember, if you want to gather honey, don't kick over the beehive."

Joy did not answer. Her face was pale and not just with cold. She rapped violently on the door with her knuckles, and when it opened she saw her aunt. "Hello, Aunt Opal," she said coldly.

Opal Tatum blinked with surprise, and her hand flew up to her mouth. "Oh, my stars, it's you, Joy—and Travis!" She stepped forward and put her arms around Joy. The young woman endured the embrace but said nothing. Travis, however, put his arms around Opal and hugged her, saying warmly, "It's good to see you, Aunt Opal."

"Come in out of the cold. Where did you two come from?" She looked at the truck that had the name of the circus emblazoned across it and said, "Are you in that thing?"

"Yes, we are. Is Albert here?" Joy asked.

Opal couldn't miss the coldness in Joy's tone. She gave Travis a look, and he only shook his head slightly. Not knowing how to interpret this, Opal said, "He's in the living room with the kids. Come on in."

Joy had looked forward to this moment of confrontation with Albert Tatum for a year and a half, and when she stepped into the living room, it gave her a fleeting pleasure to see shock run across his face. He leaped to his feet but was speechless. Olean and Witt were there also, and Olean cried out, "What are you two doing here?"

Albert seemed to have been freed from the silence that gripped him. "Well, you've come back," he said. "I'm surprised you had the nerve after runnin' away the way you did."

"I'm surprised you have the nerve to even speak to me, Albert Tatum, after the way you treated us!"

"Treated you! You're the one that run off!"

"What are you doing here?" Witt demanded. But then he seemed to remember how Travis had once soundly thrashed him, and he changed his tone of voice and said nervously, "We don't want any trouble, Travis."

"Of course not," Travis said. He strolled forward and put his hand out to Albert. "I'm glad to see you again, Uncle."

Albert Tatum flinched as if he expected a blow. He took the hand and then glanced across at Opal, who had come to stand beside him. Travis shook hands with Witt and said, "You're all looking pretty well. I'm glad to see it."

Somewhat relieved by Travis's attitude, Albert said, "Well, I didn't expect to see you two."

"I don't expect you did," Joy said, "and you won't see us long. We've just come to get what's ours."

Albert Tatum's eyes narrowed. "What do you mean what's yours? There's nothin' here that's yours."

"Yes there is," Joy said. "All this antique furniture is ours. It belonged to our parents."

"You're not getting any of this furniture," Olean hissed. "It's ours now. You ran away and left it."

"I ran away to keep Witt's hands off of me and nearly got killed doing it." She turned to face Albert and said, "We're taking everything that's in the attic, and we're taking what furniture we can haul too."

Albert shouted, his face red, "You're not taking anything! Get out of this house!"

Joy's eyes blazed. Travis had never seen her like this. She took a step as if to attack Albert, and he quickly reached forward and caught her arm. "Hold it, sis."

"You'd better hold it!" Tatum yelled. "I'll have the law on you if you try to take one thing! Now get out of here, and don't you ever come back!"

"Look, Uncle Albert, never mind the furniture, but we—"

"Don't beg, Travis!" Joy shouted. She stood there, her back straight, anger in every line of her face. "You won't even give us our folks' things in the attic?"

"I'll give you nothin'! Now get out of here!"

Joy stared at him and for a moment Travis felt her body tense. Then she said in a voice as cold as polar ice, "All right, we'll leave, but one day I'm going to find out what happened to the money that came out of the sale of our farm. And one day I'm going to have every stick of this furniture. And one day I'll see you put in jail for the thief that you are! Come on, Travis."

Travis shook his head, knowing it was no use to say any more. He followed Joy outside, and when the two were in the truck, he started the engine. He pulled away and looked back to see Albert standing on the porch, shaking his fist at them. His wife was trying to speak to him, but he simply shoved her back. Travis shook his head. "That's one unhappy man," he said. "I feel sorry for his wife."

Joy did not say a word for the next hour. She sat bolt upright in the truck, her face pale, until finally she turned to Travis and said bitterly, "He'll be sorry one day, Travis. You'll see. I'll *make* him sorry."

CHAPTER TWENTY

THE STRANGE WOMAN

★ ★ ★ ★

As soon as Travis put the brakes on and brought the truck to a grinding halt, he turned to Joy and said wearily, "Well, it was sure a long drive, but we're here finally."

Joy looked around at the setting and found it quite different from a circus. There were heavy wire cages all around, where she could see the animals were feeding. The elephants seemed to be enjoying spraying each other with water out of a pond, and the trailers were all parked in one area. "It looks nice," she said. She opened the door and got out, and Travis came around and joined her. He stretched his back and said, "I'm glad to be here."

"But you'll be leaving soon for Bible school."

Travis put his arm around her and smiled. "Yes, I will. You understand that I've got to go, don't you?"

"Of course." She hugged him and then hesitated for a moment before saying, "I'm sorry I was such a beast at the Tatums and then all the way back. I've got a vile temper."

"No you don't, sis." Travis shook his head. "You've just let your bitterness get a hold of your heart, and I'm praying that you will be able to get rid of it."

Joy did not have time to answer, for Oz came barreling up, rolling as he walked, as always. He reached up to shake Travis's hand, and as soon as he had greeted them, he said, "Did you hear about Colonel House?"

"No, we haven't heard anything."

Oz pulled his hat off, and his face reflected genuine sorrow. "I hate to be the one to tell ya," he said with some hesitation, "but we lost the colonel."

Neither Travis nor Joy were shocked, as the colonel hadn't been well in quite some time. "Was it his heart?" Joy asked.

"Yes, it was. He went to bed one night, and the next morning when Stella tried to wake him up, he was gone. Not a bad way to go," he said regretfully.

"What's going to happen with the circus?" Joy said.

"Stella's taken over. She'd been doing most of the work anyway. We'll need a new ringmaster for next season. They're pretty hard to find, but I'm sure she'll find somebody."

"Is Chase all right?"

"Working night and day. He's got a whole bunch of new cats he's training, and he hardly takes time to eat or sleep. I'm glad you're here. Maybe you can take some of the load off him, Joy." He hesitated, then said, "You got back just in time. The funeral's this afternoon at three o'clock."

★　★　★　★

The funeral of Colonel Maurice House was simple. The chapel of the funeral home was crowded with circus performers, workers, and House's many friends and acquaintances. Some had traveled long distances to be there. House had been in the circus business a long time and knew people from all over the country in both the circus and business worlds.

Joy sat beside Travis and whispered, "I wonder where Chase is. I thought he'd be here."

"He's coming. He told me he was," replied Travis.

Oz, sitting on the other side of Joy, said, "Look, there he is."

Joy looked up to see Stella coming in through a side door, escorted by the funeral home director, a tall man dressed in a black suit. Close by her side was Chase. Stella was dressed in black and wore a hat with a black veil, and she clung to Chase's arm as she took her seat in the front row. Everyone had stood when they came in. Joy was disturbed at the sight of Stella holding on to Chase like that. She had expected Chase to comfort her, but her action seemed much too possessive to Joy.

As they sat down again Oz whispered, "Stella's been leanin' on Chase pretty heavy since the colonel died. She doesn't have many real friends, you know. I guess she depends on Chase more than anyone. Good thing he's here to help her through it."

Travis heard this whisper and cast a covert glance at his sister. He saw that her face was tense, but she said nothing. Leaning back, he thought, *I hate to see her like this. She's not herself.*

The funeral was mercifully brief. The pastor of a local church read the eulogy and a group of Scripture passages, then preached the sermon. Afterward he announced that there would be a graveside ceremony for those who cared to attend immediately following the service.

"I guess we'd better go," Travis whispered.

"All right." Joy really had no desire to go, but she accompanied Travis anyway. They joined the long parade of cars, which all turned their lights on and followed the police escort. The country was flat as far as Joy could see, with flowers blooming everywhere. After being in the frozen north, it was strange to see such an abundance of gorgeous plants waving in the breeze along the road as they passed by in the funeral procession.

When they got to the cemetery, she took Travis's arm, and Oz accompanied them as they made their way to the green tent that swayed slightly in the breeze. They waited until Stella got out of the long black limousine and took Chase's arm. The two followed the minister to the tent, where they sat down together, and then the minister waved the rest of the crowd in.

Joy led Travis and Oz to the front row. She heard little that was said, for she was watching Chase and Stella closely. She could barely see Stella's face because of the black veil, but she noticed that even as they sat there, she kept her hand on Chase's arm the whole time, as if for an anchor.

Finally she lifted her veil. Her face seemed pale, but she displayed little emotion as the minister read the Scriptures.

Chase looks worse than she does, Joy thought, noticing that his olive complexion was weathered, and he looked thinner than usual. His coal black hair made a striking contrast, and sorrow reflected in his eyes as he listened to the readings.

Finally the preacher said a closing prayer, and then he went over and put his hand on Stella's shoulder and shook hands with Chase. Others began to file by, offering comforting words to Stella. Joy had no desire to do so, but Travis whispered, "We'd better go by and say something."

Joy moved reluctantly around into the short line, and when she got to Chase, he looked up at her, his eyes sad.

"I know you're grieving, Chase," she said.

"Yes, he was a good friend to me and a good man."

There was no time to say more, and when Joy got to Stella, she said, "I'm so sorry, Mrs. House."

"Thank you, Joy." No more was said, and Joy moved out from under the tent into the sunlight. She waited for Travis, and when he came up with Oz at his side, she said, "I think we'd better go now."

Oz looked back at Stella and shook his head. "Well, it wasn't too much of a marriage, but he needed somebody in his last days, and I guess she furnished that."

★　★　★　★

As Stella and Chase left the tent she was still clinging to Chase's arm. Before they got to the car, she stopped and pulled him around to face her. She looked up at him and whispered urgently, "Chase, you're all I've got left. You've got to help me."

"Sure, Stella. We all will."

"You're the one I know best, Chase. We've got to keep this circus together, and it's going to take all we've got. Please," she said, leaning against him, "help me."

"All right, Stella," Chase said, nodding slowly, "we'll do it. Try not to worry."

★　★　★　★

Joy was so tired she could barely lift her head. She had arrived at Sarasota only a week ago, and she had visualized herself spending time on the beach and enjoying the ocean, but there had been little time for that. The morning after the funeral she had gone early to meet with Chase, who had greeted her with, "I'm glad to see you made the trip back all right. Was it a good trip?"

"No, it wasn't."

Chase caught the bitterness in her tone but said merely, "I'm sorry. Are you ready to go to work?"

"Yes."

"All right. It's going to be hard. We've got mostly young animals. I had to take some that were grown in order to start the act, but I'm putting you in charge of the tiger cubs."

"Oh, that'll be fun. They're so cute!"

Chase suddenly grinned. "I'm glad you think so. They'll keep you busy, I think."

There were four tiger cubs, and they indeed kept Joy busy. She quickly discovered that like human babies, cubs had to be fed several times during the night. She also discovered that someone had to clean their bottoms before they were big enough to do it for themselves. She had to prepare their food with just the proper mix of milk, and they had to have shots. Their needs never stopped.

Joy quickly learned that each cub was different, though they all looked alike. One was pugnacious, always ready to fight the others, one was very calm and placid, and another was very curious. As the days went on, she bathed them, fed them, prepared all their food, and kept their boxes fresh. When one of them got sick, she would sit with the cub through the night just as she might have with a child.

Along with her responsibility for taking care of the four tiger cubs, Joy also learned how to train the rest of the cats. "I want them to be as accustomed to you as they are to me," Chase said on the first morning. "I'm going to show you the basics on how to train them, and then you'll take over as I move on to others. The first thing we'll teach them is to roll over."

This, as Joy soon discovered, was not as simple as she thought it would be. She had taught their dog to roll over pretty easily when she was a child, but cats were another matter. Joy started with a lion called Betty.

"You'll like Betty," Chase said. "She's quick to learn. The first thing is, you can't touch her. She has to roll over at a voice signal."

Joy learned that this was not so simple. The first part of teaching Betty was to give her a workout. She got the lioness out into the cage, and after a workout, as Chase had told her, she would lie down. Next she took a light buggy whip attached to a long pole so she could stand ten feet away. Then by touching Betty's feet lightly, and with a combination of hand and body movements, along with the spoken command, she tried to teach her to lie down. It was not easy, however, and it took almost a week to teach Betty this one simple trick. Joy grew discouraged, "We'll never teach them all these things, Chase."

"Sure we will. They learn from each other. Now, next you take Greta and teach her to roll over." Greta was a beautiful Siberian tiger, and to Joy's amazement she learned to roll over after just two efforts and never seemed to forget it. This pleased Joy greatly, and she realized she was learning more than the tiger was.

As the days passed, Chase allowed Joy to come into the cage more and more. "Never forget they're wild animals." He must have said it a thousand times, she thought. "You know what they can do from what happened to Karl, but they're good animals. They need you to respect them. Don't make pets out of them. I know it's a temptation—especially with the cubs, because they're cute—but don't allow them to play with you. They have to learn to obey."

"Now," he said, "I'll show you how to teach them to get up on their perches. That's the foundation of the act, as you know."

Joy worked hard on learning this. She quickly discovered some basic truths she had never dreamed of before. Chase taught her that Siberian tigers were different from Bengal tigers. They had much longer backs, which made it more difficult for them to sit up, and consequently they needed more time for this maneuver. Chase explained, "You can push a tiger from behind to get it into position only as long as it'll allow it—usually when it's young. They're like little kids. You push them in the right direction until they'll no longer tolerate it. But when they get big, never push a tiger."

One of the things Chase spent a great deal of time teaching Joy was exactly how to *give* commands. "Talk to them all the time, Joy. The voice means everything. Your whole relationship will be based on talk. As you already know, tigers make a lot of sounds. Lions don't usually answer you. Your tone of voice is important too. When they do something wrong, use a harsh tone. When they do something right, speak in a pleasant tone."

There was no question that safety came first with Chase. "There'll be two of us in the cage at all times," Chase emphasized. "Tigers attack from the rear. They have to really be hurt to attack from the front. Otherwise, they never do that. They're too smart. When they stalk their prey, they use surprise. Never turn your back on a tiger."

Joy learned that each tiger had to be treated individually. She had already noticed it even with the cubs, but as the winter passed, she learned that Greta, the Siberian tiger, learned almost instantly, while Brutus was rather stupid and took many, many repetitions. She never allowed herself to become irritated, though. She found out that Tom, another male tiger, had almost no balance at all. It took him forever to learn to sit up, and he was never much good at it.

One day after breakfast, Chase announced, "Today we're going to teach one of the tigers to go through a hoop of fire. Which one do you think it should be?"

"Greta," Joy said instantly.

"You're right. She's the smartest and the most obedient." He smiled and reached out to shake her hand. "Congratulations," he said, "you're becoming a wild-animal tamer."

Joy was ridiculously pleased at his praise. He gave it sparingly, but she knew he always meant it. He was not afraid to correct her when she did something stupid or dangerous, but she knew it was all for her own good.

Teaching Greta to go through a hoop was not difficult. At first, of course, they taught her to go through it without the fire. They showed her the hoop until she got used to it, and finally the day came when Chase said, "All right, it's show time for

Greta. Let's see if we can get her to go through it with the fire now."

Joy had been dreading this moment. Tigers are naturally afraid of fire, as are most animals, but Joy tried not to show her apprehension. She watched as Chase struck a match and lit the hoop, which was covered with kerosene-soaked rags. "All right, see if she'll go," he said, grinning.

"Greta, jump!"

With a bored expression, Greta took off from her perch, leaped through the fire, then turned around and looked at Joy as if to say, "What's so hard about that?"

Joy wanted to go over and hug her but knew better. "Good, Greta, that was very good! You're a good tiger!" she crooned.

In all this training Joy was amazed at how different Chase's approach was from that which Karl Ritter had used. He was firm, but there were no guns firing or whips cracking. Inexperienced as she was, she realized that Chase Hardin was getting more out of these animals, as new as they were, than Ritter had gotten out of his after years of training them. She said as much one time to Chase as they were heading for the cages to feed the animals. This was another thing. Chase had insisted that the two of them be the ones to feed the animals every night. He explained, "They've got to feel dependent on us. They have to know that we're in charge, and they depend on us for their comfort. When we're on the road, we'll go back after every performance, no matter how tired we are, and brag on them."

Now as they walked along, Chase turned to her and said, "I know you must be worn to the bone. It's been hard work."

"I've loved it, Chase."

"You have, haven't you?" He grinned at her and shook his head with admiration. "I wasn't sure it was going to work, but you've got a gift for animals. I've never seen anyone learn so quickly."

Joy felt her face burn, and she suddenly reached over and squeezed his hand. "I never thanked you for letting me do this." He squeezed her hand in return.

They stood there for a moment, and she was aware of Chase's lean, masculine strength. There was not an ounce of spare flesh on him. He was trimmed down to nothing but muscle, bone, and raw nerve.

He said, "It's good to have you here."

"It's good to be here."

Chase looked like he was going to say something else, leaning his head toward hers, but then suddenly he released her hand and said instead, "I guess we'd better go feed the cats."

Why did he do that? He was going to kiss me, and then he changed his mind. Joy suddenly knew the answer. *That woman,* she thought bitterly. *Stella's got him like a fish on a line.* Indeed, she had been much aware, despite her busy life, that Chase spent an inordinate amount of time with Stella House. He spent a lot of time in her trailer, explaining it by saying, "Everything's riding on this act, and besides, she needs help setting up the schedule." It was a feeble enough excuse, and Joy was certain there was more to it than that.

★ ★ ★ ★

"The act's going very well, isn't it, Chase?"

Stella had asked Chase to come to her trailer and go over some of the difficulties she foresaw for the next year. She had cooked a meal for him, and he had stayed until nearly ten o'clock. Now they were sitting on the couch with papers spread all over the coffee table. Chase leaned back and ran his hand through his hair. "It's going better than I ever expected."

"It's going to have to go over well if we're to survive. We're down to the bare metal." Stella was wearing a clingy silk dress and the same perfume she used to wear. He had been concentrating on the logistics of moving scores of people and animals around, tearing a circus down, and putting it back together a hundred miles away. Now he was very much aware of Stella herself. She leaned closer to him and said, "You're tired, Chase. You don't rest enough."

"Oh, I'm all right, and don't worry about the act. It's going to be fantastic. The audiences will love it."

Stella took Chase's hand and held it between both of hers as she whispered, "I don't know what I would have done without you, Chase. I would have been lost."

Very much aware of the warmth of her hands on his, Chase turned to face her. Old memories flooded through him, and he realized again what a desirable woman she was. He had never been able to put the memories of their intimacy out of his mind, and now as she leaned toward him, he could not speak. He knew he should get up and leave, but before he could bring himself to do so, she released his hand, put hers behind his neck, and drew his head down. Chase felt caught in an emotional maelstrom. He held her tightly and returned her kiss.

"Stay the night, Chase. Remember how good we used to be for each other. There's never been anyone else for me."

Temptation sliced through Chase as keenly as a knife. More than anything in the world, he wanted to yield to her softness, but with a superhuman strength that surprised him, he straightened up and removed her arms. "I . . . I can't do it. I'm different now, Stella." He got to his feet, trembling. "I've gotta go," he mumbled, almost running from the trailer.

Stella leaned back, and a smile turned the corners of her lips upward. "You ran this time, but you didn't run quick enough." She had never felt about a man as she felt about Chase Hardin. She had enjoyed Maurice's company, but had never been in love with him. Now that Maurice was gone, she could pursue Chase guiltlessly.

Outside Chase stumbled through the darkness and found himself breathing almost as hard as if he had run five miles. A form loomed up before him, and he stopped and peered at the large man. "Oh, Doak," he said.

"Hello, Chase. You out takin' your evenin' walk?"

Chase suddenly understood that Doak knew better than this. Somehow Doak knew about Stella and him, and he said, "I guess you're wondering about me coming out of Stella's trailer at this time of the night."

"People do wonder, Chase," Doak said gently, "but I'm your friend. I know what you're going through."

Chase believed the big man's words. "I don't know what to do, Doak," he said bitterly. "I love my life here with the circus, and I want to do this act more than I've ever wanted to do anything, but—"

"I know. You're worried about that woman, and for good reason. You need to be careful, you hear me? You know what it says in Proverbs five: 'The lips of a strange woman drop as an honeycomb, and her mouth is smoother than oil: But her end is bitter as wormwood, sharp as a twoedged sword.' "

"I know," Chase said huskily, "and the next verse is, 'Her feet go down to death; her steps take hold on hell.' "

"You be real careful, Chase. Don't let that woman get you. Better if you left here than let that happen."

Chase did not speak but reached out and took Doak's hand. "Thanks, Doak." He moved on into the darkness and went to the menagerie, where he was surprised to find Joy putting one of the tiger cubs back into the cage. She secured the door and came up to him with a smile. The smile faded, however, when his face was illuminated by the light overhead. She saw the lipstick on his lips and smelled the perfume and knew where he had been.

"Good night," she said curtly.

"Wait a minute, Joy!"

"Isn't one woman enough for you?" she cried, then turned and ran away.

The darkness swallowed Joy up as she left the menagerie, and Chase stood, his shoulders drooping. "What kind of a fool have I become?" he said sadly. "A man who's been burned once should know better."

CHAPTER TWENTY-ONE

SUCCESS

★ ★ ★ ★

"Well, we've sent the patch out, so it looks like we're all ready to go."

Joy had been feeding the tiger cubs through the bars of the cage when Gypsy Dan Darvo had strolled up and made his remark. Dan had spent more than a week in the hospital recovering from his injuries from his fall. He had broken his left leg in two places as well as his left arm. He had also cracked a couple of ribs. The circus family had taken good care of him as he gradually healed and got back on his feet again. Now he walked with a barely noticeable limp.

"The patch? What's that, Dan?"

Darvo grinned at her, his teeth white against his swarthy skin. "You don't know what a patch is? It's the fellow we send out to put up the posters. He always stays just ahead of the circus. Those guys have a lot of trouble sometimes. Rival circuses have been known to go by and paper over ours or tear ours down." Darvo came over and put his arm around Joy. "That was a good time we had last night."

"Yes, it was." Joy had been going out with Dan recently. Since they were still on hiatus, her nights were free, except for checking on the animals. She had found Darvo to be a witty and charming man, although somewhat forward. That, she had come to accept, went with circus life. True, there were solid families such as the Fontaines and the Martinos, but there was also a great laxness in morals. Now Dan started caressing her arm with his hand. She removed his hand from her arm and said sternly, "Dan, I'm going to hit you over the head with a two-by-four if you don't quit pawing me."

"Oh, come on now, Joy, you know you like it. I can tell." Darvo never got angry with her, and when Joy rejected his advances, he took it with good grace. He reached into the cage and stroked the head of one of the cubs, remarking, "All the tigers with this circus aren't in a cage."

Joy turned to him, not understanding his remark. "What do you mean, Dan?"

Darvo crossed his arms and tilted his head to the side. He was a handsome fellow with dark, soulful eyes that he used to good effect on young women. "I mean, I think there's a tiger inside of Miss Joy Winslow."

"What are you talking about?"

"I think if the right guy came along, you might let your wilder side show a little bit. You're a good kisser—you know that?"

Joy flushed, for she was embarrassed that she had responded a few times to Darvo's kisses but had quickly pulled away. "I don't know what you're talking about."

"Sure you do, baby. Anyway, what do you say we go out to the beach this afternoon? Since the circus leaves for Atlanta early tomorrow morning, it'll be our last chance."

"All right, that suits me fine."

Darvo stroked her cheek and shook his head. "You know, this act that you and Chase have put together—it's gonna be big. I've been with the circus a long time, and I can tell."

"We're not really ready. The cats aren't trained well enough."

"They will be. In a couple years you'll be the biggest thing. It makes me a little sad."

"Sad? Why would you be sad about that?"

"Because you won't be with this circus. You'll be with the Greatest Show on Earth. Anyway, I'll see you about one o'clock in your prettiest bathing suit. Bye-bye, babe."

Joy slowly walked away from the cages. She felt bad because

she had started dating Dan more out of spite than anything else. She was trying to get back at Chase for spending so much time with Stella. She liked Dan well enough, and he was good company, but she would never consider marrying him. He simply wasn't her type.

★　★　★　★

Chase was worn down by his responsibilities. Training such a large number of animals in itself was a killer, but in addition, he was saddled with the extra responsibilities Stella had asked him to assume. True enough Pete Delaney could work miracles in moving circuses around. Nonetheless, there were a thousand decisions to be made, and Stella had spent many hours going over all the possibilities with him. Now as he sat at the table in her trailer, he looked at the papers spread out and shook his head wearily. "I guess we'll have to pull out for Atlanta tomorrow whether we're ready or not. I wish we had another three months."

Stella was sitting beside him. The two had been going over the routes and the problems that might arise. She saw that a lock of his hair had fallen down over his forehead, and she put it back in place. "You've worked too hard, Chase."

"No harder than anybody else."

"Yes, you have," she countered. She let her hand fall on his arm and squeezed it gently. "You know everything's riding on your act. If it goes big, the circus will make it. If not—well, I don't think we'll be able to survive."

"It's a good act, Stella, but it'd be better after another year."

"We can't wait a year," Stella said moodily. She kept her hand on his arm and stroked it gently. All winter Stella had taken every opportunity to be close to Chase, and he had struggled to keep his distance. Now he gently removed her hand from his arm. "We'll make it," he said. "Everybody's worked hard this winter."

Stella pouted at Chase's reluctance to give in to her caress, but she continued talking business. "We've spent a bundle of money advertising in Atlanta. It'll be kind of a test case. A lot of people remember you, Chase."

"I always had a good reception in Atlanta."

"You'll have it again."

Chase suddenly grinned, and the smile made him look younger. "They'll come out to see if I've got the nerve to crawl back into the cage after what happened. They'll come for that or to see me get eaten alive."

"Don't talk like that!" Stella said. "You're going to be fine."

She put her hand on his arm again, but Chase stood up and moved away. She shrugged, then asked almost idly, "Is Joy working out all right?"

"Better than I thought. She's had to learn so much in such a short time. Really we're rushing it too much."

"Not much choice." Again Stella's voice seemed almost indifferent, but there was a glint in her eyes. "I've noticed she's running around quite a bit with Dan. I wonder if anything will come of that."

"Maybe so." Chase liked Dan a great deal, but their relationship made him uneasy. He knew Darvo was quite a ladies' man and pursued many of his female fans as well as some of the young performers. Chase wasn't happy about Joy going out with him, but he had not spoken of it to anyone—least of all to her. Now his mind rebelled against what Stella was suggesting, but he could not talk to her. He pulled on his jacket and said, "Well, I've got a lot to do before we pull out in the morning."

"Let's go out and celebrate tonight," she said as she stood. "You deserve a break."

She was standing close enough to him that he could smell her perfume. Chase knew he should say no to her suggestion but felt himself weakening. Not wanting to spend the evening alone, he agreed. "That'll be fine, Stella."

She reached up, pulled his head down, and kissed him on the lips before he had time to resist. "I'm so proud of you, Chase," she said. "Nobody could have saved this circus except you. We're going to go a long way together, you and me."

Chase gently but firmly pushed Stella away and cleared his throat. "I'll see you tonight, Stella."

* * * *

The band was playing, and the cats began pacing back and forth inside their cages. Chase stood beside the door along with Doak Williams, who was an important part of the act, getting the cats in and out of the big cage and serving as a watcher. Doak grinned and said, "You two gonna be fine—just fine."

Joy felt weak. She had rehearsed the act enough times that she should not have been nervous, but this was real, and the noise of the crowd, the band, and the activities swirling around her drained her strength. "Chase," she said tentatively, "I'm scared stiff."

Chase put his hand on her shoulder. "Good," he said.

"You think it's good to be scared?"

"I think being scared is a mark of respect. I want you to respect these animals and make them respect you, and I want us to respect the crowd. They are why we're here. We give them the best we have, Joy, the very best. You're going to do fine. I've never known anybody to make progress like you have. You're going straight to the top."

Joy felt a surge of emotion go through her, and she took a deep breath. His hand was firm on her shoulder, and his dark eyes were intense. "Thanks, Chase, I'm ready now."

"Okay, let's get out there, and then you can let 'em in, Doak."

"Yes, sir!"

"You first. Beauty before the beast," Chase said with a wink.

Joy obeyed and walked quickly out of the inner area into the big top. The big cage was up with the tunnel leading back to where the cats were kept. She unlocked the door, and Max Taylor, who was acting as one of the watchers, said, "Break a leg, Miss Joy."

"Thanks, Max." She stepped into the spotlight and was blinded for a moment, but she felt Chase come and stand close enough to touch her. They stood there smiling as the new ringmaster, Wilbur Whitfield, announced their act. He was a rather small man but with a voice as big as Mount Olympus. He had married Ella Devoe at the end of last season, and the two had been on a winter-long honeymoon. His big voice boomed over the speakers: "And now, ladies and gentlemen, you're in for a treat. Together for the first time in the big cage along with thirty vicious lions and tigers, I give you Mr. Chase Hardin and Miss Joy Winslow!"

Joy smiled at the applause, then turned to get into the cage as the cats came out. The first one was Major, one of her favorites. He was a huge tiger that always had an odd look on his face because one of his eyes was off-center, making him look cross-eyed. Major turned to the right and was quickly followed by Tom, who turned left, and then Brutus who went right. Brutus started to approach her, and she immediately said, "Back, Brutus, get in line there!" She made her voice harsh, and Brutus growled deep in his throat but took his place.

One by one they came on, one to the right, one to the left, until finally the cage was filled with lions and tigers. Joy could smell them and was well aware of the tension of the moment. Many of these cats had not performed before a big audience, although Chase had insisted on inviting people all winter long to watch as they were trained, both to get the cats used to an audience and to let the general public see that the animals were being well treated.

Joy stood almost in the center of the cage, turning her back on half of the animals while facing the other half. It gave her a strong sense of comfort to know that Chase was there. Since she had started working with the big cats, she could not imagine being alone with her back to such ferocious animals. It would just be asking for trouble.

The act did not go smoothly. More than once one of the cats would forget or would deliberately challenge the trainers. Betty, usually one of the mildest of the lions, decided she was not going to get up on her perch. Chase immediately approached her and tapped her on the head with his stick. "Get up on that perch, Betty!" Betty swiped at him with one paw, but Chase stood there until finally, with a grumpy growl, she went up.

When all thirty animals were up on their perches, Chase said under his breath, just loud enough for Joy to hear him, "Now, Joy."

At that instant Joy commanded, "Up!" in a loud, firm voice and lifted her hands. She heard Chase doing the same thing, and to her relief all of her charges reared up on their hind legs. Tom, the tiger with bad balance, had difficulty, but he managed to sway for a few seconds. As the applause thundered from the audience and the cheers came, Joy felt an immense satisfaction.

The time passed quickly in the big cage. Joy had no time to think of herself, for every moment was filled with tension. Brutus, a huge animal with beautiful markings, gave Chase a hard time and balked at some of his stunts. This temperamental animal could turn vicious in a moment.

When it came time for Greta to jump through the ring of fire, Wilbur Whitfield went into a long spiel about how all wild animals dreaded fire and how it took tremendous patience to teach a tiger this trick.

As usual, Chase lit the ring, and Joy instructed Greta to approach the ramp. Greta seemed to be distracted by the crowd and hesitated, but Joy insisted firmly, "Greta, you can do it! Jump!" To her relief, the great cat jumped through the ring of fire, and a wave of applause ran through the big top.

Toward the end of the act, a bad moment caught Joy off guard. The black-maned lion named Colonel was good at balancing on the big ball and rolling it. Chase had charge of him while Joy got a beautiful Bengal tiger named Grace to do the same. These two animals were the best at this trick and had never given Chase and Joy any trouble.

The trick was going well until Chase passed close to Brutus's perch. The beast leaped down and started for Chase. Chase's back was turned and his attention was on the lion rolling the ball, so he was unaware of Brutus's move.

But the watchers and Joy saw it, and in a flash she threw herself forward. She stepped behind Chase, her back to his, and called out, "Brutus, get back!"

Brutus snarled and continued to approach. She reached out with the small stick and called in a harsh voice, "Back, Brutus! Up!"

Chase had whirled around just in time to see the huge cat sulkily turn and climb back up on his perch. Brutus roared defiantly and lifted a paw to show that he was not defeated.

The crowd broke into a wild ovation.

Chase, being a natural showman, reached over suddenly and

grabbed Joy, gave her a kiss, and bowed before her. "Take a bow quick. You saved my bacon. It's great theater."

Joy felt foolish, but she bowed and held her hands up in recognition of the applause.

"That's enough. Let's get 'em out of here," Chase said.

The two of them sent their charges to the tunnel one at a time and then stood together in the center of the cage, holding hands with both arms raised. They both waved and smiled as the applause rolled on and on.

When they stepped outside the cage, Stella was there to greet them. She ignored the crowd and everyone else and threw herself into Chase's arms. "You were wonderful!" she cried and gave him a kiss. This brought another roar from the crowd, even though they did not know who she was.

Joy turned instantly and left the arena. She had barely gotten back to help Doak get the cats quieted when Chase appeared. He came to her with a smile on his face. "You were the best!" he said. "Thanks for saving my life." He put his arms around her and would have kissed her if she hadn't pushed him away.

"Go get your hugs and kisses from Stella!"

A hurt look crossed Chase's face. He said nothing but turned away, and when he was out of hearing distance, Doak said, "He was just tryin' to tell ya how fine you were, Miss Joy. Why you want to treat him like that?"

Joy felt tears rise in her eyes, but she blinked them away. "He's got a woman."

"No, he ain't," Doak said firmly. "You ain't seein' clear, Miss Joy. I'm plumb disappointed in you."

Joy wanted to tell Doak he was wrong, but in her anger and hurt, she couldn't speak, so she just turned and walked away stiffly, the triumph of the performance having been spoiled by the scene between Stella and Chase.

★　★　★　★

After the evening performance, Dan invited Joy to take a drive with him. The evening performance had gone better than the afternoon performance. The cats had cooperated, and they had received a tremendous reception from the crowd. But afterward Joy had been cool toward Chase, saying no more than was necessary. Now she wanted to get away from the circus and readily accepted Dan's offer.

The two of them drove around the streets of Atlanta until they found a café that stayed open until midnight. As they sat down, Dan winked at the waitress and said, "What have you got for a celebrity?"

The waitress, a small, perky-looking blonde with enormous blue eyes, stared at him and smiled. "Are you the celebrity?"

"Me? No. She is—Miss Joy Winslow, the most famous and daring wild-animal tamer in the world."

"Aw, you're puttin' me on," the waitress said doubtfully. "She ain't no animal tamer."

"Sure she is." Darvo reached into his shirt pocket, pulled out some tickets, and gave two of them to the girl. "You come out tomorrow night with your boyfriend, and you'll see this young lady here in a cage with thirty wild tigers and lions. It'll scare you to death."

"Gee, I wouldn't do that for a million dollars!"

Joy smiled at Darvo. "This is the real hero here. This is Captain Dan Darvo, the human cannonball. Shot out of a cannon, he flies a hundred and thirty feet through the air into a wet sponge."

The two had fun teasing the waitress, and after she had taken their order, Dan slumped down in his chair. "After a show I always feel pretty limp, don't you?"

"Absolutely boneless," Joy nodded. "But you've been at it so long."

"It never changes. Something can always go wrong. Why, last week I nearly got crunched between Nell and Alice. I got in the wrong place, and those two bulls just about crushed me."

The two talked show business for a while. Dan was enjoying his return to the human cannonball act now that his broken bones were completely healed and Travis had left to go to Bible school. He was grateful that Joy's brother had been able to fill in like that, but he was glad to have his old job back. After their food came, Dan dug in with enthusiasm. He saw, however, that Joy was not eating, and he asked, "What's the matter, doll?"

"Oh, nothing," she said, picking idly at a french fry.

"You're out with a good-lookin' guy like me, the best date in the whole circus, and you're down in the mouth? I know what's wrong with you."

"No, you don't."

"Yes, I do." Dan took a big bite of the steak before him, chewed it for a moment, then swallowed. "You're sad because you know you're never going to get me to marry you."

Joy couldn't help laughing. "Well, you've got some ego, Dan Darvo. I'll say that for you."

"I've got your number, Joy. You're the marrying kind. Not what I'm looking for."

"I know that, Dan, but you'll find a woman you'll really fall for someday. Then you'll marry her and live happily ever after."

"Do you really believe that storybook stuff?"

"It can happen. Look at Pete and Ann."

"You got me there. They're just like honeymooners all the time, but folks like that don't come along very often." He picked up his coffee cup, swirled the black liquid around, and stared into it, then finally looked up with a serious expression. "You're wasting your time with me, Joy. I like you, but it's pretty clear that your heart's someplace else," he said softly.

Confused by this, Joy said, "I don't know what you're talking about."

"Sure you do."

"Let's talk about something else."

"No, let's talk about this. You're in love with Chase, and you're mad because Stella is trying to draw him in."

Joy could not answer for a moment. "Is that what everyone's saying?"

"Not everyone's as smart and as observant as I am." Dan smiled. He put his hand over hers and squeezed it. "You can tell Uncle Dan. It's just between us. Think of me as your father."

"I don't think I'd trust you quite that far, Dan. Besides, what if he still loves her? He certainly acts like he does."

"You're a pretty smart girl, Joy, but I think you're reading him wrong." Dan released her hand and picked up the cup again, but he did not drink from it. His face serious, as it rarely was, he said, "He doesn't love Stella."

"He's got a funny way of showing it. He's at her trailer all the time."

"You think that's because he wants to be there?"

"Of course."

"You're wrong about that. Look, I know Chase pretty well. I knew him before, and there was a time when he would have stuck his head in the fire for Stella. He was crazy gone on her, but let me tell you. I don't know how to say this exactly, but it was a thing—well, it was a thing of the flesh. They were on fire for each other, and I guess Stella still is. She's got a lot of passion in her, and she wants to kindle the ashes up again, so she's out to build a fire in her old flame."

Joy stared at Gypsy Dan. There was a deep wisdom in his eyes, and she knew he understood people. He had told her once that he was a real gypsy, that he could read the fate of people in their palms. She did not believe this, of course, but she believed that his natural intelligence and years spent in the midst of the circus world had given him special insight. "I think you're wrong, Dan. I think he loves her."

"No, he doesn't, but she does have a power over him. You think a man can just walk away from a woman when she doesn't want him to?"

"Of course."

"Well, you're wrong about that. I don't know what it is, but a man can be the strongest guy in the world. He can weigh two hundred pounds and be able to pick up the back end of a truck, but a little woman weighing a hundred and ten pounds can make him do anything she wants him to. Women have that kind of power over men, and Stella's using it. She'll get him, too, if you don't wake up."

Joy stared at Dan. "What are you talking about?"

"I mean you've got to use what you've got, babe. You've got the advantage. You work with Chase every day, and he feels something for you. It's obvious. Right now he's in kind of a daze. Oh, I know he's gotten off on some religious kick, and I think it's real, but from what I understand even God's good guys get in trouble. You remember your brother preached about Joseph when that woman was after him? She tried everything she could, and most guys would have fallen right into it. Joseph was smart

278

to run away, but Chase can't run. This is his life. So if I were you, I'd wiggle a little curve at him and flutter my eyes. That's what I'd do if I were you."

"I wouldn't want any man I'd have to trap or chase."

"You don't have to trap him or chase him, but you have to give him a sign. Let him know you're interested. Chase doesn't think of you as his woman because you haven't given him a sign. Give it to him, Joy, give it to him."

When Joy got home that night she made an entry in her journal:

March 2, 1929
Dan took me out tonight and told me I should try to win Chase, but he's not right. He doesn't know as much as he thinks he does. Chase is still in love with Stella. He may not know it himself, but I know it, and I think she knows it. I can never let him know that I'm in love with him.

★　★　★　★

Two weeks later Joy celebrated her nineteenth birthday, but this time there was no time for a party. Several of the performers, remembering last year's celebration, came by to give her a hug, including Chase. She thanked him for his greeting, but felt the wall that had come between them. She remembered, on her seventeenth birthday, how he had given her the fountain pen, and on her eighteenth the silver ring with the turquoise setting. She still wore the ring, and she used the pen almost every day, and it grieved her that they weren't as close as they once had been. Their work brought them together constantly, but the closeness and affection they had shared at one time were gone.

She was even beginning to think that Gypsy Dan had been right. She could see now that Chase was fighting against his natural inclinations. Everyone was waiting for the time when he would go to Stella's trailer—and not come out until morning. That had not yet happened, and Joy was fiercely grateful for it.

★　★　★　★

All that spring and into the summer, the big-cat act went spectacularly well, so well in fact that a well-known weekly news magazine, the *Mid-Week Pictorial*, took pictures of Joy and Chase and put out a big spread. Everybody read the *Mid-Week Pictorial*, so the circus began playing to packed-out crowds as people came to see the famous duo.

Joy was excited by the attention she had gotten in every town now since the magazine had pictured their act and written a lot of nonsense about them and their private lives. She took great delight in the performances themselves. The coolness between her and Chase had not improved, however.

They arrived in Springfield, Illinois, on July tenth. They were scheduled to be there for five days, and the people of Springfield turned out in huge numbers. Every performance, even the matinee, was a straw crowd—every seat full.

After the last performance on their second day in Springfield, she had come down off of Ruth and started toward her trailer when a voice caught her attention. "Miss Winslow—!"

She turned to see a tall middle-aged man approaching her. The well-dressed man took off his hat, revealing his bright red hair with some streaks of gray in it. Joy was accustomed to people seeking her out after every show, but she was tired and purposed to cut the conversation short.

"My name is Tom Winslow. You don't know me, but I think we may be related. Are your parents Bill and Elaine?"

Joy responded, "Why, yes. Tom Winslow—you must be my dad's brother."

"That's right. I met you when you were about six years old, but I haven't seen you since. I'm sorry about that."

"My dad talked about you a lot. He said you two were real close when you were young."

"That's right." Tom Winslow shook his head sadly. "One of the griefs of my life is that after Bill left home, we never saw each other again—and we never wrote. How are your parents?"

"You didn't hear?" Joy said, stunned that he would not even know about her family's deaths. "My parents and younger sister were killed in an automobile wreck—over three years ago on my sixteenth birthday."

Shock ran across Winslow's face. "I'm so sorry to hear that," he murmured.

People were crowding around trying to get Joy's attention. "This isn't a good place to talk," she said, "but I would like to talk with you."

"That's why I came. I read the article about you and your partner in *Mid-Week Pictorial*, and I wondered if you were my niece. I had to come to find out for sure. Could we go out and have a late supper maybe?"

"That would be fine."

★   ★   ★   ★

Joy found herself liking Tom Winslow very much. She learned a lot about him while they ate. He was a lawyer, she discovered, and his children, James and Miriam, were the same ages as Travis and she. He told her about some of her other relatives. "My sister Betsy is married to a man named Wesley Stone, and they have a son named Heck. My sister Lanie is married to Lobo Smith. Their son, Logan, was an ace in the war. Shot down twenty-nine planes."

"Why, I've read about Logan Smith! They called him Cowboy Smith."

"That's him. We're all very proud of Logan. He married a Frenchwoman named Danielle Laurent. They're very happy now living in this country. And, of course, there's my brother Phil. He was always a favorite of your father's. They were very close, but Phil and his wife live in France most of the time. He's a famous painter now. And that leaves my brother John. He married a woman named Jeanine Quintana. They're missionaries in Africa and have two children." He leaned forward and said, "So you really have a big family."

"And I don't know any of them. Why did Dad separate himself from all of you? Do you know, Mr. Winslow?"

"Just Tom's fine. He got into a little trouble when he was a young man. It was just foolishness, and most of it wasn't his fault, but he always felt like an outcast, so he left. We all tried to talk him out of leaving, but he was hurt by what he had done to the family and couldn't face us. I think it was a mistake. I always loved your father. We all did."

"I wish we could have been closer."

Tom Winslow answered, "That's one reason why I came to meet you, Joy. We're having a family reunion at my house right here in Springfield in two days. The circus will still be here. Could you come and meet your family?"

Joy smiled, and her heart seemed to grow warm. "If all the family's like you, I would like it very much."

"Then you'll come?"

"Yes, I will."

"Good, and I'll make sure that the whole bunch comes to the circus to see the star of our family under the big top!"

CHAPTER TWENTY-TWO

TWO WOMEN

★ ★ ★ ★

As Chase pulled up in front of the large house set well back in an emerald yard shaded by huge oak trees, he said, "Well, looks like you've got some rich relatives."

"I guess they must be," Joy said nervously. "I really don't know whether we should have come or not."

Chase turned to stare at her. "Of course you should've come. They're your family. Come on, let's go on in."

Heartened by Chase's encouragement, Joy got out of the car, and the two of them walked up to the porch of the big house. It was a colonial-style brick house with dormers, white shutters, and four white columns in the front. When Chase rang the bell the door opened at once, and the tall redheaded man said, "Well, if it's not my niece. Come in, Joy."

Joy stepped inside and said, "This is Chase Hardin."

"Oh yes, I know that!" Tom took Chase's hand and shook it firmly. "We're so glad you could come. Come on in. Your family is anxious to meet you."

The next hour was almost like a kaleidoscope for Joy. She met Lanie Winslow Smith and her husband, Lobo, and was fascinated by both of them. Lobo wore a patch over one eye, but the other was a bright indigo. She discovered that he had been very close to being an outlaw in Oklahoma Territory but had turned honest and become a federal marshal after he married Lanie. Betsy Winslow Stone and her husband, Wesley, were there, along with their son, Heck. Joy was surprised to see Phil Winslow, a tall, fine-looking man with his beautiful wife, Cara, and their three children, Brian, Kevin, and Paige. Phil said to Joy, "I'd love to paint you in your circus costume sometime—maybe in action with your big cats."

"You should take him up on his offer, Joy," Tom said. "He's selling so many paintings, you'd be known everywhere!"

"I would love for you to pose for me, Joy," Phil said.

"Well, I don't know, Phil. The circus moves around constantly."

"Well, so do we, but I'm sure we can work something out."

Joy met many other Winslows there, including Barney and Andrew with their wives, all missionaries in Africa and home on leave for a month, and so many others that finally Tom said, "Your head must be swimming, Joy. Come on, we all want to hear about you."

Joy found herself telling her story, leaving out much of it. They were all fascinated with the fact that she was a wild-cat tamer, and she was quick to say, "It's Chase who's the real tamer. I'm just a beginner."

"Don't believe a word of it," Chase said. "She's come further in a year than I came in five. She's going to be the most famous of the Winslows."

Later they gathered in the big dining room for dinner, and Tom Winslow asked the blessing. They enjoyed a fine meal, and when they were finished, Tom said, "We have a presentation for you, Joy." He held up a finely bound leather book and said, "This is the journal of Gilbert Winslow, our family ancestor who first settled in America." He ran his hands over the cover and shook his head. "We've had good Winslows and bad, but I'm hoping and believing that Gilbert sees from heaven that some of his family loved God almost as much as he did." He walked over and gave the book to Joy and said, "God bless you. Welcome to the family."

Joy took the book and felt her eyes grow misty. She murmured her thanks but could say little. Other members of the family then began to talk about their ancestors, and Joy was amazed at the variety of Winslows who had served God and man. Some of them were judges, some were governors, three were senators, and several were college professors. All of them who spoke, however, stressed the fact that they all loved and served Jesus Christ.

★   ★   ★   ★

"I'd like to talk to you alone for a moment, Tom," Joy said after dinner.

Tom suggested they go to his study. "You've made a hit with the family, Joy. Everybody loves you."

"It's . . . it's good to know I have a family. I've missed out on so much."

"Yes, you have, but now that we know how to find you, it'll be easier to keep in touch." Being a good lawyer, Tom knew when to be silent, and now he waited for Joy to tell him what was on her mind.

"I haven't told you everything about what happened to my parents. My uncle Albert—that's my mother's sister Opal's husband—he cheated us out of everything. . . ."

Tom Winslow stood silently, his quick mind registering everything she said. When she finally finished, he asked, "So you believe he was dishonest about the sale of your dad's place?"

"I know he was. As soon as the place was sold, he suddenly had a lot of money, and he bought a big new car. I know he robbed us of our inheritance. And they took all the furniture, and all of Mom and Dad's and Dawn's personal things are up in their attic, and they wouldn't even let us have those things."

"And you want me to help you with this?"

"Could you please, Uncle Tom?"

"Of course. I'll see what I can do. I'll have one of my assistants look into it, and then maybe I'll make a little trip myself and see what can be done toward recovering your property."

★   ★   ★   ★

". . . so Uncle Tom said he would look into it, and I think he'll be able to get back what Albert stole from us."

Chase listened as Joy spoke passionately. He could feel the bitterness in her spirit, and he knew she had never shaken off her unforgiving spirit toward Albert Tatum. "Well, I hope you can get your things back. I know it's been bothering you for years."

Finally they pulled up in front of the trailer that Joy now had to herself since Ella had married. She sat there a moment and continued to speak of the Winslows. "It's so good to have a family, Chase. I used to feel that I didn't have anybody."

"Well, you have somebody now. Those Winslows—they're wonderful people."

As they sat there talking, Joy remembered what Dan had said to her months earlier about showing Chase how much she cared for him. Joy was actually more experienced in fighting men off than in enticing them, but she turned and touched Chase's arm, saying, "Thank you, Chase, for going with me tonight."

Chase was silent for a moment. Her touch and her soft voice were a sudden switch from her coldness toward him the last few months. She surprised him even more when she reached up and touched his cheek, whispering, "I'll never forget all the help you've been to me."

Chase saw the faint color staining Joy's cheeks. Her signal was coming through clearly, like a melody on a calm day. He pulled her toward him, as a man reaches for something he might lose. She smiled up at him, and he felt desire for this woman flow through him. But it was not like his desire for Stella House—that was simply a strong physical attraction, and he did not feel right about it. He wondered now if what he felt for Joy was love. Maybe she did love him after all. That seemed to be the message coming through in her eyes. Yet she seemed hesitant to fully surrender to those feelings, and he did not want to push her.

As for Joy, she sat near him, wanting him in a way she had wanted no other man. She longed to throw caution to the wind and tell him she loved him. Timidly at first, then with more courage, she reached up, put her arms around his neck, and whispered, "There's nobody like you, Chase."

Chase knew it was not easy for her to say those words, and it touched him deeply. Holding her in his arms, he kissed her, and over the lengthening moment he felt her surrender to him. Finally when she pulled away, she was silently crying, and he held her tightly with her head resting on his shoulder. He knew then that no other woman would ever stir him quite like this one. She was rich in a way a woman should be, and she was so much more complex than Stella. Stella was very attractive physically, but this girl was beautiful like a symphony that makes a man feel strong enough to whip the world.

"Joy," he whispered, "you're so sweet. You're like a drink of water to a thirsty man." He kissed her again and drew her closer, forgetful of his own strength. He held her so tightly it almost hurt her, but she did not draw back.

Joy did not understand all she was feeling at that moment, but she now admitted to herself that she was in love with Chase Hardin and she believed he was with her. She felt confident now that Stella was no longer a threat. She rested quietly in his arms and waited for him to say something, but he was silent. Finally she drew back and looked at him. His expression seemed troubled. "What is it, Chase?"

Clearing his throat, he said, "I . . . I think you'd better go inside."

"Why? What's the matter?" Joy's heart started beating faster. She was afraid that maybe she'd read him wrong after all. *Did I just make an utter fool of myself?*

Chase hesitated. "I . . . I'm just not the man you think I am, Joy. Please go in now."

Her fear turned to hurt, which turned to anger. She stared at him in disbelief. Had the embrace meant nothing to him? She had exposed her soul in a way she had never done with any other man, and all he could say was that she should go inside?

Without another word she got out of the car, slammed the door shut, and ran into her trailer. She threw herself down on the couch and fought back the tears. "He doesn't care! He's in love with that awful woman. He doesn't care that I love him!"

★   ★   ★   ★

Chase had borrowed Stella's car to take Joy to the reunion. He needed to return the keys, but he didn't want to see Stella. When he knocked on the door of her trailer, she answered immediately and said, "You're late."

Chase handed her the keys. She took them, but she could tell something was different about him. He seemed agitated . . . and she suspected it had something to do with Joy. She put her hand on his chest and held it there firmly. "We were everything to each other once. Don't you remember?"

Chase looked down, unable to meet her eyes. "Yes," he said, "I haven't forgotten."

"Then why are you fighting it? We had something very few people have. We can have it again. We can get married if that's what you want, but I want you under any circumstances."

Chase felt as though a tornado were rushing through his mind. He felt again the power that she had over him physically, and he said, "I can't do that, Stella. I'm a Christian now, and we can't do the things we used to do."

Then she threw her arms around him and kissed him firmly. "You'll never get me out of your system, Chase. You know that as well as I do." She whispered huskily, "We were meant for each other. You can't get away from me, and I can't get away from you."

★   ★   ★   ★

Chicago welcomed Chase and Joy. They played to a full house at every performance, but that was not the best of it for Joy. Travis, who was enrolled at the Moody Bible Institute in Chicago, was there for every performance, and the two of them spent every available moment together. Now as they sat in Joy's trailer, she told him all about the Winslow family, saying, "I wish you had been there, Travis. You would have loved them."

"Maybe there'll be another reunion sometime that I can go to. I know we've got some preachers in the family. Quite a few."

After discussing the preachers that Joy had heard about, she finally said, "I've got something else to tell you. It's about Albert and the way he robbed us."

Quickly Travis looked up. "What is it? I'd hoped you had for-gotten that."

"I'll never forget it," Joy said bitterly, "and I don't see how you can."

"It doesn't do any good to hate people, and refusing to for-give, as I've told you before, is a bitter pill. You're hurting your-self more than you are Albert."

"Well, you listen to this. I talked to Tom Winslow, and he's a fine lawyer. He's real smart, and he's going to try to help us." She went on to tell him how she had asked Tom to look into the set-tlement of their parents' estate, and she had said with a trium-phant gleam in her eyes, "I hope he finds out what he needs to know to put Albert in jail. I'd like to see him rot there!"

Travis bit his lip. "I hate to hear you talking like this, sis. It's not going to help any."

The next day Travis talked to Chase and told him what Joy had said about Albert Tatum. "I hate to see her this way. A woman should be gentle," Travis said.

"She is in everything except that."

Travis had become very good at reading people, and he sensed something was bothering Chase. "What's wrong with you, Chase?" he asked. "Are you not getting along with Joy?"

"No, I'm not. I've got to tell somebody this. It's Stella. Travis, I thought when a man became a Christian, he'd have an easier time of it, but it's been worse for me."

"Stella giving you a hard time? I saw that a long time ago. Everybody knows what she wants."

"She says we were made for each other, that we couldn't be happy apart, but you and I both know that's not true. I don't know why I'm still drawn to her. I hate myself for even thinking about her, but I feel like I'm losing the fight, Travis. What am I going to do?"

"Well, you remember Joseph? When Potiphar's wife tried to seduce him, he just ran out."

"But I can't do that. I can't just leave the circus. What would happen to Joy if I did?"

Travis was glad that Chase was concerned for Joy's welfare, and he said, "I'm glad that you know this feeling you have for Stella is just a physical thing. It's no secret that men have trouble with that, but you're going to win. I'm going to pray for you, and you're going to pray for yourself, and both of us are going to pray for Joy. This hatred she has for Albert Tatum is an evil thing too. She'll have to beat it, or it will destroy her."

★   ★   ★   ★

Two days after this conversation Joy met Travis after the performance with an excited look in her eyes. "A man from Hollywood was here this morning. He's thinking about using Chase and me in a feature film."

"Would that make you happy, Joy?"

"Well, of course it would. It would give us a lot of money too. Chase doesn't want to do it, though, and I don't think they'll do it with just me."

"Joy, I wish you wouldn't think so much about money. I wish you'd think more about the Lord."

The words stung, and she said, "You need money to get through school, don't you?"

"I do, but I'll get through school one way or another. They'll help me at the institute. It's just another sign that the world's getting its hooks into you. You're getting hard, Joy. You're not the nice girl who used to be my sister. I hate to see it."

This conversation with Travis disturbed Joy more than anything had in years. She respected him and loved him, and as much as she didn't want to admit it, she knew he was right. She took her frustration out on Chase that very evening. With her mind on other things, she performed badly in the cage, leaving herself vulnerable to danger. Later, back at the menagerie, when Chase tried to gently remind her that her full concentration was required in the cage, she said, "I don't have to listen to you. Here you are a big Christian and sleeping with your boss!" The words popped out before she could call them back, and she saw that they hit Chase like a physical blow.

"No, I'm not," he said quietly, then turned and walked away. She wanted to call after him, but it was too late, and the opportunity was gone.

What's happening to me? she cried silently. *I'm getting mean, just like Travis says, and I'm losing Chase. I thought all this success would make me happy, but it's not.*

★ ★ ★ ★

"Your name's what?"

"Tom Winslow. I'm a relative of yours, Mrs. Tatum."

"A relative? Why, how in the world is that?"

"Well, only in a roundabout way. Your sister Elaine was married to my brother Bill. I guess that makes us kinfolk in a way."

The Tatums stared at the man with the graying red hair. "What are you here for, Mr. Winslow?"

"I'm afraid I have a rather serious matter to bring to your attention, Mr. Tatum."

"What kind of a matter?" Tatum stood very straight, but there was a frightened look in his eyes, and he had turned pale.

"I'm an attorney, and I've been here for two days now, going through the records at the courthouse and doing a little investigating. I hate to tell you this, but I have evidence that you have committed a felony."

"What are you talking about?" Opal cried out. "You can't say that about Albert!"

"I'm afraid I have to. I have evidence that my brother's farm sold for fifty-two thousand dollars. The mortgage on it was only for thirty-two. That meant a profit of twenty thousand dollars. According to the law," Tom said carefully, "and my brother's will, the three children were to share the proceeds equally. Since Dawn was killed with her parents, that means the survivors, Joy and Travis, should have received ten thousand dollars each, and the personal property belonged to them as well, including this furniture." He saw that his words had struck Tatum so that he could not speak. "Where's the money, Mr. Tatum?"

Tatum glanced wildly at his wife, and she could see that his hands were trembling. "You get out of my house!"

"I'll do that, of course, but I must warn you it would be much easier if you would pay up."

"I'm paying nothing!"

"I'm going to try hard," Tom Winslow said, "to convince my

niece not to put you in jail, and I can tell you as an attorney, you don't have a chance of escaping it. You falsified records and embezzled twenty thousand dollars from my nephew and niece. I'm going to see justice done. If you'll pay the money and give up the furniture and the personal effects, I'll try to convince them not to prosecute you on a criminal charge."

Albert shook his head. "Get out of my house!"

"Very well. If you want it that way, I'm sorry."

As soon as Tom Winslow left and the door slammed, Opal said, "You never told me about this, Albert. We've got to give them their money back."

"I did it for their own good. I invested the money. I intended to pay it back."

Opal Tatum knew her husband. "I don't think you're telling the truth, Albert," she said sadly, tears in her eyes. "And now you're going to jail if you don't pay the money back."

"I . . . I don't have it, Opal! I've invested it in stocks, and they're rising every day."

"You'll have to sell them, and you'll have to go to Travis and Joy and beg for mercy."

"I'll never do that!"

"Then you'll go to jail, and we'll lose this place." Opal Tatum looked at her husband with pain in her eyes. "I hope the kids and I can find jobs so we can make a living, because that's what we're going to have to do—while you're in prison."

CHAPTER TWENTY-THREE

DISASTER!

★ ★ ★ ★

The circus pulled into St. Louis for a five-day run on September twenty-third. In the two months that had passed since the day Chase and Joy had shared a kiss and admitted their attraction to one another, neither one of them had been bold enough to bring up the subject of their relationship. It seemed they were destined to be stuck in this strained awkwardness forever. Joy was grateful that at least when they were working, the cats required their full attention, so casual conversation was not expected, nor even possible.

The crowds in St. Louis were better than ever, and both Chase and Joy were delighted to discover that Tom Winslow came to see the show on their third day in town. He came to the menagerie after the act and greeted the two with a smile. "You're getting better," he said. "I wouldn't get into one of those cages if you gave me the city of Chicago."

"What a surprise to see you here, Tom!" Chase said.

"I've been working on a case here for the last two weeks, but I think we've finally got it settled. I need to talk to Joy. Is there someplace we could go? You're welcome to join us, Chase."

"We could go to my trailer. Just let us get the cats settled down."

Tom Winslow watched with interest as the two spoke to every animal and fed them. "I would think you'd feed them *before* the act. Then they wouldn't be so likely to come after you," he remarked.

Joy laughed. "What do you feel like after you've eaten a big meal?"

"If it's real big, I'm hardly able to move."

"That's the way the cats would be. They'd be sluggish, and we want them to be lively out there to put on a good show."

"I never thought of that."

As soon as the cats were filled up with horsemeat, the three went to the trailer. Joy fixed coffee, and the three sat around her little dining table while Tom told them about several members of the Winslow family, for he saw Joy was interested. "My wife keeps up with most of the Winslows, and she's written letters to everybody telling about our new discovery. Joy Winslow, wild-animal tamer! We're all proud of you, Joy."

Joy flushed. "Well, I'm proud to be a part of this family. I've been reading Gilbert Winslow's journal you gave me, and it's the most exciting thing I've ever read in my life. He was some man, wasn't he?"

"Yes, he was," Tom said. "I don't know if there'll ever be another quite like him."

The talk went on for some time, and finally Tom said, "By the way, I hope you two haven't put any money in stocks."

Chase grinned. "Stocks! We're lucky to pay the meat bill for the cats. Why? Do you think something's wrong with the market?"

Tom Winslow's face grew very serious. "Haven't you been keeping up with the news?"

"It's hard to keep up with the news when we're on the road all the time. But what's this about the stock market? Isn't that something for rich men to worry about?"

"Is there something wrong with it, Tom?" Joy wanted to know.

"Nothing you can put your finger on exactly, but it seems this country's going crazy." Tom Winslow sipped the coffee that was in front of him and shook his head with disgust. "Everybody's trying to get rich. They're buying up stocks like there's no tomorrow, and a lot of people are making a killing. But I just think this boom in the stock market can't last."

"Why can't it last?"

"Since Hoover was elected, this bull market, as they call it, has smashed every record. I just wanted to warn you not to sink any money into it. I don't trust the good times to last. You can go broke real quick, and that's what's going to happen, I'm afraid, to a lot of people."

"That reminds me," Joy said suddenly. "I'll bet Albert has sunk money into it—*our* money!"

Tom looked at her with a level gaze. "That's why I came to talk to you. I went to see them, Joy."

"You did! What did you tell them?"

"Actually, I went to see them last summer when I had a few days off. Since then I've had some other business that has kept me occupied, but now I have some time I can devote to your problem. When I was up there I did a lot of investigation, but it didn't take long. I found out that your uncle cleared about twenty thousand dollars on the sale of your dad's place—I've got it in black and white."

"What did you tell him?" Joy demanded.

"I laid it out flat. I told him that he would have to pay the money back and also that he would have to give you your furniture and any other property that belonged to your parents."

"I bet he refused, didn't he."

"Well, that's what he did. I told him he'd go to jail because he committed embezzlement. A felony like that could get a fellow twenty years."

"Good!" Joy exclaimed and struck the table with her fist. "I hope he goes for life."

"Wait a minute, Joy," Chase said. "You don't mean that."

"Well, of course, I mean it! He's done wrong, and he ought to pay for it."

"There's a verse in the psalms," Chase said quietly, "that says, 'If thou, Lord, shouldest mark iniquities, O Lord, who shall stand?' "

Joy shook her head, her mouth set in a defiant expression. "I'm sure that makes sense to you, Chase, but all I know is I want that man put in jail. He deserves it."

Tom was unhappy with her decision—Joy could see that plainly—but she insisted on going after the Tatums. "You can take your fee out of the money when he pays it to us."

"There won't be any fee, Joy. This is a family matter," Tom said gently.

After he left, Chase said, "Travis won't agree with you. We talked about it the last time I saw him."

"Travis is too soft."

"I don't think it's soft to be forgiving, Joy."

"We're going to get what's coming to us and so is Albert Tatum, and I don't want to talk about it anymore!"

★　★　★　★

After the meeting with Tom Winslow, Joy found herself preoccupied with the wrongs done to her by Albert Tatum. She thought about it constantly. A couple of weeks later she received a letter from Travis telling her that Tom had written to him and described the situation. Travis wrote: *Don't get hard about this, sis. You and I have done things ourselves we wouldn't want put on the front page of the newspaper. The Bible says to forgive your enemies, and I think that's what you should do.*

Joy had ignored the letter and had gone about her work. When the show moved on to Springfield, Missouri, the quality of her work began to suffer. Chase noticed this and knew the reason, but she did not pay any heed to him.

It was on the second night in Springfield that something happened that all animal trainers dread worse than anything else. The act had gone well, and the crowd had been warm and receptive. Joy and Chase took their bows, but as they were leaving the cage, they heard someone yelling behind the canvas where the tunnel led from the big cage.

"Something's wrong!" Chase said. He broke into a run, and Joy followed him. They met Doak, whose eyes were wide with fear. "Somebody left the doors open, and three of the tigers got out!"

Joy went cold with fear. She was afraid of what would happen if other people encountered these large wild animals and did not know what to do.

"Where are they, Doak?"

"Two of them went that way and one went that way." Doak pointed in different directions.

"I'll take the two. You take that one, Joy."

"All right," Joy said. She raced away, and the thought crossed her mind, *I wonder how he can take care of two? One is enough.*

She had no idea what to do. She began to walk around the edge of the big top, searching everywhere. Since it was nighttime, she knew the tiger had the advantage, for cats could see much better than humans in the dark. She moved cautiously, carrying only the training stick in her hand. She had gone halfway around the tent when she caught a flash of movement between two of the trucks.

She moved forward slowly, and when she had cleared the front of the truck, she saw the glowing eyes of a tiger, reflecting in the dim lights overhead. Her heart sank when she realized she had encountered Brutus. She heard people over to her left and knew that if Brutus turned that way, he would encounter people who were moving back and forth between the tent and the refreshment stand. She moved to put herself between the cat and the crowd and heard the rumble of the big cat. She had never really handled Brutus. Chase had said he was too dangerous for her to handle until she had more experience. She had no choice now, however, and she moved forward, talking as Chase had taught her. "There's a good tiger. Come on now, Brutus. We're going to go back in the cage. Wouldn't you like a bit of nice horsemeat? Come on, Brutus, you're going to be all right."

Brutus eyed her steadily and switched his tail, but then he crouched slightly. Joy had enough experience to know that this was a danger sign. She knew that if they were in the familiar cage and one of the cats crouched, she would rap the tiger with the training stick or reprimand it vocally, and the cat would obey.

But here outside the cage everything was different. Brutus drew his lips back, but in the semidarkness it didn't look anything like a smile. It was frightening to stand there in front of the five-hundred-pound tiger with claws that could rip flesh off the bone in a flash, but Joy was determined not to show any signs of fear.

Keeping her voice steady, Joy edged forward, knowing that no tiger could be pushed into doing something it didn't want to do. Brutus was probably as nervous as Joy was, and he crouched even lower as Joy advanced an inch at a time. "All right, Brutus, be a good boy. Come on now, we're going to go back and get in the cage."

Brutus suddenly whirled and turned to his left and made one of those magnificent leaps that tigers are capable of. *At least he's headed back in the right direction,* Joy thought. She dashed after him and then stopped abruptly when she saw he had stopped and whirled to face her again. "Come on, boy, you're going in the right direction. Go this way." She continued to speak strongly but gently and showed no fear. As she advanced, Brutus swung from side to side, and she thought he was going to charge. But then he moved back in the direction of the cages.

The two seesawed back and forth. When Brutus tried to move to the left, Joy would step that way and wave the training stick with a stern command. "No, not this way, Brutus!" When he moved to the right, she did the same thing. It was like herding a recalcitrant kitten, except this kitten carried death in his jaws and razor-sharp claws.

How long this went on Joy didn't know, but it seemed like forever. Finally she reached the menagerie. She saw Doak appear, and he nodded at her and said quietly, "Mr. Chase has got the other two. He's comin' to help."

Relief washed through Joy, and she even heard herself breathing the words, "Thank you, God."

Joy never knew what it was that set Brutus off. They were almost to Brutus's cage when, without warning, the big cat leaped straight at her. She had no time to dodge, and she cried out, "Back, Brutus!" and struck at him. But he slashed at her with his mighty front paw and caught her on the leg. She felt the flesh tear and heard her slacks rip, and before she knew it, she was under the animal. Reacting instinctively now, she dropped the stick and punched his nose as hard as she could. That hurt the cat enough to make him rear back, and as he retreated, she felt the heat of his breath and saw the gaping red mouth and savage teeth.

Then she heard Chase, who had thought to grab his whip. He popped it at Brutus's nose, which startled the beast, and herded him into the cage. Joy rolled over and tried to sit up, despite the searing pain in her leg, but immediately felt light-headed and lay back down. Doak ran to her side and said, "Are you all right, Miss Joy?"

"No, Doak, he got my leg," she whispered as she felt the blood pouring out. She heard the sound of metal on metal as Chase closed the doors of the cage. Almost at once he was back, his face pale.

"How bad is it?"

"It's pretty bad, I think." The pain was coming now in waves, and Chase scooped her up, saying, "We'll have to get you to the hospital."

As Joy clung to Chase she knew she had escaped death by an eyelash, and as his feet pounded on the hard ground, she felt secure in his arms. She held on to him, thinking, *It must have been God. I would have been dead if Chase hadn't come when he did.*

★　★　★　★

Several nights later Dr. Knox was bent over examining Joy's leg. Chase stood over to his left. Joy was so sick she could hardly hold her head up. Chase came over and took her hand. "You all right, Joy?"

"Not really," Joy whispered. "I haven't been able to keep anything down all day." She looked at Dr. Knox and said, "Is my leg all right?"

Knox was a big, burly man with a thick southern accent. "No, it's not all right," he said quietly. "It's not healing properly. I thought we had it all taken care of the night you were brought in, but something has gone wrong. Your leg is badly infected. I'm afraid it could be blood poisoning. That may be what's causing all the nausea."

Fear gripped Joy's heart, and she tightened her grip on Chase's hand. "What . . . what can you do about it?"

Dr. Knox did not answer for a moment. He chewed his lip and said, "We'll take good care of you, but I must warn you that you might get a lot sicker before you get better."

Joy groaned. She couldn't imagine being much sicker. She hesitated to ask the question that was now on her mind. "Doctor . . . am I going to die?"

"I don't want to be that pessimistic, Miss Winslow, but in all honesty, this is indeed very, very serious. But we'll do everything we can."

Joy closed her eyes as another wave of nausea swept over her.

"I've sent for a colleague of mine from St. Louis. He's a specialist in these matters. If anybody can help, it's him."

"Don't worry, Joy," Chase said, "God will be with you. You'll be up and out of here before you know it."

Joy felt tears form in her eyes, and the vision of Chase's face swarmed so that she could not see him clearly. "Stay with me, Chase," she pleaded. "Don't leave me."

"Don't worry. The circus can do without me. They pulled out yesterday."

Joy sank back on the pillow, but she clung to Chase's hand. "Don't leave me," she whispered again, and then she descended into the darkness of unconsciousness.

CHAPTER TWENTY-FOUR

HOME AT LAST!

★ ★ ★ ★

The worst sensation was that she was falling from some terrible height—down, down, down into a black hole. She would tense her muscles and brace herself for striking the bottom, and her ears would be filled with the roaring of a tornado. Sometimes she would open her mouth and try to call out, but the howling wind would fill her lungs, stifling her cry.

Sometimes there would be no sound at all, merely an eerie quietness that seemed to have its own tiny echo deep inside. And with the quietness there would come a light—soft and gentle—bathing her in a warmth that drove away the bone-cracking chill that wracked her.

Sometimes she would dream she was on fire, her body parched with the scorching heat, but then when the heat became unbearable she would feel a coolness come over her face, and cool moisture would bathe her burning body, washing away the pain and the fear.

More than anything she had the feeling she was drowning, trapped under a horrible weight far beneath the surface, swallowed in darkness. More than once she almost broke through but would always sink back into the stygian blackness. In that dark abyss she learned to distinguish, somehow, between the hands that touched her and the voices that spoke to her. One voice and one touch was more soothing and more comforting than the rest. The voice would seem to call her up out of the dark pit, and although she couldn't understand the words, she knew this one was trying to help her.

And then everything changed. She rose out of the darkness and opened her eyes cautiously. Memory came rushing back, and although she tried to speak, her lips were terribly dry. She finally whispered, "Chase—" and saw his eyes open wide. He leaned over her and put his hand on her brow. It seemed cool, and she tried to speak.

"Wait a minute. Let me get you some water."

Joy lay there and heard the sound of water pouring. It was the most beautiful sound she had ever heard, and then his hand was behind her head and she felt the coldness of the glass and gulped the water down, grasping at the glass with her hands. The water spilled down the sides of her mouth and ran down her neck, and that felt good.

"Take it easy. Just little swallows at a time."

She stopped obediently, and he held her firmly until she had drained the glass. "You can have some more in a minute," he said. He put the glass down, then leaned over her. "How do you feel?"

"I've been so far away. . . ." She looked around the room. "How . . . long have I been here?"

"Not long," he said quickly. "You've been having a hard time, though."

Joy said, "Could I have some more water?"

"Sure."

She drank again and then said, "I remember coming to the hospital, but I got so sick."

"You have been pretty sick, Joy."

Joy looked down and said, "My leg. I remember. Brutus clawed me, didn't he?"

"Yes, he did." She saw him hesitate; then he said, "The wound got infected. You've had a very high fever. We've all been worried about you."

Joy studied him and saw that he looked pale and drawn. Her eyes went to the clock on the wall. It was almost two o'clock.

From the sun streaming in the window, she knew it was afternoon. "Why aren't you doing the act? It's time for the matinee."

Chase laughed softly and took one of her hands in his, saying, "The circus will have to wait."

Joy tried to understand this, but confusion swept through her. "Does Travis know I'm in the hospital?"

"I called him to let him know. He came down as soon as he heard about the accident, and he's been here most of the time. I sent him back to the trailer to get a little sleep. The city said we could keep one of the smallest circus trailers on the grounds for as long as you're here."

"But what about school? He'll be missing classes."

"His professors were very understanding and told him to stay as long as he needs to."

She finally asked the question that was on her mind, "How's my leg?"

He said quietly, "It has a pretty bad infection, Joy. That's why you had such a high fever."

Joy considered his answer, but then saw that he was fidgeting and avoiding eye contact. "How bad is it?"

"The doctors aren't happy."

"Would you help me sit up?"

For a moment Chase hesitated, then said, "I guess it'd be all right." He cranked the bed up, and as it slowly came up into position, she looked down at her leg. She pulled the sheet back and saw that her leg was swathed in bandages. She tried to bend it, and pain shot through her.

"Don't try to move it. Look, Joy, I'm going to go get Dr. Knox. He's here making his rounds."

Before Joy could speak, he turned and left the room. Joy stared at her leg as if it belonged to someone else. She knew there was more to her condition than Chase was telling her, and fear began to nibble at her. This was the first time she had ever been seriously hurt, and it wasn't an experience she intended to repeat.

Dr. Knox came in followed by Chase. Knox approached the bed, saying, "Well, now, you're awake." He put his large, rough hand on her brow and then took her wrist. As he stood there silently, his bright blue eyes studied her, and finally he said,

"You've given us all quite a fright."

"I'm sorry. What's wrong with me?"

Knox did not answer at once, and his hesitation increased the fright that ran through Joy. "What is it?" she cried, and her eyes went to Chase, who was standing slightly behind Dr. Knox.

"The infection in your leg has gotten out of hand. We don't know why. We've tried everything we know to do. We even went in and cleaned out the wounds again, but—"

"What is it?" Joy whispered.

"If the situation doesn't improve soon, we may have to take more . . . well, more serious measures."

Joy lay there staring at him, not wanting to hear the rest but knowing that she must. "What kind of measures, Doctor?"

Knox chewed his lower lip and then, after a moment's silence, said reluctantly, "We may have to amputate the leg, Miss Winslow."

Knox's words struck Joy like a fist, and she stared at him in disbelief. Her eyes went to Chase, and she cried out, "No, Chase, don't let them do it!" She reached out, and Chase shouldered his way past the doctor. He put his arms around her and held her. "It won't happen," he said fiercely. "God won't let it happen!"

Joy clung to him in her weakness, tears running down her cheeks. She could not face the possibility of losing her leg, and she whispered, "Please, Chase, don't let them do it."

★ ★ ★ ★

Joy did not fall back into a coma, but she slept fitfully. From time to time the nurses would wake her for a bath or to give her some medication. Chase was usually there, but once when she opened her eyes, she found Travis, and he went to her side at once. "Hello, sis," he said quietly.

"Travis, they say if my leg doesn't get better they might have to—"

She could not finish the sentence. Even saying the words frightened her.

Travis's grip tightened on her hand, and he said, "We serve a great God, Joy. He's able to do all things. You've got to believe that He's going to do a healing work in you."

Tears began to roll down her face. She cried so easily now, it seemed. "How God must hate me."

"Don't be silly," Travis smiled. "He loves you. You know that."

"But I've been so awful."

"Haven't we all? But Jesus died for awful people. He died for sinners, and that includes us. Don't think about yourself. Think about Him. He died for you."

Joy lay there as Travis spoke comforting words for a long time, mostly quoting Scripture. Finally she said, "I don't have any faith at all."

"God has dealt to every man the measure of faith, Joy, and I have faith, and Chase has faith, and our family has faith. They're all praying for you."

"What family? Who's praying for me?"

"The Winslows. Chase called Tom Winslow, and he got the word out to the family about your accident. So you've got a whole chain of Winslow prayer warriors all over this country, and we even heard from Barney Winslow in Africa. They're all praying for you."

Joy closed her eyes and held tightly to Travis's hand. She said no more, but as she drifted off again into sleep, somehow the intolerable burden seemed to have lightened.

★   ★   ★   ★

When Joy awakened, it was dark in the room except for the light coming in from the hallway. She saw Chase standing by the window looking into the darkness. She whispered his name, and he turned quickly and came to her.

"Am I any better, Chase?"

"No, the leg's still got the doctors puzzled. They don't know why it's not healing."

"I don't know either."

Chase put his hand on her head and stroked her hair gently. "Sometimes," he said finally, "God gets our attention through difficult circumstances. When we won't listen to Him, He has to stop us for our own good. I've been praying so much lately, and I think that's what's happened to you."

Joy shook her head. "I'm so scared, Chase."

"Listen, Joy, something has been coming to me over and over again. You know we don't always understand whether a thought that comes to us is from God or is something that we just happen to think of, but this has come to me so strongly that I think we have to pay attention."

"What is it?"

"God seems to be telling me that you need healing in your spirit as well as in your body. You've told me that you grew up going to church and listening to sermons, and you've heard the Gospel many times. But I think God wants you to make a total surrender to Him. Will you do that, Joy?"

"I don't . . . I don't know how, Chase."

"You know, I didn't know either. Most of the time, when I was searching for God, I was trying to think of some way that I could please Him to make Him happy. I thought if I could make God happy enough, He would forgive my sins. But don't you see, Joy, that's just another kind of work. We can no more please God by being good than we can please Him by being baptized or taking communion or going to church. All those are good things, but they're not what God longs for most." Chase's voice became softer, and he said, "I finally just gave up and said, 'God, I'm a rotten man, and I'll never be anything else. Take anything you want in me, and I'll be anything you want me to be, but I'm helpless.' I prayed something like that, and the minute I gave up my own efforts to be good, the Lord Jesus came into my heart."

Joy finally nodded and said, "I'll try it, Chase, if you'll help."

"Of course I'll help. Why don't we both pray? I'll pray for you, and you call out to the Lord. I don't think the words matter much. He sees the heart."

The two joined hands, and Chase began to pray as Joy struggled to put what was in her heart into words. She was terrified at the future, but at the same time she was conscious that there were things in her past she had to confront. Almost immediately she thought of her hatred for the Tatums, except for Opal. She had been troubled about this before, but now, in an agony of spirit, she began to cry aloud, "Oh, God, I was wrong to feel hatred for Albert and for Olean and for Witt. Forgive me for that. I'm sorry."

After crying out for forgiveness, she was silent for a moment and then finally whispered, "I can't do anything, Lord, but I want to be saved. I want to be free of all this. And now I ask you simply to come into my heart and do whatever has to be done, because I know that only you can do it, Jesus."

Joy continued to call on the name of Jesus, asking Him to cleanse her and to make her a new person. Finally the desperation seemed to lessen and, encouraged, she called out even more fervently. The more she prayed, the more she was aware that something was taking place in her spirit. She paused then as Chase prayed for her. She lay there silently with her eyes closed and her hands in Chase's, and a great peace began to envelop her. Chase continued to pray, but she did not understand his words. She was only conscious of the fact that the weight that she had carried like an army pack for years was gone!

She opened her eyes and whispered, "Chase?" and when he looked at her, she said, "I'm trusting in the Lord now. Jesus has taken away the burden!"

"Praise the Lord!" Chase whispered fervently. He leaned over and kissed her on the cheek, and his hand pressed against her hair. "Praise God for His goodness." He straightened up, and his expression was exultant. His eyes seemed to glow, and he nodded, saying, "The other thing God's told me to do is to anoint you with oil and pray for your physical healing. I'm going to see if I can find some oil." He turned and crossed the room. When he stepped outside, he saw a nurse and said, "Do you have any oil, Nurse?"

The nurse, a tall, angular woman, stared at him. "Oil! What kind of oil?"

"It doesn't matter. Motor oil, baby oil, mineral oil—anything you've got."

The nurse laughed. "I'm a Pentecostal myself. I know what you want."

"You're right. I want to anoint Miss Winslow with oil."

"Well, come along. I don't think we have any holy oil from Jerusalem, but we've got something."

Chase followed her to the nurses' station. She stepped into a storage room and came out quickly with what looked like a quart of oil. "Use all you want," she said, "and I'll be praying for God to heal that young lady."

"Thanks." Chase whirled and went back to Joy's room. He did not speak but opened the top and poured a few drops of the oil out into his palm. He set the bottle down on the table and then dipped his finger into the oil and put it on Joy's forehead. "Oh, God," he said, "you have commanded us to pray for those who are sick, and I pray for Joy. I pray that you will smite this infection, root and branch. In the name of Jesus and according to your commands, Father, we anoint this child with oil. And we are expecting and believing as we come to you, that you're going to manifest your power and your strength, and we thank you in advance for what you're going to do, and we'll thank you all of our days. In the name of Jesus, be healed!"

★   ★   ★   ★

Dr. Knox came in at dawn to check on Joy and was surprised to see her looking comfortable and alert. He removed the bandages from her leg, and then he stood bolt upright, his eyes wide open. "This leg looks better—a lot better!" He put his hands on her skin and gasped. "The fever's gone!" He put his palm on Joy's forehead, held it for a moment, then shook his head. "Well, I've never seen anything like this." He leaned over Joy and said, "How do you feel?"

Joy replied, "I feel better than I ever have in my life, Dr. Knox."

Knox turned to stare at Chase, who was sitting in a chair beside the bed. "You and your prayer team must have gotten serious."

"You're right about that, Dr. Knox. This is all God's doing."

Knox scratched his bushy silver head vigorously, then laughed. "Well, bless the Lord, I believe you're right. I know it wasn't anything we doctors did, since there was nothing more we could do for her. It's good to see that God's still in business."

Knox clapped Chase on the shoulder and then reached over and gently took Joy's hand in both of his large ones. "I'm real happy, young lady. I must admit, my wife and I have been doing some praying for you ourselves."

"Thank you, Doctor. The Lord is good."

As soon as Knox left the room, Chase came over and stood looking down at Joy. Neither of them said anything, but she put her hand out, and when he took it, she said, "Thank you, Chase."

Chase squeezed her hand and then released it. "I've got to go make some calls," he said. "Travis and the Winslows and our circus friends—they'll all want to hear about your miraculous recovery."

"Hurry, Chase, I want everybody to hear what God has done for me."

* * * *

Get-well cards were piled high on the small table beside Joy. She sat in a wheelchair now and read them carefully. Some were new, and others had been there for quite a while. She couldn't believe it was already October thirtieth. She leaned over to smell the delicious aroma of the red roses that made a splash of color in the gray hospital room. Chase sat on a chair watching her. "You look great," he said. "Only two days ago you were at the bottom of the pile, and now you look as fresh as those roses."

"Isn't it wonderful!" Joy exclaimed. "All these letters and flowers and the phone calls."

"You and Travis have a wonderful family," he said softly.

"I've got to answer every one of these. Would you get my pen and some paper? I think they're in that drawer there."

"All right."

Joy saw that Chase was more serious than usual today. Since she had been out of danger, most days he had come to her room bearing such a happy spirit that it had lifted her even more. But today he looked troubled.

"Is something wrong, Chase?"

"Well, there is a problem. I didn't want to bother you with it, but—"

"What is it? It's not Travis, is it? He's all right?"

"Oh yes, he's fine. But things have been going on in the world since you've been in the hospital."

"What sort of things?"

Chase rose and walked over to the chair where he had laid his coat. He fished a newspaper out and said, "This country is in real trouble, Joy."

Joy took the paper and read the large headline in bold black letters. " 'Stock Market Collapses.' " She looked up and said, "What does it mean?"

"It means this country's in for some hard times. You can keep that paper. You might want to show it to your kids some day. America will never really be the same again. Not for a long time anyway."

Joy began reading the paper but soon shook her head. "I don't understand it. What happened?"

"Not even the smartest men in Washington know that. All they know is that all over this country people have lost everything. Stocks that were worth a hundred dollars a share are not worth a cent now. Families have been wiped out. I heard on the radio that some very rich men have jumped out of windows, killing themselves, because they went bankrupt."

"How awful!"

Chase sat down and pulled his chair closer to her wheelchair. "It's going to be a terrible time for America. They're calling it a depression, which really means everybody's broke."

"But, Chase, the circus will still go on, won't it?"

"Yes, I suppose it will, but it'll be hard. People who don't have bread to eat won't have money to go to the circus. But America's going to come through it. It won't be easy, but we'll make it."

"What am I going to do, Chase?"

"You're going to go to Sarasota, Florida, with me just as soon as Dr. Knox says you can travel."

"But what will we do there?"

"Stella decided to cancel the winter season again this year and hope the crowds will be bigger again in the spring. So we'll winter with the circus like we did last year. The season's almost over anyhow."

"But what will we do? It may take me a long time to get well."

"Doesn't matter. We'll be all right. I don't want you to worry, do you hear me?"

Joy put her hand out, and Chase took it. "I won't worry," she said.

Chase left shortly after, and Joy spent a good part of the day writing thank-you letters to Winslows all over the world. One of them was an admiral in the United States Navy. She had never heard of him, but he had written her the kindest letter imaginable. She wrote, of course, to Tom Winslow, for she knew he had gotten the prayer chain going, encouraging Winslows all over the world to pray for her.

She was scribbling away when suddenly Stella House appeared in the open doorway. Stella was well dressed as usual, in a wool coat with a fur collar and a cloche hat over her hair. Joy stared at her and could not think of a single thing to say.

Stella came into the room and a small smile turned the corners of her lips upward. "I'd guess you didn't expect to see me."

Joy could only stammer, "Well . . . no, I really didn't."

"Can't say as I blame you. How do you feel?"

"Oh, I'm much better now. It didn't look good there for a while. Did Chase tell you?"

"Yes, he did. Among other things he told me that you were going to lose your leg, and God healed you."

"That's right." Joy asked, "Would you like to sit down?"

"No, I started to write you a letter, but I had to come back through Springfield anyhow. You're going to be all right?"

"Yes, thank God I will be."

"You'll be doing the act again with Chase next season?"

"Oh yes."

"Some people lose their nerve after they get hurt. I can see that's not the case with you." Stella looked down at Joy, and something came into her eyes that Joy could not identify. Regret, perhaps, but there was also tension there.

"What is it, Mrs. House? Everything's all right, isn't it?"

"Things are falling apart nicely, thank you." Stella grimaced, then shook her shoulders. "It's not going to be easy making ends meet next year. We'll need you and Chase as headliners. We were going so great earlier this year, and Chase tells me the big cats will be even better next year."

"That's good to hear. Chase says he's taking me to Sarasota as soon as I can get out of here."

"That's what he told me." Stella again paused, and then she shook her head. "I guess you know I tried everything I could to get him back." She saw Joy's confusion and laughed shortly. "I guess everybody saw it; I wasn't all too subtle about it. But it didn't work. Whatever we had is gone, at least for him." She put her hand out, and when Joy, surprised, extended her own, she gripped it and nodded, "Congratulations."

"For what? You mean for getting well?"

"Among other things. I've got to go. I'll be seeing you in Sarasota. I'm glad you're feeling better, Joy."

And then she was gone. Her visit confused Joy, and when Chase came in later, she told him that Stella had been there.

"She said she might be coming. What did she say?"

"Among other things, she congratulated me. She also told me she had tried everything she could think of to try to get you back."

Chase studied her face. "I told her it was all over. It took me quite a while to find that out for myself, but I did. We didn't have much the first time, Joy. It was all physical. I was young, and I thought it was love, but it wasn't."

"Are you sure, Chase—that you're over it, I mean?"

"Yes." He hesitated, then said, "Say, do you feel like traveling?"

"Yes!"

"Dr. Knox says you're well enough to leave the hospital. We can leave bright and early tomorrow morning."

"I'll be glad to get to Florida, and pretty soon I can help take care of the cats."

"You'll take it slow and easy. I'm the doctor now." He leaned over and kissed her on the cheek. "Travis told me he'd be coming in to see you later today to say good-bye."

"Okay, Chase. See you tomorrow."

★　★　★　★

Chase and Joy had pulled the trailer across the country with the big car that had belonged to Colonel House. They had taken it easy, stopping often to rest her leg and staying in hotels at night. Now as they finally pulled into Sarasota, Joy said, "It's so good to be back. Look, the ocean! I can't wait to go wading in it."

"It's pretty cool in November, but we can walk on the beach. Just short walks at first."

"My leg feels fine."

"I was worried about how you'd take the long trip."

"No, it feels good." Joy was expecting Chase to turn to the left and go to the place where the circus quartered for the winter. Instead he turned right and drove along a road that followed the coastline. "Where are we going?" she asked.

"You are a nosy female," Chase said, grinning. He seemed lighthearted and happier than she had ever seen him. The trip had been good for both of them. Now he reached over and playfully tweaked her hair. "Ask me no questions, and I'll tell you no lies."

Joy was mystified at his attitude and even more puzzled when he pulled up in front of a small stucco house on the beach.

"What place is this?" she asked with surprise.

"I told you, ask no questions." Chase got out and walked over to her side and opened the door. "Use your crutches."

"I don't really need them," Joy protested. He started to speak, and she said quickly, "All right, all right, I know. You're the doctor." She got the crutches, and he accompanied her as they walked up to the front door. He pulled out a key, opened the screen, and unlocked the door. He shoved it back and stepped aside to hold the screen. "Come on in," he said.

"This is breaking and entering, isn't it?"

Chase laughed but said nothing else.

Joy stepped inside the house and immediately noticed that a large window facing the ocean gave a beautiful view. She gazed at the blue-green sea stretching out to infinity and was delighted to see a row of dolphins as they arched their way along, breaking the water in a line.

"What a wonderful house!"

"Do you like it?" Chase asked. He leaned up against the wall, crossed his arms, and watched her.

"Yes, but why are we here?" She looked around almost with envy at the white walls, and from where she stood she could see a screened-in porch with a table and chairs. The furniture was nothing special, but the house itself had a warm feeling. "It's beautiful. Whose is it?"

Chase shoved himself from the wall and stood directly in front of her. He took her hands in his own. "It's yours," he said gently.

Joy stared at him, thinking she had misheard him. "What are you talking about, Chase?"

"I've been meddling with your business. I looked at this house when we were here last summer. It was for sale then, and I called back last week and found out it was still for sale. I made a down payment on it."

"But that means it's your house."

"No, it's for you. I haven't exactly kept you up to date on all the news. I got a call two weeks ago from Tom Winslow. Tatum has decided to pay up. The money's in some sort of legal limbo now, but half of the money is yours. Ten thousand for you and ten thousand for Travis. It'll just about pay this place off, and also you can get the furniture and the personal things that belonged to your parents."

Stunned by Chase's words, Joy freed herself from his hands and made her way to the screened-in porch with her crutches. She stepped outside the door and heard the murmuring of the surf, a sound she had always loved. The wind blew her hair, for it was strong coming off of the ocean. She heard Chase come up behind her, and she turned and looked up into his eyes. "How thoughtful of you, Chase, to do all this for me."

"Well," he said, and he flashed a grin at her, "that's not all of it. I want to live with you in this house."

"Why, you know we can't do a thing like that! It'd be wrong," Joy responded as her cheeks grew red.

"Not the way we'll work it." He pulled Joy into his arms and bent to taste the sweetness of her lips. "This is the way it's going to be. I'm going to stay in my trailer at the circus, and every day I'll come here courting you. I'll bring you flowers, and we'll walk on the beach, and I'll tell you how beautiful you are, and sooner or later you'll fall in love with me and decide that you can't live without me. And then," he smiled, "you'll marry me and let me live in this house with you."

Joy felt secure in his arms. She held him tight for a moment with her face against his chest. When she lifted her head, she said, "It's like coming home, Chase."

"You mean to this house?"

"No," she whispered and, pulling his head down, said, "it's like coming home to you."

★ ★ ★ ★

Turn the page
for a preview of

Heart of the Lion

by
Gilbert Morris

★ ★ ★ ★

CHAPTER ONE

HEART OF THE LION

★ ★ ★ ★

by Gilbert Morris

The broad river wound through the flat country in a lazy ser-
pentine pattern. As Noah and Jodak approached the water the
smell of rich, loamy earth and decaying matter hung in the air.
Jodak paused and fixed his eyes on his younger brother. "You're
too inexperienced to hunt the river beast."

"No I'm not!" Noah protested. "And you promised!"

"You don't remember when our older brother was killed on
just such a hunt as this. Maz was in his prime—only a hundred
and twenty-three years old. I saw it happen and couldn't do a
thing about it. He fell out of the boat into the river, and . . . and
the monster just bit him in two!" The bitter memory twisted
Jodak's mouth into an ugly curve, and he shook his head as if to
rid himself of the thought.

Noah had been through this before, begging Jodak to take
him on a hunt for the dangerous leviathan that prowled the
river. Jodak had always refused.

Now Jodak stared at Noah, considering his brother's plea.
Noah's heart sank as he saw refusal building up in his brother's
dark eyes. "Please let me go, Jodak!" he begged. "I'll be careful.
I'll do everything you say."

Jodak shook his head and started to speak, but a movement
caught his eye. He turned to his left and stiffened as an old man

came toward them. Jodak muttered, "It's the seer. What's he doing here?"

The man who approached was not tall, and his body was lean, almost emaciated. He leaned on a staff as he came steadily toward the two. His piercing eyes were an odd yellowish color, like burnished gold, and at times when he was speaking of his visions, or when he was angry, they would burn like twin flames. A rough mane of silvery hair hung over his shoulders, and his beard matched it. His name was Zorah, but he was called the *seer*, for he saw visions. It was whispered that he had even seen the Ancient One with his own eyes! Some called him the *sayer* for his habit of appearing before the clan and proclaiming a startling message directly from the Ancient One.

Noah had always been a little afraid of Zorah, and he involuntarily took a step backward. For some reason the old man with the golden eyes had seemed to select him for special attention. More than once the seer had stopped and stared at Noah, and a few times he had questioned him sharply. Noah had never noticed him doing that with any other young man, and he could not imagine why the frightening old man had selected him for special attention. As Noah felt the pressure of the seer's penetrating eyes, he swallowed hard, attempting to show no fear.

Zorah turned his gaze from Noah to his brother. "Jodak, come with me. I would have a word with you."

Jodak nodded and walked away with the seer. Noah stood nervously watching the two men talking from a distance, their voices inaudible. From time to time one of them would turn and examine Noah. *They're talking about me! What have I done now?* Finally he saw Zorah put his finger before Jodak's face, and although Noah could not make out his words, he knew they were harsh. Zorah gave him one final look, then turned and walked away. Jodak returned, a strange expression on his face. He said nothing, keeping his eyes fixed on Noah.

"Well, what did he want, Jodak?"

"He's worried about you. He warned me not to let anything happen to you."

"Why does he care?"

"I don't know, but it's not the first time. He's always had a special interest in you, Noah. Another reason for me to keep you from going on the hunt."

"Did he say I couldn't go?"

"No, he didn't say that, but—"

"Then I want to go, and you *promised*."

Jodak gave up, throwing his hands in the air. "All right, but you do *exactly* what I say. You understand? You'll take no chances."

"Anything you say," Noah responded quickly, relieved and pleased that he would not be sent away.

The two hurried along the riverbank, so thickly lined with tall reeds that at times they could not even see the river itself. But Noah was always conscious of its soft, swishing melody, and through the reeds he could spot the rippling backs of crocodiles in the shallows. Noah was more aware of the world about him than most, and his eyes moved constantly, missing nothing.

Finally Jodak said, "There they are. We're late."

The two approached an open area on the bank where several reed boats were pulled ashore. Noah ran his eyes over the hunters who were waiting for them. Nophat, the best hunter of the clan, was a huge man with only one eye but great strength. Next to him stood Ruea, not much of a hunter but a fine singer. He might not be able to kill a river beast, but he would surely make a fine song about it! Close to him was Boz, only two years older than Noah. He was a cheerful fellow, always getting into mischief, and he winked at Noah as the two arrived. Kul, a husky young man with a wild mop of kinky hair, and Senzi, an older man with a sour look, made up the hunting party.

Senzi spoke up with irritation. "We've been waiting for ages. Where have you two been?"

Jodak hurried to one of the boats and glanced at Senzi. "Sorry to be late." Turning to Nophat, he said, "We're ready now."

Nophat scratched his wild beard and grunted. "Are you sure you want to take that tadpole with you?" He stared at Noah, seeming to find him wanting.

"Oh, let him come along, Nophat," Boz urged. "We can use him for bait!" He laughed at his own joke, his teeth white in the morning light.

"All right," Nophat grumbled. "Get in the boat. But don't get in our way when we go for the kill."

"Wait a minute," Jodak said. "Let's ask the Strong One to give us strength and keep us safe."

Nophat did not believe in anything but the strength of his own arm. Impatiently he muttered, "Go ahead and ask—for all the good it will do."

Ignoring Nophat's indifference to the power of the Strong One, the others all looked to Jodak, who lifted his hands and closed his eyes. "O Ancient One, keeper of those who trust in you, we ask you to keep us safe. Make our eyes quick and our hands strong."

A silence followed the simple request; then Nophat snapped, "All right, we go now."

As they climbed in their boat, Jodak whispered to Noah, "I offered a dove to the Ancient One before we left home, so we'll be all right."

The three lightweight reed boats moved swiftly into the muddy river, one man at the back of each boat poling along with the current. Noah found no difficulty keeping his balance as he poled.

The water rippled in the morning quiet as the pointed prows sliced through the river. Noah spotted several crocodiles lying just below the calm surface of the water. Brilliant white birds flew up from the banks as the boats skimmed past. The vegetation in the river began to thicken, a sign that they were approaching the favorite haunt of the river beast.

Without warning a scene flashed into Noah's mind, causing him to miss a stroke and drawing a sharp admonition from Jodak. The scene was from a dream he'd had a week ago. It came back now, sharp and clear, and he realized it was a dream of this very hunt, in which he had been on the water and was very frightened. He saw the open red mouth of a mighty river beast and then heard the terrified cries of his own voice.

"There's the beast!" Nophat whispered hoarsely, the gleam of battle blazing in his single eye. "Ruea and I will go first. Boz, you bring your boat on the end to help. Noah, you and Jodak stay back."

Noah's sharp eyes were quick to pick out the rounded hump of the river beast, its body mounded like a small hill, its eyes and nostrils punctuating the surface. Although it appeared awkward, the river beast could move with terrible speed, and its powerful jaws could bite a crocodile in two, or snap a reed boat if it so chose!

Noah felt light-headed as he watched Nophat stand in the front of his boat, holding his spear ready and staring at the river beast. Behind him Ruea continued poling slowly but was ready to grab his spear at the right moment. Boz guided his boat around, and Senzi and Kul stood with their spears poised. The boats converged on the beast, which continued chomping on river vegetation, ignoring their approach.

With a mighty yell Nophat lifted his spear high and plunged it down into the flesh of the startled river beast. Noah's shouts rose while the other hunters moved their crafts closer to the animal that was now thrashing in the bloody froth.

Without warning, the boat containing the three men rose high into the air, and with wild cries, Boz, Kul, and Senzi were catapulted into the water. Terrified for their lives, Noah screamed, "What can we do, Jodak?"

"Come on! We must help them!"